Mark Sowers

The Blackfire Chronicles

Volume 1

Mark Sowers

Cover design by: Arcane Book Covers

Created in the United States of America

For Mom. If you hadn't read to me before I could read for myself, this book would not exist.

For Marcy – who always believed

Acknowledgements

The publication of this book would not have been possible without the incredible support and tireless work of the most wonderful wife a man could ask for – Marcy. She not only reads everything I write, but edits, formats, and has created cover art for some of my books. Without her I'd be just another writer with manuscripts clogging up the hard drive of his computer. Thank you babe!

Thanks must also be given to the writers who have inspired me to write: Stephen King, Terry Goodkind, Dean Koontz, Robert Jordan, Peter Bacho, Primo Levi, Dan Simmons, Dickens, Celine, Solzhenitsyn, Dumas, and so, so many others.

Cover Art by Arcane Book Covers
www.arcanebookcovers.com

Map illustrations by Jeff Mathison
www.mapsbymathison.com

Thank you to Igino Marini who created The Fell Types fonts are digitally reproduced by Igino Marini.
www.iginomarini.com.

Thanks to Paul Lloyd for creating the free font Bridgnorth.

i

Table of Contents

Acknowledgements... i

The Three Kingdoms Map iii

The City of Kessar Map iv

Chapter 1..1

Chapter 2..25

Chapter 3..39

Chapter 4..47

Chapter 5..55

Chapter 6..67

Chapter 7..77

Chapter 8..87

Chapter 9..95

Chapter 10..103

Chapter 11..113

Chapter 12..139

Chapter 13..145

Chapter 14..157

Chapter 15..167

Chapter 16..173

Chapter 17..183

Chapter 18..191

Chapter 19..213

Chapter 20..223

Chapter 21..229

Chapter 22..235

Chapter 23..255

Chapter 24..271

Chapter 25..293

Chapter 26..305

Chapter 27..315

Chapter 28..323

Chapter 29..335

Chapter 30..343

Chapter 31..349

Chapter 32..361

Chapter 33..371

Chapter 34..383

Chapter 35..409

Word of Thanks...445

About the Author...447

Next in Series...451

Blackfire Chronicles Volume 2, Chapter 1..........457

Books by the Author..463

The Three Kingdoms

DESERT SEA

DESTRUCTION BAY

THE PIT

JARRADAN

LAVAN'S GAP

BLUE CRAG MTS.

NORTHERN DESERT

KESSAR

XANDEI RIVER

HEFTEN

GRASSLANDS of DRISAVA

ENRAT

SILVER ARM BAY

COASTAL MOUNTAINS

BARRENBAUG

DRISAVA

CANTA GLOBZ

CANTA

BENTRAVIRRI

REGRA

MIDSWIFT CUT

FACELESS MOUNTAINS

VINEYARDS

JURSAFAR

BLACKFIRE

EASTERN SEA

J. MATHISON

iii

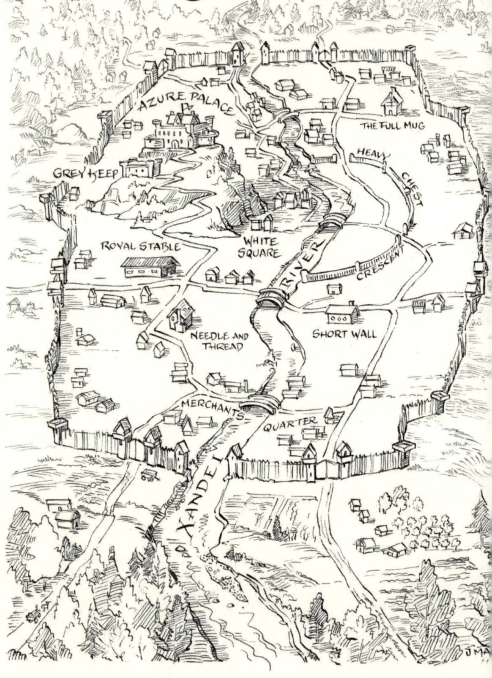

HESSAR

AZURE PALACE

THE FULL MUG

HEAVY

CHEST

GREY KEEP

ROYAL STABLE

WHITE SQUARE

RIVER

CRESCENT

NEEDLE AND THREAD

SHORT WALL

MERCHANTS

QUARTER

XANDEL

From whence did it come? The accepted theory of our age contends that it has always been, as if it sprang, fully formed, from the ground, in that long ago age when the land was created. Yet questions persist. If the Blackfire has always been, then what is it? What purpose does it serve? Or does it even have a purpose? Most simply gaze at its ominous and striking presence in the southern sky, watch its slow spinning, the mountains within it thrusting up with their unfathomable force, then crashing down as if their very foundations suddenly vanished. Perhaps they did, like so many who have attempted to cross its boundary. I have devoted my life to the study of the Blackfire, and it often seems I know less now than when I began, so many years ago.

Transcribed from a lecture by
Wurfavend Mentrana, Udron
Library, Enrat, Turning 3480,
Era of Calm

Chapter 1

he crack of Bhinja's lash tore a furrow across the skin of Revan's back, sending small streams of blood oozing down towards his waist. The map of scars that crisscrossed his flesh would have another road soon. Revan arched his back with a quiet grunt, as if stretching after getting out of bed, and drove his pick into the iron hard ground. He'd long ago become numb to the pain of lashes; they were nothing more now than Bhinja's way of saying work faster. Even the pain and blood was simply something to shrug off, a minor annoyance deserving of minor acknowledgement. He could vaguely remember a time when the lashes had caused him to cry out in pain, when he'd had to sleep on his sides to avoid aggravating the fresh injuries. But those days had passed long ago.

Chips of light brown earth sprayed out from the tip of his pick, ricocheting off the others toiling near him. None even bothered to look up. The young man closest to him had a small red nick on his ribs from a particularly sharp piece. From his lack of reaction, it seemed he hadn't even felt it. Most of them didn't. At least the ones who had been there for a time.

"Swing those tools faster or it's the lash for the lot of ya," Bhinja growled. His crooked and broken teeth enhanced the menace in his eyes, one of which was cloudy white and sometimes spun around in its socket like a rock rolling downhill. Sweat dripped off his bald head and ran down the bulging muscles of his chest and shoulders, making him glisten in the baking sun.

The master's aide, that was what he was called officially even though everyone knew he was nothing more than the muscle with the whip, was fully aware well that his admonition didn't have much influence with the men and boys toiling in the heat. It was a tired old game between himself and those wielding the picks and shovels, pushing the carts full of dirt. He issued the orders, swung his short dark leather whip, and those upon whom it fell increased their efforts for a moment, only to fall back into the dreary rhythm of digging. When Bhinja really wanted them to move, he resorted to other, more persuasive methods. One of his favorites was the short wooden rod with narrow spines of sharp metal running from its tip almost to the leather wrapped handle.

"The Master has ordered that we are to make ten units today," he called out. "Any of you worms who don't put your back into it will visit the camp."

This too was part of the game, albeit one that was taken more seriously – a visit to the camp. It was rare that someone sent there ever returned. Those who did were not the same as they were before they'd left. They all came back with a vacant look in their eyes, as if whatever force had inhabited their bodies had fled, leaving behind nothing more than the breathing, moving husk of what had been once a person. Work was all they knew, then. Words were rarely, if ever, spoken, tasks were undertaken without comment or complaint, and most only lived a few days, at best a few weeks. When they dropped lifeless to the hard ground, or didn't wake in the morning, their bodies were collected, placed in small carts pulled by tired and undernourished horses, and disappeared up the winding circular road out of the excavation. Everyone feared the camp, which lent a morbid weight to Bhinja's threats. Most who visited it were new arrivals or established diggers who had simply given up. There was a colloquialism among the diggers for what happened when one of them died – it was known as 'the last ride'.

Revan believed that he was about sixteen turnings of the sun. He was tall, at least a half head taller than others who were about his age. His hair was a glossy black, when it wasn't covered in dust, and his eyes were a sparkling blue almost the color of the cloudless sky. He had strong angular features with high cheekbones, a wide, prominent chin and jaw, and thin nose. Skin tanned by endless days in the sun had not lost its olive complexion. In another place, another time, another life, he might have been said to have been regal looking.

Revan had no idea how long he'd been digging in the pit, as the excavation was called. His earliest clear memories were of riding in a wagon with several other young boys through a desert of towering orange sand dunes and arriving at the enormous excavation where he had lived ever since. It seemed at times that he could remember a man and woman, he thought they might be his parents, and grass. It was the grass that was clearest in his memory from that distant, foggy time– the green color, the soft feel of it, and right on the edge of memory, a smell of freshness, cleanliness. There were times he could almost recall that it when a breeze that had somehow made its way deep down to where Revan dug brought with it a hint of that smell. It was fleeting but held within it a world of promise and possibility that dissipated as quickly as it had arrived.

There was no green grass in the pit, only the hard ground and the massive edifice slowly emerging from it. He wished sometimes that the faces of the man and woman he seemed to remember were clearer, but they were fuzzy, indistinct, like a dream that fades on waking or the last moments of a sunset. The vibrance of the colors is soon gone and the only thing that remains is the feeling of having seen something of incalculable beauty. He thought that if he could pull those two faces up, force them to become clear in his mind, then perhaps he'd find something in them that could replace the feeling of hopelessness that pervaded his days. But they never quite came into focus.

Bhinja had moved on along the line of men, watching their limbs and tools moving in monotonous rhythm as they slowly dug deeper. Revan paused a moment to look up at the enormous structure rising out of the ground in front of him. It was at least three thousand paces long on each side and rose an equal number into the broiling blue sky, blocking his view of the far side of the pit. Its walls were made of dark grey stone, small precise square blocks each about three hand widths wide and tall, and dotted here and there by clumps of the stubborn dirt that clung to it tenaciously. Each block was fitted so precisely that it was often hard to discern the joints where their edges met. There were no windows or doors visible, no openings in the smooth walls at all. Nor was it adorned with any carvings, writing or symbols. It seemed to be nothing more than a huge grey box buried no one knew how deep in the unforgiving and reluctantly yielding earth. It was said among the workers that the master had been working to uncover the building his whole life, and that there had been many other masters before him working towards the same goal. Revan could imagine it was true. In his entire time digging, the pit had descended by perhaps thirty paces. He could tell because one of those clumps of dirt clinging to the wall had a shape like a drop of water that had fallen on a stone - one large irregular shape surrounded by smaller dots of earth. He'd seen it the first time he'd swung his pick. At that time, it was barely a pace above the level of the earth. Now, if he was close to the wall, he had to crane his neck to see it.

If anyone knew what the structure was, they didn't say. Speculation among the workers at night, over their meager supper, was that it was a place full of riches, perhaps a palace or repository where magnificent weapons were stored. Those who claimed to have seen a palace, said that it couldn't be one. Palaces had doors and windows, towers and ramparts. The arguments over what it was were subdued and quiet. No one really had the energy or spirit for heated debate after a day in the pit. When they bedded down for the night on their thin pallets and drew their meager covers over themselves, they would sometimes talk softly about what would happen if they ever found an entrance. They all agreed that it would probably be their last day alive.

It was understood by everyone that the lives of the workers were of no importance to Bhinja and the other aides. Every few weeks wagons full of men and boys would roll over the rim of the pit and wind their way down the narrow road circling the inner walls to the camp at the bottom. The new workers were ordered out of the wagons, lashes whistling and cracking, their shackles and chains clanking. The cries and wails as the whips found flesh didn't even make anyone look up from their digging, so common were the sounds. Most of those newly arrived were young, having seen at most twelve turnings. A few were older. Many were younger. They were herded from the wagons by the aides to the tool area where the implements of the dig like picks, shovels, and dirt carts were stored. Their shackles were removed, exposing the raw and bleeding sores where they had chafed and rubbed their wrists and ankles, and they were told to pick a tool and join the line of workers. Those who moved too slowly or protested that they couldn't were subjected to the curses and lashes of the aides. If one cowered or fell to the ground, he felt the fist or the boot. Some didn't get up and they invariably joined the others in the carts that left the pit. The ones who did rise, and those who had seized a tool without receiving a beating, obeyed the commands of the aides and set to laboriously removing the hard earth.

That was how Revan had met Arval. He'd come in a wagon about half a turning before. The scene that day had been like any other. The lashes cracked, the curses were levied, the captives had cried and begged. That time two had made the last ride back out of the pit, their lifeless bodies heaved into a cart like so much offal. Arval hadn't uttered a sound as a lash took him across the shoulders. He hadn't even flinched. Revan, still new to the pit, had stolen a look when the wagon arrived, and was slightly amazed to see a boy about his age who could withstand the bloody burn of the lash. Most cried out or at least shed tears. Arval hadn't done either. Revan had marveled a little at his stoicism.

It happened after Arval had chosen a pick, that he'd ended up on the line next to Revan. Glancing at him out of the corner of his eye, Revan said "How did you not cry out when that aide hit you?"

"I'm used to it," he replied.

Revan took in Arval's appearance. Not as tall as he was, Arval was stockier, with broad shoulders, rounded features and expressive dark brown eyes. A mop of reddish-brown hair adorned his head. His hands were large but delicate looking, as if they were made for smelting silver, then crafting it into fine jewelry. He moved with a litheness that implied speed and agility.

"Still, they don't swing the lashes softer because we're young. They use equal force on everyone here."

"When you come from where I have, you learn to tolerate pain. To hold your cries and not show weakness."

"And where would that be?" Revan asked.

"Kessar."

"What's Kessar?"

"A city far from here."

"What's a city?"

Arval gave Revan a look of utter bafflement and incredulity. "You don't know what a city is?!"

"No."

"It's a big place full of people and buildings. This is a little like a city in that there are so many people here," he said, looking out over the pit, the hordes of men and boys digging. There were so many that the furthest away looked to be no more than insects crawling over a midden heap in high summer.

"This is like a city?" asked Revan.

"Yes. Haven't you ever been to a city before?"

"No."

"Well, where have you been?"

"Here."

"Always?"

"Almost. I remember coming here in a cart when I was very young. And I remember grass, that it was green and soft, and had a smell. And two people – a man and a woman. But I can't really remember their faces. Sometimes I try, but they're blurry, like when sweat gets in your eyes."

"So, you don't remember your home? You don't know where you're from?" asked Arval.

"No. I think maybe the grass I remember was there, at my home, and probably the people, but that's all."

"Sorry," Arval said, dropping his eyes.

"Quick, dig," said Revan. "Bhinja is coming, and you'll get the lash again. He's the worst of the aides. If a week goes by without him killing someone, he gets mean."

Arval glanced sideways at the big man with the dark whip. His enormous bare arms and chest were covered in black tattoos of swirling, spiky designs. Sweat dripped from his bald head, browned from the sun, and down onto the leather suspenders that crisscrossed his massive chest and held up his tan trousers. Black boots with square toes poked out. Arval could see splattered drops of something reddish brown dried on them. He gazed over his charges with a look that promised pain, as if his glare alone could unbury the massive edifice before them. His mouth being slightly open, Arval could see crooked and broken teeth, and a thick ropy white scar running from his left shoulder diagonally across his chest where it cut through the tattoos almost to his waist. The burning sun had done nothing to make it blend in with the rest of his tanned skin. His eyes, the right normal but fierce, the left a sightless white that rolled around haphazardly, scanned the workers intensely with the promise of pain. This man had seen his share of violence.

Bhinja had passed them by that day, giving Arval and Revan no more than a cursory glance as he moved on, always alert for malingerers. But other days he hadn't. Their backs both told the story of the times Bhinja had stopped.

"I thought this was the camp," Arval said one night not long after he'd arrived.

They were lying on their pallets, the rest of the workers laid out haphazardly around them. Snores came from some, muffled crying from others, probably the ones with fresh wounds from lashes. The stars glittered overhead, sparkling, distant and cold.

"This is our camp. The workers camp," Revan replied.

"You mean the slaves' camp."

"Well, yes, I guess so. It doesn't seem so bad if you call it the workers' camp."

"What do you mean it doesn't seem so bad? You're a slave! We are all slaves! Workers get paid. Get to go home at night. Have families. Drink in taverns."

"What's a tavern?"

"Never mind," Arval said with a frustrated sigh.

Ever since he'd met Revan the boy had been peppering him with questions about everything. What's this? What's that? He was so exasperated with explaining everything that he felt like not talking to him at all. Or hitting him in the mouth so he'd shut it.

"The camp is up outside the pit," Revan said.

"Outside?"

"Yeah. Its where they take those who don't work fast or hard enough."

"Have you ever seen it?"

"No."

"Then how do you know that's where it is?"

"Because the wagons and carts leave the pit with the people who are sent there. Or when someone dies."

"I guess that makes sense. I didn't see it when I was brought in. Did you?"

"No. At least I don't remember seeing it."

"Well, you've been here a lot longer than I have. Has anyone ever seen it?"

"I don't know. No one has ever said they have. And the ones who do come back never talk about it. But I guess that kind of makes it real doesn't it?"

"They must have been taken somewhere, those mostly dead diggers you described. The camp is as likely a place as any. I suppose it doesn't really matter since we could all be dead tomorrow."

"Yeah, I guess so. Not many here talk. But some do. They usually say how they're going to kill Bhinja and escape someday. But that's always the older ones, the ones who are newer here. Those of us who've been here a long time don't talk about escape. We just try to live through the day."

"I'll tell you something," Arval said in a soft voice. "I'm going to escape."

"Don't say that! It's better if you don't talk about it. About hope. There isn't any."

"Have you tried to escape?"

"Not me. But I saw three boys try to escape last turning. They waited til night, then tried to sneak up the road. They didn't even get to the second circle."

"The second circle?! That's it?! But there are at least fifty!"

"Yes. I know. I've counted. There are fifty-four circles of the road you would have to travel to get to the top. It takes a long time just for a wagon to get down here."

Arval remembered his recent wagon ride circling the road to the bottom of the pit, remembering how long it had taken and realizing how hard it would be to get all the way to the top without being seen. The walls between the circles of the road were far too steep to climb. "They should have been smarter," he said. "How did they get caught?"

"There are aides all over the road. They hide somehow. You can't see them at night, and only sometimes in the day. But they're there."

"Like sentries."

"I suppose. What's a sentry?"

"A guard."

"Yes, well, sentries then. They caught them. I heard the yells of the sentries and the screams of the boys. It woke me up. They were brought down here to our camp. We were all woken, those of us who weren't already awake. There were at least a hundred aides. The boys were brought to that platform over there by where they serve the food-"

"Food?! There is no food here! Its rancid swill!" Arval said, rolling on his side to face Revan.

"It's what we have. Eat it or we starve."

"I know and I do but believe me – it isn't food."

"I believe you, ok? Can I finish?"

Arval sighed and rolled his eyes. "Go on then."

Revan continued, gesturing toward the wide wooden platform in the distance at the base of the wall of the pit. "So, they took them all up on the platform. Bhinja was there but he was just standing to the side. It was another aide who looked to be in charge. I'd never seen him before; I have no idea where he came from, but he looked meaner than Bhinja. He told us all to gather around. It took a couple minutes because there were so many of us. But we've all gathered around the platform before. Sometimes they give us orders from there, tell us about something special we have to do for a day or a week."

"What could be special here?" Revan ignored the question. "When we were all awake and around the platform, the aide I'd never seen before started speaking to us. He told us that the three boys on the platform with him had been caught trying to escape. That they were going to be made examples of, to show us what would happen if any of us were to try the same thing. He took a big knife from his belt. I could see torch light reflecting off the blade as he held it up so we could all see. It was huge. He took one boy's arm and drew the blade down from his shoulder to his wrist. Then made a cut all the way around his arm at the shoulder and the wrist. I could tell the cuts were deep because I saw how much they bled and because of how the boy screamed. He was about my age. The other two were a little older. When he'd finished with the last cut, he grabbed one corner of the skin and tore it right off the boy's arm. He took all the skin and most of the muscle with it. I could see his arm bones. I'll never forget the scream he let loose when that happened. I've never heard one like it since I've been here. It didn't last long. He either passed out or died. I don't know. He just fell. They left him lying on the platform. The aide went to the next boy and did the same thing, except to his head. He took all the skin off his head by cutting it just like he had the other boy's arm, except those cuts were around the boy's neck. It was like he'd pulled a sack off the boy's head, but it was his skin. Hair and everything. We could all see his skull. His eyes were still there, looking at us. Past us. He didn't scream long either. I put my head down because I didn't want to see what he was going to do to the third boy. But one of the aides hit me in the back with his fist and told me to watch. Others had quit looking too, and they got hit. With a fist or a lash. We all watched. The aide stood in front of the last boy and told him to choose which way he wanted to be punished – his arm or his head. The boy was sobbing, begging, pleading to be spared. But the aide just looked at him. No one spoke. It was so quiet that all we could hear were the boy's sobs. The aide waited a moment and said it once more – 'Choose'. The boy didn't say anything. I don't think he could. He was too terrified. He was shaking so hard the aides had to hold him up. The man with the knife just looked at him. Then he suddenly grabbed his head and took the skin off it. Just like he had the second boy. I'll always remember how he struggled, but the aides holding him were too strong. There were too many of them. When he had fallen down, the aide looked out at all of us. His arms and chest were covered with blood. It was dark and shiny in the torch light. All he said was, 'This is what happens to anyone who tries to escape.' No one spoke. He waived his hand, and we all went back to our pallets." Arval decided he didn't want to hear about the special pronouncements that were sometimes made from the platform, so he didn't ask about his unanswered question.

Revan's story finished, they lay on their pallets, looking at the strip of faraway stars. The black form of the building they were excavating blotted out half the sky to their right, the rim of the pit on their left much of the rest of it. Arval felt like he was a corpse in a grave, taking his last look at the sky before dirt covered him forever. Neither spoke.

Revan and Arval worked side by side as the box, as they'd come to call the massive grey stone structure, slowly emerged from the ground. Arval had lost some of his enthusiasm for escape since hearing the story of the three boys who had tried. But he still watched for weaknesses and distraction among the aides. The pit sank slowly deeper as they dug. The army of men and boys toiled unendingly under the hot sun, each day just like the last and so many others before it. Rise from sleep, a small bowl of mostly clear liquid, sometimes with a bit of wilted vegetable or rancid meat for breakfast, and a cup of water. The same at night for supper. The only things that changed were the faces of the slaves around them and the depth of the pit. And that was what Revan had come to think of himself and his fellow workers – slaves. Arval had explained the difference to him, and he realized now that he was nothing more than a tool to the master and his aides. As easily replaceable as a broken pick or the wheel of a cart. That realization had awakened something inside him, a feeling was growing. He looked at the aides differently now. Before they'd simply been objects to be obeyed, their whips and fists were implements of pain one tried to avoid. The toil and drudgery of his life before meeting Arval had worn away any emotions he'd had before he'd come to the pit. They'd been so eroded, so buried that he hadn't even realized they were there. It was Arval's descriptions and stories of cities and the things in them that had made Revan aware of the possibility that there might be something outside the pit, some life that didn't involve picks and shovels, aides and whips. The notion that food could be something more than the thin, nearly inedible gruel that he forced down his throat each morning and night was a revelation. Arval's stories of roasted meat that didn't smell like a corpse left too long in the sun, of vegetables that crunched in your mouth instead of melting, of sweet pies and candies that could be had for the exchange of something called coins or links made his imagination spin with potential. He found himself wanting to see and taste what Arval described. He wanted to see a city, to walk its streets among the crowds, to see the vivid colors of the clothes, hear sounds that weren't cries or the crack of whips, or curses. Most of all he wanted to see the whole sky. Not the strip of it that showed between the box and the walls of the pit. He'd always been fascinated by the sky, the shapes of its clouds and the mystery of the stars. The truncated sky, to him, had come to symbolize his imprisonment. Free people could gaze at the stars and clouds unimpeded by the box and the pit walls. He wanted to do the same. Arval had told him of prisons, and he'd begun to equate the pit with those places where men were taken and rarely seen again. The pit had been home for so long that Revan had known nothing else. He'd now begun to understand that there was much, much more to the world, that it was a very big place. And he wanted to see it.

But it was anger that began to overtake his dreams of food, of crowds of people not digging and grand buildings in which people lived and worked that gradually began to dominate his thoughts. He started to see the aides, particularly Bhinja, with a new clarity. Before meeting Arval he'd simply accepted his life as it was. Dug as he'd been told. Toiled until his hands bled, and his back ached. The aides simply were. They were always there, always ready with the whip, as constant as the box and the sun. They'd been objects, purveyors of pain, a part of life. He'd been ambivalent towards them, toward almost everything. Their curses and lashes hadn't elicited an emotional response. He'd absorbed them and continued. Now they were people. Like him, but not like him. They were worthy of his anger, of killing.

That was a new thought for Revan – killing. He'd never even imagined killing someone, let alone that the aides were possible to kill. Aides had always been the ones to do the killing. He'd never even seen one bleed. He'd thought them invincible. Arval had disabused him of that notion. He'd explained that they weren't omnipotent, untouchable wielders of the lash, but men. Just like them. It was possible for them to bleed, to die.

"I saw a man much like them die in Kessar," he told Revan one day. They'd been digging close to the smooth, featureless face of the box, its grey stone form soaring far above their heads. The sun was behind it at that time of day, leaving them in blessed shade, although the air around them still boiled with heat. Arval had told him that the place where the pit was located was called a desert. He'd explained that the sun almost always shined there, that it was always hot. When he spoke of mountains and snow, cold and frost, rain and fog, Revan was mystified. He couldn't conceive of cold. To have to wear more clothes than the thin shirt and ragged trousers they all did, not to mention boots instead of the sandals everyone had, was a completely alien concept. But that was the way of things with Arval, most everything he told Revan created a fresh mystery in his mind, something else to be explained, examined, imagined. Experienced.

On this occasion Arval had been telling him a story about picking pockets in the busy streets of Kessar. He and his friend Plistral were working the crowd, searching for wealthy looking people in their fine colorful and embroidered garb, preferably with a purse tied to a cord on their belt or a pocket in a jacket or robe. They'd had a good day up to that point. Arval said they each had about ten links, one of them even gold. They would be able to eat for a week on just that one coin. They slept in a small space under a building somewhere in the city. But during the day they were out among the throngs, eking out their meals by way of thievery or begging. Stealing too was foreign to Revan. In the pit there was nothing to steal. Except someone's gruel. And that was usually eaten so fast that there wasn't even a chance for it to be stolen.

Plistral and Arval had just come up empty on what they'd thought was a promising mark. The man had been well dressed, wearing a bright red jacket and wide, baggy white trousers, with what looked to be deep pockets on each side. Plistral had acted as if he'd dropped something on the ground right in front of the man, while Arval had crept up behind him waiting for him to be distracted. When Plistral suddenly bent over in front of him to search for what he'd pretended to drop, Arval had quickly stuck his hand in one of the pockets, but it was empty. The other was too far away to reach without the man noticing, so Plistral shifted over, forcing the man to turn which moved his unsearched pocket closer to Arval. They'd performed this move so many times that it was automatic. They didn't need to exchange glances or signals to know what the other was doing. When Arval's hand came up empty from the other pocket, he quickly moved away into the crowd. Receiving the man's curses with downcast eyes and a deferential "pardon me Sir," Plistral stood and moved away towards where Arval had gone.

As they neared each other ready to search for another mark, they heard a commotion from close by in the crowd. Shouts boiled up and the hiss of steel being drawn caused the throng to part in front of them. As they turned to watch, a huge man with what Arval had said were tattoos just like the ones Bhinja had, was raising an enormous axe as he glared towards a slender man in close-fitting light grey leather armor. He wore a cloak of dark blue, it's hood covered his head, only his mouth and nose were visible. The man in grey and blue stared calmly at the man with the axe as he brandished a long, curved slender sword, a silver scabbard at his hip.

"You Jix think you can fight?!" the big man had growled.

"From the way you're holding that axe Nojii, it appears you'd like to find out," he answered calmly.

"Then shall we taste steel?"

"As you wish."

The big man had lunged forward, the axe whistling through the air as he swung it towards his adversary's head. The man in the grey leather had moved to his left with a grace, speed and fluidity that had made Plistral and Arval's eyes bulge. With an effortless whip of his right arm, the sword had flashed up and across the belly of the man with the axe. His eyes widened in surprise, both with how quickly the man had moved, and with what he surely knew was the feeling of his death as the sword parted both the leather suspenders that held up his trousers and the skin of his stomach. His lunge carried him past the man in grey, a grunt of pain escaped him as his hands fell off the handle of the axe and went towards the wide gash in his stomach. He staggered a few steps towards the watching ring of people and collapsed to the ground, his hand not coming close to preventing his blood and entrails from spilling out on the ground. His life was over in moments.

The man in the blue cloak and grey armor nonchalantly wiped his sword on the dead man's trousers, which had fallen around his knees when his suspenders had been cut, and calmly returned it to its silver scabbard. The circle of onlookers murmured quietly amongst themselves, some of them staring openly at the mess on the ground, others at the man in grey armor moving away nonchalantly through the crowd. Someone picked up the dead man's axe and disappeared, others stepped gingerly around him, avoiding the blood and viscera and continuing about their business. Plistral and Arval had watched until the crowd began to disperse, then made their way towards a shop that sold soup and bread, their bellies telling them it was time to eat in spite of the gory scene they'd just witnessed.

"So, what happened to the body?" Revan had asked, his eyes wide with wonder at this firsthand account of someone like the aides bleeding, dying.

"There are cleaners who go about the streets with carts. They usually just clean up after the horses or gather other trash. But if there is a body, they clean that up too."

Revan had been incredulous to find out that one like the aides had been killed.

"What did the man in grey mean when he said Nojii?"

"I don't know," Arval had admitted. "I've never heard the word before or since."

"Was it his name, like Bhinja?"

"Like I said, I don't know. It could have been. Or it could have been the name of his people."

"His people?"

"Yes. There are many peoples in the three kingdoms. There are Drisavans, Bentravirri, and Jarradanis, to name a few. Their names tell you which land they're from."

"Three kingdoms? What does that mean?" Revan asked.

"The world is made up of three kingdoms, the people I just mentioned draw their names from the name of the kingdom where they live. There are Jarradan, Drisava and Bentravirri.

"I think I'd like to see a city and visit these other lands, these kingdoms," Revan said.

"If we can get out of here, I'll take you to Kessar. We'll be able to live there with Plistral and the others."

"Others? There were more than just you and Plistral?"

"Of course. I was part of a Khet."

"What's a Khet?"

"It's a name for our little group in Kessar. There were about twenty of us. We survived by taking things from the pockets of the wealthy. Or cutting their purses. I was told there are Khets in every city in Jarradan."

"Where is Jarradan?"

"You're in it."

Chapter 2

he corpulent man in the lavish green and gold robe lay back on the cushions in his tent. His thick fingers held the roasted leg of some animal. Grease ran down his wrists to his forearms and was smeared and glistening across his chin. The tent was large with a ceiling three paces high, its walls about twenty apart, forming a square. The floor was covered in lush carpets with piles of cushions arranged along the walls. Two guards with swords on their hips stood just outside the opening, its cloth door rolled up and tied in place, allowing a hot breeze to blow in. In the middle was a fire pit, but with the heat inside the wood lay unburning. In the back, opposite the curtained entrance, was a long wooden table covered with stacks of papers, books, a wooden box with a brass latch, candles and a scale. A plain wooden chair rested in front of a small ink and pen set. Two battered wooden chests sat to the right side of the table.

"What news from the pit?" the man asked the angry visitor in front of him.

"Nothing today, Master Otarab," Bhinja muttered between clenched teeth.

"Ah, then it's a day like any other. The dig continues, the walls grow higher, the sun burns. Perhaps tomorrow will be different."

"Perhaps," Bhinja said disinterestedly.

"Have the new arrivals been performing?"

"Most. They work as instructed or they feel the lash. One didn't make it to the tool selection. We tried to persuade him to see reason, but the boot of Nillit did for him before he decided that he wanted to work."

"Then he will have to be replaced. Note it down on the ledger. I'll have to send the order in to Hento in the next day or two."

Bhinja stalked towards the table and sat down in the chair. The mention of Hento seemed to have increased his ire. Picking up the pen and dipping it in the ink jar, he angrily made a notation on a piece of paper on top of one of the stacks. He pushed the pen so hard that it tore the paper in two spots.

"That makes six that have made the journey out of the pit this week," Bhinja said.

"Yes, I recall your last report. Something about them simply dropping in place as they dug?"

"They were young, perhaps ten turnings. We hadn't received any water in two days. In this heat I'm surprised we haven't lost more."

"It does seem to have been hotter lately," Otarab said, fanning himself with one pudgy hand. "But it's always hot in this tent. Even with the vent at the top. Sometimes I dream of being back in Kessar, cooling myself in the shaded courtyard of my villa. But King Vraniss' bidding is that I, and you, remain here to control things. He's not a man to be crossed. Especially with those Jix of his."

"Yes, yes, the Jix. We all know how deadly they are," Bhinja said irritably. "But they aren't here now and never are. I don't care whether or not any of the diggers live or die, but without water, we will fail the king. And then the Jix will be here. Neither of us would want that. And thank you for reminding me that I'm stuck here like you are. You can have your villa in Kessar. I'd rather be drinking, whoring and slaughtering. That's what Nojii are for. Not babysitting and digging holes."

"I will include a note to Hento to see to it that the water shipments arrive more regularly," Otarab said. He pointedly ignored Bhinja's comments about the man's preferred activities.

"Good. If there is nothing else, I must return to the pit. By now I'm sure that someone there is not putting his back into it. I'll find him and he'll feel my lash."

"The heat getting to you Bhinja?" Otarab said with a sly grin. "Using your lash only makes you sweat. It'll feel even hotter. If you'd been a good boy to begin with, maybe King Vraniss wouldn't have sent you here."

"You stick to your orders, notes, and… meat," he said, waving a hand towards the greasy leg Otarab was gnawing on. "Let me worry about my lash. And where I am," Bhinja growled with a glare at his interlocutor.

Otarab waved him away with a soft chuckle.

"Bhinja's in a mood today," Arval whispered to Revan as they swung their picks. They'd seen him circling the road down to the pit earlier, the hooves of his horse echoing on the hard roadway. When he'd finally made it to the bottom, he'd wasted no time in screaming curses at the diggers, and while he was always free with his lash, he was especially vigorous in its application this day. Casting sidelong glances at him as he'd worked his way toward them, Arval and Revan had seen him flog no less than twenty diggers. By the time he was halfway to where they were, heat and fatigue had caused him to lose some of his pique. They could see rivulets of sweat running down his chest and arms, cutting small channels through the dust that coated his muscular torso. He'd finally found another aide, growled something to him in a low voice, and stalked off toward the small tent where he slept.

"I'm just glad he didn't get to us. He might have used the rod instead of the lash. In the mood he was in, we both could be dead," Revan said.

"Here comes Pinsi, keep digging."

They both turned back to the ground in front of them and swung their picks. Pinsi, another aide, who favored his fists over a lash, strolled past them, barking orders and curses. One aide was a vocal as any other.

The ground was as unyielding as it ever was, the rock-hard dirt coming off in chips. Revan and Arval were pickers, shovelers stood behind them, scooping up what they loosened and loading it into small hand-drawn carts that were wheeled over to other, larger carts pulled by horses. The contents of the small carts were shoveled into the larger carts and when they were full, the horses began their long, slow circuitous trip up the road out of the pit. None of the diggers knew where the carts full of dirt went once they were out of the pit, only that they left full and came back empty. It didn't really matter. Each day was just another closer to whatever their ultimate fate was. And in the minds of those digging, that fate was invariably death. The only question was how and when they would make their last ride. And how much it would hurt before they got there.

Revan and Arval were digging close to the wall of the box, once in a while stopping to let one of the shovelers remove the debris that accumulated at the base. These pauses were tolerated by the aides, most of the time. After Bhinja's outburst earlier, none of them seemed to care much about the two boys not swinging picks while shovelers cleaned up after them. Bhinja's mood affected them in much the same way it affected the diggers – it made them draw into themselves in order to appear invisible. Even Bhinja's fellow aides were not completely immune to his lash. Or fist. It was late in the day, the sun had dipped below the rim of the pit, its last golden rays were bright on the opposite rim, leaving the depths of the pit in welcome shadow. The air, while still hot, had cooled considerably.

Revan and Arval, both slim but well-muscled from their days of digging, resumed swinging their picks after the shovelers had finished. They had each only taken a couple of swings when Revan's pick dislodged a large chunk of the iron dirt. He'd never seen a chunk this big break off before. Once in a while a piece as big as his hand, maybe a little bigger would break loose, but this was the size of three shovel heads. Astonished, Revan paused a moment to stare. The chunk hadn't come completely out of the ground, just shifted a little, like a bowl not quite sitting level on top of another. In the gap between the edge of the chunk and the wall, he could see the edge of a brick but not another one beneath it. Behind appeared to be a void, a recess of some kind. He quickly shoved the chunk back in place, concealing the edge he'd found, and moved back a few steps to dig further from the wall. Arval, still close to the wall, eyed him askance and said, "What are you doing?"

"Move back. Dig by me."

"Why?"

"Just do it. I'll tell you later."

Arval did as Revan had asked, both of them swinging their picks in the monotonous rhythm they were so accustomed to. Minutes later a horn blew, signaling the end of the digging day.

As they both shuffled with the other workers towards the tables next to the platform to be served their meager dinner, Arval asked again what Revan had been doing.

"Tonight. When everyone's asleep, I'll tell you," he said quietly.

"Fine, but it better be worth waiting for."

"Shut up and get dinner."

When they'd consumed the gruel that had been served that night, each not so delighted to have had a piece of rancid meat in their bowl, Revan had suggested moving their pallets to the far side of the group of diggers, closest to the box.

"Why?" asked Arval.

"So, we can talk without the others hearing."

They both rolled up their thin pallets, they were just mats of woven reed with a thin sheet to cover them and made their way through the crowd of men and boys who were beginning to lay down for the night. Ignoring the stares and occasional curse when they stepped on someone, they finally made their way past the last boy on the edge of the group.

"Don't go too far away, we don't want to attract the attention of the aides," Revan said.

"This is your game, just tell me what you want me to do."

"Lay down, but don't go to sleep."

"Alright, but I'm tired. This had better be worth losing sleep over."

"It will be."

As they lay on their pallets, waiting for the rest of the diggers to fall asleep, Revan could barely contain his excitement. In the years of sameness - same food, same box, same pit, same pick, same death and pain - he'd finally found something different. It's what they had been looking for – an opening in the wall. When he was sure everyone around them was asleep, he nudged Arval. Whispering quietly, he told him to roll up his pallet and follow him. Frowning with perplexity Arval did as he was instructed.

"Don't talk, move quietly and stay low," Revan said.

The boys, pallets tucked under their arms, stole quietly towards the box. There were only a couple of aides who stood guard over the camp at night. Their confidence that the diggers were so tired from working and cowed by their lashes caused them to be lax in their vigilance. Revan could see three of them sitting at the table where meals were doled out talking among themselves in low tones. The night was very dark; clouds had moved in obscuring the stars that usually provided a faint light to the sleeping pit.

"Why did we have to bring our pallets?" Arval asked.

"So, the aides won't notice we're not in them if they look."

When they came up next to the wall, Revan looked down and began moving along parallel to it, muttering under his breath. Arval followed, mystified. Suddenly Revan squatted down and prodded at the ground with his hand. "Here it is," he said. Squatting beside him, Arval saw the chunk of dirt pivot as Revan pushed on one end of it.

"I found this today. Its why I moved back when we were digging. Look under here," he said, pulling up the edge.

Arval leaned over to peer into the small hole as Revan pulled the chunk out.

"It's so dark. I can hardly see anything."

"Look closer."

Arval leaned in a squinted into the dark hole. "It looks like an opening!" he quietly exclaimed.

"Yes!"

"How deep does it go?"

"I don't know. That's what I want to find out."

"Pull it out," Arval said.

With a soft grunt Revan got his fingers under the chunk and twisted it up and out of its hole. He reached down and pulled up a handful of sand, its grains draining out between his fingers like water from a cup riddled with holes.

"It's sand! We can dig this easy!" Arval said.

"Help me," Revan admonished.

Together they scooped out sand by the handful, enlarging the hole where the chunk of dirt had been. As they excavated, they realized that they needed to remove more of the hard dirt in order to see where the door, as they both now thought of it, led.

"Dig under it, make a void," Arval said.

They both jammed their hands in under the sharp lip of the hard dirt into the soft sand beneath.

"That's good. Now kick it down into the hole."

Revan kicked and another large piece of the rock-hard dirt broke off. He scooped it out and quickly dug more sand out from under the new edge. Arval did the same. In minutes they had a hole large enough for one of them to climb into.

"Now dig straight down and towards the wall."

"Wouldn't it be easier if we had a shovel?" Revan asked.

"Do you want to try to sneak over to the tools and get one without the aides seeing you?" Revan shook his head.

"Neither do I. Use your hands. The digging is easy enough."

Stopping to glance over towards the aides, Revan saw that they weren't paying any attention to anything other than what they were talking about.

"I'll go in," Revan said.

"Ok, I'll help you out if you need it."

Revan pawed at the sand, scooping and throwing it out over his shoulder. Arval moved to the other side of the hole to keep from getting a face full. There was indeed what seemed to be a doorway in the wall. About a pace in from the soaring face, Revan reached stone. It was far too dark to see, but he could feel something carved into the slab making up the recessed part of the wall. As his fingers traced the carvings, his mind conjured the image of a triangle inside of which were shapes and symbols he couldn't define.

"I think there's a door here," Revan whispered up to Arval. "There's something carved in it."

"What?"

"It feels like a triangle with other things carved inside. I'm not sure what they are."

He dug down deeper towards the bottom of the door and hit a ledge. The opening in the wall he'd discovered was now a little higher than the height of an average man. He'd also found, beneath the triangle on top of the door, another one on the bottom, only this one was inverted. But it too had strange symbols he couldn't quite define carved into it. As he ran his hands over the door, searching for a handle of some kind, he felt a tingling in his fingertips. The sensation was faint, but it made him pause. He took his hands away from the door for a moment and looked at it, it's form and carvings obscured by the inky darkness. The tingling stopped. Not seeing anything he resumed feeling around; the tingle returned.

There was no door handle, nor could he feel anything other than the triangles and strange symbols. The tingling grew stronger and began to make its way up his wrists and arms.

"I feel something strange," Revan said. "My hands and arms are tingling."

"Does it hurt?" Arval asked.

"No. It feels good actually, but it's strange. Like when you've slept on your arm and it starts to wake up, but different from that, not as deep. It's just on my skin."

"Can you find a way to open it?"

"Give me a minute. I'm trying."

The tingling had reached Revan's shoulders and was moving down his torso and up his neck now. The not unpleasant feeling was making him a little nervous, but didn't seem to be doing any harm, so he kept searching. He could hear Arval breathing above him. That did seem strange. He didn't recall hearing Arval breathe until now. Maybe he was as excited as Revan himself was. That was probably it.

The tingling had reached his cheeks. His eyes. His vision wavered, like looking through waves of heat. Suddenly it was gone. He was blind. In a panic he tried to pull his hands away from the door, but they wouldn't move. His arms didn't seem to be his. He could feel them distantly, but it was like something else was controlling their movements. He could feel the stone under his fingers, the heat in the air that still lingered this long after dark, and the smell of unwashed bodies and dust. He hadn't remembered smelling the diggers in the camp that strongly since he and Arval had made their way to the box. They weren't close; how could he smell them? His hands suddenly stopped moving. They held in place completely still for a moment, Revan was still unable to pull them away from the door, when they slowly glided up on their own to the tip of the triangle on top. Each index finger paused together at the tip and slowly began tracing the outline of the triangle down its sides, to the bottom corners and back towards the middle. When they met at that point, Revan realized there was another line moving straight up back towards the tip. Both fingers followed it and about in the middle, moved apart. They encountered the symbols carved inside the triangle, and each began to trace their sinuous shapes, their sharp angles.

As suddenly as it had begun, it was over. His fingers remained at the end of the last symbol they'd traced. A faint hum began to throb deep in his chest. It seemed like he could both feel and hear it. He tried to ask Arval if he could feel it too, but his mouth wouldn't work. Not only was he blind, but now he was apparently mute as well.

He felt himself squatting down, his hands running lightly over the door to the bottom triangle.

Again, his index fingers found the tip of the form, this one towards the ground. The process repeated, fingers tracing the outline of the triangle to the line in the middle, and out across the symbols. The hum grew more intense, his whole body vibrated with it. In front of him, the blackness began to abate, and a faint green glow began to appear in front of him. He still couldn't talk, but at least his vision had returned. The glow intensified; he could faintly see the triangles and symbols in front of him. That was where the glow was coming from – the carvings in the door - the glow came directly from them. His mouth suddenly could move.

"Quick," he called up to Arval, "cover the hole."

Arval seemed to understand what he wanted without having to ask. Maybe he could see the glow as well. He quickly lay down across the hole, his torso covering it completely, sealing in the strange light. They couldn't have the three aides seeing it.

It wasn't black in the hole in front of the door anymore because the glow was getting very bright. The light coming from the symbols pulsed in rhythm with the hum. The light grew in waves so bright that Revan closed his eyes to it, when without change or warning it stopped. The light and the hum were gone as he slowly opened his eyes. In front of him a door had swung open silently and a dimly lit passage drew out before him.

"Come down here! There's a tunnel of some kind," he said excitedly to Arval.

Revan moved a few steps inside and noticed that a faint green light was emanating from the walls themselves. They seemed to be made of the same blocks that constructed the outside walls he'd been looking at for so long. Except that these glowed the same way the symbols had, albeit not as brightly. Ahead about a hundred paces he could see the passage turn to the left. Arval dropped down behind him.

"What is this place?!"

"I don't know," Revan said. "But let's find out."

"After you."

As they moved further in, Revan glanced behind them. The door had swung shut.

Chapter 3

ook, the door closed."

Arval turned and noted the new development. "We're trapped," he said, a hint of fear in his voice, a touch of panic in his eyes.

"Maybe. Let's keep going. There might be another door further on. Whoever built it must have added a way out along with the way in."

They crept slowly along the passage, wary of they knew not what. There was no telling what might lurk around the corner up ahead, what traps may lie unsprung, what manner of death might greet them. Fear welled up in them both with the unknown dangers that could be waiting, but their excitement at being the first inside this place in who knew how many eons overrode it.

As Revan turned the corner he saw the passageway begin to slope upwards. The stone walls were unchanged, their ethereal green glow did not abate, but didn't intensify either. The air was still, but strangely didn't have the musty, stale odor of age. It was as if the air outside the box was the same as inside. The only sound was their footfalls on the stone and the light rasp of their breath. Their thoughts were as loud as anything inside.

They followed the passage up, through numerous turns and landings. There were no side passages, no obvious doors, no symbols. Whomever had built this place had apparently intended anyone entering it to follow this path. It must lead somewhere, but where that was the two boys still had no idea.

After what seemed to be at least an hour of steadily climbing, Revan noticed that the light seemed to be getting brighter. Arval had noticed it too. He tapped Revan on the shoulder and said, "It's getting brighter in here."

"Yes. We have got to be getting near to the top now. The box is tall, but we've been climbing for quite a while."

Ahead of them the passage turned to the right off a landing. Rounding the corner Revan found himself in an enormous room. It looked as if it must be as large inside as the box was outside. The walls stretched far off into the distance. The green glow had increased to the point that it was as bright inside the huge room as it would have been at midday outside. The stones making up the walls and floor were glowing in such a way that it seemed as though they were almost transparent. The room itself, aside from its size, was utterly plain. There was no furniture, no columns, no other passages that they could see. Nothing but the vast empty space.

"What do we do now?" Arval asked. His brown eyes were ripe with anxiety.

"Let's look around. There has to be something here. Why would someone build this place and not put anything in it?"

They walked out into the room, each scanning to the sides, searching for anything to tell them more about the structure they were in. It was all the same though, all the way to the far end; there was the floor, ceiling, and four walls. The only feature was the opening to the passage they had just traversed. The stones glowed brightly, the walls and floor stretched on before them. Revan found it hard to believe that this was all there was – a huge empty room. Was this what he and Arval had been digging for? Had all those men and boys died to discover this? Absorbed all those lashings, both from whip and tongue, just to find the box empty?

Arval nudged his shoulder and pointed ahead of them. "The floor looks different there. See?"

"Maybe. Keep looking."

As they grew nearer to what Revan judged to be about the middle of the room, he noticed that the floor did indeed look different. It didn't glow green like the rest of the stone that made up the walls and floor, but looked white, like a late afternoon cloud passing in front of the sun.

"Be careful," Arval whispered as they approached the anomaly.

"You don't have to whisper; we're the only ones in here."

"Oh yeah," he said, his face turning a light crimson.

Revan could now see that the stones making up the floor in that spot actually were glowing white. As he edged up to it, he realized that it was an area three stones by three, making a perfect square in the middle of the room. They both gazed down on the white stones, perplexed.

"Should we touch it?" Arval asked.

"Do you have something you can throw on it? It could be a trap of some kind."

Arval took off his sandal and tossed it into the middle of the eerily glowing white stones. Nothing happened.

Revan knelt down up against the edge, holding his hand out over the stones. He was bathed in the white light radiating up from them.

"I don't feel anything."

"Are you going to touch it?" Arval asked.

Revan didn't answer. Taking a deep breath, he quickly dropped his hand to the stone closest to him. There was a distant rumble from far below them. The whole room seemed to vibrate. Arval, eyes wide backed away a few steps. Revan kept his hand on the stone. It felt like any other stone he'd ever touched. There appeared to be nothing special about it, except for its effulgent white light.

The rumble grew louder and louder, like some huge boulder was being rolled away from the entrance of a cave. Suddenly the stone on which Revan's hand rested began to rise from the floor. It moved slowly, as if some long unused mechanism was gradually waking and putting its shoulder to its task. Revan stood as it rose, glancing back at Arval who stood, mouth agape and eyes wide, watching.

When it had reached about the height of his waist, it stopped. Directly above it about a hand's width, the air began to shimmer. It looked like the waves of heat he saw in the pit when the sun was at its worst, except that it was more substantial, thicker somehow. Thin red and gold streaks twisted and danced within it, like pieces of thread caught in a wind. The walls and floor behind it blurred into twisted and melted shapes, indistinct and constantly changing with the movement of the object.

Revan lifted his hand from the stone and gingerly stretched his fingers towards the pulsating form. As his fingers made contact with its outer edge he felt a flash of power course through him, freezing him in place. Unlike when he'd opened the door, he could still see, but he couldn't move his limbs; his hand remained where it was. The twisting mass began to move towards him, slowly encasing his whole hand in its formless wavering shape. His body felt as if all the blood in it had suddenly quadrupled in volume and force, as if he had four hearts pumping it instead of one. As the shape moved up his arm, the red and gold threads dove into his skin, like swift snakes careening into a hole in the ground. It seemed he could feel them swimming up his arm, spreading throughout his body. His senses grew sharper too; he could hear Arval's ragged breathing and tell that he was terrified. The smell of the dust from the pit and the sweat on each of them was cloying and nearly overwhelming. He thought it strange that he hadn't noticed it before. He'd smelled something like it when he'd been digging out the door, but he'd thought it was from the other diggers in the pit, even though they hadn't been close. The glowing stones that made up the structure were far more distinct than they had been. He could clearly see the joints between them, even in the walls farthest away. On the stones closest to them, he was able to discern small irregularities, little divots and pits that he knew he'd never seen before.

Suddenly he heard a voice. It came from all around him, as if there were a ring of people circling him, all saying the same thing in perfect synchronization, their timing so precise that all the voices melded into one.

"You have awoken me," it said.

"Who are you?" Revan said. At least his mouth was able to work, even if the rest of his body didn't.

"Who are you talking to?" Arval asked.

"Long have I slumbered. Long have I waited for wakening. What is your name?"

"Revan."

"That is an ancient name. It is known to me."

"Revan who in the dark depths are you talking to?" Arval asked, fear tinging his voice.

Revan tried to tell Arval that it was alright, but he couldn't form words to say to him. His mouth wouldn't work. Maybe he was only able to speak to the disembodied voice addressing him. He thought to test the idea.

"My name is ancient?" he was able to say.

"Yes. It is a name from the time before the departure."

"What departure?"

"The departure of magic."

"Magic? What's magic?"

"It is what you feel now, within you. You first felt it when you opened the door."

Revan realized that the voice must be talking about how his hands had moved on their own when he'd traced the outlines of the triangles and the tingling he'd felt.

Arval had backed away several steps. He nervously eyed the doorway far behind them, ready to run if he sensed danger. His survival instincts had been honed and polished from his time thieving with his Khet back in Kessar. They were all at his disposal now and told him to run, but he didn't want to leave Revan. They were friends, and he was not one to run when a friend was in trouble. Except he couldn't tell if Revan actually was in trouble. He wasn't moving, but he was talking. To whom Arval couldn't tell. And what was this magic he was talking about?

"Do you sense the difference in you?" the voice said to Revan. "Are your senses more acute? Can you hear, smell, see more clearly than you could a moment ago?"

"Yes. I can see the joints between the stones on the far wall. I can hear Arval breathing. He's afraid," Revan answered.

"He does not need to be. There is no harm here. Unless you bring it with you."

Revan ignored that last comment. "Who are you?" he asked.

"I am a remnant of those who lived before the departure. I was placed here so that one might someday come whom I could tell of what happened. Who could receive what you have been given. Who may be able to bring about the return."

"Return?"

"The return of magic. Come with me, I will tell you."

Revan noticed now that the undulating mass had disappeared; it seemed to have all been absorbed into him. All that remained was the voice. He felt his vision drawn down towards the white stone jutting from the floor. As he stared at its flat surface, he felt himself pulled towards it, the white light intensifying as the stone grew larger in his vision. The room suddenly ceased to exist and the world went white.

Chapter 4

evan felt as if he were in a tunnel of white light. But unlike the passage he'd come through to reach the room and the white stones, this one was perfectly round, its walls strangely discernable even though the light seemed to be of a uniform brightness. He had no sense of his body, couldn't see his limbs or feel anything tactile. It was as if his mind had left his body behind and was now adrift in this tube of white nothingness. He tried to speak, but nothing happened. His sense of smell detected nothing, and his ears picked up no sound. There was only the tube of light and a sensation of movement. Movement that seemed to be picking up speed. There were no features to tell him that he was rushing past something, but he knew he was flying through the lighted tunnel, following twists and turns like he had back in the passage. He had no sense of time, the light and movement simply were, he was powerless to do anything but flow along.

The sensation of movement suddenly stopped. He could tell that there was something in front of him, an indistinct yet vaguely human shape, its form obscured by the brilliant light surrounding it. He was in a room, its walls were close together, about large enough for two people to stand comfortably.

"This is the place where magic used to dwell. It has been long since I have seen it. Once there were many who flowed through these conduits. You are the first to be here in untold ages."

"Where is this?" Revan asked.

"This is nowhere. It only is. It is the home of magic."

"Oh. I don't understand."

"If you must think of it as a place, think of it as somewhere inside yourself but outside as well. Between life and death but not fully of either. Here all things exist, all things do not exist. It is nowhere and everywhere. It is the conduit through which magic once flowed."

"What is magic, where did it go?"

"It is the force on which all life depends, but which also makes up all life. With it, things you've never imagined are possible. It left the world long ago."

"Why?"

"It was dying. Once many were open to it, were able to wield it to create the most wondrous things, to perform miracles beyond imagination. But over the eons faith in magic was lost. Abilities were discarded or ignored. And some sought to use it for ill or avarice. Magic began to wane, its purpose melted into obscurity like a candle that has burned to the end of its life. Eventually there were only a few remaining who remembered it, who still bore the ability and desire to interact with it, to create as had been done before. Most had rejected magic, either intentionally or through neglect. Some held it in contempt and sought to destroy it or to use it for evil. Those left who truly understood magic decided that they must remove it from the world until such time that the world was again ready for it. Thus, was conceived the idea of the departure. A council was convened of those who wished to preserve magic and a plan was formed. Magic needed to be isolated from the world. It was determined that the only manner in which to do that was to send it away, to a place where it couldn't be reached. From this council the Blackfire was created. Magic departed."

"Where did it go?"

"Away from this world. It can be seen now in the sky. It is the Blackfire."

"Blackfire? In the sky? I've never seen it. What is it?"

"It is magic. Magic is aware."

"Do you know how I ended up in the pit?"

"That I cannot tell you. Since the departure some things are lost to magic. There is very little of it left in this world. Most of what remains supports the Kryxaal."

"What's a Kryxaal?"

"It is where you found me – it is the structure which you are inside of at this moment. The Kryxaal was created at the time of the departure to house certain knowledge critical to the return, and to serve as a place where one who would bring it about might make contact with me or one like me. It is also where a small repository of magic was stored to be bestowed on the one who entered. As you have been."

"I have magic?"

"Of course. When you opened the door you were infused with a small bit of magic. When you called me from slumber, you received yet more."

"You mentioned one like you. You mean there are others?"

"Yes. There are four Kryxaal throughout the world. This is only one."

"Where are the other three?"

"Hidden. After they were created they were concealed from the eyes and minds of those who would use them for ill or destroy them."

"How did you do that?"

"This one was constructed in a deep valley that was then filled with dirt, buried where none would find it for eons. The others were concealed in different places around the world. The remaining magic was used to eliminate the memory of the Kryxaal from those who knew of their existence."

A strange thought occurred to Revan. "So, are you the Kryxaal?"

"No. I am the remnant of one who lived before. The Kryxaal are objects within which I, and those like me, repose."

"So, if I were to find another Kryxaal then I would find another… person?"

"I am no longer a person. I am a remnant, as are the others. My existence was created and is sustained by the magic that was placed in the Kryxaal. The stone you touched was imbued with a fragment of my magic, as was the Kryxaal itself. This bound a part of me to the Kryxaal. You do not yet understand, but if it helps, then yes, you may think of me as a person."

"You're right, I don't understand. So how was this Kryxaal found?"

"That I do not know. The Kryxaal were concealed but were ultimately meant to be discovered. You did not find it. I know not who did. Yet you are the first to enter the Kryxaal since it was built. As such you are to whom I pass this knowledge and its attendant magic."

"Why me? Why not Arval?"

"You had the courage to activate the initiation stones. Not he. Also, you carry within you the means to reawaken the Kryxaal."

"What do you mean 'the means'? What's inside me?"

"Those who are able to commune with magic, to employ it, each carry within them a small part of it. All living things possess this, but it is stronger in some than in others. In the time of the departure this force, this spark, had begun to die. Fewer and fewer were born with it."

"What caused it to die?"

"We were never able to determine the cause. As I said, many had abandoned magic, or used it for evil, but this was not the cause of its decay. We worked to halt the process, to restore magic to life and life to magic, but we failed. Had we been able to ascertain the cause, it is possible that a remedy would have been found.

Since we were unsuccessful in our efforts, the departure was conceived and the Kryxaal created."

"So, what do I have to do with all this?"

"You are the first in millennia to enter the Kryxaal, you also have within you that spark of magic. Most do not. If you had not had it, you would not have been able to gain entrance here. But you have awoken me, activated this Kryxaal. If magic is to be restored to the world, it must begin with you. Or with another who may enter one of the remaining Kryxaal."

"Me?! I'm a slave. I've spent my entire life, well most of it, almost all I can remember anyway, digging the Kryxaal out of the pit where its buried. And what do you mean another who may enter?"

"The Kryxaal will provide you with knowledge and abilities with which you can begin the process that will lead to the return. If another enters one of the other three Kryxaal and they have the spark as you do, they may be able to bring about the return the same way. They would also receive knowledge and abilities."

"Abilities? Knowledge?"

"Do you not recall your heightened senses? How well you were able to see, hear and smell?"

"Well... yes."

"Those abilities will remain with you when you leave here. You may be able to add others over time. And knowledge will be imparted as I have imparted some to you. This is what is meant by activating the Kryxaal. Once you have these things, the magic contained within the Kryxaal will be no more. I will be no more."

"You mean you will disappear, be destroyed? Will the same thing happen if someone else enters a Kryxaal and gains these things?"

"Yes, if that person has the spark, they will receive the same things you have. Now that you have received magic and knowledge, I and the Kryxaal will cease to exist."

"Do you at least have a name?"

"I was known as Drannal in life. We must return. The magic remaining in the Kryxaal is fading and there is yet more to do before I pass from this world forever."

Revan suddenly felt himself moving again, the white tunnel before him stretched away as the shape he'd seen dissipated like smoke on a strong wind, and the sense of speed increased. Again, there was no time, nothing but the white light, the tunnel, and Revan's thoughts, which were whirling in confusion.

As quickly as it had begun, the journey was over and he found himself back in his body, still looking at the white stones in front of him.

Chapter 5

evan stood dazed, the nine white stones glowing brightly before him, his mind whirling with what he'd just experienced. It was too much for him to comprehend. Until this moment his entire life had been digging, exposing the very structure he now stood inside of. He'd never truly contemplated what might exist outside the pit, what else there was other than Bhinja and his lash. Arval's arrival half a turning ago had made him aware that there was an entire world he'd never known that there were things he'd never imagined. The idea that food could be something to be enjoyed, not just hurriedly swallowed to fill the void in his stomach was a revelation. He'd never thought that there could be something like a city, a place that contained all that Arval had described. His only true connection to that phantomlike other world had been the vague memory of grass and the people he thought might be his parents. He suddenly realized that he'd never asked Arval how he'd come to the pit from the city of Kessar. It just hadn't seemed important; it never even occurred to him to ask. The lives of the other diggers were immaterial. Diggers came, diggers died. There was digging and the lash. Life plodded on one dreary day at a time. The thought that his life could be something other than endless toil simply hadn't formed in his mind. He'd spent his life waiting for his eventual last ride. But now, coming into the Kryxaal, meeting Drannal, hearing what he had, experiencing his sharpened senses, had finally driven home to Revan the possibility of leaving the pit, of actually seeing Kessar, and maybe the rest of the world - of having some purpose beyond just wielding a pick. He found, somewhat startlingly, that he wanted to live. Not just exist like he had in the pit, but really live. The thought of his final ride up the circling road clinging to the walls of the pit, as a corpse, heated his anger, made him want to destroy Bhinja and the other aides. Destroy them! It hadn't seemed possible. The thought itself had been so far beyond any idea of potential, so outside the boundaries of his reality, that it had never wended its way into his conscious thoughts. Now he lusted for it. He fiercely desired to see Bhinja's blood splattered across the dirt of the pit. Or anywhere. The song of the lash combined with Bhinja's screams of agony seemed a wonder that was becoming all too possible. Revan suddenly realized he was experiencing the notion of revenge. Arval had mentioned it in passing, in some story about a beating he'd administered to one of his Khet who'd stolen something from him. It had been an alien concept. Now it felt real, tangible, something he wanted for himself and for all the others who'd never had a chance at it. For those who had suffered and died in the pit. Who had toiled their precious lives away at mindless digging until they had made the last ride. It felt attainable, near. Possible.

The other white stones began to rise from the ground as Revan's mind was pulled from the thoughts tumbling through it and back to what was in front of him. As they reached the height of the first stone to have risen, they stopped, creating in front of him a small platform. The light above them began to shift and move, its brilliance spewed forth, muting the glowing green that pervaded the rest of the room. It looked to be forming itself into some kind of shape. As Revan watched, he could hear Arval behind him, backing up another few steps, his breathing ragged.

"It's alright Arval," he said. The prohibition on speaking to his friend had been removed. Perhaps Drannal was done with him. As soon as the thought occurred, he heard the voice again.

"Follow the light to find the way out."

Revan watched as the light coalesced into a brilliant white ramp running from the platform of risen stones towards the ceiling. Its shape hung suspended by nothing in the air. Revan thought that if he trod it, he'd simply step right through and fall.

"How can I walk up a ramp of light?" he said.

"It is the only way to leave the Kryxaal. You must traverse it to reach the exit."

"But it just goes to the ceiling..."

"You must also trust in the magic that has created it. As you must trust in the abilities and magic you've been given."

"What abilities? My senses are sharper, but that's all I can feel."

"When the other stones rose from the floor to create the exit path, you were given other abilities that you will discover in time. You must trust them. Most of all you must trust yourself. You have been given these gifts, these abilities, in order to help you may bring about the return. It will not be simple. The danger will be great. You will be challenged, perhaps mortally, and your life will be forever altered. You will have choices to make. The first is whether or not you wish to pursue the task that has been presented to you. It truly is your choice; you are not bound by any covenant. If you decide not to try to bring about the return, your abilities will fade as the magic that made them possible dies within you. You will mourn their passing, but you may yet be able to live a life of your choosing. One that does not involve any more danger to you than you have already faced. If you choose to follow the path of the return, the magic within you will grow, your abilities will grow, but so will the personal danger you will face. This is not a test. It is your choice, and one you must make freely. You have one turning from this day to make it."

"One turning? What happens if I don't attempt the return?"

"Nothing. Except that the magic and your abilities will begin to fade. And another will eventually discover one of the other Kryxaal, and they may choose to bring about the return."

"How do I choose? What do I have to do?"

"If you make the decision in your heart, that will be enough."

"If I choose the return path, will I be able to have revenge on Bhinja?"

"That too is your choice. But know this: revenge may not bring you what you believe it will."

"What do you mean?"

"I can say no more. Our time is at an end."

"Will I ever… talk to you again?"

"If you choose the path of the return, then one day we may meet again. That is possible with magic."

"How?"

"If you are successful then you will come to know. You must leave now. The Kryxaal will soon exist no longer."

Revan turned to the still wide-eyed Arval, "We have to go. This ramp is the way out."

"Ramp?! It's just light!"

"Trust me; it's the only way. Come on."

Revan hoisted himself up onto the platform. As he did, he felt a subtle rumble similar to what he'd felt when the first stone had risen from the floor. Except this felt stronger. He could actually see the stones of the walls and floor vibrating with its intensity.

Looking down at the ramp of white light in front of him, Revan hesitantly placed one foot on it. He could feel its solidity under his sandal.

"Its solid. Let's go," he said over his shoulder to Arval.

As he began to walk up it, he could hear Arval scramble up on to the platform. They both moved gingerly as they walked, fearing at any moment that the light might disappear like a lamp blown out at night before bed. It was as wide as the passage they'd followed to the enormous room, so they didn't fear falling off, even though there were no railings. It was the thought of walking on light that made them both hesitant.

Nearing the top Revan looked up, wondering how they were to get through the ceiling. He noticed the glow around another square of stones begin to change from green to white. It looked as if the ramp went straight to them. He wasn't sure what was happening, but he was still alive, and the ramp held, so he kept climbing. Glancing from the ramp to the ceiling, he saw the now completely white square of stones turn translucent. In moments they had disappeared, and he could see the night sky above, the shadowy blackness just acquiring its first hint of the orange colors of dawn.

"The sun is coming up," he said back to Arval. "We've been in here all night."

"It feels like it. You didn't move for a long time after you talked to whatever it was. I didn't know what to do so I just waited. Then you just suddenly started talking again."

As Arval glanced up to the opening in the ceiling, he said, "I can see the sky! Those stones just disappeared!"

"Yeah. Let's hurry, I don't think we have much time."

The rumbling had increased to a low roar all around them. Revan noticed that the stones of the walls and floor had begun to turn white like the spot in the ceiling had.

"We'd better run. I think this whole building is going to disappear soon like those stones above us did!"

They both began to jog. The opening in the ceiling was near and they both burst out on the roof of the box into the warm morning air. Revan was astounded at the sight of the sky unimpeded by either the walls of the pit or the box. His view of it for as long as he could remember had been obstructed by one or the other. The mass of stars was disorienting. Even with dawn brushing its fingers lightly across the dark, there were still far more stars than Revan had ever believed possible.

Directly ahead of them he could see another ramp of light extending from the edge of the roof they were on towards the rim of the pit. Since the box had been buried so deep, its top was much lower than the rim of the pit, giving the ramp of light a relatively steep incline.

"We have to get to that other ramp. Quick, we have to run," Revan yelled back. The roar had become deafening. The entire building was now glowing a brilliant white and quaking violently. Some of the stones had turned opaque, as if they were on the edge of translucence. Revan recognized that when they got to that point, the whole of the Kryxaal would disappear. And probably their way out too. They'd be lucky if they even survived. The bottom of the pit was a long way down. He could picture them both falling as the Kryxaal vanished. Trust in yourself, Drannal had said. Revan shoved the thought of falling away and sprinted for the ramp. Arval, seeming to understand the danger, was close behind.

As they made it to the ramp and started across, Revan snatched a glance down. He could see the bottom of the pit far below. It was bathed in the brilliant white light emanating from the stones of the Kryxaal. His vision, enhanced now from the magic he'd received, told him that the entire camp was awake. He could see aides and diggers running for the road, heard the confused shouts and the crack of lashes. Even under these circumstances the aides were attempting to keep order among their slaves. Bhinja sat atop his horse, screaming, and swinging his wooden rod. He felt sadness for those receiving its blows, and rage at Bhinja for using it. One day, he silently vowed, Bhinja would feel the rod and its sharp metal spines. Or maybe something even worse.

Revan knew that if they didn't make it to the far end of the ramp, and soon, that they were dead. A glance over his shoulder showed him that the stones of the roof were now translucent, some had even disappeared. The roar coming from the Kryxaal was the loudest sound he'd ever heard. Fear driving him, he realized that he wasn't running as fast as he could. His legs weren't at all tired, even though he hadn't slept in a day. He stretched them out, pumping harder and harder, and was amazed to find that he was moving at least twice as fast as he had been. And it seemed he could even go faster. The lip of the pit was rapidly approaching. Another glance back showed him that the roof was entirely gone, the walls below it were disappearing as well. Arval was a good distance behind him, and the far end of the ramp, where they'd begun their escape, was disappearing, washing out of existence at an ever-increasing rate, racing up behind them to destroy the path beneath their feet. In an instant Revan judged that the ramp would be gone long before Arval ever reached safety. He himself, with his newfound speed, would be across, but Arval would plunge to his death.

Fear for his friend ignited something in his mind. A flame was kindled in the farthest recesses of his consciousness. The light it cast seemed to illuminate his thoughts, imbue them with clarity. He felt that he'd been asleep his entire life and was now waking. No, that wasn't it. It was like he'd been dead and had somehow returned to life. The essence of that light suffused his entire body with a feeling of vitality, strength and an awareness that surpassed anything he'd heretofore felt. At the same time, an image formed in his thoughts like a vibrant and well-remembered dream. It was as if he was back in the tube of white light with Drannal, only the tunnel was inside him now. His mind and body were bent on escaping, his awareness on running, but some other part of him, one he had never known existed, was back in that place of white light, but within himself. He saw, yet didn't see, the red and gold threads again. They twisted and undulated as they had before, but they were his now. With a jolt of understanding he realized that he could control them, move and manipulate them. Revan's instincts took over; his conscious mind didn't understand what he was doing, but he instinctually knew what he had to do if he was to save Arval. His mind sent the threads shooting out of him, towards Arval. There were far more red than gold, but they were both there; he could see them penetrate Arval's chest.

"Run faster! You'll never make it," He called back.

Arval, fear writ large on his face, amazingly increased his speed. He was now moving as fast as Revan was. A moment later Revan reached the rim of the pit. He turned, panting to watch as Arval raced the rapidly disappearing ramp of light. It was gaining on him. He was almost to the rim of the pit, but the ramp's vanishing edge had nearly reached him.

"Jump!" Revan yelled.

A look of comprehension on his face, Arval took two lunging steps and leaped, the rim of the pit seemed impossibly far away from him. As he flew through the air, Arval looked down, morbid understanding flashed through his mind: he was going to die. He reached his arm out with everything he had, hoping to just maybe catch the rim of the pit. It didn't look like he was going to make it.

At the last instant Revan reached out as far as he could and caught his hand just as he began to fall towards the distant road below. With a smack, Arval's torso crashed into the wall below Revan. Their grip slipped a little, but they were able to maintain it. With a grunt Revan heaved Arval up and onto the rim next to him. It seemed he was stronger as well as faster; Arval hadn't felt very heavy.

As they both stood panting from the run, they watched the Kryxaal disappear before them. The brilliant white light was dissipating as the stones vanished. The roar was still audible but had diminished markedly. Mesmerized they gazed at the object of their imprisonment as it disintegrated into nothingness. The process that had begun slowly had sped up considerably, and it wasn't long before the roar died away and the last of the stone blocks had disappeared. From their vantage point at the rim of the pit, they could see the enormous square hole in the ground where the first stones of the Kryxaal had been laid in some epoch long past. It wasn't very deep. Glancing at each other, they both reached the unspoken conclusion that their lives hadn't had much more time. It would have only been a matter of a few weeks, perhaps a month or two before the bottom of the structure would have been found, and they most likely would have taken their final ride out of the pit.

"We should get out of here," Arval said. "The aides will probably kill everyone left down there, and then they'll be coming up here. We need to be away before they arrive."

"I agree. Where should we go?"

"Let's head southwest, towards Kessar. We can join up with my Khet."

"Sounds good to me. I'd like to try some of this food you've been telling me about."

As they turned away from the pit, Revan looked at the sky to the south and stopped, dumbfounded. He was looking at an enormous wheel of turbulent and undulating black flamelike clouds. It was huge, blotting out most of the southern sky, but he could also tell that it was a long way away. A spiral of curved and rotating black arms of flame emanated from an angry black ball at the center. The arms stretched out into the vastness of the sky and towards the earth, obscuring the stars that lived behind them. The farthest fringes were illuminated with red and gold lightning. They looked to Revan very much like the threads he'd seen in the Kryxaal and which he'd somehow shot into Arval. The black of the object's arms was not uniform, but morphed from a glistening shade of obsidian, to the flat and dull black of the tomb. Within in it were valleys and peaks, growing and subsiding. They followed no discernable pattern, but twisted and rolled, rose and fell at random. The black ball at the center looked like nothing so much as a mass of inky black clouds swirling and crashing together, like they were attempting to annihilate one another. Its violence, even from this distance, was mesmerizing. The lowest edge of the wheel-like arms descended past the southern horizon, obscuring the entire sky to the south. Revan stood, frozen, unable to tear his eyes from the massive wall of black flame spinning slowly through the sky.

"What in the dark depths is that?!" Revan asked, his voice just above a whisper.

Arval smiled at Revan's amazement. "That's the Blackfire," he said simply.

Chapter 6

hat do you mean it's gone!?" King Vraniss roared.

"Gone Sire. The entire structure," the man standing in front of the king gulped. No one enjoyed giving the king news they knew he wouldn't like. And this was almost the worst news anyone could ever give him. "The initial report has been verified. The structure is no more."

"Where did it go?" Vraniss asked, the heat in his voice and fury in his eyes made the man in front of him shuffle a small step back, his eyes downcast.

King Vraniss was an imposing man even without the authority his station provided. Tall and broad-shouldered, he moved with a lithe grace that testified to his physical prowess. Tales of his exploits with weapons were legendary. It was said that he'd once killed, alone, fifty men who'd tried to assassinate him on a hunting trip. His penetrating brown eyes stared out from under a wide brow, the prominent cheekbones and wide mouth above his strong chin lent him an authoritative air. Everything about the man whispered command. Except his nose. It was abnormally large for his features, protruding out asymmetrically from his face, with a hook at the tip that gave it a beak-like quality. The effect was jarring and made him seem more than imposing; it made him look sinister. His dark hair was shot through with grey and just brushed the shoulders of his embroidered silver jacket. A white shirt with ruffles down the front and brown trousers of fine cloth tucked into highly polished black boots completed his attire.

"No one knows Sire," the man responded, fear making his voice croak just a little.

"Where is that pompous fat man Otarab?" King Vraniss' voice had lowered from the raging scream it had been, to almost a whisper, dripping with menace.

"He is en route, the messenger said."

"When he arrives, he is to brought directly to me. Post guards at the city gates and give them these instructions: he is not to visit his villa, a tavern or a pleasure palace. He is to come here. Instantly."

"By your command Sire," the terrified man responded.

"See to it at once."

The man turned abruptly and without another word, scampered off.

Vraniss went to the window behind him and looked out. From this room in the Azure Palace, he could see out across the city of Kessar to the gates off to the north. The road leading to those gates was empty all the way to the nearby mountains that formed the border between the forested land to the south, and the desert wastes north of them. The Bluecrag Mountains were a natural barrier that had served to defend Kessar from northern invasions for centuries. The stones of the Azure Palace had been quarried from them. The mountains and the palace were both aptly named – their stone was a brilliant shade of blue, shot through with veins of white and yellow. The palace itself gleamed on sunny days, visible on its hill at the center of the city, for ranges in all directions. The room where Vraniss now stood was his private study. It contained an ornate carved wooden desk with matching chair. Bookcases lined the walls to either side of the large window set in the center of the wall opposite the doorway. The heavy wooden door stood open, the shoulders of guards out in the hall to either side were visible, their long pikes resting upright. They would be lowered across the door to prevent anyone from entering without the king's permission. The tall window in front of King Vraniss was of clear glass, its mullions of thick lead separating the individual panes into a grid. A map table stood under it. Vraniss glanced at it, noting on the large vellum map that lay open, the location of the excavation where the structure had disappeared well over a week ago. He realized that Otarab might not arrive at the city for another few days; it was many ranges to the pit. The Nojii messenger who had brought the news had ridden hard for a week. His horse, pushed beyond exhaustion, had died underneath him, and he'd run the final distance on foot. By the time he'd arrived at the city gates, the man had been nearly as dead as his horse actually was.

How could it have disappeared, Vraniss thought. The excavation had been going on since long before he'd ever gained the throne. His predecessor, King Travorik, had left behind a diary concerning the structure and the excavation. The digging had begun during the reign of one of his ancestors. The diary hadn't made clear how the structure was found, only that it was believed to contain immense power. Vraniss was a man who enjoyed power, who sought it and relished it, reveled in its application. He didn't know what the power was that the structure apparently contained, the diary didn't mention anything of its nature, but it must have been something worth all the effort expended to reach it. Since coming to the throne, Vraniss had doubled, then doubled again, the size of the crew of diggers he had working.

Vraniss tolerated Otarab's fawning ways because the man had produced results. In truth he detested the man. Sycophants made Vraniss want to cut their throats. He expected obedience and was quick to punish failure or sloth, but Otarab brought murder to his thoughts. It didn't help Vraniss' mood when he remembered that Otarab was a Nojii noble. He had other issues with the Nojii; that Otarab was one of them simply bolstered his ire.

As he paced the room, his mind on the catastrophe at the site, he pondered what he was going to do with Otarab. He could confine him to the dungeons. No, that seemed too easy. A public spectacle would be better. He'd use Otarab to send a message to the populace: disappoint King Vraniss and this was what would happen to you. Also, by punishing a Nojii noble, he would send a message to that unreliable and bloodthirsty race that he was King in Jarradan, and they were yet his subjects. Keeping them in line was vitally important. But what would he actually do, or have done, to Otarab? He'd seen men tortured to death by some very talented and very ruthless people. Perhaps that – torture? Yes, but of what variety? Burning? Otarab's screams as he burned would be most pleasant. Too fast, although very painful. Disembowelment? He wouldn't die fast enough. His men who were experienced with that method were very good at keeping their victims alive for long periods. Vraniss didn't want to wait that long. He could order them to speed it up a bit. But no. It was too predictable. Wouldn't make enough of a spectacle. Although Otarab's exquisite pain would be very satisfying to behold. Peeling? Yes, that was the method! Otarab liked to have his lackey Hento peel his slaves at the pit when they misbehaved. Vraniss would peel Otarab. But not just one limb or his head, his whole body. Slowly. And he'd have his most trusted lieutenant perform the deed. That's the exercise of power that would send just the right message, not only to the Nojii, but to all.

"Bring me Barittin," King Vraniss called to the guards outside the door to his study.

"At once Sire," one of them responded.

The man shouted commands down the hall to someone else; Vraniss could hear that person's footsteps echoing on the blue marble of the hallway floor as he ran off.

The question Vraniss now asked himself, having decided what to do with Otarab, was what to do about the Nojii and the missing structure. He wasn't sure there was anything he could do about the missing building now, at least not until he'd heard Otarab's report. But the Nojii were a more tangible problem. The excavation was staffed and overseen exclusively by them, and Vraniss had been paying them to keep order among the slaves there. Now that they no longer had that task to keep them occupied, they would probably return to raiding and pillaging throughout Jarradan. The Nojii were a hardy people who came from the very desert where they had, until several days prior, been taking out their aggressions on slaves.

When Vraniss had usurped the throne from his predecessor, the Nojii were roaming all over Jarradan, sacking villages and small towns, and making off with plunder and slaves. While Vraniss cared little for the lives of the people the Nojii brutalized and slaughtered, he did not care for disorder. One of his first actions upon ascending the throne had been to make a deal with the Nojii. If they were to stop rampaging, he would offer them employment where their darker appetites could be sated, and they would receive a salary for their efforts. They'd been quick to accept. Especially when he'd threatened to loose the Jix on them. No one in Jarradan wanted the Jix' attention turned their direction.

And that was another problem - his relationship with the Jix. Their prowess at fighting and ruthlessness in carrying out the orders of their king was legendary. It was said that they'd never lost a battle in which they'd been engaged. Even against staggering odds. Their order had existed for millennia, and their history had been recorded, but it was locked away in their stronghold on the lower slopes of the hill below the Azure Palace. Requests to view their records were met with polite but firm refusal. And no one had ever been brave enough, or stupid enough, to try to take them by force or stealth. The origins and exploits of the Jix were known only to them. Vraniss cared about the history of the Jix, only to the extent that they did his bidding when he called upon them. Theirs was an uneasy alliance. Vraniss' predecessor King Travorik had come from a very long line of hereditary rulers, all of whom had had the Jix at their disposal. And the Jix had been loyal to them. Vraniss was not of that line – he was a usurper. And the Jix, while obedient to whomever occupied the Azure Palace, had their own agenda. And lately it was one that seemed to diverge from Vraniss'. He'd thought that perhaps a reading of their history could provide some clue as to how to deal with them, but they'd politely refused every effort he'd made to gain access to their records. That problem would have to be solved another day.

So, what should he do with the Nojii? Vraniss was lost in thought, considering, when Barittin walked in.

"You wanted to see me Sire?"

"Yes. By now I assume you've heard that the structure in the desert has disappeared."

"I am aware of the reports."

"Your ears don't miss much do they?"

"No Sire."

"So do you also know that Otarab is on his way here?" Vraniss' voice dripped with loathing as he uttered the hated man's name.

"I've also heard that he will be arriving soon. Presumably to make a report on the incident?"

Vraniss wasn't fooled by the question. He knew Barittin had ears throughout the palace which listened for him and reported things. And Barittin knew he knew. It was an old game they played with each other. Vraniss sometimes feigned ignorance of Barittin's knowledge in order to figure out how much he actually knew, how effective his network was. As the king's most trusted lieutenant, Barittin was privy to information that no one else possessed. Even as close as their relationship was, Vraniss didn't fully trust Barittin. No king could ever fully trust anyone if he expected to keep his throne, let alone his head. So, some things Vraniss kept even from him. This was not one of those things.

"I despise that man," Vraniss said. "Once he's made his report to me, we are going to make an example of him. Failure by any of my subjects or those in my employ will not be tolerated. He has failed in the most important task in this kingdom. And he will be punished publicly."

"What do you intend to do to him?"

"Peel him. Like he peels his slaves. Slowly. His whole body. One small piece at a time. And you're going to do it."

"By your command Sire," Barittin said with a deferential nod. "I'll have carpenters begin erecting a platform in White Square."

"Good. And afterwards we will have to discuss what to do about the Nojii. Now that the structure is gone, we have no need of them. Once they no longer receive wages from the royal treasury they will go back to their marauding ways. I will not have such disorder in Jarradan."

"I have some ideas Sire. When I'm done with Otarab we will talk."

"Very well. See to it."

Barittin turned towards the door and walked out.

Chapter 7

evan and Arval had been trudging through the desert for most of the day after they escaped the Kryxaal. They'd been following a road of sorts that led through the enormous orange sand dunes in the general direction of Kessar. It was made of hardened dirt like what they'd both dug for so long. Parts of it were covered in with drifted sand, but enough was visible winding its way through the dunes that it was easy to follow. Arval remembered it as being the road to the pit that he'd traveled when he'd first been brought there. Both had been listening closely for the sound of anyone coming up behind them, and about an hour after they'd set off, someone was. Revan had heard it first – the sound of a horse galloping at full speed.

"There's a horse coming up behind us, fast" he said.

"I don't hear anything. How do you know?" Arval replied.

"Believe me. We have to get off the road. Now!"

Arval hadn't argued, although he hadn't really believed Revan. They both veered off the road into a cleft between the dunes, smoothing out their tracks behind them with their hands. In the sand a trail left by two people walking would be as good as a bonfire at night for attracting attention.

"The sand doesn't look the same even though we covered our tracks," Arval said.

"I'll bet whoever is on that horse isn't looking for us. I think they have more important things to do than search for a couple escaped slaves. If they even know we're missing."

"I hope you're right."

Hunkering down behind a ridge of sand, they peered over it and down at the road, waiting for the rider to pass. They didn't have to wait long. Mere moments after they'd concealed themselves, a dust cloud became visible behind a turn in the road not far away. A rider appeared soon after, laying low over the horse, urging it on with a short whip. As he rode into view in front of them, they could tell it was one of the aides. He was past them and gone without a glance in their direction.

"You were right," Arval said, slightly amazed. "How did you know?"

"I heard him."

"You heard him?! How could you have heard him from that far away?"

"How did you run faster than you ever have when that light ramp was about to disappear from underneath you? Magic."

Revan had told Arval a little of what he'd learned about magic in speaking with the remnant, Drannal.

He'd told him about magic and how it had begun to die and been sent from the world in some long-gone age. And he'd mentioned his new abilities. He supposed he had to since he'd been able to give Arval a little of what he himself had.

"I guess one of my new abilities is better hearing too."

"Much better I'd say," Arval said.

Revan didn't reply. His thoughts were still occupied by what he'd learned in the Kryxaal. The idea of magic was still so new and alien that he wasn't sure what it really meant. Yes he could run faster, see farther, hear better, and felt the world open to him in ways he'd never imagined, but what was magic? What did it do? What was its purpose? He glanced up at the Blackfire, swirling dark and gibbous in the southern sky, and marveled that it had something to do with magic. And him. Somehow that immense mass of black fiery cloud, it's red and gold threads streaking through the fringes like lightning, and he, Revan the digger, Revan the slave, now Revan the free man, were intertwined, their fates linked. He hadn't told Arval about the Blackfire and what Drannal had said about it. He wasn't sure he would tell anyone anything about that until he knew more himself. But how was he to learn more? Drannal had said that there were four Kryxaal in the world. He had to find one of the others. But was it buried like this one had been? If so he'd never get into it. It had taken years upon years to get to the doorway he'd found. If the others were buried as deep, Revan would be long dead before anyone ever found the way in. What to do?

Where to look? Revan had no idea. He sighed quietly. Drannal had said he had a year to decide if he even wanted to pursue the return, as he'd called it. Maybe he'd find out more in Kessar when they got there. He suddenly realized that he was very thirsty. He'd not had anything to eat or drink since dinner the night before, prior to entering the Kryxaal.

"I'm thirsty, are you?" asked Arval as if reading his mind.

"Parched."

"I wonder where we could find something to drink out here..."

"I know as much as you."

"What about the camp? Think there's water there?"

Revan shrugged. "Do you even know where it is? I don't."

"No. I didn't see it when they brought me here."

"It can't be too far. Let's climb a dune and look around."

They angled off the road to the right and began to climb a particularly large orange dune. The sand kept slipping out from under their feet, making the ascent strenuous. By the time they reached the top, they were panting with the exertion and sweating profusely.

"We've got to get some water soon or we're going to die out here," Arval croaked, his dry throat making it hard to speak.

"Look around," Revan said.

They shielded their eyes from the burning sun with their hands and gazed out across the dunes for some sign of the camp. Or anything that could provide water.

"What's that?" Arval said, pointing out ahead of them.

"Where?"

"Straight out from where we are, just over the third dune."

Revan's eyes narrowed as he peered where Arval was pointing.

"It's a tent!" he said.

"You sure?"

"Yes, I can see the stripes in the fabric."

"Are there any people around?"

"I don't see any. It looks like the road passes close to it. If we're careful, we should be able to sneak up without being seen. If there's anyone still there."

They scrambled down the face of the dune they were on and made their way back to the road. The possibility of water and food made them nearly run; they had to remind themselves that there could be aides there. Even the master himself. He wasn't one that they wanted to meet.

As they reached the final dune before where Revan said the tent was, they moved to the side of the road, walking slowly, and listening for any sounds of life.

"Hear anything?" Arval asked.

"No. It's completely quiet."

As they edged around the dune, the tent came into view, as did the rest of the camp. There wasn't much to it. Behind the tent was a latrine dug into the sand, two canopies made of white cloth and held up by posts, under which were tables, chairs and assorted crates and barrels. A few paces beyond the canopies, out in the desert sun, were three wooden crates, each about a pace long and half that wide. And a wooden table with sets of iron shackles affixed at either end. Its wood was stained a dark brown. There were no people around.

"Let's wait a few minutes, see if anyone comes out," Revan said.

"We've waited this long, I guess a few more minutes won't matter. Besides, that table looks like it's meant for holding people down. I don't want to find out what it's like to be on it."

Watching the tent for movement, Revan found his eyes returning to the three crates out in the sun by themselves. He couldn't imagine what they would be there for. Everything else was under the canopies. Why were those just sitting there?

Finally deciding that their need for water was greater than their fear of whomever might be lurking in the tent, Revan nudged Arval and they both moved cautiously towards the camp.

"Let's go to those crates and barrels under the canopies first. See if there's water there," Revan said. Arval nodded his assent.

When they arrived under the first awning, each went straight to a barrel, shaking it to see if it contained anything.

"There's something in this one," Arval said, as he worked to get the cap off the top. Grunting with the effort, he managed to work it free, and looked inside.

"It's water!"

Revan had already found two beaten tin mugs on one of the tables, and both of them quickly dunked the mugs into the clean but warm water. They drank greedily for a few moments, relishing the wetness washing the dust from their mouths and throats. Arval moved away from the barrel, his thirst slaked for the moment, and began rummaging through the crates. With a triumphant smile, he held up something he'd pulled from one of them.

"What is that?" Revan asked.

"Dried meat!" Arval said. "You're about to have your first taste of what real food is. And this isn't even the best way to have meat. They dry it so it will last longer. Undried meat rots very quickly. People take this with them on journeys when they know food might be hard to come by. Try some." Arval tore off a chunk and handed it to Revan.

So, this was what real food looked like, he thought, looking at it for a moment. Its texture was rough and hard, but it smelled wonderful. Revan gingerly bit off a piece and began chewing. As the meat ground between his teeth and began to release its flavor, he smiled at Arval, and started chewing more vigorously. Arval tore off another strip and handed it to him. Revan devoured it in seconds.

"There's more in that crate," Arval said. "Don't eat it all. We'll bring it with us for the trip to Kessar."

"Ok," Revan said, wiping his mouth. "I never knew food could taste so good!"

"Wait 'til you try it roasted with gravy and potatoes," Arval said. "And ironberry pie for dessert!"

"What's dessert?"

"Questions, questions. I'll tell you about dessert on the way to Kessar. Let's see what's in that tent. We could use some better clothes than these. And boots. These sandals are not going to serve us well when we get to the Bluecrag Mountains."

Thoughts of dessert and roasted meat left Revan's mind as he turned towards the tent. They crept up to it cautiously, listening for voices or any other sign that there might be someone inside. When they reached the flap of fabric that served as a door, Arval dropped to the ground and gingerly lifted the bottom corner.

"I don't see anyone inside. Come on."

He stood up and pulled aside the flap. Revan followed him in and gazed around in wonder at the colorful carpets covering the ground and the pillows of myriad sizes strewn around the walls. The fire pit in the middle was cold and unlit. It really was empty.

"Looks like the master was called away to see his master in Kessar," Arval said.

"Let's look around," Revan said

As they moved deeper into the tent, Revan noticed the table and chair in the back. Next to it were two simple wooden chests. He walked over to them and opened the one closest to the table. Inside were an assortment of wildly colored robes, covered in geometric patterns and embroidered designs.

"Look at this!" Revan said.

Arval walked over and looked at the garments Revan was pulling out.

"Looks like the master liked to dress well. These are huge. He must be a pretty big man."

"I think three of us could fit in this one," Revan said, and he marveled at the colors and softness of the fabric.

Finding nothing of real use in the first chest, Revan opened the other. Inside he discovered several sets of well-made pants and shirts, and sturdy leather boots with good soles.

"Now this is what we needed," Arval said. "Quick, let's change into them before someone comes along."

Both boys quickly shed their threadbare clothes, rags really, from the pit and donned the new clothes they'd found. Surprisingly, everything fit fairly well. Even the boots. Arval dug down to the bottom of the chest after they'd dressed.

"What are you doing?" Revan asked as Arval flung aside yet more clothes.

"I'm looking for coats. We'll want them in the mountains." He stopped suddenly. "Well, well, look at this," he said as he pulled something up from the bottom. In his hands were what looked like belts, hanging from them were two swords in dark brown leather scabbards.

"Swords?" Revan asked.

"Yeah! Ever held one?"

"Of course not. Just picks and shovels."

"Here, take this one. I don't need two."

Revan, his eyes wide, hesitantly reached out and grasped the scabbard. He turned it over in his hands, slightly amazed that he was actually holding a real weapon. The scabbard and belt it was attached to were worn with use, the leather cracked in spots. As he looked at the hilt, he could see that it was wrapped in dark, sweat-stained leather below the straight crossguard. Taking a grip on the hilt, he drew it from the scabbard; it made a quiet rasp as it emerged. The blade was dull in spots, with small patches of rust along its length. It had been some time since anyone had polished it. Small nicks here and there provided ample proof that it had met other blades in the past. Revan thought that it felt natural in his hand as he held it up in front of his face. The balance was excellent, the whole seemed sturdy and solidly constructed. This was a utilitarian weapon, not some showpiece like the ones Arval had described seeing on rich people in Kessar. Revan thought that his must be what a soldier would carry. A weapon that would not betray him by breaking in combat. He took a couple swings through the hot air in the tent, relishing the way it felt. An image of Bhinja flashed into his mind. Would he someday use this weapon, or one like it, to slay that hated man and have his revenge? Revan imagined Bhinja's face showing incredulity and fear, pictured his sword piercing the man's chest, the mist of blood that would spray up from the wound. Yes, he decided, he would kill Bhinja with a sword. His mouth turned up in a small smile at the thought.

Chapter 8

e should leave," Arval said. "The aides might be on their way. If they are then they'll probably stop here."

"Ok," Revan said.

They'd both strapped swords around their waists. Arval had not found jackets in the chest, but he had found more shirts that they could layer on in the mountains. He'd also found a pack that he'd thrown over one shoulder.

"We'll need to find waterskins and load this pack with as much food as we can carry. I don't know how long it will take to get to Kessar. Once we're in the mountains we can probably find at least some food. And there should be water too."

They walked out of the tent and back to the canopied area. As he looked towards the crates and barrels, Revan again noticed the three crates out in the sun by themselves.

"Why are those crates out there instead of under the awnings with the rest?" he asked Arval.

"I don't know. Maybe they're empty."

"I'm going to take a look."

"Fine, but we have to leave. Soon."

"I'll just be a minute."

As he approached the crates, he could see small holes drilled in the tops and sides. All three were closed with simple but solid metal latches. Going to the one on the far right first, Revan opened the latch and threw up the lid. It was empty. He moved over to the chest in the middle and did the same. It too was empty. He still couldn't imagine what chests with holes in them were doing out here. Holes wouldn't keep things in. Why would someone drill holes in a perfectly good crate?

As he approached the final one, he heard a muffled thump.

"Arval, come here!" he called.

Looking up from his packing, Arval gave him a questioning look.

"There's something alive in this one!"

Arval walked over, drawing his sword as he neared the crate.

"Do you even know how to use that?" Revan asked.

"I've seen them used. It can't be that hard. See the threat and swing the sword at it."

Revan grunted. "Just be ready to use it when I open this thing."

Arval stood a couple paces away from the crate, facing it, sword brandished. Revan unhooked the latch, cast open the lid and quickly stepped back. Nothing happened. Cautiously he craned his neck out to look down inside. What he saw was a person lying on his left side, knees pulled up to his chest, arms wrapped around them, his head bent down. He just barely fit inside. A low moan could be heard emanating from his cracked lips. His only clothing was a cloth wrapped around his waist that barely covered him. Livid bruises covered his arms and sides. His legs and what Revan could see of his back bore the familiar stripes of lashings. He was glistening with sweat.

"Arval help me! There's someone in here!"

Arval lowered his sword, stepped to the chest, and looked down.

"Let's get him out," he said, reaching down to grasp the arm closest to him.

They gently got their hands under him and lifted him slowly up. When they'd gotten him upright, they could see he was a boy about their age. His eyes were closed, his breathing ragged and strained. Now that they could see him from the front, they saw more bruises and lash marks on his chest, and also sores with blackened edges.

"Those look like burns," Arval said.

"Can you hear us?" Revan asked the boy.

"Water," he rasped in a voice so quiet they could barely hear him.

Arval, dropped his sword and ran back under one of the canopies. He picked up a waterskin he'd found and dashed back to the boy Revan was holding up.

"Here, drink slowly," he said, tipping the waterskin to the boy's mouth.

A bit of water dribbled down his chin, but enough got into his mouth to whet his thirst and he began to gulp the liquid.

"Not so fast," Arval said. "You'll get sick. I'll give you some more in a minute."

The water seemed to have revived the boy somewhat and he was able to open his eyes. He looked at Revan and Arval uncomprehendingly.

"Who are you?" he asked, his voice a little stronger and not as raspy.

"We're from the pit. This is Revan and I'm Arval. Who are you? Are you from the pit?"

"I'm Kanar. Yes. I was in the pit…"

"How did you get here?" Revan asked.

"They brought me. The aides. They said I wasn't working fast enough. I told them I couldn't work faster." He coughed, a long and rattling hacking that shook his whole body. "Could I have some more water?"

Arval tipped him the waterskin again. He drank slowly but greedily.

"Better," he said, a slight smile forming on his lips.

"So, they brought you here because you told them you couldn't work any faster?" Arval asked.

"Yes. That's what I told them. Then Nillit gave me the lash. It was the worst I'd ever had. Or ever seen anyone have. I couldn't walk when he was done, so he had a couple other diggers put me in a cart. He told the aide who was driving it that I was to go to the camp."

Revan and Arval shared a glance at the mention of the camp.

"So, this actually is the camp," Revan said quietly. "We know of it. And of those who have gone to it. Most never came back. The ones that did almost never lived long."

"I wouldn't have lived if you hadn't let me out. They beat me more when I got here. With lashes and fists. One of the aides used tongs to get coals from the cookfire and burned me with them."

Revan and Arval didn't ask about those wounds; the grim sores on Kanar's chest and arms told that story.

"If you're from the pit, how did you get here?" Kanar asked.

Revan and Arval looked at each other again. Revan nodded.

"The box is gone," Arval said.

"Gone? How is it gone?" he asked, another cough rattling his body.

"We can tell you later. Right now, we need to get out of here. Can you walk?"

Kanar was kneeling in the box. In response to the question, he rose, shaking and unsteadily, to his feet. He stepped gingerly out of the box, his arms supported on each side by Revan and Arval.

"I think I'll be ok. Everything hurts but the water is a helping a little. Do you have more?" Arval handed him the waterskin.

"There are clothes in the tent. You'll need to get dressed. We're going to Kessar. I know people there," Arval said. Kanar seemed steadier, so they both let go of his arms. He walked, albeit slowly, on his own towards the tent.

"The clothes are in the chest on the far wall. Get some extra shirts. Arval says the mountains are going to be cold and we don't have coats."

Kanar nodded his understanding and disappeared into the tent.

"Are you going to tell him the real story of how the Kryxaal disappeared?" Arval asked as he picked up the sword he'd dropped and returned it to its scabbard.

"Not for now. We'll tell him about how it disappeared, but not that we were in it. Our story is that we were able to escape in the confusion."

"Ok. But why not tell him the real story?"

"I don't know. I just don't think I want to. Maybe later, after we know him better, we can tell him."

"Ok. Just doesn't seem right keeping him in the dark."

"Here he comes."

Kanar, changed into clothes from the chest, was walking towards them, extra shirts draped over his arm. He was moving considerably better than he had been. Revan noticed for the first time that Kanar had longish blond hair that touched his shoulders; it had been wet with sweat and matted from being in the box when they'd first seen him. The brief time in the hot tent had dried it some. He was a little shorter than Revan, but taller than Arval, with dark brown eyes and narrow, angular features.

"Is there any food here?" he asked.

"Here's some dried beef," Arval said, handing him a large strip. Kanar tore off a chunk in his teeth and chewed heartily.

"I don't remember the last time I ate," he said.

"I'd never had dried beef before in my life until we got here a little while ago," Revan said.

"Really?" Kanar asked a hint of disbelief in his voice.

"I was so young when I came to the pit that I don't remember much of anything. Arval has been telling me about cities and food for half a turning."

Kanar, still chewing, turned his gaze to Arval.

"He knows nothing," Arval said. "I was going to tell him about dessert on our way to Kessar."

"Well, I've never been to a city, but I know about food. My parents owned a Traveler's Rest on the road to Bentravirri. We did a lot of cooking for our guests. I was taken from there last season."

"So, you were taken too," Arval said quietly.

Revan looked at him questioningly.

"I never told you how I came to be in the pit. I was taken," Arval said.

"How? By who?" Revan asked.

"Let's go. I'll tell you the story on the way."

They each picked up two waterskins; Arval had found several, as well as two more packs. When they'd stuffed their extra shirts and as much of the dried beef as they could into the packs, Arval shouldered one, Revan and Kanar the others, and they set off for Kessar.

Chapter 9

s the camp disappeared into the dunes behind them, Arval told them his story.

"I never knew my father. My mother told me that he died just after I was born. She was a maid for some rich people in Kessar. One of the men who owned a house she worked in used to take her into his bedroom. She would come out crying, sometimes with a black eye or breathing funny and holding her side, like her ribs hurt. I was young, but I remember it; I was about six turnings. She had no one to watch me so she used to take me with her to the homes she cleaned. She told me one day that she was going to inform the city wardens that he had been hurting her. Not long after that, the wardens came and arrested her."

Revan and Kanar looked at the ground as they trudged along the hard dirt road, occasionally skirting some of the larger dunes that had swept over it. Neither spoke as Arval continued his story.

"We lived in a very small shack on the outskirts of the city, close to the outer wall where the poorest people live. My mother didn't make much money being a maid, and it was all she could afford. Some nights we didn't eat because she had no money to buy food. They came for her on one of those nights. The shack was just big enough for a bed, a small table, and an old chest she kept our things in. We were in the bed; we both slept in it because it was all we had. I can remember how hungry I was, and that mother had said we'd have food tomorrow. I was almost asleep when someone pounded on the door. I heard a man shouting my mother's name, telling her to open up. She jumped out of bed and rushed over to open it. When she did, four big men in steel breastplates and black cloaks came in. They could barely all fit in the small room. One of them was older than the other three. He had a grey beard but no mustache. One of his front teeth was missing. He said he was Corvan, that he was in charge of the city wardens, and he was there to arrest my mother for thievery. She tried to tell them she hadn't done anything, but he didn't listen. He signaled to his men and two of them took her by the arms and dragged her out the door. The other one picked me up. They didn't even let us get dressed or take any of our things."

"When they got us outside, there was a big wagon with a tall wooden box on the back of it. Corvan opened a door in the side, and they shoved us in. There were benches inside, so we sat on them. Two of the wardens came in with us. The held short swords that were out of their scabbards, ready to use. As if a woman in her nightdress and a boy of six turnings could be a threat to men like that."

"What was your mother's name?" Revan quietly asked.

"Erte," he answered.

They all walked on for a time, not speaking. Arval coughed a little and finally continued.

"They took us to a huge building made of black stone somewhere towards the Azure Palace. When we got inside, they took my mother away down one corridor, and me down another. I can remember her screaming for me, reaching her hand out. One of the wardens punched her in the side of the head and she went limp. They took me to a little room with an iron door on it and threw me inside. I remember smacking my head on the stone floor. I was crying for my mother, but the warden just closed the door. I could hear him slide the bolt closed. I don't know how long I was there. Sometimes they would open the door and put a bowl of soup inside for me. It wasn't really soup, more like the gruel we had in the pit. However long it was, they finally came and took me out. One of the wardens held me by the arm as we walked out of the building and into the street. There were more wardens outside and when they saw us, we all started walking towards the Azure Palace. They had other people with them. Some were adults, some children like me."

"It wasn't very long before we were in White Square. There was a huge crowd gathered. I could see a big wooden platform at the end closest to the palace. The wardens walked us through the crowd to the front and towards the left side of the platform. There were stairs there that went up to it. At the bottom of the stairs was a group of people, all with their hands tied behind their backs, their heads drooped forward. We waited there a few minutes when I saw Corvan walk past the little group and up the stairs. He went right to the front of the platform and held up a hand to the crowd. When everybody had quieted down, he spoke. He said that today a group of dangerous criminals was going to have judgment passed on them, by the decree of the king and so on. I don't remember the words. Three other wardens walked up on the platform with him. One of them carried a huge sword. It took two hands for him to carry it."

"Some wardens on the ground in front of the platform made the crowd move back about ten paces, leaving an open area in front of it. The white stone of the square was sparkling in the sun. I remember thinking how beautiful it looked and wondered why I was there. I just wanted my mother and to go home. Corvan called out to bring up the first criminal. Two wardens dragged a man up onto the platform. He was begging and screaming that he was innocent. The wardens brought him right to the front of the platform and forced him to kneel. They untied his hands and held his arms behind him and out to the sides in a way that forced him to lean forward. Corvan said something about 'by order of King Vraniss' and 'judgment', that the man had been caught visiting harm on a merchant of the city, then the man with the huge sword swung it down and cut off his head. I can remember how the blood sprayed out of his neck, the sound of his head hitting the stones of White Square. But most I remember how red the blood on those white stones looked. I'd thought it was so beautiful before. Now it just looked horrible."

"The wardens threw the man's body off the platform and Corvan called for the next criminal. A couple cleaners came from the other side of the platform and took the body and head away. A woman in the group with me started screaming. Wardens took her away."

Arval was quiet for quite a while, and they trudged along in silence. Revan took a drink from his waterskin and stared ahead of them at the road as it twisted around an enormous dune a ways ahead. The sun was beginning to go down, hints of purple were visible in the eastern sky.

"They brought several more people up on the platform, and all of them had their heads cut off. People and children in my group screamed and cried for most of them. A couple of the people killed didn't have anyone cry for them. I guess I must have known, somehow, that my turn to cry was coming, so I wasn't really surprised when I saw my mother. They brought her up on the platform just like all the others. She was the only one whose head wasn't drooping forward. She was looking straight ahead. At the top of the stairs, she turned a little and saw me. She didn't say anything, but she gave me a smile I'll never forget. It was like she was telling me that she loved me and that I'd be alright. That's when I started crying and screaming. I knew she was going to die, and I wanted to save her. But the wardens were far too strong. I couldn't get away. And what could I have done against them anyway?"

"They made her kneel too and held her arms to the sides and behind her. Corvan said his words, something about my mother being convicted of stealing from a distinguished citizen of the city, and the man with the sword swung. I can still hear the sound of her head hitting the ground. The wardens dragged me away from the platform as the cleaners came out for her. When we got out of the crowd and onto one of the side streets, they threw me to the ground and told me to leave. I got up and tried to run back, but one of them backhanded me and I blacked out. When I woke up, Plistral was there."

"Who is Plistral?" Kanar asked.

"He's a friend of mine who lives in Kessar. I lived with him and the Khet for years before I came to the pit."

"Khet? What's that?" said Kanar.

"It's a group of children like me. Orphans and castaways. We picked pockets and stole things to live. Khet is what a group like that's called. I was told there are other Khets in other cities."

"So how did you end up in the pit?" asked Revan.

"I'd been with Plistral and my Khet for a long time, about ten turnings when one day we were working a crowd in one of the markets. Plistral had found a fruit vendor and gotten us a couple sun fruit. Ever had one?" Revan and Kanar shook their heads. "They only grow in summer, and only in remote places. I think they're the most delicious fruit I've ever tasted. Plistral was so excited that he'd been able to filch two of them from the vendor and not get caught."

"We were walking through the crowd, sun fruit in our pockets. You don't want to be caught eating one in public. The wardens know that boys like us couldn't afford them and would arrest us if they caught us with them, so we were going to a barn we knew of where there were never any people so we could eat our sun fruit and decide what to do next. When we got to the barn, I went in first. It was dark inside except for a little sun that was coming through a few cracks in the walls. Plistral was right behind me. As I got through the door, I heard someone talking in a low voice. I couldn't make out what was being said, but I could tell it was a man. Plistral must not have heard him because as he came in he said something about how lucky we were to have sun fruit. The talking stopped. I turned to Plistral to push him back out the door when I felt a hand grab my collar. Plistral's eyes went wide at something behind me. I felt a crack on the back of my head, and I blacked out."

"When I woke up I was in a wagon with a bunch of other boys and two men, all of us were bound. We were in the mountains, and it was cold. There was snow all over the ground. Everyone was shivering. None of us had clothes for being in the cold, except the two men up front who were driving the wagon. They weren't shivering. I could see the heavy fur cloaks they were wearing. I heard horses' hooves and looked behind us, and there were four more men with fur cloaks on horses following the wagon. They all had weapons hanging from their belts. One had a big bow and a quiver of arrows on his back, another one a huge axe with a long handle. One of the boys next to me was watching me.

'Looks like you're awake,' he said. 'Where are we going,' I asked him. My head hurt and it was hard to talk. I was so thirsty too. He told me we were on our way to the pit. I found out later, when we actually got there, that the men who'd been traveling with us were the same kind of men who were aides at the pit."

"Nojii," Kanar said.

"What? What does that mean? I've heard that name before." Arval asked.

"The men who took you are Nojii. They're from this desert. Like someone from Kessar is called a Kessari, they're called Nojii."

"So that's what that Jix meant. I never knew that." said Arval thoughtfully.

Revan realized then that Bhinja and his aides were part of a larger group. They weren't just his former captors and tormentors. His enemy now had a name. And it was Nojii.

Chapter 10

ight was settling in over the desert. Its inky tendrils crept across the sky towards the west, chasing the sun as it dropped lower and lower until it was gone behind the enormous dunes to the right of the three boys. The temperature had fallen from the searing heat of earlier in the day making walking comfortable.

"We should probably look for a place to sleep," Arval said. "Somewhere off the road in case someone comes by."

"Over there, behind that big dune should work," Kanar said. "If we walk single file, it'll be easier to cover our tracks in case someone does happen by."

"That's a good idea. Where did you learn it?" Revan asked.

"There were woods close to where I grew up. My friends and I used to try to hide from each other in the forest when we were kids. My father taught me to track animals and survive in the wilderness. He liked to hunt and one of the things he taught me was how to hide in case I was ever in danger. I got pretty good at hiding from my friends. And also, some of the guests that stopped at our Traveler's Rest weren't the most honorable or savory of folk. Since it was just the three of us, my father taught me things about living in the wilderness in case any of them ever gave us trouble and we had to run. I learned to track and cover my tracks, hunt, fish, all kinds of things that could help me survive." Kanar's tone was flat, unemotional, and made Revan and Arval a little uneasy. After what he'd been through, they weren't surprised, but he had them both on a little uneasy, nonetheless.

"You'll be handy when we get to the mountains then," Arval said, trying to lighten Kanar's spirits.

"Over here, let's go through this way," Kanar said, gesturing towards a small cleft between the towering orange dunes.

As they walked in, Arval went first, followed by Revan who took care to step in Arval's footprints. Kanar brought up the rear. He'd taken a couple of the extra shirts they'd brought, bunched them together, and was sweeping the sand behind them as they went, effectively covering their tracks. No one would ever know that they'd been there.

"Neat trick with the shirts," said Revan.

"You have to make do with what you have," he said.

"Normally I'd use a piece of wood with a cord tied on either end and just drag it behind us. But we'll be able to sleep tonight without anyone knowing we're here."

Between the dunes they found a small depression in the sand. Night had almost completely taken over the sky and the stars were shining brilliantly. Revan marveled again at how many there were. He still couldn't believe that he was free of the pit, of the endless digging. The mystery of magic and how he fit into it still tumbled through his mind, but the immediacy of his release from slavery overpowered it. He'd eaten real food for the first time he could remember just a few short hours ago! What he would experience once they got to Kessar filled him with excitement. He was finding it hard to sleep. His life had been changed completely in just a few short hours. He idly wondered if it was that way for other people. The ones who hadn't lived as slaves. Could their lives change so dramatically in such a short time? Arval and Kanar had drifted off almost as soon as they'd lain down in the sand. Revan couldn't help just staring up at the stars, marveling at his new life, at how suddenly it had been thrust upon him. Finally, he did drift off like the other two. It had been a day and a half since he'd slept, after all, and weariness had at last ushered him from the waking world.

It was the smell that woke him. Something familiar was in his nostrils. It smelled like unwashed bodies, but not his or his traveling companions'. He'd come to know his own smell and those of Kanar and Arval. This was something else. It wasn't the smell of toil; it was the smell of pain. Revan sat up with a start. He could hear the soft rasp of footsteps on sand, and he suddenly knew what the smell was - Nojii. They were close. A fleeting thought ran through his mind as he silently stood: the Nojii smelled different from the diggers. They had a sour, angry scent. The diggers had smelled a little like the rancid meat they'd sometimes gotten in their gruel. It was almost like they'd been rotting before they even died. Maybe they had been. He hadn't realized until this moment that there was even a difference, but he knew without doubt that there was. He'd taken off his sword when he'd lain down to gaze at the canopy of stars; the blade was close to where he'd lain. He reached over now and picked it up, slowly and quietly drawing it from its worn leather scabbard. The feel of it in his hand felt encouraging, empowering. It wasn't like holding a pick or a shovel, some tool he used to follow orders and avoid lashings. This was something that would give lashings. Worse, or maybe better, he thought, it would give death. To Nojii.

He could tell they were very close now. He heard one of them whispering something about trying to hide from Nojii in their own desert. Soft chuckles followed the comment. There was no time to wake the others; they would be too groggy from sleep to do anything, and the Nojii would be on them at any moment. Revan moved to his right, closer to the cleft between dunes where they had come in to this spot and away from his companions. He'd keep the Nojii away until they could wake and help him.

He was right at the edge of a dune; as the Nojii came around it, he'd see them before they saw him. The first one was only paces away. He thought he could hear four of them breathing, their smells were all similar, but different enough that he was sure there were four. Kanar and Arval were still asleep; Arval was snoring softly.

As the first one came into view, Revan swung the sword at his head. He was amazed at how quickly the blade carved through the air. It moved so fast that he barely felt the impact as it caught the man across the bridge of the nose. There was a mist of blood and the top half of his head slid off, brains and blood poured out from the cleft skull. As the man dropped, his companions let out a shout and rushed past his falling body, two had swords, the third an axe, all held high and ready to use. The first one past the dead man raced towards Arval and Kanar; the shout had awakened them, and they were both scrambling to their feet. The second saw Revan out of the corner of his eye and turned toward him, his sword sweeping down in a killing arc. Revan saw the blow coming easily; it seemed as if time had slowed, and the man was swinging through mud. He knocked the sword aside with a backhanded swing of his own sword, and on the downswing he curled it around, it's tip angling towards the ground, and brought it up straight across the man's belly, laying him open from navel to chin. The gaping wound spilled viscera and a torrent of blood as the man pitched onto his face, his killing and lashing days done.

The man with the axe held high over his head, seeing his companion down, let out a scream of rage and swung his axe at Revan. He sidestepped the blow easily, pivoting away from the big man as his momentum took him past where Revan had been standing. A straight thrust from his sword penetrated the man's back and burst out through his chest, dispatching the third of Revan's attackers. As he yanked the sword out of the man's dying body, Revan spun towards the final attacker and saw him swinging his sword wildly at Kanar. The shifting sand caused his movements to be jerky and erratic, making him miss. But if that blade made contact, Kanar was dead. Arval was up and away from the man but hadn't remembered to pick up his sword. The Nojii was standing right over the top of it as he tried to cut Kanar down. He just missed cleaving off Kanar's shoulder and left arm with one wild swing. Kanar dove to the side at the last instant and got a face full of sand for his efforts. The Nojii's sword had crashed into the sand where Kanar had been, stalling his murderous efforts for a moment. Revan saw his opportunity and dashed the few paces towards the man as he lifted the sword up for another try. The Nojii must have heard him because he began to turn towards Revan as the sword came up in his hand. He was too late. With one swing Revan's blade cut through the Nojii's throat and embedded itself in one of his neck bones. A fountain of blood spurted from the gaping wound in the man's neck as he gurgled, drowning and dying as his life poured out on the sand and down his opened throat. With a yank Revan freed his sword and stood watching as the Nojii crumpled to the ground.

"Tradan's Pocket, how did you do that?" exclaimed Kanar as he got up, brushing sand off his face. It was the first real emotion he'd shown since being freed from the crate.

"Tradan's Pocket, what does that mean?" asked Revan.

"It's just something people where I come from say when we can't believe we've just seen something. Like how you just killed four Nojii by yourself!"

"That was easy."

"Easy?! They were armed! That one almost killed me!" he said, gesturing at the corpse on the ground.

Arval hadn't moved. He was a few paces away, staring wide-eyed and slack mouthed at Revan.

"They were trying to kill us. I killed them first," he said with a shrug.

"I saw," Kanar said.

Now that the action was over, Revan suddenly felt very tired. His legs started to shake, and his vision began to darken.

"You've gone white, sit down a minute," Arval said, finally speaking.

Revan flopped to the ground, his hand fell off the hilt of the sword and lay at his side. The magnitude of what he'd just done began to dawn on him. Four of the aides from the pit lay dead around them. By his hand. He'd done it! He'd actually killed Nojii! Not Bhinja, the one he'd been fantasizing about killing, but four others. Four! Who they were didn't matter. He'd killed four of the enemy, ended their lives as they had ended so many others. It had been necessary. If he hadn't acted, they would all be dead right now and the four Nojii would be alive, probably eating their dried beef and drinking their water. But then again, these had been lives. Perhaps they'd had mothers much like the one Arval had spoken of earlier in the day. For a moment he regretted their deaths. The blood soaking into the sand reminded him of the blood Arval had described on the stones of White Square and he felt sorrow for those who'd died there. But these men had chosen their lives. They had been free, able to leave the pit at any time, to choose a different life for themselves. They hadn't been diggers, subjected to the lash and the curse, the fist and the camp, with its crates in the sun. They'd been the ones to administer the lash, to put people, boys like Kanar, into those boxes and leave them there, broiling alive in the heat. Their deaths had been deserved, warranted, necessary. The regret Revan had momentarily felt was gone, replaced by an emotion he didn't recognize.

"They were horrible, evil men," he said to Kanar and Arval. "It was men like them who put you in that crate. Who gave us all the scars on our backs with their lashes. Who caused so many to take their last ride out of the pit. And they were going to slaughter us. They deserved to die. We did nothing to them. Never harmed their families or stole from them. But they did harm us. I'll kill as many of them as I can. One day I will kill Bhinja too."

"You're proud... of killing them," Arval said slowly.

Proud. Yes, he was. He was proud of himself that he'd killed them, protected his friend Arval and their new companion. Proud that he'd found in himself the courage, through need, to face and slay them. Proud that he hadn't run but had stood and bested those who'd been his tormentors all these years. Arval was right – he was proud.

"Yes I am," Revan said simply.

"They're dead and the world is better for it," Kanar said frowning. "If I'd had a weapon I'd have killed them with you," he said as the picked up the sword that had belonged to the man who'd tried to kill him. He unbuckled the scabbard from around the dead man's waist and fastened it around his own. The look in his eyes as he gazed at the corpses around them told Revan that he wasn't boasting. Kanar would have fought with him. Arval, he wasn't so sure about. He was still staring at Revan with awe, and more than a little fear. Kanar showed no fear. His dark brown eyes glowed in the starlight with something Revan thought looked very much like hate.

Chapter 11

he days following Revan's killing of the four Nojii passed uneventfully. They walked on through the massive orange dunes, following the road as it wound through them. It angled steadily to the southwest in the direction of Kessar, bringing them closer every day to the mountains Arval had talked about. Kanar talked about them too, about how he'd come through them in a wagon in summer when there wasn't any snow on the ground. But he knew all about cold. His home to the south had been cold in winter he'd said. His father and he would go out in the summer to cut down trees for firewood. They'd used an enormous iron saw to cut the logs into small round pieces they would then split with an axe. Those pieces were hauled to their home in a cart pulled by two draft horses they'd owned. When Kanar had gotten older, he'd cut the trees by himself. He'd enjoyed the work, it was fun to be out in the woods on his own, working away the day instead of back at the Rest, as he called the family's business now. He hated the chores around the Rest – cooking, cleaning, washing bedding and clothes, serving the rude and drunken travelers who rented rooms from them. But what he especially hated was emptying the night buckets from the rooms in the morning. Each room had one for their guests to relieve themselves in at night, and since he was the child, it was his job. His parents told him, when he complained about it, that they'd done it for years before he was born, and that it was now his task. Kanar would cut down an entire forest, split and stack it all, alone, before he ever wanted to empty one more night bucket.

Revan and Arval had laughed at his story of slipping coming down the stairs with one, its contents spilling everywhere.

"It's not funny!" Kanar admonished them. "I had to clean everything off the stairs with a rag and a bucket of soapy water! Do you know how bad... solids... stink?!"

Revan and Arval had laughed so hard they had to stop walking. Finally, Kanar had joined in the laughter, the three of them holding their sides as their howls caused their stomach muscles to ache.

"You'll never... have to do that... again!" Arval had gasped as he tried to get his hysterics under control.

"No... I won't," Kanar said, his laughter fading. His face took on a grim cast, his eyes dropped to the ground in front of him and he started walking again. Revan, gasping for breath as his laughter eased, shot Arval a questioning look. Arval shrugged his shoulders in response as he started walking after Kanar. He didn't speak when they caught up with him, and his mood told Revan and Arval that he didn't want to talk anymore. They trudged on in silence for the rest of the day.

After they'd been traveling for a week, the dunes and the road never changing, Arval suggested finding a very tall dune and climbing it to see if they could tell how much farther they had to go before they reached the mountains. Revan and Kanar agreed, and they all started looking for a dune taller than the others. Some time later Kanar pointed to the left and said, "How about that one? It's a lot taller than the others." Revan and Arval looked where he was pointing and agreed that it was a very tall dune that would probably give them a good view toward the southwest.

"Let's go have a look," Revan said.

Starting the long climb to the top, it had to be over three hundred paces tall, Revan unslung one of his waterskins to have a drink. It was empty. So was his other one.

"Does anyone have any water left?" he asked.

"I have a little in one skin, but the other is empty," Arval said.

"Both mine are empty," said Kanar. "Have been since yesterday. I was hoping one of you had some left."

"We'll need water very soon," Arval said. "We can split what I have left three ways, but we've got to get to the mountains."

"Let's see where we are, come on," Revan said.

As they reached the top of the dune, they could just see the snowy tips of mountains in the far southern distance. The heat from the day rose off the sand, making the vista waver and shimmer like oil in water. The Blackfire loomed over everything, much further away to the south.

"So that's what mountains and snow look like," Revan said.

"They're too far," Arval said. "We'll die out here before we get to them."

"There must be some way to get water out here," Kanar said. "The Nojii have lived here for ages, and they survive. Where do they find it?"

"Maybe they bring it in wagons from the mountains?" Revan asked no one in particular.

"It wouldn't be practical," Kanar said testily. "They'd have to have wagons doing nothing but bringing water all day, every day. There are a lot of Nojii, from what I've heard. If that's true then to get everyone enough water it would take an endless line of wagons just going back and forth." He looked at Revan like he thought he was dim.

"Well how should I know?" Revan said defensively. "I've never been here before. I was just trying to think of something."

"Maybe there's a well somewhere," Arval suggested, trying to defuse the sudden tension.

"It would take more than one. Have you seen any?" asked Kanar sarcastically.

Arval frowned at the tone in Kanar's voice, "No, but how else do they survive out here?" Kanar had seemed angry since the night Revan had killed the Nojii. And it had gotten worse since the story about the night bucket. He wasn't sure what was going on with Kanar, but his company was starting to become very unpleasant.

"I don't know, but we're going to have to find out fast or we're dead."

Revan was gazing at the mountains and trying to forget about Kanar's attitude. He imagined what it would be like to walk through them, to see the snow, trees and streams his companions had talked about. They were so far away that he knew Arval was right, that they'd never make it to them without getting water from somewhere. As he looked at them, he noticed, off to his left a bit, something sticking up from between two dunes a ways off. It looked like some kind of brownish orange square. Just the top of it was visible over the closest dune.

"What's that over there," he said pointing.

"Where, I don't see anything," Arval replied.

"Neither do I. Where are you looking?" asked Kanar.

"Right over there. Look down my arm," he said.

Arval and Kanar leaned in, one on either side, and looked along Revan's extended arm towards where he was pointing.

"I still don't see anything," said Arval.

"I don't either."

"Well, there is definitely something out there. It looks like a square of some kind. Maybe a building."

"Are you sure?" asked Arval. "This heat can make you see things."

"I'm telling you there is something there. It looks man made. Like the box back in the pit, but not nearly as big. And it's kind of brown and orange. It blends in with the sand; I guess I can understand why you don't see it." Revan still wasn't sure how much he should let Kanar know about his abilities, he just wasn't sure he trusted him enough yet to share that knowledge. He realized just then that he might have slipped up and inadvertently let Kanar know he was different. He hoped his statement about the object blending in had covered the mistake. Kanar's change in attitude was making Revan more hesitant than ever to tell him anything about his abilities, and he reminded himself to watch what he said.

"If you say so," Kanar said, a disbelieving tone to his voice.

"Let's go see what it is. Maybe there's water there," Arval said, sensing tension.

They set out across the dunes toward where Revan had seen the object, still walking single file, but not bothering to cover their tracks. Since Revan had killed the four Nojii, they hadn't seen any others. Or anything living. There'd been no sign of life at all. No ashes of campfires, no tents, no wagons, just the scorching heat and the endless, enormous dunes of orange sand.

Up one dune and down another they trudged, not speaking. Their thirst was beginning to dominate their thoughts. The heat was squeezing the water out of them, and their throats were almost too dry to talk. It even hurt to breathe. The last of Arval's water, and there hadn't been much, had been shared between them when Revan had first spotted the object.

After they'd cleared several dunes shorter than the tall one they'd climbed, Arval and Kanar finally got their first glimpse of what Revan had seen.

"I see it," Arval croaked.

"I do too," Kanar managed. "You must have incredible eyesight to have seen that from so far away," he said to Revan. "It does blend in."

Revan felt a strange relief that Kanar didn't seem to suspect anything amiss, other than that Revan's eyesight was preternatural. Why was he so hesitant to let Kanar know about his abilities? The boy hadn't done anything to them, in fact he'd been a decent companion, mostly, except for the snide comments and his anger, which did seem to be growing. There was just something that told Revan that he should keep his secret… well, secret. He'd noticed that Kanar's strength had come back remarkably fast from his ordeal in the camp. The wounds not covered by his clothes were healing nicely; Kanar never complained about them. It was no use dwelling on it. Kanar hadn't turned against them so far. Maybe he wouldn't.

"You go on ahead of me," Kanar said. "I have to, you know - go. I'll catch up in a minute," Kanar said.

"Don't take too long," Revan said. "We've got to get there and see if there's water. It's not much farther."

"I said I'll catch up," Kanar replied, irritation evident in his voice.

Revan frowned at him a moment, wondering what had made him irritable, but decided to just leave it be. He and Arval continued up to the top of the dune they'd been climbing and paused a few steps down the slope on the far side

"It's close," Revan said. "I'm going to tell him to hurry up."

He turned and walked back over the top of the dune towards Kanar. As he looked down the slope, he saw Kanar taking a long pull from one of his waterskins. Revan froze, anger boiling up inside him. Kanar must have heard him because he turned and met his eyes. They stared at each other in silence for a moment. Slowly Kanar lowered the waterskin from his mouth and replaced the cap, his eyes never leaving Revan's.

"I thought you said you were out of water," Revan said quietly.

"Yes I did," Kanar replied, just as quietly.

"So, you lied to us."

"I'm not going to die out here if I can help it."

"We will all die out here if we don't work together. Arval shared the last of his water with you when you still had some." He glared at Kanar, his anger seething. Kanar simply glared back, his fists balled at his sides.

"We should move on. The tower's close," Revan said as he turned away. Arval, standing just on the other side of the dune waiting, had heard everything. He looked questioningly at Revan as he walked past, stone faced. A moment later Kanar crested the dune. Arval glared at him but didn't say anything. Kanar walked past him without a look or a word.

The three boys had been walking up and down dunes for the better part of two hours when, as they crested one, Kanar in the lead now, quickly gestured to them to get down as he dropped to the ground. Arval and Revan crawled up next to Kanar and peered over the top of the dune. Revan's initial impression of the object had been right – it was a tower. About a hundred paces tall, it was about thirty per side, and was made of big rough blocks that looked like the dirt of the road, mixed with sand from the dunes. The color produced by the mixture gave it a tint that made it blend in with the sand just enough to hide it from a casual glance. A small square window looked in their direction about three quarters of the way up its side, another, about the same size opened at the top. It sat in a wide clearing between the dunes; the ground was the same hard brownish dirt the road consisted of. There were no people or wagons around, nor was there a well or any other sign of life. The place appeared to be deserted.

"Do you see a door?" Arval asked.

"No," Kanar replied. "Maybe it's on the other side."

"Let's go have a look," Revan said, tossing a glare Kanar's way. He was still seething over Kanar's lie about the water.

They walked slowly and cautiously down the face of the dune to the clearing at the bottom. All three drew their swords when they reached level ground and stood still for a moment, listening. Not even Revan's enhanced hearing detected anything. They began edging around the tower to the left, still listening, their heads turning from side to side as they scanned for danger.

There was another small window about three quarters of the way up and another at the top, just like on the side they'd first seen, but no door. Coming around the far side of the tower, they saw again two windows at the same heights as the others, and still no door. All three constantly glanced around, searching as much for a threat as a door.

"One side left we haven't seen," Kanar said. "I hope there's a door on it."

Arval and Revan didn't say anything, their anger over his betrayal kept their mouths sealed.

When they'd reached the last of the four sides, it was the same as the other three.

"How is anyone supposed to get into this place?" Arval asked, frustration apparent in his voice. "We can't climb it; we don't have a rope."

"Who would build a place like this and not put in a door?" Kanar said. His frustration was obvious too.

"Let's look closer at the building," Revan suggested. "Maybe there's a handle or something we missed. I mean we didn't look that close at the walls; we were too busy making sure we wouldn't get ambushed by Nojii." Revan walked up close to the wall; the others followed. He ran his hands over the rough blocks, feeling and looking for anything that seemed out of place. Although the blocks were rough and not made with the precision of the ones that had made up the Kryxaal, they were still fitted tightly together. Revan had thought for a moment that they might be able to climb up to one of the lower windows, but his examination of the face of the tower told him that there would not be enough handholds. If they only had a rope. Then again, they didn't even know what was inside. There might not be any water. The effort of crossing the dunes to this place, abandoning the road they'd been on, might have just cost them their lives. If they left and made it back to the road, it was doubtful they'd be in any shape to travel any meaningful distance. And if Nojii happened along, they'd be in no condition to defend themselves. There had to be water here. Or it would be their grave.

Arval and Kanar had begun examining the face of the tower too, running their hands across it like Revan was.

"What are we looking for?" Arval asked.

"I don't know. Anything out of the ordinary," Revan said.

"Well, that could be anything," Kanar said flippantly.

Revan didn't reply; he was lost in scrutinizing the tower. As he rounded a corner toward the side next to the one they'd first seen from up on the dune, he thought he felt something under his fingers. He stopped and looked closer at the spot. There seemed to be something there. He couldn't quite tell what it was. When they'd realized they were alone and weren't about to be attacked, they'd sheathed their swords. Revan now pulled his from the scabbard and used the tip to scratch at the spot on the block. Small clods of dirt fell out as he scraped. Whatever it was had been carved into the face of the tower and filled in with grit over uncounted years.

Arval and Kanar heard the rasp of the blade on stone and turned to look. Seeing that Revan had found something, they walked over and stood silently watching. Revan kept scraping, occasionally digging the tip of the blade into the emerging carving to remove a particularly stubborn chunk of grit. The carving seemed to be small, and it didn't take long to expose it. When he thought he'd gotten all the grit out, Revan stepped back and looked at what he'd found. It was a circle about three hands wide, with strange squiggly symbols following the curve of the circle inside, and more conforming to it outside. At the center of the circle was a four-pointed geometric star incised into the block. Revan had a strange feeling that he should know what it was. His caution about revealing too much to Kanar kept him silent as he gazed at the symbol.

"What is that?" Arval asked.

"I don't know. Do you?" Kanar said to Revan.

"No."

Arval traced his hand over the strange symbols. Kanar just stared.

"Kanar, see if you can find something like this on the other walls. Arval you look too," Revan said.

"Who made you the leader?" Kanar asked angrily.

"No one. But we do have to work together. So just look," Revan replied. His voice was cold, his stare colder. He'd had about enough of Kanar, and thirst had evaporated any desire to persuade or cajole. Kanar would look or they would settle their differences now.

Kanar saw something in Revan's stare and decided not to argue the point anymore. Wordlessly he moved off to look at the other walls of the tower, a glare set firmly on his face. As Arval turned to walk off, Revan grabbed his arm.

"I feel like I should know what this is," he said quietly, making sure Kanar was out of earshot.

"Really?"

"Yes. I think it's a type of writing. And I think I can read it. I just don't want Kanar to know about the things I can do. Go keep him occupied and give me a minute to work on it."

"Are you sure? Why don't you want him to know?"

"I can't really say. He lied to us about the water and his attitude has gotten a lot worse, but there's more to it than that. Something tells me that I shouldn't let him know too much. Just go keep him away from me for a few minutes."

"Ok," Arval said hesitantly. "But I'm not sure I want to be alone with him after how he's been acting."

"Just do it for me will you Arval? Please?"

As Arval walked off around the tower, scowling at having to distract Kanar, Revan turned back to the symbol. Looking closely at it, he noticed a small carved square at the bottom point of the star that he hadn't noticed before. It wasn't dug out completely, but the scraping had exposed enough of it that he was sure it was there. A couple quick scratches with the sword confirmed his initial impression. He focused on the squiggly symbols that he was sure now were a type of writing. He'd never actually seen writing, but Arval had told him about books and how they contained written words. He'd said there were enormous places called libraries that contained endless volumes, so much knowledge that no single person could ever learn it all. Revan concentrated on the symbols he now thought of as words and as he did, he began to feel that he was sinking into himself. His vision began to darken from the edges until all he could see were the words right in front of him.

Suddenly he felt himself drop out of the world and into the white tunnel. Again, he felt the sensation of rapid movement, as if he was flying through the tunnel, its twists and turns coming at him insanely fast, then falling away behind him as he wound around within them. He didn't control his movements, rather it was like he was being pulled along by some unseen force. He wondered if this was another of the Kryxaal. No, Drannal had said they were hidden. This building wasn't hidden; it blended in with the sand dunes, but it certainly wasn't concealed. Anyone could have found it had they climbed a tall enough dune. No, this wasn't a Kryxaal. He didn't know what it was. Maybe being in the tunnel didn't have anything to do with the tower.

The sensation of movement abruptly stopped, and Revan found himself in a room, much like the one where he'd met Drannal. This one was a little bigger, but still the same brilliant white. It seemed he could see a tunnel on the far side; the light was too bright to be sure, but the hint of an opening was there. As he looked around, he noticed dark blotches appear on the walls.

They swirled, spun and undulated in no discernable pattern but grew darker and darker until they were an inky black. The movement of the blotches began to slow, and they started to form themselves into shapes. As he watched them solidify, Revan realized they were the same as the shapes in and around the circle on the face of the tower. And he understood them.

There were four lines of them on the wall to his left, another four on the wall to his right.

"Is anyone there?" he called out. There was no response. Apparently no remnant dwelled in this room in the white tunnels.

As he scanned the words on the wall to his left, he somehow understood that it was an ancient language, and he knew it was called Denoran. Revan had no idea how he knew that he just did. Drannal had said that he'd gained knowledge from the Kryxaal; maybe this was some of it. The words on the left, he understood, were a warning:

YOU WHO HAVE REACHED THIS PLACE HEED

WELL

FOR TO ENTER WITHIN TO GAIN ITS SANCTUARY

YOU MUST PROVIDE THAT WHICH SUSTAINS

TO WITHHOLD IS THE PRICE OF BLOOD

Revan didn't understand what that meant, and he turned to read the words on the wall to the right.

UNDERNEATH IS SALVATION

BEHIND IS ALL

WiᴛHiŋ i8 LiFE

WiᴛHOVᴛ i8 ŋoᴛ

Puzzled, Revan turned from one wall to the other, reading and re-reading the words. He couldn't imagine what they meant. Frustrated, he turned from the words back toward the tunnel from which he'd come. He stopped a moment and glanced back at what he had thought might be a tunnel on the far side of the room, the suggestion of it was still there. For a moment he considered seeing if he could get to it. No, his companions were waiting, and they needed water. He didn't know if he could survive in these tunnels. His body, he knew, wasn't really here. It was his mind in this place; his body was still in front of the tower, in the heat. If he died out there, would he die in here? He didn't want to find out. As he moved towards the tunnel, back the way he'd come, he was instantly flying again. Faster and faster through the tunnel he went, until he realized he was beginning to see the wall of the tower again.

His eyesight took a moment to return to normal. Looking at the words around the circle on the wall, he understood that these were the same words he'd read inside the white room. Somehow he'd entered the tunnel and translated the words. Another ability perhaps? It was something he'd ponder another time. Right now, they needed to find water. Soon.

Arval and Kanar still weren't back. He thought they must still be looking on one of the other sides of the tower. Now that he was out of the white tunnel, he could still understand the words on the wall; they were as clear as if he'd been reading them all his life. What did they mean? That which sustains? Within is life? Without is not? Underneath? Behind? Was it a riddle he had to solve to enter the tower? He thought that maybe it was.

Arval and Kanar came around the corner of the tower in front of him. How was he going to keep his new knowledge from Kanar? He wasn't sure that he could. If they were going to find a way in, he was going to need their help.

"Did you find anything?" he asked.

"No. We went slowly and looked from the ground to as far up as we could see. We even scratched around with our swords. This seems to be the only thing carved anywhere," Arval said.

"Did you find anything?" Kanar asked.

With a sign, Revan decided he'd tell Kanar.

"These squiggly lines are writing. I can read it."

"What?!" Kanar asked frowning. "I thought you said you'd spent most of your life at the pit. They don't teach reading there. How can you read these things?"

Revan sighed, "I'll tell you some other time. Right now, we have to figure out what it means. I think it's a riddle."

He told them what the words said. Arval and Kanar looked at him a bit strangely, like he'd just sprouted a thumb from the middle of his forehead.

"Are you sure that's what it says?" Arval asked.

"I'm sure."

"Does either of you have any idea what it means?" Kanar said.

"No," Revan replied. "But after you left I found this little square under the star shape, here," he said, pointing to the obscure little shape. "I hadn't noticed it until you both left to look at the other sides again."

"I wonder if it has to do with the riddle?" Arval pondered.

"Maybe, but what?" Kanar said.

"Well, the main shape is a star," said Revan. "Could it have something to do with the stars in the sky?"

"Could be," Arval said thoughtfully. "But a shape like this is also used as a compass on maps."

"What's a compass?" Revan asked.

"Another time question boy," Arval said playfully.

Revan smiled a little at the jab. "So, if it is an actual star, which one does it represent?"

"Who knows," Kanar said. "There are thousands of them in the sky. Without more information we don't know which one it could be. Or what it means even if we did know."

"What do the points of the star indicate on a map?" Arval asked.

"Usually the four directions," Kanar said. "North, south, east, and west."

"That doesn't tell us much then," Revan said.

"It might," Kanar replied. "We are on the east side of the tower right now. If this is a compass, and it's oriented like it would be on a map, then this small square is to the south."

"Well, let's go look on the south side then, see if there's anything there" Arval said. He was glad that for the moment Kanar seemed to have forgotten his anger and sarcasm.

They turned away from the carving and moved around the tower to the south side.

"I wonder if we're looking in the right place?" Revan said.

"What do you mean? This is a tower. Towers have doors. Therefore, there should be a door into this tower," Kanar replied.

"I'm sure you're right. I've never seen a tower that I remember, but this one is obviously different from towers you've seen. Maybe they put the door somewhere else."

"Where else would they put it?" Arval asked.

"Well, imagine that the compass isn't carved into the wall, but laid out flat on the ground with the tower in the center. And let's say the small square is the door. Then the door wouldn't be on the tower, but on the ground somewhere to the south."

"On the ground?" Arval asked, a hint of skepticism tinging his voice.

"Why not? Maybe there's something valuable in there and whoever built it wanted to hide it. Wouldn't you hide the door too in order to keep someone from finding it?"

"I guess," Arval said, still skeptical.

"That actually makes a strange kind of sense," Kanar said. "But what would be 'that which sustains?'"

"I don't know. It could be anything," Revan replied.

"Then again, it could be something that will kill us all," Arval interjected.

"I don't think so. It said, 'within is life, without is not,'" said Revan. "I think that means that if we get into the tower we live if we don't we die. Why go to the trouble of carving the riddle into the stone, leaving it for someone to solve, only to kill them once they figure it out and get inside?"

"Maybe the Nojii built it," Arval said. "They like killing. It'd be just like them to make someone think they're about to be saved, only to kill them after all."

"I think Revan's right," Kanar said grudgingly. "Let's search the ground to the south."

Arval, grumbling under his breath about death lurking just out of sight, dropped his eyes to the ground and started looking. Revan and Kanar did the same. It seemed to be the same kind of hard brown dirt they'd trod for days on the road. There wasn't anything to distinguish it from that hard surface. Maybe all the ground under the towering sand dunes was made of this same unforgiving substance. Revan got down on his hands and knees and was searching closely.

"You're too far to the left," Kanar said.

Revan, puzzled, looked up at him questioningly.

"The small square was directly underneath the southern point of the compass. You're way off to the left of where it should be if we're following it like we would a map."

Revan glanced around and realized Kanar was right. He scooted over about five paces to his right and glanced back at the tower to make sure he was lined up with the center of it and resumed his search. Arval was just to his right, walking slowly, peering intently at the ground, Kanar to his left, doing the same.

The thirst was becoming overpowering. They'd been talking a lot over the last several minutes, and Revan's throat felt as dry as the sand. Once in a while he coughed, a dry rattle that spoke of the desperation they were all beginning to feel. He was still so angry at Kanar that he didn't bother to ask if he had any water left in his skin. He'd find water himself or die trying before he'd ask him to share what he'd withheld.

Revan was a little behind Kanar and Arval, since they were standing, and he was on his knees. So, he didn't notice that Arval had stopped and was looking closely at something on the ground. It wasn't until Arval said something that Revan even noticed him.

"Come look at this," he said.

Revan glanced up and saw Arval about five paces ahead of him, looking down and to his left. As he scrambled closer, Revan saw what Arval was looking at. It was a small, square depression in the hard dirt.

"Let's clear it off," Kanar said as he reached them and saw what they were looking at.

All three pulled their swords and started chipping away at the dirt. It came off in small chunks just like it had at the pit.

"Never thought I'd say that I wished I had a pick in my hands, but I do," Arval said. Revan grinned at the irony; Kanar didn't. It wasn't easy trying to dig with a sword. They had to hold them by the hilts and stab downwards. It made their hands hurt and wasn't very effective at digging.

"Move back," Revan said. Arval and Kanar, looking at him questioningly, backed off a couple steps. Revan held his sword high over his head and brought it down with all the force he could muster. The blade carved into the dirt as it had the Nojii's flesh. He tugged it out, leaving a big gash in the hard soil, and swung again, a little to the left. Pulling out the sword left another big gash. He turned perpendicular to the gashes and swung again, driving his sword into the ground across the center of the cuts.

"Now stick the points of your swords in and pry up the dirt," Revan said. They found that it was fairly easy to clear the dirt that way. In a few minutes of hacking and prying, they'd cleared an opening about two paces by two paces and half a pace deep.

"We should have done this at the pit," Arval said.

"If we had, we'd all be dead by now," Kanar replied.

Arval looked at him, a startled expression on his face, realizing he was right.

"There's something down here," Revan said. "It feels like stone."

"Well, we're digging in the dirt, of course there will be stone. There are always stones buried in dirt,"

Arval said. Kanar smiled coldly at the sarcastic comment.

Revan shot him an annoyed glare and started scraping at whatever he'd found with the edge of his sword. "Help me," he said.

Arval and Kanar got down on their knees and started scraping next to Revan, scooping out debris with their hands when it built up. In a few moments they had exposed a stone block about a pace and a half square. Its edges seemed to drop down into the dirt. There were no carvings on it that they could see.

"Dig around the edges, see if we can lift it," Revan said.

As they worked to clear the dirt from the sides of the stone, Revan kept looking at the face of it. There should be something carved on it, he felt, but there wasn't. He'd examined it thoroughly and it was just a rough stone block.

"It just keeps going," Kanar said. "Even if we get to the bottom edge, there's no way we'll be able to lift it."

Revan sat back, baffled. This was where the map on the wall said something should be, and they'd found something. But was it just a stone block? He didn't think so, but what was it? An entrance to the tower? A decoy to throw off someone trying to get in? He sighed in frustration. The work of digging had sapped his strength; he was very tired. So were his companions. They weren't sweating much even though it was blisteringly hot, and they'd been exerting themselves. Revan didn't think that was a good sign.

"Let's take a break for a minute and think," Revan said.

Arval and Kanar sat down, their legs stretching into the little pit. Revan was morbidly amused to find that they were digging again. After all they'd gone through to find the Kryxaal, here they were digging yet another stone out of the ground. A wry smile stole across his face at his private amusement.

Arval was idly playing with his sword, turning it this way and that, gazing at the blade, when it suddenly slipped from his hand. As it fell, the blade slid along the edge of his calf, opening a hole in his trousers and a cut in his leg.

"Ouch!" he said, quickly covering the cut with his hand.

"Didn't your mother teach you not to play with swords?" Kanar asked sardonically.

Arval glared at him. Revan reached for his pack and took out one of their spare shirts. He tore the sleeve off and handed it to Arval. "Bind the cut with this," he said. Arval rolled up his pant leg and began to tie the shirt sleeve around his bleeding leg. The cut wasn't very deep, but rivulets of blood rand from it and dripped onto the stone they'd been excavating. Revan watched as Arval bound the wound.

"Look at that," Kanar said, wonder in his voice, his finger pointing at the stone.

Revan looked where he was pointing and saw Arval's blood seeping into the stone like water would sink into the sand. Arval, his eyes wide scooted back away from the small pit. Revan pulled his legs out of the pit and stood. As the last drop of blood disappeared, they heard a low rumble. The stone started to lift on one side, like the lid of a chest being opened. In a moment it stood upright, exposing a staircase leading down into earth. It was dark in the hole. "It makes sense now," Revan said.

"What does?" Arval asked.

"The riddle. We had to provide what sustains, to withhold was the price of blood. The last two sentences were the key - the price of blood. If we hadn't given the stone blood, it wouldn't have opened, and we'd have died out here. But what sustains is blood. It sustains life. The last two sentences were both a warning and instructions. Arval cutting himself accidentally solved the riddle."

"We could still die out here," Kanar said.

"I don't think so," Revan said. "I'll bet if we go in there, we'll get to the sanctuary the riddle mentioned."

"Even if we do, there may not be water there. And I still don't understand how you could read those squiggly lines."

"Like I said, I'll tell you some other time. I think we should get down there quick. That stone might not be open for long."

"After you, "Arval said.

Revan picked up his sword, pack and empty waterskins, and followed by Arval and Kanar, descended down the stairs into the dark.

Chapter 12

ing Vraniss waited impatiently in his study for Otarab. A messenger had arrived minutes before, bearing the news that the man was finally in Kessar. It had been almost two weeks since the incident at the excavation, and the king was seething at the lack of news. That would change when Otarab arrived. Barittin had carried out his orders and had a platform erected in White Square. All that was lacking for the gruesome spectacle to come was the object of Vraniss' ire, and he was now here.

He considered sitting at his desk to await Otarab's arrival, then thought better of it. Standing would show his displeasure and reinforce his position of authority. Sitting would make it appear that Vraniss was not terribly concerned with the incident. He wanted Otarab to squirm. The king had learned long ago that his size intimidated people, and he'd learned to use it, to loom dangerously, to great effect. Rare was the person who didn't cower before his intense gaze when he locked it onto them. He would make Otarab positively quake before he had him taken to the platform.

There was a commotion outside in the hall that pulled Vraniss' thoughts back to the present. Muffled voices came to him, one of them unmistakably Otarab's. It was only a moment before the hated man sauntered into the study accompanied by four of the king's personal guard.

"King Vraniss," Otarab said with an obsequious bow.

How fare you this day?" Otarab wisely kept his gaze on the floor before him, instead of meeting the furious gaze of the king.

"I wish to hear your report on the incident at the excavation," Vraniss said, his voice quiet yet powerful and seething with anger.

"Yes, I thought that might be the purpose of my visit. My report is as follows: the structure, as I'm sure you're aware, is gone," He replied simply.

"Yes, I am aware. What happened?" Vraniss was tempted to remove Otarab's head himself, right then, for his flippant attempt at a report. Instead, he simply stared at the man before him.

With a grunt Otarab continued. "I wasn't there when whatever happened, well… happened, Sire. But the reports I received from my aides state that there was a rumble that shook the earth. It woke the entire camp. As it grew in intensity, the stones of the structure began to glow with a bright white light. As the rumble grew louder and the ground shook ever harder, the light intensified until it was almost too bright to look at.

When these phenomena had reached a point of such intensity that my aides all believed the world was about to end, the blocks of the structure began to turn translucent and disappear. This happened at an ever-increasing rate until the whole structure was simply gone. All that was left was a hole in the ground where the foundation used to exist."

"How could it have just disappeared?!" Vraniss screamed. His rage had been building as Otarab spoke, and the disappearance of the structure combined with his hatred of the Nojii noble had caused him to momentarily lose control of his emotions. Otarab didn't flinch, but he didn't meet the king's furious eyes either. "How does stone glow and disappear?" he asked still heated, but no longer screaming.

"Sire, there is simply no explanation for the events I've just described. I'm a learned man, and nowhere in my studies have I ever encountered an account of something remotely akin to this incident."

"There has to be an explanation, a reason," Vraniss said. He'd regained some composure since his outburst.

"If you might permit, Sire, I have a theory."

"I'm listening."

"Well, in Nojii culture there are tales, legends really, that pertain to the time before the Blackfire."

"There was no 'time before the Blackfire'; it has always been," Vraniss interrupted.

"I beg your forgiveness and indulgence Sire, but there are tales from several cultures that pertain to the time before the Blackfire."

"I've not heard of them."

"Again Sire, I plead your pardon, but there are books, very, very old books in the Udron Library in Enrat, that describe things from the time before the Blackfire."

"I've never heard of them. Why should I believe you? Have you seen them?" Vraniss asked, his skepticism evident in his tone.

"Not me personally Sire, but I have it on unimpeachable authority that they exist."

"And what authority might that be?"

"Sire, as you have your eyes and ears throughout the three kingdoms, I have mine. Some are in, shall we say, very sensitive positions, and have whispered things to me in the strictest confidence. Surely you wouldn't ask me, in your wisdom and mercy, to divulge the sources of my information. Their lives would be in danger if they were ever discovered."

"I care not for their lives or yours. What I do care about is how and why that structure disappeared. You will tell me what you know, or, as a subject of the kingdom of Jarradan, you will come to understand the nature of our laws against treason. I'm sure I don't have to explain to you what that would mean."

The four guards standing around Otarab stiffened at the king's words. Their attention had been on their charge; they were good at pretending not to hear what was said in their presence. But the threat the king had just issued brought them to a higher state of readiness. At a small gesture from the king, they would seize Otarab without question or hesitation. They were well trained.

Otarab sighed in resignation, understanding full well the king's meaning. "Very well Sire. I have a contact, a distant relative actually, who is one of the most trusted resident scholars of the Udron Library. Within the library is a small room, hidden deep in its lower levels, where books and records of a the most delicate nature are kept. The area is heavily restricted, indeed, very few even know of its existence. I visited Enrat some years ago on business and met my relative for a libation at a pleasure palace in the city. We'd not seen each other since we were children and he wished to celebrate. I'm sure you can imagine that the life of a scholar can be very dry, without distraction, and being Nojii, he was wont to experience some of life's simpler enjoyments. I agreed to indulge him with an evening of drink and, uh, well, companionship. Towards the end of our visit, just before I departed to my lodgings, him being in his cups, he told me that he had something he wished to impart to me, some bit of secret knowledge. I dismissed our... guests... and he proceeded to describe to me this hidden room and its contents. His station in the library provided him access to this repository, and he'd used it to acquire knowledge that had been deemed too dangerous for unscrupulous eyes."

"And what might that knowledge have been?" Vraniss asked, his gaze intent on Otarab's still downturned face.

"He told me that the Blackfire had not always been. That it had been created in eons long past."

"Created? By whom? And for what reason?"
"To remove magic from the world."

Chapter 13

evan descended the stairs into utter blackness. He walked slowly, one hand on the wall to his left, the other held out in front of him.

"It's as black as the dark depths in here," Arval said.

"Where exactly are the dark depths?" Kanar asked sarcastically.

"It's just an expression," Arval replied testily. "Like you saying, 'what in Tradan's Pocket.'"

Kanar chuckled softly. He seemed to enjoy needling Arval. He'd been doing it since not long after they'd freed him from the box. Arval wasn't sure what to make of it. Did Kanar like him and do it because he felt some kinship with him? Or did he do it because he thought himself somehow better or smarter? He wasn't sure. All he knew was that Kanar could get under his skin quicker than just about anyone he'd ever met.

"Keep quiet you two," Revan said testily. "If there's something or someone in here with us, I'd like to be able to hear them. And I won't be able to with you two jabbing at each other."

"I strongly doubt there is anything alive in here, other than us," Kanar said. Arval remained silent.

"We don't know anything about this place. Who knows what could be down here? We didn't think Nojii would find us when we were sleeping that first night after we found you, but they did, and we still don't know how. Now keep your mouths shut, both of you." Revan's tone silenced Arval and Kanar. Since they'd been together, Revan had seemed to grow in confidence. Arval had been astounded at how he'd killed the Nojii by himself. Combined with his abilities that incident had made him more confident. He even stood taller, his head up instead of drooping to his chest the way it had in the pit. Like everyone's had in that dismal place. Arval and Kanar had found themselves doing what Revan said, although Kanar frequently pushed back. It was obvious that Revan was smart, that his instincts were acute, but there was something new in him. His sky-blue eyes gleamed when he looked at them; they weren't dull and flat like they'd been in the pit. Arval wondered idly what else they might experience in the future, and how they'd all react to it.

"There's a wall here. It feels like the stairs turn," Revan said.

He was still in front, followed by Arval, with Kanar bringing up the rear. When they'd started down the stairs from up above, they'd been moving directly away from the tower. When Arval reached the spot Revan had just mentioned, he felt the wall and realized it turned to the right. They were now moving parallel to the face of the tower. The stone that had lifted out of the ground had closed behind them not long after they'd started down. And it had closed quickly, coming down with a crash that shook the walls and caused dust to billow up in their faces. As thirsty as they all were, the dust had not been a welcome development. Since they were now trapped in the stairwell, the only thing to do was to go on and find out where the passageway led.

"Still going down," Revan said.

"I wonder if we'll ever come back up?" Kanar said sarcastically.

The quips were beginning to wear on Revan, and he knew that they were really getting to Arval. Maybe once they'd gotten through this passage and found some water, or whatever awaited them, Revan would talk to him about his attitude.

They had plenty of room in the stairway. Its walls were about two paces apart; they could touch the ceiling over their heads by reaching their hands up, so they didn't feel terribly confined. It was just dark, and they didn't know what lay ahead. When the stone had opened up above, they'd noticed that the blocks that made up the stairway looked to be of the same material that made up the tower. If that assumption was correct, then whoever had built the tower had probably built the stairs too. Therefore, it seemed logical that the stairway would eventually take them to the tower.

The stairs descended ever deeper into the pure and unbroken dark. Revan could hear Arval and Kanar breathing behind him. Their breath had a rough, grainy quality. As did his. The dust they'd inhaled when the stone had dropped closed on them hadn't helped their dry throats. It was hard to even get a mouthful of spit to purge the dust coating their tongues and teeth. Revan thought he'd trade just about anything at that moment for a small cup of water.

His hand found another wall in front of him, another turn to the right. "The passage turns again," he said. Neither of his companions replied. Revan was on a small landing at the turn. As he probed forward with his foot, looking for the edge of the next step down, he realized there wasn't one. He took a cautious step forward, then another. The stairs seemed to have ended; maybe they'd finally reached the bottom. "It looks like the passage has levelled out," he said. "I don't feel any more stairs."

"So, we've truly reached the dark depths," Kanar said.

"Shut your mouth Kanar," Revan said, unable to keep the irritation out of his voice. "None of us likes this, and your comments aren't helping."

Kanar didn't respond. Revan thought he could feel Kanar staring at his back in anger. Maybe he was. Whatever Kanar was thinking, Revan didn't care about it at that moment. He was focused on trying to find their way out of this and get water. Kanar's feelings didn't matter to him right then, and his comments were starting to anger both Revan and Arval.

Moving forward again, Revan still kept one hand in front of him and one to the side, feeling the wall. He walked slowly and deliberately. It wouldn't do to come across another set of stairs and fall down it. The stone blocks the passage and stairs were made of would break bones. Maybe kill. Revan was certainly not ready to die down here. He didn't think the others were either. Fortunately, Kanar didn't have any quips about how slowly Revan was walking. It seemed he understood the danger and had no more wish to fall down a flight of stairs than Revan did.

They'd gone on for a time, back towards the tower, when Revan's foot suddenly kicked something in front of him. "Wait, there's something here," he said as he came to a halt. He could hear the other two shuffle to a stop behind him. He felt gingerly ahead of him but didn't find a wall. Kicking around with his foot, he thought maybe it was a set of stairs going up. He stepped up onto the object and felt another step above the one he was on. "It's a stairway," he said. "Be careful going up."

"You don't need to tell us," Arval said. "We haven't come all this way just to fall now."

Kanar remained silent. Maybe his feelings were hurt. Revan didn't care. As he began to climb the stairs, his only thoughts were of water. Strange that a simple drink could consume one's thoughts to such a degree. Even in the pit, when they'd had a drink of water in the morning and one at night, sometimes one during the middle of the day, he'd never felt this thirsty.

The stairs climbed up and up, not turning, not changing, just ascending. Revan, his thoughts momentarily distracted from his thirst, wondered if they would end up in the tower when they got to the top, and what they would find when they got there. The darkness was still solid, unabated.

They'd been climbing for some time when they reached a landing where the stairs turned to the right. Revan's legs burned with effort; his breath scorched his parched throat. "There's a landing and the stairs turn," he said. As he continued up a few steps, he reached another landing and another turn to the right. "I think we're in the tower." After several more landings and turns, he thought he detected a change in the darkness. "Stop for a minute," he said, gasping. "I think there's something up ahead. It doesn't seem as dark." Arval and Kanar, breathing just as hard, didn't reply. After catching his breath for a moment, Revan set off again.

Several more steps up the seemingly endless stairs, he was sure – there was light ahead. He could faintly see the stones that made up the walls. As they ascended the steps, he could see the stairs more distinctly. When the light had gotten as bright as very early morning, Revan signaled to stop again. He could clearly see where he was going now; there was a landing and another turn, this time to the left, just ahead. Rays of light spilled through it, illuminating the wall opposite the opening. Revan slowly drew his sword, Arval and Kanar did the same; understanding between them about potential danger didn't need to be spoken.

They crept cautiously and quietly up the stairs until they reached the landing. Revan slowly poked his head around the corner and found himself looking into a fairly large room; it appeared to be empty. He could see a window directly across from him. He thought it was about the size of the windows they'd seen on the tower from the outside. The walls and floor were made of the same stone as the exterior of the tower and the passage they'd just traversed. Other than the window, the room appeared to be empty.

Motioning Arval and Kanar to follow him, Revan stepped out into the room, scanning left and right for any threat. There wasn't any. His initial impression that the room was empty had been correct. He looked up and noted that the ceiling was about ten paces from the floor. He walked to the window and poked his head out. They were definitely inside the tower; he could see one of its walls dropping away to the ground where they'd been earlier. He looked up and saw another window towards the top of the tower. He'd lost track of time while in the passage, and the sun was low on the horizon. Looking at it, he realized he was facing west. Revan turned to survey the rest of the room. The opening to the stairway they'd just come through was in the center of a large stone column within the room that stretched all the way to the ceiling. It was like a tower inside the tower.

Arval and Kanar had each gone around a different side of the column, and it was Kanar that called out first. "Come look at this," he said, excitement in his voice.

Revan hurried around to see what Kanar had found. As he came around the column, he saw a skeleton on the floor. Dust and cobwebs covered it; the bones were a sickly grey and mottled with yellowish brown spots. A tarnished steel breastplate covered the rib cage, its leather straps corroded and broken. A helmet of steel lay to the side of the skull, obviously having fallen or rolled off long ago. Boots of mostly disintegrated leather clung tenaciously around the lower legs and gauntlets of steel around the forearms. Scraps of red and blue cloth clung here and there to the rest of the skeleton, indicating that whomever it was had once been wearing clothes under the armor. A cloth pack lay against the wall next to the remains, its leather straps as rotten as the ones on the armor. Pouches on what remained of a belt around the waist had fallen apart and spilled their contents on, around, and in the skeleton. There looked to be the remains of smokeleaf, a pipe with a broken stem, a few very old coins and some other things that time had degraded so badly that it was no longer possible to tell what they were.

"So, this is how we'll end up," Kanar said. "Skeletons in a deserted tower in the desert."

Revan glared at him but said nothing. Kanar might be right, but Revan wasn't about to acknowledge it. Arval just stared at the remains. Kanar looked at Revan, his eyes full of resignation and anger. Was there a hint of reproach in there for him, Revan wondered. He thought there might be. Breaking the look, Kanar stalked off around the column. Revan turned from watching his back as he walked away and looked down at the skeleton again. Maybe there was something in the pack, he thought. Squatting down he began to rummage through it; the fabric disintegrated under his hands. Arval had wandered over to one of the windows and was staring out.

Revan ignored him and continued his search. The pack was filled with what had once been clothes. They were mainly rags now, and turned to dust as soon as

Revan touched them. Still, he kept looking. He decided that it wouldn't matter at this point if he destroyed the pack and the clothes in it, and it would make searching easier, so he ripped the pack down the front. Its rotted material gave way easily and spilled dust and scraps of cloth on the floor. He stuck his hand inside and felt something in the bottom. Extracting his hand, he realized it was a flint and steel. He set it aside absentmindedly; a flash of a thought told him that it might be useful if they ever gained the mountains. Reaching back into the pack he resumed his search.

There didn't appear to be anything else in the pack, and he was about to give up, when his fingers felt something off in a corner. It was small and slippery. When he finally got a good grip on it, he pulled it out and saw that it was a silver ring with a round, flat face. Incised on it was the image of a sword superimposed over what looked like a scroll. Revan turned it over in his fingers, looking for any other markings. There were none. He'd never seen a sigil like it, not that he'd seen a lot of sigils. Maybe Arval had. "Arval," he said. "Come look at this."

Arval shuffled over. His eyes looked vacant, like he was looking beyond Revan at something known only to himself. Revan held up the ring to him. "Have you ever seen something like this before?"

His eyes came into focus, and he looked closer at the object Revan was holding.

"A ring? Sure. I've seen lots of rings."

"No, the sigil on it. Have you ever seen it before?"

"It looks like the same symbol on the grey leather armor the Jix wear. But that doesn't make sense. How would it be on a ring that's been in this place for ages?"

Kanar had come over to see what Revan had found; he must have heard them talking. Revan hoped he wouldn't speak. He didn't want to listen to him right then. He was disappointed when he did.

"I guess you've found yourself a treasure," Kanar said. "Too bad whoever he was didn't have any water to wash the dust off that ring."

Revan stood quickly from where he'd been squatting in front of the skeleton. "What is your problem Kanar?" he asked, glaring.

"My problem is that I've followed you into this tower and now we're going to end up like whoever that was. I should have left you two as soon as I got out of that box!"

"If it wasn't for us you'd never have gotten out of it!"

"Hey, calm down," Arval said.

"Stay out of this," Kanar growled, pointing a finger at Arval.

"He's one of your companions Kanar," Revan said. "Don't treat him like he's a digger and you're a Nojii."

"I'll treat both of you however I want to. Want to stop me? Try it." Kanar clenched his fists and stared at Revan, hate filling his eyes.

"Maybe we should have left you in that box. You'd be dead by now and we wouldn't have to listen to you," Revan said angrily. He regretted it instantly but didn't have time to apologize. With a yell Kanar charged at him, fists swinging. Revan dodged to the side, surprised, but not quite fast enough. One of Kanar's punches landed a glancing blow on his jaw. The force spun his head to the side and caused him to lose his balance for a moment. Kanar took quick advantage of the opportunity and grabbed him around the waist. They both crashed to the ground. The back of Revan's head cracked on the stone floor; a flash of light blinded his vision. Punches from Kanar rained down on his face and chest, but Revan recovered quickly and with strength he was still getting used to, threw Kanar off him. He landed with a thud a couple paces away. Arval stood gaping at them. Revan decided to end the fight right then and jumped on Kanar, straddling his chest. He raised a fist and held it above Kanar's face. "Want to keep going?" he growled. "I will end you right now if you want to. I'll leave you here to become skeleton company to our friend over there." Kanar stared up at him, the menace in his eyes unmistakable. He didn't speak.

Revan stared at him a moment longer to make sure Kanar realized he was serious, then slowly got up off him. Arval just stood silently. Without a word Kanar stood and walked off to the far side of the room. Revan had dropped the ring when the fight started, and he scanned the floor until he found it, bent down and picked it up.

He looked at the ring a moment, then with a sigh, tried to put it on the third finger of his right hand. It was too small. He moved it to the short finger next to the third and slid it on. It fit perfectly. He'd only gazed at it for a brief moment when the world went white.

Chapter 14

e was in the white tunnels again. The now familiar sensation of rapid movement was back, the walls of the tunnel flying by, its twists and turns negotiated as effortlessly as breathing. Revan expected to end up in a room, and when he felt himself slowing, he was not disappointed to find that's exactly where he was. Except this room was much larger. He had the sense of a wide-open space, not the small bubbles he'd been in before. The room appeared to be about the size of the one in the tower; on the far side he thought he could see the openings of two other tunnels. On the floor in the center of the room was a small patch of, well, whatever the tunnels were made of, light, he thought, that was a shade of grey. Within it twisted and undulated several of the red and gold threads, just like the ones he'd seen in the Blackfire and shot into Arval during their escape from the Kryxaal. He moved (he thought of it as walking, but he didn't have a body in this place, so walking wasn't really right) towards the spot where the threads whirled around inside the grey spot.

As he approached it, a few of the gold threads stopped their unpredictable movements and rose up towards him, their ends looking much like the heads of snakes waiting to strike. The red threads kept on about their mysterious undulations. Revan hadn't seen them behave quite like this before. He wasn't sure he wanted to find out what they were going to do. Except that he had no choice, really. He approached closer and they suddenly shot towards him, drove in to where his chest would be if his body was there, and exploded within him with a force and violence he'd not realized was possible here. It seemed as if his body was there with him and that it was filled, every part of it, with fire made of molten gold. It was pain and ecstasy combined. He wanted it to both stop and never to end. As quickly as it had begun, it was over. Revan felt a wave of relief and a pang of loss as the feeing faded.

The red threads continued to swirl about over the grey spot on the floor of the room. If he'd been breathing, he'd have gasped at the recently departed sensations. As he thought about what he'd just felt, he understood that he could sense water. It was out there, in the room in the tower with his body. But how could that be? He'd searched the entire room. The only thing in it had been the skeleton. The ring? He'd entered the white tunnel when he'd put on the ring. Maybe it had something to do with all this. Revan felt elation and relief that he knew now where to find water, that he and his companions would live. Now he just had to get out of the tunnels and back into his body. Before he could turn away though, the red threads slowly changed their pattern of movement. They began to rise straight up into the air, twisting around each other like the strands of a rope. As they grew taller and taller, they began to widen and lengthen until they formed roughly the shape of a human. Revan could see arms, legs and a head made of the still turning and twisting red threads. They were thick and wide now, more like ribbons, many the width of a large belt. He wondered what this remnant, if that's what this was, had to say. As soon as the thought occurred to him, the figure spoke.

"You've found me," a voice said to him. There was no mouth on the figure. It didn't even have a face, just the shape of a head – no ears, hair or any other feature identified it as anything more than a humanlike twisted mass of red.

"Who are you?" Revan asked.

"I am Jinirlyn. Have you have found my ring?" the figure said.

"Is it made of silver, with a sword over a scroll on it?"

"Yes."

"Then yes, I did find it. I'll give it back to you if you want it," Revan said. He realized as soon as he said it, how absurd it sounded. The man was long dead; he had no need of his ring anymore. The ring wasn't even here with him, in this place, it was with his body back in the tower.

"It is yours now, I have no more need of it," Jinirlyn said, confirming Revan's self-admonishing thought.

"Did it bring me here? To you?" he asked.

"Yes and no. You have the spark of magic within you. When you found my ring, that spark brought you here. My ring has tied my essence to the world of life. Now that you have found it, I will depart this world for the next. But before I do, there are things you must know."

"My friends and I are dying of thirst. I need to get back to them and get them the water I know is in that room where I found your ring."

"Patience. You will return to them soon. Time has no meaning here. When you return it will be as if you'd never left."

"But I've been here before, in these white tunnels. When I got back one of my friends told me that I'd been in here for a long time."

"Was it in a Kryxaal?"

"How do you know that name?

The figure laughed, not mockingly, but an indulgent laugh, as a parent would laugh at a child who had just discovered that screaming and running towards a bird on the ground would cause it to fly away squawking. "I know it because I helped build them."

Revan was astounded at this information. "You did?!" he exclaimed incredulously.

"Of course. I did not have magic myself, but my order found the locations where they were constructed."

"You know where they are?" Revan asked in awe.

"No. I know where one is: not far from here. I imagine that's the one you've been inside."

"Yes," Revan said simply.

"The others are not known to me. That was a deliberate intention of those who constructed them. They were meant to remain concealed. As such four groups of us were dispatched around the world to find four places where Kryxaal could be constructed. We all set off on our journeys at the same time and all in different directions. We never saw each other, or our homes, again. But our mission was successful. The Kryxaal you entered was in a place my group found."

Revan couldn't believe what he was hearing. This was a man from before the Blackfire was created! He'd actually been among the group of people who'd constructed that massive building! He'd helped decide where to build it. His mind was whirling and confused. Out of the morass of thoughts a question occurred to him.

"So how did your ring bring me here?"

"Those who created the Kryxaal infused it with a touch of magic. It allowed me to communicate with them, give them updates on my group's progress. I myself was given a small bit of magic that I might be able to use the ring, although I had no talent for magic myself. It was through this process that my essence was tied to it. When you put it on, it activated both the magic in the ring, and what was left of my essence, which combined with the magic within you, brought you here."

"That was eons ago. How have you remained sane? Surely your mind would have disintegrated after all these ages," Revan said.

"As I told you, time has no meaning here. For you it has been eons, as it has been for my body, which must surely no longer exist. But for me, the essence of me which resides in this place, I only just arrived."

Revan couldn't understand how that was possible, but he didn't argue. There were many things that had happened to him recently that he'd never dreamed of, let alone thought possible. This was just another object in that sack of mysteries.

"When I was in the Kryxaal, I spoke to someone who called himself Drannal. Do you – did you, know him?"

"Yes, I know of Drannal. He was powerful with magic. How did you speak to him?"

"He told me that he was a remnant, sustained by magic in order to give whomever entered the Kryxaal knowledge and a little magic of their own."

"And have you received these things?"

"Yes. I can run faster, see farther, hear and smell better than I ever could. I also can read Denoran. I know it's a dead language that hasn't been spoken or read, probably since your time, but I can read it."

The figure sighed, the bright red threads darkened for a moment, then brightened again. "Then the Kryxaal has done what it was intended to do."

"It did?"

"Of course. You are here now. Without the magic from the Kryxaal you would never have been able to read Denoran or activate my ring. Its magic doesn't work the same way that the Kryxaal's does. The Kryxaal would grant magic to whomever entered it, all they needed was the spark of magic inside them, and they would receive the Kryxaal's gifts. To activate my ring, you must have more than the spark, you must have ability with magic."

"But I thought you just said you didn't have magic of your own?" Revan asked, confused.

"I did not. But the ring was created specifically for me, and the magic that was given to my body interacted with it in order to activate it, for it to serve its purpose. In that way it was bound to the small spark of magic within me, within all life. I was able to activate it to communicate with the Denoran Synod. Anyone other than me who wished to use it needed to have more than a little magic, they needed to be born with the ability to wield and control it. If they bore only a small spark, it would have done nothing."

"So, I have more than a little magic? I can, as you said, wield and control it? And what's the Denoran Synod" Revan asked.

Jinirlyn chuckled softly. "You have many questions. I was once young, and had many questions too," the figure said, a touch of melancholy in the voice. "If you have activated my ring, you have more magic than you seem to realize. And yes, you are able to wield and control it. My ring would not have activated for you if you couldn't. My people and our language were known as Denoran. The Denoran Synod was the name of the group tasked with constructing the Kryxaal. It was made up of those with great knowledge of, and power with, magic."

"But I can barely use it," Revan protested. "I was able to make Arval run faster when the Kryxaal was disappearing beneath him, but that's about all I can do."

"You just said your senses are more acute, that you can run faster. Are these not magical to you?"

"I guess so. I hadn't thought about them in that way. Magic to me seems to be these white tunnels, and the red and gold threads. Like what you are made of."

"I can tell you nothing of these... threads. They are beyond my understanding of magic. You must learn more if you are to discover their true nature."

"Where do I learn more?" Revan asked. He'd learned much since meeting Jinirlyn, but he felt more confused than ever.

"Find the other Kryxaal. Now that one has been found, there are those who will try to find the others. If their intentions are ill, then it does not bode well for the world."

"What do you mean? Will they bring on some catastrophe? Is it up to me to find them?"

"I know not what they might do. Men have desires known only to them. Some seek power and influence in order to improve the lives of all. Others choose to use their power to enrich themselves or to enslave others. Their motives are mysteries. You do not seem to carry evil in your heart. I have known many who did. If you wish to prevent those who do from obtaining the power of the Kryxaal, then you must be the one to find and enter them, to receive their power. I can tell you no more; that is all I know. The mysteries of magic were not something I understood in life. What I have told you was told to me when I was given my ring and my small bit of magic. Since I have not lived in your time, I can tell you nothing of the world as it is for you. The rest of your questions you must answer for yourself. My time is ending. I will leave soon for the world beyond this one."

"Jinirlyn," Revan said. "Earlier you mentioned your order. What's it called? Maybe I can find someone from it if it still exists."

"My order was known as the Jix. I created it."

Chapter 15

evan shot through the white tunnel again, ending up back in his body in the room in the tower. Arval was still staring out the window. Kanar was nowhere to be seen. It seemed that Jinirlyn had been right – that no time had passed in the tower room while they'd been speaking. Revan wondered how much else there was to know about the tunnels and threads, about magic. If he was going to find out, then he'd have to commit to bringing about the return. Drannal had said he simply had to decide in his heart that he would choose that path. In that moment Revan knew that his choice had been made. He had a full year to decide, but it had only taken him a matter of days. He would do what he could to find the other Kryxaal and return magic to the world. The things he'd learned and experienced since he and Arval had escaped from the pit had kindled within him a desire for life. He wanted to see the world, to experience all that it held, and to discover more about magic and how to use it.

At the moment that his decision was made, he began to see, all around him, the red and gold threads.

They twisted, turned, and flowed within everything. He saw red ones and a few gold flowing and twisting around and through Arval, all through his torso and up and down his limbs, even across his face. He held up his own hand and saw more of the red threads interspersed with gold coursing through him, flowing up and down his arm. The stone blocks of the tower contained thousands of gold threads, but no red ones. This was a new phenomenon Revan hadn't seen before. He wondered fleetingly what it meant. And what did it mean that he could now see them everywhere when before, except for when he'd given them to Arval, he'd only seen them in the white tunnel and in the Blackfire? Did it have something to do with having made the decision to pursue the path of the return? So many questions. He had no idea if he'd ever answer them all. Maybe it didn't matter if he did. He was alive, out of the pit, and had abilities he'd never imagined. Maybe that was enough.

Water! The thought crashed into his head as if it had fallen from the sky and hit him in the back. He knew there was water in the tower; it was in the room with them now, and above them somewhere. He'd been fairly certain that the windows at the top indicated there was another room up there, and now he knew there was. That was where the water could be had. But how to get to it? They'd explored the room; there was no entrance or exit other than the one they'd come in through via the stairs. But there had to be a way to get in. Revan stood from where he'd been squatting next to the skeleton of Jinirlyn and began to look around. The gold threads flowed around the stone blocks of the room, up and down, side to side. There seemed to be a pattern to their movements, but he was having a hard time figuring out what it was. The sheer number of threads and how they crisscrossed each other was making him a little dizzy. He walked past Arval, who was still staring out the window. He didn't seem to notice Revan's passing. That was alright, Revan thought. Once he'd found a way to get to the water, Arval would snap out of it.

As he walked around the column in the middle of the room where the stairs were, he saw that many of the gold threads were running from the exterior walls, across the floor to the column, and were shooting up it towards the ceiling. He walked closer to the column and looked up. He expected to see the threads hit the ceiling and then branch out back towards the outside wall. But they didn't. They went straight up through the ceiling. Looking closer he saw that the threads that were on the ceiling seemed to be coming from above. It was as if there was a passageway along the wall of the column where threads from below went up and threads from above came down, passing each other on the way. He stretched his hand out and touched the wall. He could actually feel the threads moving through the blocks under his hand. Somehow he could also tell that his suspicion was correct – they were going up past the ones coming down. An image began to form in his mind of the room at the top of the tower. It was the same size as this one, although not as tall, maybe six paces high, and in the middle there wasn't a column but a fountain. He could see water shooting up in a gentle fan from a stone pillar in its center, falling back down into a large basin that surrounded it. How could water get up there? He understood as soon as the question formed: this place was old and infused with magic. Magic from before the time of the departure. Apparently not all magic had been sent away when the Blackfire had been created. It seemed that he could see the entire structure of the tower in his mind, as if it had been drawn on paper or carved into a block of stone. He saw the stairways and passage they'd come through to get to this room, and the tower itself. Within the four walls of the column that surrounded the stairs were four round channels. They'd been bored straight through the blocks. The channels, tubes really, converged at the fountain where they all melded into one tube which was encased by a pillar in the center of the basin. As he looked down the image of the tower, he saw that the channels descended far below the depth of the underground passageway they'd come through, deep into the earth where they terminated in what he understood was an underground river. The magic of old had somehow caused the water from that source to be sucked up through the tubes in the blocks and into the fountain on the top floor. Revan also realized that he knew how to get into the room where that fountain was.

He pushed the image of the structure out of his head, and without really knowing what he was doing, he summoned the white tunnel. It came easily. He flowed through its contours at the speed of thought, looking for the room he knew was somewhere ahead. It didn't take long to find it. When he felt himself slowing as the room approached, he realized that he was aware of his body and the white tunnels simultaneously. It was like he could see both places at once. The room where his body was felt like it was far away, while the room in the white tunnel seemed somehow more real and substantial. As he focused his concentration on the white room, he noticed that it contained thousands upon thousands of the gold threads. They flowed and twisted through the whole structure of the white room, as they had back in the room where his body was. Revan intuitively understood that he could manipulate them. He reached out to them with his mind, and they responded by ceasing their movement, as if awaiting his command. An image of the fountain came to him and without quite knowing how he did it, he showed it to the threads. They seemed to know what he wanted. He heard a rumble and a section of the ceiling began to descend. Revan left the white tunnel instantly this time; there was no going back through it like he had before. As he did he noticed the gold threads that had been flowing through the ceiling all converging on one spot up against the outer wall.

A gap between the stones in the ceiling opened to his right where all the threads had gathered. They were now shooting up through the blocks towards the room above. With a loud groan the whole ceiling began to twist in towards the center of the room. The turning motion caused a set of curved stairs to drop down slowly from the spot where the threads had gathered, eventually coming to a stop on the floor just ahead of where he stood. The ceiling was now lower by about five paces. The sound and movement of it had caused Kanar to come running and Arval to drag himself out of his reverie.

"What in Tradan's Pocket made that happen?" Kanar exclaimed, amazement on his face, his anger, for a moment, forgotten.

Arval just stared. He was getting used to strange and unexpected things happening.

"Let's go see what's up there," Revan said, pointedly not answering the question.

They moved slowly up the stairs, always ready for danger. As they neared the top, the sound of tinkling and splashing made them stop and look at each other.

"Water!" Arval practically screeched.

He didn't wait for the others to respond but dashed up the stairs, danger forgotten.

Chapter 16

hey spent the night in the room with the fountain; the three boys all drank so much water that their stomachs swelled noticeably. Arval seemed to take particular delight in relieving himself out the windows. Revan just smiled as he cackled, watching his stream fall to the dry ground below. Kanar's attitude had improved a bit, Revan thought. Or maybe it hadn't. Whatever the case, at least he hadn't made any snide comments or started fights since they'd found water. The room with the fountain was no different than the one downstairs, except that it held the fountain and no skeleton. Revan wondered if there was another way out of the tower without having to go back through the long stairs and passage they'd come in by. The gold threads had disappeared once the stairway had come down from the ceiling in the room below. He still wasn't sure if he'd made them go away, or if they'd done it on their own.

In the morning, after they'd eaten a bit of dried meat and drunk from the fountain, Revan sat down under one of the windows to ponder how they were going to get out. As he sat back against the wall behind him, he thought maybe he could use magic again. Focusing his attention inside himself, he called the tunnel; it came easily. That was new. Before it had just come. This time he'd actually made it appear. When he'd flown through it to the room at the end, he found the gold and red threads floating just above the floor and showed them an image of the outside of the tower and the ground below. A low grating rumble began from outside and Revan stood to look out the window. Below him he saw a number of blocks emerging from the outer walls of the tower. They formed a descending stairway that wound around the outside of the structure several times until, he was sure, it reached the bottom.

This latest use of magic confirmed to him that the threads somehow understood what he needed. The question he pondered now was, had he somehow created the stairs up to the fountain and down the outside of the tower, or had they been there all along, just waiting for his magic to activate them?

Arval and Kanar heard the sound and walked over; Revan moved back to let them see out the window.

"Where in the dark depths did those come from?!" Arval asked.

Kanar just looked at them, then turned to Revan. "Did you make this happen?" he asked, an accusatory tone to his voice.

"Does it really matter how it happened?" Revan replied.

"Yes, it does. Ever since I've met you, weird things have been happening. And if you know something about it, I want to know too. If I'm going to travel with you, then I deserve to know."

Revan sighed. "Fine, I'll tell you. Yes, I made it happen."

He proceeded, grudgingly to tell Kanar about how they'd found the entrance to the Kryxaal and what had happened inside. He told him of crossing the light bridge from the top of it out of the pit and how Arval had almost fallen. Revan didn't mention how he'd used the threads to make Arval run fast enough to escape though. Nor did he tell him about the departure and the Blackfire, or that he was going to attempt the return. Sharing with Kanar the knowledge that he commanded a bit of magic was enough. Arval, thankfully, didn't fill in the gaps in the story that Revan intentionally left. When he'd finished, Kanar just looked at him, his expression inscrutable.

"We should probably fill our skins and get moving," was all he said.

Revan and Arval didn't disagree. They filled all their waterskins and gathered their packs. Revan climbed out the window first. As he stood on the first step high above the ground, he was reminded of being on the ramp of light as they escaped the Kryxaal. The drop was dizzying, and although not as dramatically terrifying as the drop from the ramp had been, he would be dead if he fell. He began descending carefully, watching his step closely as he made his way down. It was not easy. The blocks were not lined up directly under one another, so he had to step out over a void to reach the lower one as he descended. They were also about a half pace apart in height, making each step down a jarring affair. He held his left hand to the wall of the tower to steady himself as he stepped, more like fell he thought, from one block to the next. Arval and Kanar were behind him; he could hear their steps as they negotiated the treacherous path.

After several minutes of stress and anxiety, they reached the bottom and stopped for a moment.

"Which way should we go?" Arval asked.

"I think we should head due south towards the mountains," Kanar said. "I don't think we should chance the road again. Besides, we'd have to backtrack a full day or more to get to it. Our water might not last long enough for us to get to the mountains."

"I agree with Kanar," Revan said. "We'd have less chance of running into Nojii or whoever else might be on the road if we stay off it."

"It'll be hard traveling over the dunes," said Arval.

"Yes, but we can try to find ways around them instead of having to climb over them like we did to get here," Kanar answered.

"Alright then, we go through the desert," Revan said, thankful that for once he and Kanar agreed on something. But there was something in Kanar's voice that hadn't been there prior to their fight. It was a coldness, an aloofness that made Revan wonder what he was thinking. He'd watch him closely from now on, he decided.

Once the decision was made, Kanar and Revan climbed back up the stairs a bit to have a look at the desert in hopes of finding a fairly direct route south that would avoid the worst of the dunes. There appeared to be a series of clefts and valleys between them that meandered in the general direction of the distant mountains; nothing was direct in these dunes.

"You've spent more time in the wilderness than I have," Revan said to Kanar. "How long do you think it will take following that route to reach the mountains?"

"At least four or five days. Maybe longer if we have to do some climbing. You should use your magic to move the dunes and make a road for us," he said, some of the old sarcasm back in his voice.

"I don't think it works that way," Revan replied, shooting him an annoyed look.

"Well, maybe if we run out of water you could just create a lake with it next time."

Revan ignored the jab. "Let's go," he said roughly.

The three set off towards the mountains, Revan again in the lead, Arval and Kanar following.

The journey was uneventful. They didn't see any other towers or meet any Nojii. It was just the three of them in the vastness of the great orange sand dunes. At night Revan and Kanar would climb a nearby dune to ascertain their position relative to the mountains and the tower they'd left behind. They seemed to be following the path they'd found. Each day the mountains were a little closer, the tower, which they could still see, further behind. Having learned how quickly they could deplete their supply of water; they'd rationed it strictly. By the time they'd been away from the tower for four days, they each still had one full skin and about a quarter of another. None complained; they knew what would happen if they drank too greedily.

At the end of the seventh day, Revan and Kanar climbed a dune, as was their habit, and arriving at the top, saw how close the mountains really were. They loomed up in front of them, the snow on their peaks glinted, the stone purple and red in the setting sun.

"We should reach the foothills by midday tomorrow," Kanar said. It won't be long after that until we should be able to find a source of water. We can drink all we want tonight."

"I'll keep rationing mine until we actually do find some," Revan said.

"Suit yourself, but I'm going to enjoy mine." He turned away from Revan and muttered under his breath, "It'll be about the only thing I've enjoyed since I met you."

Revan sighed as Kanar turned and walked back down the dune to where Arval was lounging, head on his pack. He'd heard the comment clearly, although he didn't think Kanar knew he'd heard. He wished somehow that they could mend the rift that had opened between them. But he didn't see how that was possible at this point. Kanar was determined to be angry with him. He looked back toward the mountains, marveling at their size, the snow, and the dark patches of trees on their flanks. Tomorrow would bring new sights and experiences to Revan's burgeoning catalog. Kanar was one of those experiences he'd rather not think about.

"Looks like we'll be in the foothills sometime tomorrow," he said to Arval when he'd descended the dune.

"Wonderful! I'm looking forward to having something to eat other than dried meat."

Revan silently agreed. While he'd loved his first taste of a food that hadn't been from the pit, he was getting tired of dried meat too. And their supply was beginning to run low anyway. They'd have to find both food and water in the mountains if they were going to make it to Kessar.

"Let's get some sleep, I'd like to start early in the morning. The sooner we're in those mountains, the sooner we get to the city," Revan said.

Arval and Kanar followed Revan's lead and lay down using their packs for pillows. Before long they were asleep.

Revan was the first to wake. He sat up groggily rubbing his eyes and looked around. IT was just he and Arval.

"Arval! Wake up! Kanar's gone!" He said, shaking Arval by the shoulder. His friend sprang up from the ground where he'd been lying, eyes wide and alert. Morning grogginess was not an affliction he appeared to suffer from.

"Where is he?!"

"I don't know. I just woke up and he's not here."

They were both looking at the indentation in the sand where Kanar had lain down to sleep. They could see his tracks leading off towards the mountains.

"Let's go after him," Arval said.

Hastily donning their packs, they set off after their departed companion.

"I wonder why he left?" Arval asked.

"You wonder? After the problems we had with him? If I hadn't beat him in that fight, I'm not sure he wouldn't have tried to kill me. Somethings wrong with him. I really didn't like him much, but we'd have been better off if we'd stayed together."

"He knows the wilderness. Remember what he said about his father teaching him all those things?"

"Yes, it's the main reason I want him with us. He does know more about surviving out here than we do."

"If we can't find him, we'll make it. I know a few things. And you have magic. That must be worth something."

They followed Kanar's tracks throughout the morning. Fortunately, it seemed that Kanar had chosen to follow the route they'd picked out days before, so Arval and Revan weren't too concerned about losing time or moving away from the direction they'd chosen to travel. As morning turned into afternoon, they noticed the dunes had gotten markedly smaller, the gaps between them larger. It wasn't long before they saw the tallest of the mountains rearing up ahead of them.

"We'll be in the foothills very soon," Revan said. "I remember that mountain from last night. It's the tallest one I could see. The foothills were right below it."

Minutes later, they passed the last of the dunes, a tiny example only about twenty paces high. Before them stretched a series of ever larger hills that rose right up to the base of the enormous peak. Their lower slopes were covered in clumps of short grass, an occasional shrub dotted the landscape. Further up, about halfway to the mountain proper, a treeline separated the relatively open lower slopes from the forested higher regions. Kanar's tracks disappeared at the end of the sand.

"Which way did he go from here?" Arval asked.

"I don't know," Revan replied. "He was the tracker, not us. I don't think we'll find him unless he wants us to."

"I guess we're on our own then," Arval said a bit dejectedly.

"Looks that way," Revan sighed. "Forget about Kanar for now. We have to find a way through these mountains. There's no way we can climb that tall one, so we'll have to find a gap between them that we can follow."

"Let's try to the right," Arval said. "If we don't find a way, then we can try to make for the pass where the road to the pit comes through the mountains."

Revan nodded his agreement, and he and Arval began trudging up the slope towards the tree line.

Chapter 17

anar raced along the faint path through the forest. He was elated to be back in familiar surroundings. The woods had been his second home, where he'd spent almost all of his free time away from the Traveler's Rest. The smell of tree bark and moss, rotting leaves and wet dirt brought back sweet, but also painful memories. The worst were those of the day he'd been taken. He'd not told that part of his story to Revan and Arval; Kanar hadn't wanted to talk about it with them. Those memories were closed off in his mind, behind a barrier that no one would ever breach. But they came flooding back to him now as he ran through the woods, the enormous peak he and Revan had been using as a landmark rising up to his left.

It had been a day much like this one. The sky was overcast, as it often was back home. The humidity in the air caused water droplets to form on the leaves of trees and shrubs. Kanar would sometimes get showered with them if he wasn't careful ducking under a tree limb. His clothes were made of good wool which kept most of the water off him. If he fell in a stream or pond he'd be soaked, but a shower from a tree wasn't too bad.

He'd been out most of the morning hunting for small game. His father had shown him how to set traps to catch the rabbits and other creatures that lived in the forest, and he'd put out several the day before. So far the basket strapped to his back held two rabbits and one tree skimmer. He was particularly proud of the skimmer; they didn't come down to the ground much, preferring to stay high in the trees, hopping, flying really, from limb to limb, their long hind legs propelled them through the air where they flew for great distances. But their meat was exceptionally tasty, and their pelts were yellowish brown and very soft, much prized by those who made clothes out of fur. He'd get good coin, maybe a gold link, for that one pelt, and a few copper links for the rabbits. It was shaping up to be a good day, and there were still half a dozen or so traps to visit.

Kanar was about one range from home when he heard a clamor coming from the direction of the Rest. The sound of anything loud from home other than his mother calling him for dinner was extremely unusual. And it was not dinner time. Kanar turned and began trotting back down the path in the direction of the Rest, a bubble of anxiety forming in his stomach. The sounds grew clearer as he got closer and within a very short time Kanar could tell the sounds were not happy. There was screaming - a woman's voice, yelling and cursing - men's voices. Kanar broke into a dead run, the sounds of whatever was happening at home growing along with his dread. He smelled smoke, and it wasn't smoke from the cookfire in the hearth. This was wood and something else, something sickly sweet.

As he broke out of the trees and into the clearing on the road where the Rest stood, he saw that the building was in flames. A large group of men was gathered around, all of them bald with black tattoos of swirling, spiky designs running up their arms, across some of their chests, and even up the side of the head of one man. They were shirtless, even though the weather was chilly, and very muscular. Every one of them carried some kind of weapon from enormous axes to short swords. And they looked as if they knew how to use them.

Kanar slid to a halt at the sight of his mother, her arms each held by one of the huge men. The sound of gravel under Kanar's boots caused one of the men to look his way. "Well now, there's the foal!" he said, grinning at Kanar menacingly. "Let's have him over here, get a better look at 'im." Two men Kanar had not seen each seized one of his arms and dragged him toward the man who'd spoken. It was the man with the tattoo up the left side of his head. It curled around his left eye and crept out on his cheek towards his nose. The stench coming off the man was almost overpowering. It smelled as if he didn't bathe. Ever. Kanar thought it strange that he'd noticed the man's reek above the facts that his home was burning, his mother was screaming, and his father was nowhere in sight.

"Shut up you," the stinking man said as he backhanded Kanar's mother across the mouth. Her head snapped back at the force of the blow, a stringy rope of blood flew from her split lips and splashed across the shoulder of the man holding her left arm. The man just grinned, gaps showed between his teeth where some were missing. She'd stopped screaming; her head hung down to her chin, a line of bloody drool dripped towards the ground.

Stink Man, that's what Kanar had absentmindedly decided to call him, turned back to look at him. "Now, you'll do just fine as a digger," he said. Kanar had no idea what he was talking about, but he had to find a way to help his mother and himself get away from these brutes. Where was his father?! If he were here he'd have been cutting them down with his sword or picking them off from the forest with his bow. Kanar looked around, hoping to spot a sign of him somewhere.

"Looking for dear old daddy then are we?" he asked Kanar, his voice rich with scorn. "Can't you smell 'im?" Kanar suddenly realized what the sweet smell was that he'd detected in the smoke back in the forest. It was burning flesh. He screamed then, a guttural, furious sound, and began thrashing against the men holding his arms. He had no chance; they were far too strong. Still, he kept at it, kicking and twisting wildly, to no avail. Stink Man watched him, laughing. "We pinned him to a table in there with knives through his arms and legs," Stink Man said. "The knives we found in your kitchen were nice and sharp. They went right through his skin. My, my how he howled! But he didn't really start making noise until we lit a fire under 'im."

Kanar stopped thrashing, he wasn't getting anywhere, just tiring himself out. A clarity, an acceptance came to him – his mother and he were going to die. These men were going to kill them both. But if he could get away, he vowed that he would kill every man he ever saw who bore tattoos of the kind these men had. He marked the face of Stink Man well, memorized every line and contour of it, every twist and spike of his distinctive tattoo. This man he would kill slowly if he ever got the chance. This man would suffer and bleed before death took him.

"Calming down a bit are you?" Stink Man said to him. "Good. You can watch us have some fun with your ma before we leave."

Some of them had come on horses, others in a wagon which waited a few paces up the road from the burning Rest. The wagon had canvas covered sides and top and was pulled by two horses. The men holding Kanar's mother dragged her, still senseless, towards the wagon and heaved her in. Stink Man climbed up after her. At the top step he paused and turned back to Kanar and the men holding him. "I want that one awake for this. Don't let him loose and don't knock him out. He needs to remember what we do to those who make us displeased." With that he disappeared into the wagon. Kanar heard the sound of cloth ripping, then his mother began screaming again. The sound of fist meeting flesh was audible; the wagon began rocking from side to side, but the screams didn't stop for a long time.

A short time after they did, Kanar's mother came flying out of the wagon and bounced across the ground, a spray of blood fanned up as her head hit the hard dirt of the road. She rolled to a stop on her back. Kanar saw her head lolling at an impossible angle; her throat had been cut. There was blood all down the front of her torn dress and down her legs which the torn bottom part of the dress had left exposed. Kanar knew exactly what Stink Man had done to her. Rage seethed within him, and it must have been evident because Stink Man smiled at him when he looked him in the eye as he climbed out of the wagon, his hands dripping red. "So, there you have it," he said. "This life of yours is over. Another one just started. You'll do well in the pit with that anger." He laughed at Kanar and gestured to the men holding him. They dragged him up into the wagon and bound his hands with iron shackles that were fastened securely to the floor. Kanar wasn't going anywhere until they let him. The wooden boards of the wagon floor glistened with a large dark stain. His mother's blood.

The wagon set off moments later towards the north, stopping occasionally. Every so often Stink Man and his cohorts would shackle another boy inside with Kanar. It was from one of these boys that he learned the name of his new enemy: Nojii. And their leader, the one who'd killed his mother, he learned, was called Hento.

Kanar ran most of the day after leaving Revan and Arval. At night he found a cleft in a stone wall that afforded some shelter from the cold wind that blew up this unused pass. He'd followed a game trail for a long ways until it disappeared near a marshy area. He covered the cleft with tree branches to disguise it from anyone glancing its direction, also laying some on the ground to cushion it's hardness and slept as he hadn't slept since before the Nojii had taken him.

In the morning he rose with the sun, feeling as refreshed from sleep as he could ever recall feeling and set out again through the pass, making his own trail as he went. His thoughts drifted towards the Nojii and how he was going to have his revenge. He'd learned a bit about fighting from his father, primarily how to use a bow, and a few basic moves with practice swords they kept in their barn, but he had no formal weapons training. He would have to change that, he thought. He'd heard tales of the Jix, that legendary fighting force that belonged to the king of Jarradan. If he could join them, somehow, they'd teach him to use weapons. He'd stay with them just long enough to master whatever they'd teach him, then he'd desert and begin his hunt for the Nojii, especially the Stink Man, Hento. Kanar smiled at the plan he'd just formulated. And he had Arval and Revan to thank for setting him free so he could pursue it. His smile faded at the thought of Revan.

Chapter 18

rval and Revan staggered through the forest. They'd been working their way through it for several days and had been out of food for the last three. Catching game hadn't been nearly as easy as they'd thought it was going to be. And there was no path or road through the forest that they'd been able to find. Going cross country was hard enough. Without food it was doubly difficult. The one thing they did have in abundance was water. They'd followed a stream for several ranges which had replenished their waterskins, and from which they'd drunk heartily. They both agreed that this water, coming as it did from melting snow high on the mountains, was the best tasting water either of them had ever had. Revan had been amazed at the sheer volume of it. He watched, mesmerized as it tumbled over huge boulders, around and over fallen trees, and meandered slowly around bends in the streambed. The trees also filled him with awe. Their towering trunks, sheathed in leaves and needles, and sprouting enormous branches were unlike anything he'd ever imagined.

"I never dreamed there was this much water in the world," he told Arval when they'd first found the stream. "If only we had this at the pit!"

"Well now, if we'd had all this water at the pit, then we'd not have been in the desert would we?! That's why it's called a desert – because it hasn't got any water," Arval said jokingly.

Revan smiled sheepishly, "I know. I was just imagining it."

Arval laughed and elbowed him in the ribs. "Wait 'til you see the ocean. Now let's find somewhere to sleep before it gets dark."

They'd turned from the stream and found, a short distance away, a small clearing covered in soft green moss and overhung by the enormous branches of giant leafy trees. Spending the night there had been bliss.

But that was several days ago, and now they were getting weak with hunger and fatigue. Revan felt he could lay down on a rock and sleep as well as he had on that bed of moss. He'd tried calling the tunnel and the threads a couple times, and they'd come, the threads coursing through he and Arval as well as the trees and shrubs that dotted the forest floor. Except that he hadn't been able to do anything with them. Magic, it seemed, wasn't going to help him fill their bellies. He'd told Arval about his failure to get food by using magic. Arval had shrugged and grunted something about the dark depths and magic going to live there. He was hungry too.

Night was drawing close, and they needed a place to sleep, hungry or not. Revan thought that if they found another of those clearings of emerald moss, that he'd go to sleep and just stay that way forever. Well, no, he wouldn't, but hunger made one entertain exaggerations. Even if they were just in his own thoughts.

Revan was leading this time, breaking trail through the undergrowth, which fortunately for him wasn't very dense in this part of the forest, when he stopped suddenly.

"Do you smell that?" he whispered back towards Arval.

"What?"

"Smoke."

"I don't smell any... Yes I do smell smoke. Where's it coming from?"

"Somewhere up ahead I think. Let's go look. Be quiet though."

"Of course, you'd smell it before me," he muttered.

They crept forward slowly and as quietly as they could. Neither of them knowing much about woodscraft, they broke twigs and branches frequently and caused shrubs and bushes to rustle. Anyone listening in the stillness of the forest would have heard them long before seeing them. They hadn't gone more than a hundred paces when Revan held a hand out behind him, stopping Arval. He pointed up towards smoke drifting through the trees. Arval nodded to indicate he saw it. They both scanned the forest ahead of them, trying to determine where the smoke was coming from when a man's voice called out. "Well come on out of there," it said. "I don't much like visitors, but I won't skewer ya."

Revan and Arval stepped cautiously out from behind a screen of shrubs and trees and walked towards the voice.

"Come on now, I'm no threat," it said again. "If I'd wanted to string you up and cook you over my fire, I'd have done it long before now."

Seeing no need to hide anymore, Revan, his hand on his sword hilt, walked calmly and steadily the last few paces through the forest until he emerged into a small clearing. A sturdy hut made of logs stood at the far end. Smoke curled from a chimney on its left side. There was a door in the middle, flanked by two small windows, and overhung by an eave that covered a rough plank porch. A chopping block with a number of wood rounds and an untidy stack of split firewood lay to the left of the cabin, a small barn and a fenced off pen containing three goats stood to the right. A vegetable garden lay right in front of them. On the porch, in a rocking chair, sat an old man with shoulder-length grey hair smoking a long-stemmed pipe. He was dressed in what might once have been white robes, but which were now so dirty and worn that they were a sickly brown. His dark brown eyes though, they were as clear and alert as they would be in a man one quarter his age. An ancient dog lay next to his chair, its head on its paws.

"The stew will be ready in half an hour. Come have a wash before we eat," the man said.

"Stew?" Arval asked, his hunger overpowering his caution.

"Are you daft? Yes, I said stew. You got bugs in your ears from sleeping outside at night?"

Arval rubbed his right ear absentmindedly and frowned thoughtfully. Revan stepped away from him and walked around the vegetable garden. "Sir," he said, "we've been out of food for three days and would be indebted to you for some... stew."

"I've got plenty, and you can have as much as you'd like. As I said, I don't get visitors out here too often. It'll be nice to have some company."

Revan nodded his head in thanks and approached the man on the porch. "I'm Revan and this is my friend Arval."

"I'm Fendalon." They shook hands all around. "And this is Growl."

"Your dog is named Growl?" Arval asked. "Why did you name him that?"

"Because he never does. Growl that is. I got him a long time ago to be a guard dog for me, but all he really does is what you see him doing now. If anyone came up here meaning me harm, Growl would probably sleep through the ensuing fracas."

Revan and Arval looked at the dog laying on a threadbare rug next to Fendalon's chair. Growl looked back at them with mildly curious eyes, as if hoping they had a piece of mutton to share. When they offered nothing, he snorted through his large black nostrils and promptly went to sleep.

"He didn't even raise his head when we heard you two crashing through the forest. Sometimes I have to shoo him outside or he'll pee on the floor. At least he never goes... er, does, the other thing. On the floor that is. Inside. He goes out in the trees for that. I was able to train him to do one thing well anyway." Fendalon sighed. "So, what brings you two through here?"

Revan didn't answer right away, but instead asked a question of his own. "Have you seen, or heard, anyone else come through this way in the last day or two?"

"Chasing someone are you?" he cackled. "I've chased a few in my time. Women mostly," he muttered. "By the looks of those swords you're wearing, I'd say you've already caught someone. Or a couple someones."

Revan smiled a little. "We did meet with some people who didn't, let's say, have our health as one of their foremost concerns."

Fendalon laughed uproariously and slapped his knee. "Your health! That's the funniest thing I've heard in years! You boys are more than welcome to some stew and to stay the night! I'll bet you've got one mountain of a story to tell." Fendalon got up from his chair and motioned them inside.

Revan and Arval smiled at each other as they followed. Revan mulled over the fact that Fendalon hadn't answered his question any more than he'd answered Fendalon's.

The stew was incredible. Revan thought that if this was what all food was like, then he would sample every food in the world. In fact, he'd travel to every distant land that he could, trying everything. He was in ecstasy as he chewed. Arval commended Fendalon on the quality of the stew. "I know we haven't eaten in three days, but this is the best stew I've ever had." They were sitting together at a small table in front of the hearth inside the little cottage.

Fendalon smiled at the compliment as he lifted a spoonful to his mouth. After he'd chewed and swallowed, he gestured toward the kettle hanging from a rack over the fire. "I've learned a few things about cooking in my time. Eat your fill," he said. "I'll make more tomorrow. Or the next day. Whenever I feel like it. Living alone out here allows me to do whatever I wish, whenever I wish. All I really have to do is make sure I have enough food to last me through the winter. Since it'll be several months yet until that season comes again, my biggest concern is keeping the rabbits and tree skimmers out of my garden. And that's easy enough to do with a few traps."

"How long have you been out here?" Revan asked between mouthfuls of stew.

"More turnings than either of you has been alive," Fendalon said.

"Don't you like people?" Arval asked.

Fendalon didn't answer but looked at Arval with an unreadable expression. "When you're done with the stew, save a bit of room for an ale. I've a keg here somewhere that needs to be finished off before it turns."

"You're about to try ale for the first time," Arval said to Revan with a sidelong glance.

Revan grinned at him, "Ever since I met you I've been learning and trying all kinds of new things."

They finished the stew in their bowls, then refilled them and ate silently. Fendalon rummaged around in a cluttered corner of the small abode until he found his keg. With a grunt he pulled the small wooden cask free and put it on the table. From a shelf next to the hearth, he picked up a small hand axe and used the blade of it to pry the top off. When he had it open, he bent over it and inhaled deeply.

"Ah, nothing like a keg of Kessari winter barley ale," he said in a tone of near reverence.

Arval, his bowl of stew empty, asked, "Are you from Kessar then?"

"No, but I lived there for a long time. I grew up in a small fishing village called Heften on the shore of Silver Arm Bay." Fendalon plucked three mugs from a cabinet next to the hearth and used a ladle to fill them.

"Is that near the sea?" Revan asked a bit of awe in his voice.

Fendalon picked up on it and said, "Have you never seen the sea then?"

"No."

"Well, where are you from?"

Arval jumped in, "I'm from Kessar -"

"I'm from the pit." Revan interrupted.

Arval looked at him incredulously. "What are you doing? Why did you tell him that? We don't know him!"

Revan looked calmly back at Arval and said, "We can trust him. I don't know how I know, but I do. I didn't trust Kanar, but I do trust Fendalon."

Arval, looking unconvinced, just stared at Revan. Fendalon, who had been glancing from one to the other, now fixed his gaze on Revan.

"From the pit you say?" his eyebrows furrowed a little.

"Yes," Revan replied simply.

"So, you were among those diggers out there. How did you escape?" He asked quietly.

Revan picked up the mug of ale and took a sip. "This is delicious," he said, his eyes widening.

"Glad you like it. Don't drink too much of it or you'll be very unhappy tomorrow. I'd like to hear your story, if you're willing to tell it. And I'll tell you mine in exchange."

Arval sighed, "I suppose there's nothing for it now but to tell him."

Revan proceeded to tell Fendalon the whole story, from how he'd no memory of coming to the pit or much at all before it, to Arval's arrival and their subsequent escape. He left out no detail, even including his conversation with Drannal in the Kryxaal. He told Fendalon of magic and the threads, how he'd been able to manipulate them, even sending them into Arval to make him run faster. When he reached the part about the tower, he reached into his pack and took out the ring he'd found on the skeleton of Jinirlyn. He'd put it in the pack several days ago after it had fallen off his finger when his hands got wet filling a waterskin; he didn't want to lose it. He held it out to Fendalon as he told the story of his conversation with the ancient man, moving on to Kanar's departure and finishing with their arrival at the small cottage in the woods.

Fendalon, holding Jinirlyn's ring in his hand, looked from Revan to the ring and back. "You say you found this on a skeleton in that tower in the desert? And that you actually spoke to that dead man in those white tunnels? He said that he'd created the Jix?"

"Yes."

Fendalon exhaled slowly, his eyes wide but somehow vacant. "From the dark depths it comes, magic is back in the world." He shook his head as if coming out of a reverie and said, "I've heard of Jinirlyn. He's a legend among the Jix. It's said that he was the fiercest and most deadly warrior who ever walked the earth."

"Where did you hear of him?" Arval asked.

"My dear boy, all of the Jix are taught the history of their order."

"You were one of the Jix?!" Arval exclaimed.

"Of course. How else would I know about Jinirlyn? The Jix do not share their history with outsiders, but it is taught to members. Those of us who join take an oath to never reveal our secrets or history to anyone outside it. I'd not have told you anything of what I know, except that you already know some of it."

"What else can you tell us?" Revan asked.

"First let me tell you my story," Fendalon answered. "Have another mug of ale. I'll put on some tea as well. The ale is almost gone, and the story is long in telling." Night had closed in completely around the cottage as Fendalon picked up an iron tea kettle and went outside to fill it from a rain barrel next to the cottage. When he came back inside, he opened a small wooden box and pinched out some tea leaves, scattering them across the water in the kettle. He put the lid on it, then hung the kettle from the rack in the hearth where the stew had cooked, that kettle long since empty and set aside to cool on the stone floor in front of the fire. Revan and Arval, both working on their second mugs of ale, watched silently as Fendalon went about preparing tea. When he seemed satisfied, he sat back down at the table, finished off his mug of ale and looked at each of them in turn. "I was just a boy about your age when I decided that the life of a fisherman wasn't for me," he began.

I'd been a fisherman my whole life, up until the time I decided to leave. My father, like most other men in Heften, had a small boat and several nets, and we'd go out almost every day into Sliver Arm Bay to catch whatever fish we could. There were Red Flashers, Flat Fish, Strongbranch, all sorts of fish. Some days we caught a whole boat load, other days none. What we did catch we either kept for ourselves to eat, traded with the other villagers, or dried and sold to traveling merchants who came through our village. My mother tended a small garden next to our little house, which I helped her with when I wasn't out with my father. Its where I learned how to

grow vegetables, a skill which has served me well since I came out here to live.

I was always good at sport. We had a festival in Heften at the end of every summer where there were footraces, wrestling and pole racing. I was always fast in the races, and pretty good at wrestling, but pole racing was my event. There was a collection of old pilings standing in the water from some long rotted dock; they were just poles poking up at different heights out of the sea. The object was to jump from one pole to another until you'd gotten to the farthest one out in the water. There was a red handkerchief there that you had to pick up, then make it back to shore. Ten contestants at a time would try for the handkerchief. If you fell in the water, you were out. Other than that, there were no rules of conduct except that weapons weren't allowed. You could push or punch someone to knock them off the piling, or just try to evade them. If the person holding the handkerchief went in the water, then the game paused. The handkerchief went to the contestant closest to the pole from where the bearer had fallen, and the game resumed. Whoever made it back to shore with the handkerchief won. I won three years in a row before I left. The prize for winning wasn't links or riches, but the acclaim that came from besting your peers. The winner did get to sit at the mayor's table during the feast that marked the last day of the festival, but most no one liked the pompous old fool of a mayor, so that seemed more a punishment than a reward. But the food was incredible!

My mother had taught me to read when I was a small child, and I'd always loved it. But books were very rare in Heften. One of our neighbors, an old man like I am now, named Colwig, had some books that he let me read. He'd lived in Kessar for many years before he came to our village. I never knew why he left there to come to our little fishing town; he never said. But his tales of all the amazing things in the city, combined with the few books he let me read (they were all tales of adventure and danger!) made me realize that there was more to the world than fishing, gardening and pole racing.

Winter had just begun to set in when I left; the festival was a few weeks gone. There was frost on the ground in the mornings, and the sun didn't really warm you like it had a few short weeks before; you had to wear a coat and hat even in the warmest part of the day. The wind off Silver Arm Bay would cut right through you.

One evening after dinner I told my parents that I wanted to leave, to go to Kessar and see the world. My father wouldn't have it. He said that the city would corrupt me, turn me into a criminal. My mother understood the restlessness of youth better than my father. She begged me to stay, but I'd already decided; I was going. My plan was to leave the next day, but my father was so upset that he told me to leave right then. I was as angry as he was, so I gathered my few belongings and stormed out the door.

I traveled northwest until I reached Kessar, eating what I could and sleeping wherever I found shelter. Since I'd never been to a city, I had no idea how things worked there, like how I needed money to pay for food, or a room in an inn or Traveler's Rest. I spent my first night in Kessar in an alley amid stinking trash. I'd tried to sleep in front of an inn, but the big man who threw out the drunks kicked me in the ribs and told me to move on.

The next day I was wandering the streets, looking for a way to make a coin for something to eat, when I felt a tugging on my pack. I turned quickly and saw a young boy with one of my shirts in his hand starting to run away; he'd pulled it from my pack. I chased him, and since I was a fast runner, I caught him easily. He screamed and some of the city wardens came. So did a man in light grey leather armor and a dark blue cowled cloak. There was a symbol embossed on the armor – a sword overlaid across a scroll. The same as on your ring.

The wardens questioned me and the boy; he claimed I'd given him the shirt. One of the wardens took the shirt from him and when he did, the boy ran off into the crowd. I chased him again and caught him again. The wardens, surmising that his attempted escape proved his guilt, named him a thief right there and took him away. They gave me back my shirt though. I put it in my pack and started to walk away, when the man in the grey armor took me by the arm. He asked me where I was from, and I told him my story, leaving out the row with my father, and he told me to come with him. I asked if I'd get something to eat or a link if I did and he replied, rather cryptically, that I might get more than that. He didn't seem to mean me any harm, so I followed.

He took me to an enormous keep made of grey stone on the side of the hill below the Azure Palace. We walked up a twisting road that ended in front of it. The hill all around was empty of other buildings except for the palace looming above. I can still remember how the sun shone off its blue stone walls and towers. I thought it must have been the most beautiful structure in the world. The keep had two huge wooden gates made of black wood and bound with tremendous iron bands. They opened a crack when he walked up to them; he didn't have to call out or even knock. We passed through and they *closed behind us. Inside was a wide courtyard, to the left were stables full of different animals. To the right were archery targets and wooden figures of the shape and size of a man. Straight ahead was a smaller wooden door into the keep proper. We were the only ones in the courtyard. I looked up and could see windows, ramparts, and four enormous towers, one at each corner of the keep's walls. But still no people. I remember wondering if we were alone there. At that instant the man drew a sword and swung it at my head. I'd never seen someone move so fast. It was lucky I was fast too, because I was just able to duck his swing. I dodged away from him as he turned to face me fully, and out of the corner of my eye I saw another man in the same grey armor step out from behind one of the archery targets. This man held a very tall bow and he loosed an arrow at me. I'd shot bows before and was always amazed at how quickly arrows got to their targets. This arrow moved far faster than any I'd ever seen. It seemed the man had barely released it when the arrow was on me. I was able to turn aside just in time to avoid dying, but it did graze my right shoulder. I still have a scar. The man who'd brought me was standing in the same place, sword in his hand, but lowered to his side, watching me. I couldn't see his eyes under the cowl of his hood, just his chin and mouth. He asked me if I'd like something to eat. I couldn't believe it. He and the other man had just tried to kill me, now he was offering me food. I think I managed to say something like 'yes, as long as the food didn't try to kill me too.' The man with the bow had walked up to us by then, and they both laughed when I said that. The bow man said that if they'd wanted me dead, I would be. The sword man clapped me on the shoulder and bade me follow him. What else was I going to do? I followed.*

As it turns out they were Jix, and they'd been testing me to see if I had the natural ability to join their order. The man with the sword was named Ulviq, the one with the bow was Ulvar. They were twins; you couldn't tell one from the other, they looked so much alike. They took me into the keep, fed me some wonderful roasted meat and vegetables, and introduced me to more of their order. I learned later that when one of the Jix brings in a prospect, like I was, that everyone stays out of sight, but watches to see how he fares in the tests. The whole keep had seen me almost die. If a prospect fails, he is given a meal and a few copper links, and treatment for his wounds, should he have any, and sent on his way. There are no women members of the Jix. I don't know why that is. In my time I've met women whose gaze alone would strike fear into the strongest of my order. I've always thought that some women would make wonderful Jix.

Since I'd passed the tests, I was offered a place among them. I accepted, and the following day my training began. I won't bore you with details, but I learned to fight with any weapon imaginable, and even a few you never have, and after two years, I took the oaths and became a wearer of the grey, as Jix are called among themselves.

I had many adventures, participated in many military campaigns, and killed many, many men. The Jix became my life; I was totally devoted to them. Until the usurper King Vraniss stole the Throne of the Firmament from King Travorik and murdered him. When that monster took the throne, I decided I'd had enough. Most of my life had been spent with the Jix, in service to the king and my order. I refused to serve that brutal man. So, I asked for my release from the Jix, and it was granted. I did not give the real reason;

the Jix are honor and duty bound to serve whomever sits on the throne, and have for generations. Opposition to the king, no matter his level of despotism, is not tolerated. I told my superiors in the Jix that I was old and tired and wished to return to my ancestral home of Heften, to live out my remaining years fishing like my father had. My request was granted, and I left.

I took passage on a boat from Kessar down the Xandei River to its mouth in Silver Arm Bay, where I disembarked and walked the shore until reaching my old home. It was abandoned. Most of the homes had burned down, boats had been smashed. It looked as if an invading army had sacked the village. The only life I saw were birds nesting in the ruins. Here and there were bones which I recognized as both human and animal. They were long bleached white. Whatever happened there was far in the past, many years. My old home was one of the ones burned. I found it easily and rummaged through the ruins. There was nothing left. Whatever hadn't burned had been pillaged in some bygone year. My sadness was deep. I'd hoped to see some of my old friends and tell them of my adventures, perhaps even one of my parents was still alive; I'd not seen them since I'd left so many years before. But if there was anyone still alive from my little village, they'd long since moved on somewhere else. I realized that this was no longer home to me. It was just a ruin and a memory. For a time, I was at a loss as to where to go. Returning to the Jix was out of the question with Vraniss on the throne. I sat on a large rock and stared at the sea for a long time. It hadn't changed; the sea is eternal. Most of the pilings from that old pole racing game were even still there.

As I sat pondering my future, and my past, I remembered this place here in the mountains from one of the campaigns I'd been on in my youth. I'd passed through it with a squad of my fellow Jix and knew it was unvisited and uninhabited. It had everything I needed to live – game, water, relative shelter from the worst of the weather, so I determined to come here to live out my days. I wanted nothing so much as to be away from people and war. So here I am. I've been here for over twenty turnings, and you are only the second and third people I've seen since I came here.

Revan and Arval were astounded to be actually sitting with one of the Jix. Even if he was old, this man could probably still kill them both with one hand while stirring a pot of soup with the other. Revan was the first to speak, "Who was the first person you saw?"

Fendalon grinned slyly. "It was a woman I knew back in Kessar. Her name was Endanna. I sent word to her on the way from my village to this place that I was coming here and bade her visit me if she chose. Some years ago, she did. If you ever get to Kessar, look in on her for me, tell her I'm still alive and thinking of her." He smiled wistfully at memories that were only his.

"We will," Revan said.

"Where do we find her?" Arval asked.

"She owns a small clothing store not far from White Square called The Needle and Thread. There was once a wooden sign hanging above the door with that name and the image of a needle and spool of thread carved on it."

"I know that shop," Arval said. "I've never been in it, never had the links to buy anything, but I've been past it countless times."

"Then you'll have no trouble finding it."

"It's the first place we'll go when we get there," Arval said.

"Yes, good," Fendalon replied. "Now about this return business, the return of magic that is. How do you propose to go about it?"

"I have to find the other three Kryxaal. If I can locate them and get inside, then I'll learn more about magic and receive more of it. I suppose if I learn enough then I'll figure out a way to bring magic back."

"There are records of these Kryxaal in the archives of the Jix. You'll need to get to them in order to figure out what they say. I myself didn't spend much time poring through old books; I was more interested in traveling and fighting. My lessons in books and history consisted of what was required of me and nothing more. Books are for scholars, which I am not; if I'm going to read, and I do enjoy reading some, I prefer an adventure story to some dusty old tome on history or politics. But there are those among the Jix who are very learned and spend much of their time poring over books. One of them would be able to help you find what you are looking for."

"But how do we get in? The Jix don't let anyone see their archives," Arval said. "I heard some of the city wardens talking about it one day. They said they'd asked to read something in the archives and been refused. If they won't let them see it, why would they let us?"

"You'll have to join them, become one of them. Or convince them, somehow, to help you. No one that I know of has ever done that, so your options seem to be limited to one."

"Great," Arval said. "Join the Jix. Just what I envisioned for my life."

"You didn't envision much at all for your life when we were in the pit. You had two options there – escape or death," Revan said. "And no one had ever escaped, so you really only had one option there too. Until we got into the Kryxaal."

"What are you saying? That we have no choice but to join the Jix or we'll never find the other three Kryxaal?"

"No. I'm saying that it seemed there was only one real option in the pit. Something else came along and provided one we hadn't even known existed. The same thing could happen once we get to Kessar. My point is that we don't know what's going to happen, so don't get too anxious about joining them. Could be that another way will present itself."

"Wise words," Fendalon said. "Your friend here, for all his time digging in that horrid place, seems to understand things beyond his experience."

"Well, all this magic has certainly swelled his head a bit," Arval said.

Revan and Fendalon chuckled.

"What do you know of the pit?" Revan asked.

"More than most, less than some. The history of the Jix that I was forced to study made mention of it in a vague way. It told of how Jinirlyn and a few others were tasked with finding locations where they were to be built. Those locations were not revealed to me, nor was anything about magic. The tale was told simply to illustrate the details surrounding the founding of the order. One of King Travorik's ancestors somehow discovered the location of the Kryxaal where you were slaves, and it was he who began the excavation. Every king since that one, I forget his name, has continued the project. When Vraniss stole the throne and murdered Travorik, he must have discovered something about it because he doubled, then doubled again, the number of slaves digging out there. It's one of the reasons I left the Jix. He reached an agreement with the Nojii, those barbaric raiders from the northern desert, to kidnap young boys and men and force them into slavery in order to excavate the site. Slavery is a curse on humanity. Would that I could have chained and shackled Vraniss and sent him to the dig. That's all I know about your mysterious Kryxaal."

Revan's head felt light on his shoulders from the two mugs of ale. It was not an unpleasant feeling, but it was making him sleepy, in spite of the tea he'd also had. "It's getting late. Let's get some sleep and we can talk about it more in the morning," he said with a yawn.

"Agreed," Fendalon said. "Here, I've a couple of pelts I use for blankets in winter. Spread them on the floor in front of the fire and you'll stay warm all night," Fendalon said as he pulled two enormous fur pelts from a trunk against the far wall. "I'm off to bed too. Sleep well," he said as he disappeared through a doorway into his bedroom. Arval and Revan, both yawning now, spread the pelts on the floor, and were asleep moments after they'd lain down.

Chapter 19

hey awoke the next morning feeling as if they'd slept for a year. The wonderful stew, combined with ale and the warm animal skins they'd slept on had made them both sleep as soundly as they had on the carpet of moss back in the forest, maybe better.

Revan stretched as he sat up and went outside to relieve his night water. There was a light mist in the air that obscured the tops of the trees, sunlight shone through it jagged beams, illuminating small patches of the forest floor. Birds sang as they flitted about, filling the morning air with songs Revan had never heard. He stood for a moment, looking and listening, marveling that such a scene could exist. They'd rarely heard birds in the pit, and those were usually hunting for carrion; their songs were more like anguished cries. His hearing told him that some small rodent was rooting around next to a fallen log a few paces away, surely searching for its breakfast. He smiled and walked to one end of the log, deciding that a spot of dirt there would receive his water. As he stood relieving himself, he looked up into the misty treetops and watched the birds he'd heard before as they went about their business. If he could find a scene as beautiful as this a few short days after entering the forest, then what else would the world have to show him? He was lost in daydreams of the world, his senses turned inward, so he didn't realize he wasn't alone until the monstrous creature lumbered out of the trees in front of him.

It was easily two paces taller than he was and walked on four gigantic legs. The knees on the front legs were as high as his waist, wide hairy paws tipped with wicked looking claws smashed flat anything they trod on. Broad and powerful shoulders topped those legs and formed a frame for the gigantic head. It was the head that Revan focused his attention on. It was wider than his torso with deep set eyes and a short snout. Its nose was wide and flat, the mouth wider still with jaws that looked like they could crush rocks and short stubby teeth that looked like they had. A long pink tongue lolled out of the mouth; a silvery rope of drool dangled off it. A pelt of reddish fur covered the head above which tall pointy ears poked up. The same fur covered the rest of the torso, which had to have been at least six paces long. Revan had never seen such an enormous beast. His first instinct was to flee, but he knew that with those long legs, the creature would have him in its jaws before he could make it halfway back to the cottage. Instead of running, he stood his ground.

The huge creature ambled slowly towards him, its nose sniffing the air as it approached. Revan could see a long bushy tail swishing behind it. When it was within two paces of him, it stopped. The gigantic head looked down at him, as he looked up at it. Stretching forward it sniffed his face and down his torso. Seeming satisfied, it sat back on its haunches and just looked at him. Revan had expected to be bitten in half, but the creature didn't seem aggressive. Cautiously he stretched his hand out towards it, ready to jerk back at the slightest sign of danger. The creature just sniffed his hand. He took a step closer to it and it lowered its head to about the level of his chest. Revan's initial fear had abated some, curiosity took its place, and he let his hand drop to the top of the giant head. The fur was wonderfully soft, but wiry too. He scratched between its ears and the creature let out a contented sounding snort. It suddenly dropped all the way to the ground and laid its head on its enormous paws.

"I see you've met my friend Korpa," he heard the voice of Fendalon say from behind him.

Revan turned, startled that someone was behind him. His attention had been focused on the beast in front of him and he'd not heard Fendalon approach. "You know this creature? It's not going to attack us?"

"Of course not, he's my friend. You've been in my home, and he probably smells it on you. Any friend of mine is a friend of his. If you were just some random traveler, you'd probably be dead by now."

"Where in the dark depths did you learn to make friends with something like that," Arval said, having wandered out from the cottage.

"I found him when he was a pup not long after I came here. He'd been injured somehow, been separated from his mother. I gave him a bit of meat and some water, and he let me tend his wounds. He had long gashes down his right side and had lost a lot of blood. You can still see the scars, even under that fur. We've been friends ever since."

"What kind of creature is this?" Revan asked.

"Most people call them Forest Mashers. It fits, what with the size of those paws. If they were ever called by another name, I don't know it. I've run across them from time to time in these woods. They usually leave me alone and I them. The trick is to stay away from them; they won't attack you unless you get too close. The adults are solitary animals; you'll never see two of them together unless its mating season, then you'll see several of them in the same spot. They're particularly dangerous then. Their howls will shake the trees when the rut is on. Korpa seems to like you."

Arval had walked up to Revan and was watching him scratch between Korpa's ears. He reached down and did the same. He turned to Revan and smiled, a look of childlike wonder on both their faces at being this close to such an enormous beast.

"I've heard stories of the Forest Mashers, but I never thought I'd see one. This is amazing!"

Korpa was making a rumbling sound deep in his throat that Revan thought meant he liked his head being scratched.

"Will he chase us if we walk away?" Arval asked.

"No. He'll probably follow us back to my cottage and lay down by the animal pen. He likes the goats."

"He doesn't eat them does he?" Arval asked anxiously.

Fendalon laughed, "Of course not! They're his friends as much as I am. As you two are now. Come on, you'll see."

Revan and Arval reluctantly stopped scratching their new friend's gigantic head and turned to follow Fendalon. They'd only taken a couple steps when they heard Korpa stand up behind them and begin to lumber after.

When they reached the cottage, Korpa did indeed lay down next to the pen. The little goats were running and jumping in their excitement to see the big creature. Their bleats rang out in the morning air. Korpa raised an enormous paw and dropped it over the fence. He gently pushed the goats around with it and they seemed to love the game, darting around trying to stay away from Korpa's paw. He was incredibly gentle for such a large creature. Revan was slightly amazed that he didn't crush one of the little goats.

"Where did his name come from?" Arval asked.

"I named him after one of the Jix from a long time ago," Fendalon said. "Korpa was a friend of mine. He was one of the fiercest warriors I've ever known, and one of the gentlest humans. I named this big fellow in honor of him."

Revan and Arval just watched Korpa playing with the goats. His wide mouth was open in what they both would have sworn was a grin.

"Well, he does seem to like the goats," Arval said.

"He won't hurt them. They'll play like that until they're all tired, then they'll sleep the day away. Let's leave them be and get some breakfast," Fendalon said, turning towards his cottage.

He made an enormous meal with help from Arval. Revan, who knew nothing about cooking, simply watched as they sliced and cut vegetables, mixed some white powder with milk and butter, and kept putting things over the fire. When they were done he had a large plate filled with what Fendalon said were potatoes, onions and peppers, with biscuits on the side. The biscuits were a revelation to Revan. He'd have eaten the entire batch if it had been up to him.

"So, you've never had biscuits before either, eh?" Fendalon asked.

"No. They are amazing!"

"When you get to Kessar, go to the tavern called The Short Wall. Tell Yelun, the owner, that I sent you for biscuits and gravy. He'll make sure you eat well. And tell him I said hello. But don't tell him where I am. In fact, don't tell anyone where I am. And don't mention me to anyone other than Yelun and Endanna."

"We won't tell anyone," Arval assured him. Revan nodded his agreement around a mouthful of biscuit.

"Good. I'm trusting you both because I think you are honorable. I like my life out here and don't want to be disturbed. By anyone. There are some in that city who would come looking for me if they knew where I was and that I was alive."

"Were you in some trouble then?" Revan asked. He realized as soon as he said it that the question was invasive and impolite.

Fendalon looked at him for a moment, considering. "No. I just don't like people anymore. Most of them anyway. And I'd rather not be involved in their troubles again. I like my simple life and want to keep it the way it is."

Revan, chagrined, just nodded.

"Do you know how far it is to Kessar from here?" Arval asked.

"If you follow the valley where we are, it will bring you through the Bluecrag Mountains into the lowlands just to the east of Kessar. Getting to that point will take you probably four or five days. The city is another two beyond that. If you don't run into any trouble that is. I doubt you'll have a problem in the mountains, but once you get to the lowlands, there will be people around. Many of them will, like you said last night, not have your health in their interest," Fendalon said with a snort of laughter as he remembered Revan's quip from the day before. Arval and Revan smiled.

"We should get moving soon," Revan said, his food eaten. "We've still a long way to go and we need to get to Kessar. I've got to find out where those other three Kryxaal are."

"Patience lad," Fendalon said. "If you go rushing out of here, you're liable to get lost, take a wrong turn somewhere in this pass and never find your way out. Let me draw you a simple map you can follow. There are lots of dead-end valleys and draws that branch off from the route you'll need to follow. If you take one of those, you'll spend too much time backtracking. You may run out of food, or worse, run into an unfriendly

Forest Masher. They can be killed like any other animal, but you'd end up hurt or dead yourselves in the attempt. My map will keep you away from where you're likely to see one. They're territorial and keep to their own areas most of the time. And there are other things in the wilds that should be avoided if possible."

"Sounds good to me," Arval said. Revan nodded.

"Why don't you two collect your things and fill your waterskins from the rain barrel. I'll start working on the map. But you also have to promise me that once you're out of the mountains, you'll burn it."

"Agreed," Revan said. "I found a flint and steel in Jinirlyn's pack. I'll use it to start a fire and burn it once we're clear of the mountains."

Fendalon grunted an acknowledgement and went to a chest against the wall. He withdrew a pen and ink and a piece of parchment paper and sat down at the table to draw the map. Arval and Revan went outside and filled their waterskins. When they came back in, Fendalon was almost done. He began to explain the route as he finished drawing. There were several landmarks noted on it, a couple mountains with distinguishing features, a river, and a huge boulder that marked the end of the path through the valley.

"When you reach that boulder, the path starts down into the lowlands. Start your fire and burn the map there. A fire beyond the boulder will be visible for miles. You might attract unwanted attention."

"It will be done," Revan said.

"Once you are in the lowlands, head due west for about half a day. There is a road you should find easily that will lead you straight to Kessar."

"How can we thank you?" Arval asked. "You've been such a gracious host and I feel indebted to you." Revan agreed with a nod.

"Just look in on Endanna and Yelun for me. Tell them I said hello and that I'm thinking of them. That will be thanks enough."

"We will, assuredly," Arval said.

"You'd best be on your way," Fendalon said. "Put the map in your pack. It's well made and should keep it dry. Unless you fall in the river," he said with a chuckle and a smile.

"I'll remember the route," Revan said as he shouldered his pack.

"Good."

Arval stuffed the map in his pack and put it on. They both picked up their swords and buckled them about their waists. Fendalon had given them the leftover biscuits and some more dried meat. He'd also admonished them to ration their food so that they'd have enough to last until they reached the lowlands. "You can survive two days by foraging for berries and such down there," he'd said. "And the city isn't far at that point. You'll find food easily enough."

As they stood in the small yard in front of the cottage, they shook hands with Fendalon and thanked him again for his hospitality.

"It's been nice having company again," he said. "You're both good lads and I wish you the best. If you ever get back this way again, look in on me. I'll make biscuits if you'll bring a cask of ale."

"It's a deal," Revan said smiling.

"I'll bring you four if you'll make that stew again!" Arval said.

Fendalon smiled. "Off with you then," he said. "Go find your adventures!"

They both smiled at the old man and turned away, walking into the forest and towards Kessar.

Chapter 20

tarab sat in the courtyard of his villa in Kessar, sipping from a glass of the best Cloud Wine he could find. The warm summer air was redolent with the smell of the flowers that grew in pots and small beds around the inner walls of the courtyard. Green vines climbed up the columns that supported the balcony that ringed the large square space and twisted laconically around the ornately carved stone railing. A small pond in the center contained lily pads and dozens of small colorful fish that darted around in their fishly pursuits. A pair of servants in white livery stood to either side of a set of wooden double doors under the balcony opposite the large gate leading into the courtyard from the street outside. Otarab could hear hawkers selling all manner of wares as they pushed their carts down the road. The villa was in what was known as Heavy Chest Crescent, the most affluent section of the city, hence the constant presence of merchants seeking to part its residents from their links. Outside that gate could be found any number of luxury goods from casks of the Cloud Wine Otarab was now enjoying, to the finest garments and foods, to delicately crafted jewelry made with rare metals and gems. On this day Otarab wanted nothing to do with any of it. He'd bought a cask of Cloud Wine on his way here from the Azure Palace because he'd wanted a drink, or several, after his meeting with King Vraniss.

Otarab was no fool. He knew exactly how close he'd been to dying the moment he'd walked into the King's study. The look on Vraniss' face was one he'd worn himself any number of times. It was a look that meant someone was about to die. What truly galled him was that he'd had to give away information he'd wanted to keep to himself. Just to stay alive. Information was currency, best kept in one's pocket until it was needed to pay a debt. Except that Otarab hadn't known he'd owed anything. And really, he hadn't. Telling Vraniss about the Kryxaal and magic had been an act of desperation born out of necessity. For three turnings he'd overseen activities at the pit. In that time the progress had been more rapid than at any time since Vraniss had usurped the throne. He'd actually, in the past, congratulated Otarab on the efficiency of his workers. Their lives didn't mean anything to the king, nor did he care what methods Otarab and his Nojii henchmen employed to motivate them. He cared about results. Otarab could sympathize; he too cared about results. But what Vraniss didn't realize, or simply didn't care about, was that his workers, as he called them, were tools being used to perform a job, a function. If a tool was cared for - sharpened, oiled, maintained - it lasted longer and performed better than a neglected one. To that end Otarab himself was simply a tool of the king.

One that could be replaced as easily as a broken shovel. Being a man who valued the finer things in life, and, even more so, life itself, Otarab had determined to do what the king should have done and maintain himself upon his assignment to the excavation. To that end his sole motivation was to make himself as indispensable to the king as possible. The disappearance of the Kryxaal had ended that plan and instantly made him as disposable as yesterday's salad. Telling the king of the Kryxaal, and, more importantly, his own connection to a source of information about them, had purchased him his life. He'd been very careful not to betray the name of his relative in Enrat. It wouldn't do to have King Vraniss send a delegation to the library to ferret him out. There was no telling what the man might reveal under duress. Scholars were not known for their stoicism in the face of torture. Yes, information was indeed currency, and Otarab had spent a fortune.

He was fully aware that King Vraniss and his lieutenant Barittin had ears and eyes all over Jarradan. Any good king would do the same. But so did Otarab. He'd received regular reports at his camp near the pit from his network of spies. Hento brought the small notes they wrote to him when he delivered fresh diggers. The burn pit in the center of his tent had never had a fire fueled by wood in it; the heat of the desert made fires for warmth unnecessary. But hundreds of small notes containing all manner of information had been burned there.

Before Vraniss had assigned him to the pit, Otarab had been well on his way to becoming the

Holder of Sand, the position that for all practical purposes functioned as King of the Nojii, if Nojii could be said to have a king. His time at the pit had delayed those plans somewhat, and consequently his larger plans. But no matter, he'd still been able to manipulate events to his favor among those Nojii with influence. It was only a matter of time before the current Holder of Sand was deposed and Otarab assumed the position. The disappearance of the Kryxaal had changed some things though.

He'd received a report from an aide he trusted that when the Kryxaal had begun to disappear, a ramp made of light had been seen stretching from the roof of the building to the rim of the pit. Two figures had been seen running across it at incredible speed, far faster than anyone should be able to run. The diggers had attempted to flee when the incident began, and it had taken every available aide to stop them. Many had been killed. The rest had been herded into a small corner of the pit and heavily guarded. When the news had reached Otarab at his camp, he'd ordered an extensive search begun to find the two who had escaped. He'd also ordered the remaining diggers questioned as to the identities and possible whereabouts of the two missing diggers. Several search parties had been dispatched to scour the desert for the escapees, and Otarab had immediately left for Kessar after giving his Nojii their orders. It was only after arriving back at his villa that word had reached him that one of the search parties had never returned. Any number of things could befall a lone person, or even two, in the harsh desert. But there should have been word from at least one member of a four-man group. These were, after all, Nojii. Born and raised in the desert, they were at home in the sand, climbing the dunes. And they knew all the hazards. At least one of them should have returned. This was a most unusual and concerning development.

None of the diggers had been of any assistance. The names and descriptions of the diggers were not recorded, just numbers, and there were so many that it was an impossible task to pick out two who might have been the ones seen escaping from the pit. Otarab thought it would be easier to simply track them through the desert, so he'd sent out the search parties. All but the one had returned, and all with the same thing to report – nothing. The messenger who'd just departed from his villa carried orders to continue the search and to liquidate the remaining diggers and dispose of their bodies in the hole left behind by the vanished Kryxaal. If any were still alive out there. The food and water shipments had been reduced to the minimum required to fill the needs of the Nojii on guard duty, leaving no food or water for the imprisoned diggers. Otarab had issued that order himself just before leaving the camp. Vraniss wouldn't know about events at the pit for some time, and Otarab had seen an opportunity to skim a little coin from the royal treasury for himself in the interim. After all, it was the king who paid the bills, not Otarab. Reports to the king would state that the full measure of supplies were still being bought and shipped, while a very small percentage actually was. Otarab would pocket the balance. His salary for overseeing the excavation, while generous, was not nearly enough to support his lifestyle.

Otarab sighed as he rose from the comfortable chair in front of the pond. With a quick swallow he finished his Cloud Wine and gestured to one of the servants as he walked toward them.

"I'm expecting Hento soon. When he arrives see to it that he is brought directly to me."

"Understood Master," the servant replied.

"And bring me another glass of Cloud Wine. I'll be in my study."

"As you wish."

Otarab walked through the double doors and down a short hallway to his study. He sat down at his ornate goldenwood desk and removed a piece of parchment paper from a drawer. Ruminating for a moment, he picked up a pen, dipped it into an inkwell, and began to write to his relative in Enrat. It was time to learn more about these Kryxaal and magic.

My dearest Clatri, it began. There is a development I think you should be aware of....

Chapter 21

King Vraniss paced from one wall of his study to the other. He'd worn a spot in the elegant carpet behind his desk from his frequent trips back and forth across the room. A small voice in the back of his mind whispered that he'd have to replace it soon. The big voice in the front of his mind was screaming at him about Otarab. How had he managed to wriggle off the fishhook that Vraniss had baited and set? The king was not used to feeling like someone had gotten the better of him, and it had made him furious. He'd even briefly entertained the thought of having his guards fetch the man back and dispatching him right there in the study. The bloody mess created by venting his anger would certainly make him replace the carpet. Vraniss stopped pacing for a moment and stared at the ground, his breathing shallow and ragged. He had to get himself under control. It wasn't good for subordinates to see their leader in such an agitated state. Unless he meant for them to see him that way. At this moment he did not. He forced himself to take a deep breath and called for

Barittin. One of the guards immediately ran off down the hall.

The king sat down at his desk and worked to compose himself; it would only be moments before Barittin arrived. Just as the thought occurred to him, he heard the unmistakable sound of heavy boots on the sky-blue stone floor of the hallway. The man had a distinctive tread – authoritative and decisive. It wasn't like the sound of the guards, who moved purposefully, but somehow restrained, like they were shackled.

"You wanted to see me Sire?" Barittin said.

"I didn't pour any salt on that slug Otarab. I let him go."

Barittin was nonplussed. "I don't understand Sire," he said frowning. "I thought you wished to make an example of him in White Square. The platform is ready."

"I changed my mind," Vraniss said testily.

"May I ask why?"

"He provided me with information that could be of great value."

"I see," Barittin said, still frowning. It was clear he didn't see.

"No, you don't," Vraniss said, not in the mood to be patronized. "And I may or may not enlighten you. What you need to do is prepare an emissary from Jarradan to Drisava. He is to carry a formal request from me to Queen Andissa."

Barittin erased the frown from his face. He knew the king's moods well enough not to push his questions any further. Besides, his ears would hear something, his eyes see something, and he'd ultimately know anyway. He really had no need of Vraniss' explanations.

"I will summon your scribe at once to draft the correspondence. What is the message?"

"I am going to request that a group of scholars be allowed to conduct research in the archives of the Udron library. There is an internal matter of some import pertaining to the lineage of my predecessor that I wish to know more about. One of our scholars here has informed me that he's heard of a volume of history in their library that deals with this particular issue."

"That seems a simple enough request. Which scholars will you be sending?"

"I've not yet decided on any but one – Clammalod."

"You will be sending your chief librarian and archivist?" Barittin said, even more perplexed.

"Yes. And bring him too when you have the scribe brought to me."

Barittin's eyebrows went up slightly. It was unprecedented for the chief librarian to be dispatched anywhere, for anything. This was a most interesting development. The subject seemed rather trivial to Barittin. Why would the king send his primary scholar to research something any scholar could? He would have to spread the word among his spies that whomever brought him solid information first would be well rewarded.

Barittin acknowledged the order with a nod. "By your command Sire. When the delegation departs, you may wish to send an armed detachment with them. I've had reports of unrest between Drisava and Bentravirri. It seems their old border dispute has flared up again. It's said that contingents of troops from each kingdom are moving toward the disputed territory."

"Then Queen Andissa will have to deal with Bentravirri and their empty skull of a king, Zeryph. If anything happens to our delegation, I'll go to war against both of them. And I'll see to it their heads take leave of their bodies in White Square." Vraniss sighed exasperatedly. "Send some soldiers with them when they go."

"As you wish Sire. Which reminds me, there is one other matter before I summon your scribe and Clammalod. What to do about the platform? The people have been waiting for their spectacle since it was erected. We will need to give them something to satisfy their curiosity and sate their bloodlust."

Vraniss thought for a moment then said, "The four guards who escorted Otarab in to see me. They are guilty of treason against the throne. All four of them will lose their heads. That should satiate the masses."

Barittin struggled to keep his jaw from dropping. This was truly an exceptional day. He'd never seen King Vraniss execute his own guards. He was not at all averse to executing political enemies or others he felt were insubordinate or treasonous. But his guards were well trained to remain silent and obey orders. It suddenly hit him – Vraniss was silencing them. They'd obviously overheard something he didn't want them to repeat. Barittin understood that his king was a hard and brutal man, but he'd never gone this far before. Whatever

Otarab had told him must have been incredibly important. If he could only get some of his ears into the fat man's villa. With the guards about to be executed, he had no hope of obtaining any information from them. Barittin blinked away his thoughts and bowed to King Vraniss. "As you command Sire, they will be executed by sunset."

"Very well, see to it."

Barittin waited until he was clear of the doorway to the king's study before he shook his head in wonder and bewilderment.

Chapter 22

evan looked down the slope of the mountain toward the forested flatland below. He and Arval had emerged from the mountain pass earlier that day. As they'd promised, they'd lit a fire and burned the map he'd drawn them. Revan had been pleased to use the flint and steel he'd taken from Jinirlyn's pack to start it. "This hasn't been used to start a fire in thousands of turnings!" he'd said excitedly. Arval had just smiled as he'd watched the small twigs and dry grass catch fire.

They'd rested a bit after burning the map, looking out from their vantage point high above the tree-covered lowlands of Jarradan. The world was a carpet of green as far to the south as he could see. Until the Blackfire rose up from the horizon. From here though, it seemed beautiful and not sinister the way it usually did when he saw it. The enormous spinning black ball in the center and the threads of red and gold on the fringes of its arms almost looked like they belonged in this verdant setting, like they were caressing the trees and sky. Usually, the undulating and rotating arms of the Blackfire looked like they were scourging the skin off the world. Maybe, somewhere far to the south, they were.

The slope of the mountain they would soon descend was barren of trees, but the pass through which they'd traveled was full of them. Arval told him that trees didn't grow up high on mountains because the weather was too severe at high altitudes. When Revan had questioned how trees grew in the pass, Arval said something about it being sheltered from the worst of the weather. It sounded like a thin reason to Revan, but since he knew very little about mountains and trees, he didn't push the issue.

When they finally did start down, Arval told him that they would probably see the Azure Palace on its hill in Kessar in the distance off to their right. There was an enormous wall of rock protruding out from the mountain, so they would have to get beyond or below it before they could see Kessar, but Arval was sure they would.

"I can't wait to see it – a palace made of stone the color of the sky!" he'd said.

"It's beautiful," Arval replied. "But it's just a building. Big. With towers. And gates. And guards with weapons. And dungeons."

"Still, I've never seen one before."

Arval sighed. "I know. You're going to see a lot of new things soon."

They'd rested for a bit, chewing lazily on dried meat, and drinking from their waterskins. Revan was reclined against the huge boulder that marked the end of the pass, using his pack for a cushion. Arval lay flat on his back, his pack behind his head, staring at the sky. High above puffy white clouds drifted lazily along, occasionally obscuring the sun, but it was overall a beautiful early summer day high above Jarradan. Revan turned to look behind him at the sound of a low rumble in the distance. Far up the side of a towering mountain, he saw a huge white cloud of snow flowing down a deep draw. He watched mesmerized as the enormous mass of snow crashed into the treeline below. Even from this distance he could hear the crack and snap of trees breaking under the force of the deluge.

"Avalanche," Arval said.

"What?"

"All that snow coming down the mountain – it's called an avalanche."

"Oh."

"You don't want to get caught in one of those."

"I can hear trees breaking."

"You can?"

"Yeah. I have great hearing remember?"

"Oh yeah." Arval sometimes forgot that Revan's senses were far more acute than his.

"We should get moving soon. I'd like to get down there into the trees before dark. We should be able to find a good place to spend the night, then find the road tomorrow and start towards Kessar."

"Anxious to get there are you?" Arval asked, shaking his head of reddish-brown hair at his friend's exuberance.

"Well, yes. I can't wait to see a city and try some of those foods you've been telling me about."

Arval sighed and stood up. "We aren't getting anywhere just sitting around here. And I would like to see Plistral again. I'm sure he's been worried about me since I've been gone. He probably thinks I'm dead."

Revan shouldered his pack and waterskin, making sure he'd put the flint and steel away, and turned towards the open mouth of the pass. From here he couldn't see the downslope of the mountain; it looked like it ended in a cliff. He felt a moment's fear that they wouldn't be able to go that way and would have to backtrack all the way to the desert. A few steps towards the edge disabused him of that notion as he saw the steep slope fall away into the trees far below.

"We're going to have to be careful going down. It'll be easy to fall, and if one of us does, we'll roll all the way to the bottom. I doubt we'd survive," Arval said looking down the slope. It was made up mainly of loose rock that looked like it would slide right out from under their boots. Boulders of varying sizes, smooth and jagged, poked out of the surface here and there.

"Let's go down, side by side. If we go down single file and the one above falls, he'll take both of us down," Revan said.

"Good idea."

Together they started down the slope.

They'd been descending for about a half hour when Arval spoke up, "There it is."

"What?" Revan asked, his eyes on where he was stepping.

Arval had stopped, so Revan stopped too. "The Azure Palace."

Revan looked up and off to his right. Far in the distance he saw it. The Azure Palace gleamed in the morning sun on top of its hill. The first thing that struck Revan was its size – it was at least as long as the Kryxaal but not nearly as tall. The blue stone that made up its walls reflected the sunlight back in sparkling, blue-tinged yellow beams. It looked like the palace was lit from inside with some ethereal light. Revan thought he'd never seen anything so beautiful. Its numerous towers rose grandly into the morning air. In the middle of the hill and about halfway down its southern side, was a smaller but more imposing building made of grey stone with a road leading up to its gates that wound back and forth in a switchback pattern up the steep side of the hill.

"I can see another building below the palace. Is it the Grey Keep?" Revan asked.

"Yep, that would be it. The home of the Jix. Can you really see it from here?

"Yes. The hill the palace is on looks like grey stone so the keep blends in with it some, but I can see it."

"We should be there by the day after tomorrow, or the day after that at the latest," Arval said. "Let's go. It's even more impressive up close."

It took them the rest of the morning before they reached the bottom, and they were both very tired from the effort. Revan said something about halfway down that he'd always thought going up was harder. Going down was just as hard, but in a different way.

"Something else new that you've just learned?" Arval said playfully. Revan just glared at him; Arval laughed. After a moment Revan grinned back.

It had been hot on the slope with the sun beating down on them most of the way, and they were both sweating freely when they reached the shade of the trees. They found a fallen log and sat on it for a few minutes, drinking liberally from their waterskins.

"How far did Fendalon say it was to the road once we got to the trees?" Revan asked.

"About half a day," Arval replied.

"Ok, let's walk for a few hours, then start looking for a good place to sleep. We won't be far from the road then and can make good time tomorrow."

"You really are in a hurry to get to Kessar," Arval said.

"I'm in a hurry to find the other Kryxaal."

Arval sighed. "Let's go then. The sooner we get there, the sooner we can leave."

"You don't really want to go to Kessar do you?"

"Not really. There are a lot of bad memories there. Since we escaped the pit, I've never felt so free in my life. And I'd like to keep it that way. You don't know the city wardens in Kessar. They'll throw you in a dungeon because they have a headache from last night's ale. They'll execute you because they got a sliver in their short finger."

Revan looked down, remembering the story Arval had told him about his mother being killed, and felt sad for his friend. Maybe he had been a little too eager to get to Kessar. He'd have to remember in the future that the things he did affected others, not just him.

"And we'll have to hide these swords somewhere before we go into of the city."

"What do you mean?" Revan asked.

"No weapons are allowed in Kessar."

"But you told me about that Nojii being killed by the Jix warrior, and that the city wardens carry weapons."

"I know. The Jix are the Jix. No one would dream of taking their weapons. They don't cause problems anyway. The city wardens are supposed to be the peacekeepers, so they get to keep theirs. I don't know about the Nojii. The one I saw the Jix kill had that axe. I don't know how he got it into the city or why the Wardens didn't take it from him."

"Well, what if we get attacked? How are we supposed to defend ourselves?" Revan asked, incredulous.

"We run. And hide."

"I'd rather fight. Especially if its Nojii attacking us."

"I know, and so would I. But we will be in a dungeon before we get three steps inside the city gate if we show up with these swords."

Revan sighed in frustration. "Who wants to keep us from protecting ourselves?"

"It's a law that King Vraniss made when he took the throne. At least that's what I've been told. Apparently he fears an armed revolt against him and doesn't want any of us to have weapons."

"But people get attacked there anyway! You've told me stories of seeing people beaten and murdered in the streets!"

"Some people carry knives to protect themselves. But they are taken away to some dark hole somewhere if they're caught with them. The point is that we have to hide the swords before we go in. Unless you want seeing a dungeon to be your first experience in Kessar. If that's the case, you can forget about that ironberry pie."

Revan smiled at that, his frustration draining away. "You're right. Dessert sounds much better than a dungeon."

"Then quit complaining and let's go!"

Several hours later they'd found a good place to spend the night in a cleft between a group of downed trees. After sleeping soundly on a soft bed of needles, they'd risen refreshed and set out to the West in search of the road.

The forest in this part of Jarradan was easy to travel. There wasn't much undergrowth and the trees themselves were soaring specimens with enormous leafy canopies pierced here and there by even taller pines, their needled branches protruding into the leaves like spears. There was no path to follow, but it was another sunny day, and they could tell from the sun's position which direction they were travelling. Colorful little birds flitted about in the high branches, once in a while swooping down almost to the ground, then darting up to the safety of the heights again. Revan enjoyed watching them, and was amazed at how fast they were, how they could turn in midair so quickly. When they'd come through the pass, there had been a wet, swampy place that smelled of rot and gave Revan a feeling like something evil was watching them. This forest smelled clean and fresh, like it harbored nothing with ill intentions. He knew neither feeling was based in any fact, but he liked to think that this place, this forest, was welcoming and danger free.

"There's something ahead," Arval said.

"Is it the road?," Revan asked.

"I think so. Be quiet and walk slowly. If there's someone out there, we don't want them to see us unless it looks like they're friendly."

"How will we know if they're friendly or not without talking to them?"

"I was hoping you'd use your magic power and delve their minds to see if they were intent on harming us," Arval said, a glint of mischief in his brown eyes, a hint of a smile on his lips.

Revan gave him a good-natured slap on the shoulder and said, "You know it doesn't work that way."

"Well, you had an idea about Kanar. I think you were right too."

"But I'd talked to him some. I'd have to talk to anyone we meet out here to see if I get the same feeling," Revan said. "And I don't think magic has anything to do with it. Like I said, it's just a feeling."

"Well, we could try that."

"Let's just be careful."

They crept up to what they could now clearly see was the road winding through the forest and paused behind a couple huge trees. There didn't appear to be anyone in sight.

"Well, there's nothing for it but to take the road if we want to get to Kessar. At some point we have to come out of this forest anyway. Might as well be now," Revan said. Arval nodded his agreement, and they made their way out onto the hard dirt surface of the road. There were two sets of wheel ruts side by side. Carts and wagons could go opposite directions and pass each other without moving aside. The trees were cut back from the road itself for about five paces on each side, providing a small buffer between the road and the forest. As they began walking towards Kessar, each rested a hand on the pommel of his sword.

About midday Revan nudged Arval and pointed to the side of the road. "Someone's coming. We need to get into the trees."

"We can't run away every time someone comes along this road, Revan," Arval said. "Some of them will be bad, some good, some won't be either. I'm staying here."

Revan sighed, realizing Arval was right. "Ok. We'll just keep walking like we don't have anything to worry about."

A few minutes later Arval heard the rumble of wheels on the road. It wasn't long before three wagons came around a bend and quickly reached them. The driver in the lead wagon pulled back on the reins and called out to his horses to slow. As he rolled to a stop, he looked down at the two boys. They looked back calmly. The driver was much older than them, with sandy brown hair that was at least half grey. It hung to his shoulders and the effect of the grey made it look like he'd had a bucket of stone dust dumped on his head. His deeply tanned face was crisscrossed with age lines and his mouth had a sour twist. But his eyes appeared kindly.

"Where are you fellows headed?" he asked.

"To Kessar Sir," Revan replied.

"Looking for trouble?" the man asked, gesturing to the swords they were wearing.

"No, we just like to have something to protect ourselves if it comes looking for us," Arval said

"You won't be able to bring them into the city."

"I've heard," said Revan.

"Well, we're bringing in a load of early summer wheat to sell to the bakeries. That is myself, my wife and son are. They're driving the other two wagons."

Revan and Arval looked back, and sure enough, a woman about this man's age was driving the second, a boy not much older than them drove the third.

"We'd be inclined to give you a ride if you'd give your word that you aren't up to any mischief."

"We aren't Sir. We're just trying to get to the city and get a good meal. We'd be in your debt for a ride, and we promise we don't mean you or your family any harm," Arval said.

"Alright. There isn't enough room for you both to ride with me, so one of you hop up here, the other can ride with my son in the last wagon."

Revan nodded to Arval to go to the son's wagon while he climbed up next to the man. When they were both seated, the wagons set off again.

"My name is Anden," the man said, extending his hand. Revan shook it and introduced himself and Arval. "My wife's name is Poli, my son is Denen. We're farmers from the south. Been on the road to Kessar for near a week."

"So long? Isn't there somewhere nearer to your home where you could sell your wheat?" Revan asked.

"Sure, lots of places. But no place pays as well as the bakeries in Kessar. Even though it's a long trip, it's worth it to us in the end. What we make from selling it there will take care of us, and then some, for the next turning."

"Well, that makes sense," Revan said.

Anden glanced at him. "Don't mean to pry son, but I've told you the truth of my situation. I'd like to have the truth of yours. Especially if you're going to share my wagon."

The wagon bounced and jolted over the ruts and rocks in the road, making its occupants sway from side to side. How to begin? He didn't get a bad feeling from the man; he seemed honest, and Revan didn't detect any threat from him. Still, he wanted to keep his business to himself. What could he tell him that was believable?

"My friend and I ran into an old hermit in the forest some time back. He gave us food and shelter for a night, and in exchange we agreed to visit some friends of his in Kessar to let them know he was alright and thinking of them."

"Well, that sounds like a nice thing to do. I know a lot of people in Kessar. Maybe I could help you find them. What are their names?"

"Endanna is one. She owns a clothing store called The Needle and Thread. The other is named Yelun. He owns a tavern called The Short Wall."

"Well, I don't know either person, but I know both businesses. My wife likes to buy a new dress from The Needle and Thread every year once our crop is sold. And The Short Wall is a place my son and I have had an ale once or twice on our visits. They won't be hard to find. Did your hermit friend live in Kessar? I might know him. What's his name?"

Revan was caught off guard momentarily. He'd agreed not to mention Fendalon to anyone else, and now he was being questioned about him. In a panic he seized on the only name that came to mind but changed it a little: "Bhenjor," he blurted out.

Anden frowned as he searched his memory. "Can't say as I know that name. Well, no matter. There are lots of people in that city. I'm not surprised I don't know it."

Revan let his breath out slowly; he didn't realize he'd been holding it after Anden had asked about Fendalon. They rode on in silence, the only sounds were the creaking of the wagon and clopping of the horses' hooves.

The sun was beginning to set in the west and the shadows of the enormous trees were long on the ground. Night insects had begun to come out and Revan had a couple welts from their bites to prove it. He glanced back and saw Arval and Denen laughing animatedly about something. Anden's wife Poli gave him a polite smile. He smiled back and turned to the road in front of them. As they rounded a bend, he saw a wagon resting diagonally across the middle of the road, one wheel was laying on the ground, the wagon itself up on wooden blocks. A team of horses stood tethered to some trees just off the road. Three men were bent over, apparently working to repair some damage. It's cargo, a number of crates, was stacked to the side of the road in a jumbled pile. Anden reined his horses to a halt and got down off the wagon. Revan followed.

"Hello there, anything we can do to help?" he asked as he walked closer. One of the men stood up and wiped a grimy hand across his brow, leaving a dark streak of wheel grease across his forehead.

"Well yes, matter of fact there is," the man said. "Our wagon lost a wheel, as you can see, and we're having some trouble getting it mounted again. Had to tether the horses and unload our cargo just to lift it onto these blocks. Would you have a large mallet? If we give it a good pounding, that might get it to seat."

"Don't have a mallet, but I've got a hammer that might help," Anden replied. He walked back to the wagon and lifted the front of the driver's seat. It rose on a hinge like a chest, and he reached into the space underneath, fishing out a hammer with a large square head. He handed it to the man who nodded his thanks.

Revan hadn't liked the look of the man. As he'd taken the hammer, he'd been glancing around nervously. Revan's hand gripped the hilt of his sword as the man bent to do something to the wheel. As he raised the hammer, he suddenly stood and turned towards Anden and swung the hammer at his head. Revan instinctively drew his sword and swung it at the man as the hammer whistled through the air straight at Anden's face. His blade caught the man's arm at the elbow and severed it in a mist of blood. The bodiless limb, still holding the hammer, sailed off into the woods and crashed into a shrub. A scream from the man brought several more men running from where they'd been concealed behind the crates and some of the gigantic tree trunks. At a glance Revan counted seven coming towards him, plus the three they'd initially seen pretending to work on the wagon. One of those men was coming at Revan with a knife and a grimace of anger.

As the man lunged at him, Revan smoothly sidestepped him, whipping his sword up and across the man's chest. His flimsy and threadbare wool shirt parted, as did his flesh. He crashed to the ground and didn't move. The man who'd lost the arm was writhing on the ground screaming, great gouts of blood pumping from the stump of his arm and decorating his broken wagon a vibrant shade of red.

The third man also had a knife, but he took two steps and threw it by the blade at Revan's chest. It seemed to come in slow motion and Revan was able to easily knock it aside with the flat of his sword. The man screamed in frustration and ran straight at Revan as if to tackle him. With a quick thrust, Revan's sword found the center of the man's chest and exploded out his back. He was dead before the blade could be withdrawn.

Out of the corner of his eye, Revan saw Arval running towards him sword in hand, Denen right behind him, a large wooden club gripped tightly in his fist. The seven others had split up. Four came towards him and Anden, the other three were heading for Arval and Denen. Poli was still on her wagon, eyes wide and fear etched on her face. All the men had either clubs or knives. No swords, Revan thought. That was strange. Couldn't they afford them? Ten men out here trying to rob people and not a sword among them. Did they want to die? The thoughts flashed through his mind as he waited for the first man to reach him. He had a big wooden club held high over his head as if he was about to drive a fencepost into the ground. Revan was slightly amazed that the man was so reckless; he didn't have a chance, and he proved it to the man with a slash across his throat as he pivoted away from him. The man stumbled forward several steps, blood spraying from his neck in a fan. The second man had a knife and swung it at Revan's head as if it was a sword. A flick of his blade took the man's knife hand and half his forearm off in one swing, he then brought it arcing back up and caught him under the chin, splitting his head up to his eyes. The third and fourth men hesitated a moment, then charged him together. Each of these fellows had clubs that they swung at Revan, one high and one low. He jumped back from the low swing, ducked the high one, and swung his sword in a long and graceful, but incredibly swift arc, taking off both their heads before they could recover to swing at him again.

As the men dropped lifeless, Revan turned and ran towards Arval and Denen. He could see that Arval had wounded one man severely in the thigh, although he was still swinging his knife at him. The other two were attacking Denen. He was fending them off with his club, but it was clear to Revan that in moments one of them was going to land a blow and do for Anden's son. He ran towards him first, knowing Arval would be alright.

The men didn't hear Revan charging up behind them, so their expression betrayed their surprise when his sword took them each across the back, laying open their skin so deep that their backbones and ribs were exposed. A quick thrust to each ended their lives. Denen dropped his arms to his sides and stared at Revan, who had turned to Arval, only to see him pulling his sword from the man's chest. It had only been moments, but ten men lay all around them. The first man whose arm Revan had cut off was the only one still alive; he was writhing on the ground and screaming. But his voice was weakening; he wouldn't last long.

As Anden and Poli made their way to where the three boys stood, their eyes were wide in disbelief at what they'd just seen. Poli's mouth was agape with amazement. Anden's was closed, but his eyes were practically bulging out of his head.

"You just killed nine men. By yourself. And you're not even breathing hard," Anden said softly, the awe evident in his voice.

"They were going to kill us," Revan said simply.

"I've never seen someone move so fast." Denen and Poli nodded in dazed agreement. "How did you do that?"

Revan shrugged. "I just did it. I didn't really think about it."

"Well... thank you. From all of us," Anden said. "We'd be dead now if it wasn't for you." Denen walked up and clapped Revan on the shoulder, smiling his gratitude. When he stepped back, Poli suddenly hugged him so tightly he couldn't breathe for a moment. "We owe you our lives," she said. "If there is ever, and I mean ever, anything at all that you ever need, you just ask us."

Revan smiled sheepishly and nodded. Arval took his turn at clapping him on the back. "Just another day's work for my friend," he told the stunned family.

"Killing doesn't get him excited, but you should be there to see his reaction when he tries ironberry pie for the first time!"

Chapter 23

essar was more than Arval had described, more than Revan had imagined. As they walked its streets, Arval had to keep elbowing him to close his mouth; it kept dropping open in awe. Nothing Arval had told him prepared Revan for the reality of this enormous, bustling mass of people, sounds and sights.

They'd come out of the forest in the early afternoon and into the open treeless area where the city lay. Revan had seen the Azure Palace from the side of the mountain when they'd made their descent out of the pass, but since then it had been screened from view by the gigantic trees of the forest. As they'd emerged from those trees onto a low hill overlooking the city, Revan could see how far the city spread across the flat land before them. To the right the Blue Crag Mountains rose up, separating Kessar from the desert to the north. To the left, beyond the edges of the city's southern reaches, the forest stretched away as far as Revan could see. But it was the city and not the surrounding natural features that commanded his attention and fed his incredulity.

The city was about fifteen ranges across and was laid out in a rough circle and surrounded by a wall made of upright logs. Watchtowers interrupted its length at irregular intervals. The Azure Palace, on its tall hill, was just to the left of the center. The wide, greenish blue Xandei river flowed in from the north and cut the city almost directly in half, skirting the palace at the base of the hill on the eastern side and wending its way through the city and into the forests to the south. The Grey Keep lay on the southern side of the hill; Revan could see the road to its imposing black gate twisting up the steep slope. Nothing moved on that road, but down below, among the multitude of buildings, throngs of people moved in every direction. From their vantage point above it, Revan stared, amazed that so many people could inhabit one place. The warren of streets teemed with people, carts and noise. Even from here he could detect such a myriad of sounds and smells that his head nearly spun trying to make sense of them all.

"Well, there it is," Arval said. "The fabled city of Kessar."

Revan looked at him with a new sense of respect. "You actually lived in that?! It looks so crowded."

"It is. Now do you want to stand here gawking at it, or do you want to go see it up close?"

Revan smiled then. "I've been waiting weeks to see it – let's go!"

They'd parted ways with Anden and his family earlier that morning. They'd been effusive with their thanks for Revan and Arval's actions against the thieves and reminded them that any time they were ever in need, of anything, to call on them. Handshakes all around, and fierce hugs from Poli had marked their parting. As the family drove away in their wagons, they'd smiled and waved, Revan and Arval had returned the gesture.

"There are good people in the world," Revan had said. "They aren't all like the Nojii."

"Of course not," Arval replied. "Fendalon is a good man too."

"I know. It's just that that's the first family I've ever met. And they were all good people."

"Most people are good," Arval said. "Or at least they aren't as bad as the Nojii. I'll bet that even some of them are good too. People are just people. They do what they have to in order to survive, like I did in my Khet, like we both did with those thieves. Sometimes where they end up in life means they have to do bad or distasteful things, but that doesn't make them bad. The truly bad ones are people like Bhinja. He actually enjoyed hurting all of us; you could see it in his eyes. But a few of the other Nojii at the pit I don't think really liked using their lashes. Don't get me wrong, most of them were like Bhinja, but there were a few who, if you watched closely, didn't swing as hard as the others, and their eyes didn't light up when they drew blood. Those are the people I'm talking about. Don't let Bhinja and the monsters like him make you think everyone who does something bad really is bad."

Revan nodded his understanding. "I just thought of something."

"What?"

"Poli is the first woman I've ever seen. That I remember."

Arval paused and stared at Revan a moment, considering. "That's probably true. There weren't any women at the pit. I hadn't thought of that. Well, you'll see plenty soon. I have a feeling the pretty ones are going to like you."

"What?! Why would they?"

Arval grinned wickedly at Revan and clapped him on the back. "Oh, you'll find out soon enough."

Revan was mystified but suddenly felt warm and strangely uncomfortable. A hand to his face told him his cheeks were burning with heat. He quickly changed the subject. "We should find a good place to hide these swords."

Arval just smiled at him.

They'd walked into the woods a short distance and found a fallen tree with a small gap underneath it. After stashing the swords under the tree and covering the opening with branches and leaves, Arval stepped back and surveyed their work. It looked natural.

"How will we find this place again?" Revan asked.

"I'll show you," Arval replied. He'd walked back to the road and found a particularly large tree with a gigantic trunk; its roots resembled a small mountain range as they pushed up from the dirt. Arval picked up a fist sized rock and placed it between two of the bigger roots.

"When we come back for the swords, we just have to find this tree and this rock. The hiding spot will be easy to find from here."

They'd made their way down the road off the low hill and through the gate in the wooden wall into the city itself. The outer fringes consisted mainly of small, ramshackle dwellings cobbled together from whatever scraps of material the inhabitants could find. Arval had told him that the poor lived in places like this, as he and his mother had. The poor quarter, as this region was colloquially known, formed a ring almost all the way around perimeter of the sprawling city, right up to the outer wall. At the southern end, on either bank of the Xandei river, was the area known as the Merchant Quarter. It was made up of docks and warehouses where the goods coming and going from the city were loaded and unloaded onto river boats and wagons. The closer one moved toward the center of the city and the river, the more affluent the residents and their homes became, and also, the more plentiful the city wardens. The area closest to the palace and directly across the river from it was known as Heavy Chest Crescent. Its name referred not just to its shape, which was a crescent formed to the west by the river, and to the east by a tall stone wall that separated it from the rest of the city, but also because of the great wealth of its residents. It was assumed that everyone who lived within the walls possessed a chest, or several, heavy with gold and other riches. The name, while not recognized officially on any map, had become a source of pride for those who lived there, and a pejorative term for those who didn't.

"So, you lived in the poor quarter?" Revan asked. "Seems like the poor quarter makes up most of the city."

"It does," Arval answered. "My mother told me that there have always been far more poor people than wealthy. It's just how things are. Most poor people are actually fairly happy. As long as they can feed their families, have a home, and be left alone, they're usually content. They get angry when they're treated unjustly, or the Wardens hassle them for little things."

Revan pondered this bit of information as they walked through the edge of the city. As he looked around he realized that Arval seemed to be right. The people he passed were mostly smiling as they went about their lives. Women chatted together as they hung wet clothes on lines. Women! He'd never imagined so many even existed. They were everywhere – young and old, skinny and round, beautiful and hideous. With a surprise that he was becoming accustomed to, Revan realized that women were as varied in their appearances as men. Maybe more so. They certainly wore dramatically different clothes than men did. Their hair was short and long, tied up in a knot on the top of their head, or hanging all the way to their waist. And many painted their faces in the most garish of colors. The red of one woman's lips was so unnatural that Revan couldn't help but gape. Arval elbowed him in the ribs when the woman gave them a fierce scowl. "It isn't polite to stare," he said to his chagrined friend. Revan had yet much to learn. A group of girls about their age were glancing at the two of them as they walked by, smiling shyly and giggling. Revan looked at Arval, the question in his eyes unspoken. Arval just shrugged and smiled at him again. "I told you they'd like you," he said.

As for the men, they seemed to be in much the same mood as the women. They weren't frowning or yelling as they drove carts or carried loads of goods. And everywhere Revan saw dirty children running and playing, their laughter and cries of delight at whatever games they were in the midst of made him smile for them. It also gave him a pang for the childhood that had been stolen from him. A memory surfaced at that moment – of the man he thought of as his father chasing him through green grass. He remembered quite clearly laughing in much the same way the children of this city were.

"You look happy," Arval said.

"It's great to see all these children running around playing. It reminded me of when I was a child before I came to the pit. I hadn't remembered it before, but a man was chasing me through the grass, and I was laughing like they are."

"Good memory. Hang on to it."

Revan smiled at Arval. They'd traveled about halfway to the river when an unfamiliar smell reached Revan's nose.

"What is that smell?" he asked.

"What smell?" Arval asked back.

"The one that's making my mouth water. It smells like the dried meat we ate, but better."

"We're getting close to a spot where there are several taverns and shops. Maybe it's coming from one of them. Wait! The Short Wall is close to here. Let's find it and say hello to Yelun."

At that moment, a group of six heavily tattooed Nojii came around a bend in the road and cut across their path. Their appearance caused everyone to pause briefly in their doings. Furtive and angry glances were cast their way, glares and frowns were directed at their backs. For all the overt hostility exhibited towards them by the people of the city, the Nojii seemed unaware, or maybe just unconcerned. All of them carried weapons – swords and axes, one had a bow – while none of the common people had so much as a knife. At least not one that was visible. The mood of the people towards the Nojii was apparent to Revan and Arval instantly for it was the same as their own. They all hated these men. An old man in ragged clothes muttered something under his breath at the Nojii, but not loud enough for them to hear. Revan heard it though.

"What did you say?" he asked the man.

"I said their time is coming soon."

"What do you mean?"

"I mean that we are going to do to them what they've been doing to us."

"And what's that?"

"We're going to kill them. There are plans." The man gazed vacantly off into the distance, shook his head and started to walk away from Revan.

I've said too much," he muttered.

"Wait, what plans?" Revan asked, taking a few steps after him.

"Let him go," Arval said. "Don't make a scene. Those Nojii could decide to come back."

Revan sighed with frustration. He wanted to know what that man had been talking about. What plans? "Let's go find this Short Wall place then."

A brief time later they were standing outside the tavern Fendalon had told them about. It was a single-story building with a sign hanging above the door, the image of a low stone wall carved and painted on it. The name was emblazoned above the image in bright red paint. Several people walked in ahead of the two boys.

"It's close to the end of the working day," Arval said. "Most of these people will be going in there for a meal and an ale. Or several."

"Let's go get a meal ourselves – I'm starving," Revan said.

"We don't have any money to buy a meal."

"Then how are we supposed to eat?"

"I'm hoping when we tell Yelun that we've seen Fendalon that he'll give us a meal for free."

"What?!" Revan said. "You don't want to pay for it somehow?!"

"When you live on the streets like I did, you learn how to survive. Trying to get someone to give you a free meal is one thing you learn very quickly."

"It doesn't seem right though."

"Remember what I told you about people doing what they have to in order to survive? That was one thing I had to do. And you'll have to learn it too."

"Maybe we could offer to work for him or something. To pay for our meal."

"Ah, Revan," Arval sighed "Your sense of morality is highly defined for someone who didn't even really know what the word moral meant not long ago. Let's go in and just see what happens."

As they walked through the door, Revan realized that the smell he'd detected earlier had definitely come from this place. They were in a large room filled with wooden tables and chairs; an enormous stone fireplace stood on the back wall surrounded in an arc by more chairs. A long wooden bar took up the left wall, at the end of which a doorway led to the back part of the building, presumably to the kitchen. Several people sat on stools at the bar, drinking from greyish metal mugs, others sat in groups at tables eating heartily from plates of steaming food. Two men sat in the chairs by the fireplace talking animatedly and drinking.

Arval walked confidently to the bar and gestured to a woman working behind it. She ambled over and smiled at them. "What can I get you boys?"

"Is Yelun available?" Arval asked.

"He's in back cooking. Something I can help you with?"

"We have a message for him. From an old friend."

"Let me see if he can get away for a moment," she said as she walked through the door into the back. A moment later she returned followed by a huge man. He was probably about as old as Fendalon and totally bald except for a long drooping white mustache. He wore a stained leather apron and no shirt which gave Revan and Arval a view of his massive arms. He looked strong enough to pick one of them up in each hand and throw them all the way back to Fendalon's cottage.

"What can I do for you boys?" he said in a not unfriendly tone.

"Could we speak to you in private a moment?" Arval asked.

Yelun regarded them pointedly, as if assessing them for threats. Apparently thinking he could handle two striplings, he gestured to them to follow and led them into the kitchen.

"Now what is it that you have to interrupt my cooking for?" he asked, folding his gigantic arms across his massive chest.

"We bring you greetings from Fendalon," Arval said.

"Fendalon?!" he said incredulously, his arms falling to his sides. "How could you possibly know Fendalon?"

"We met him several days ago," Arval said simply. Revan remained quiet. He was new to this kind of social situation and decided to let Arval do most of the talking.

"And where would that have been?"

"He had us promise not to tell anyone where we met him. But he did ask us to tell you he says hello. And to ask you for biscuits and gravy."

"Ha! That does sound like Fendalon. He did love my biscuits and gravy. And he was always secretive. What can you tell me about him that proves you met him without betraying your promise to him?"

"Well," Arval said, "he was a member of the Jix. He left not long after Vraniss became king."

"That be true," Yelun said. "But did you know he wasn't just a member of the Jix?"

"What do you mean not just a member?" Arval asked.

"He was the captain," Yelun said quietly.

"He was?!" Revan asked, amazed.

"Well, it speaks," Yelun said good-naturedly, glancing at Revan. "Yes. He was captain of the Jix for a number of turnings. He didn't tell you that part apparently."

"No," Arval and Revan said almost in unison.

"You met an important man," Yelun said. "He is still known and widely respected here. There are many who wish he was still captain. The man who replaced him is good, but Fendalon had a way about him. You'd forget his station if he talked to you. He came across like any other man who works for a living. Not to say he didn't work, he did. As hard as any Jix captain as far as I know. But he didn't hold his position over your head like some do. He could come in here for a meal and have the patrons all laughing at his stories. Of course, they feared him, not just because of who he was, but also because of how good he was with weapons. He could kill everyone in The Short Wall and not break a sweat, but you'd never know that by talking to him. People who were deathly afraid of him on first meeting ended up being his friends by the time he left here. I miss that man."

"We understand what you mean," Revan said. "He was… an excellent host."

"So, you stayed with him then?"

Arval elbowed Revan to bite his lip. Revan glared at him and continued, "We can't tell you where we met him, but yes, he let us stay with him one night. He fed us the best stew we've ever had."

"Ah, the stew. He did tell me about his stew. Even brought me a bowl of it once when I told him it couldn't be as good as he'd boasted. But it was. I even tried to get the recipe from him. He wouldn't give it up for anything. And believe me, I tried everything I could think of to get it out of him."

Yelun was silent for a moment as he appraised his visitors. At last, he sighed and led them back out into the main room of the tavern. "You boys look hungry and I believe I can spare some biscuits and gravy for friends of Fendalon."

"We can't pay Sir; we have no money. But we'll be happy to work for it," Revan said. Arval rolled his eyes at the offer, annoyed that Revan had destroyed his plan for a free meal.

"No need. I'm happy to have news that Fendalon is alive and thought enough of me to have you tell me hello. Besides, if he hadn't liked you, you'd both be dead right now. There isn't a man alive that I know of who could have bested Fendalon in a fight. So, since you're obviously friends of my friend, a bit of food as thanks for you visiting me is a small price."

The biscuits and gravy were as wonderful as Fendalon had told them they were. Revan chewed lustily, talking around mouthfuls of them about how delicious they were. Yelun smiled as the boys each cleaned a heaping plate of his specialty. When they were done they said goodbye to Yelun, promising to return again for more biscuits and gravy. He shook both their hands and wished them well, making sure to tell them that if they ever saw Fendalon again, to tell him he still wanted the stew recipe.

"Where should we go now?" Revan asked.

"Let's try to find Plistral. He'll know where we can sleep for the night. The Needle and Thread will be closed by now, so we can visit there in the morning, then get on with whatever else it is you want to do here."

"I want to find a way to get into the Jix' libraries. We need to find the other Kryxaal before someone else does."

"Do you think someone else knows about them? About what they are I mean?" Arval asked.

"I don't know. But I need to find them. I am going bring magic back to this world."

They walked the streets in silence for a time. Arval knew the city, so Revan was content to just follow him. After a time, they came to the river and a wide stone bridge that spanned it. Arval began to lead them across, but Revan stopped in the middle to look down at the water flowing by below them.

"Look at all this water," he said. "I never thought there could be this much water in the world."

"There's a lot more in the ocean, from what I've heard," Arval said. "It would make this river look like a puddle."

"I want to see it too. The ocean. Maybe even get on a boat and sail around the world."

"One thing at a time adventure boy," Arval said. "Come on, it's getting late. We need to find a place to sleep soon. If Plistral is still around somewhere, I'll find him. If not I know a couple places."

As they crossed the bridge, Revan looked back across and to the north. He saw the big homes surrounded by the tall stone wall that designated that area as Heavy Chest Crescent. The homes within the wall were spectacular. They had innumerable windows and balconies, columns and doorways. Most were painted in a myriad of vivid colors, and he could see people moving around inside and outside them. Servants, staff or owners, he didn't know. But he couldn't imagine being wealthy enough to own a home like one of those. Another bridge spanned the river from approximately the center of Heavy Chest Crescent. Across the river from that prosperous district, he could see a huge open area paved with white stone. That could only be White Square where Arval's mother's life had ended. And so many others. Revan didn't say anything about it, knowing that the memory was painful to Arval. But he marked it in his mind.

A short time after they crossed the river, Arval turned off the main road they were on and down a narrow side street. The buildings to either side were two and three story examples. The sun had sunk low on the horizon and combined with the height of the buildings to either side, the street was deep in shadow. As they turned a corner to the right, they were stopped in their tracks by a group of ten young men about their age. One who stood slightly in front of them eyed them menacingly. Revan turned to walk back the way they'd come, but eight more had closed in behind them. They were trapped. The boy who'd been eyeing them spoke then, "Well, well. Looks like a couple of pockets have shown up for us to search," he said. The groups in front and behind began to move toward Revan and Arval. There was nothing friendly or welcoming in any of their faces.

Chapter 24

here's Plistral?" Arval asked quickly.

"Plistral? Who's Plistral?" the one who'd spoken laughed. He appeared to be the leader of this gang.

Don't know any Plistral. Now give us what you have, and you won't bleed."

"We don't have anything," Revan said. "But if you'd like to take our clothes, you're welcome to try," he said calmly. Revan stared directly at the boy, unblinking. He was about their age but skinny, like he missed more meals than he ate.

"So, this one thinks he's tough, eh fellas?!" the boy said. "Should we show him how tough he is against all of us?" Some of the other boys laughed and agreed. Others didn't laugh. Something in Revan's eyes had given them pause. Only half of either group continued to advance.

"If you want to see how 'tough' I am, keep walking," Revan said. His words caused a couple more boys to slow, hesitation in their eyes. The leader appeared not to notice that his original eighteen had dwindled to six very quickly. Suddenly Revan could see the threads. He hadn't tried to see them, they just appeared. The gold threads flowed all around in the buildings, the stones of the street they were standing on, and in a cart on the side of the road. Red threads interspersed with a few gold ones twisted and streamed through the gang of boys that confronted them. But what really caught Revan's interest were the red threads in the boy who spoke. They were moving sluggishly and almost all were a dull, dark red, not vibrant and bright and shiny like those of everyone else. He wondered what that meant. He thought maybe he knew.

"You're too pretty to be any threat. Those blue eyes of yours might make the girls giggle, but they don't scare me," the leader said.

"Revan, we don't have our swords. I'm sure we could take them all if we were armed, but it's just our fists right now," Arval muttered under his breath. Revan ignored him; he just continued to stare at the leader. Three more boys stopped moving, and just watched Revan and their leader facing off. Despite their numbers, the boys who had stopped were all fearful. It was obvious they weren't used to being challenged. The leader was just three paces in front of Revan and Arval now, one of his gang still next to him, another stood menacingly behind them.

"What are you going to do to stop us, hmm? We'll take what we want, and you won't be able to do a thing about it." he said.

Revan remained silent. He was watching the boy next to the leader. He looked sick, with greyish skin and dull eyes, but was apparently loyal to the leader since he'd come this far. He noticed that the red threads in this boy were moving almost normally. But their color was the same dull, dark red as the leader's. Revan glanced back at the other boy behind them out of the corner of his eye. This one was big and looked well fed. And healthy. His threads were perfectly normal. He'd be the strongest and would have to be dealt with first. He stood less than two paces behind them, leaning forward and grinning in anticipation of violence. This one enjoyed it like Bhinja had, Revan could tell from his expression. Yes, he would go down first. If Revan took him, the others would scatter. Except maybe the leader - he didn't seem to lack for courage, although he probably still thought he had a whole gang to back him up. Strangely, he didn't seem to notice that most of his gang had ceased to support him.

Silently, but as fast as he could, Revan spun towards the boy behind him, his fist flying out from his side so quickly his target didn't see it coming. When it connected with the side of the boy's head, there was a loud crack, as if a piece of wood had just snapped. The boy crumpled soundlessly to the ground. Whirling back around to face the leader, Revan glared at him, silently daring him to advance another step. The leader's eyes were wide with shock, as were those of the rest of his gang, the sickly boy included. Several turned and ran away.

"Looks like the soldiers are deserting the army," Revan said. "Would their general like to continue the battle?"

He seemed to have forgotten his intentions and just stared at Revan for a moment until he finally said in amazement, "How did you move so fast?"

Revan ignored the inquiry and just glared at him.

"Really. How did you do that? No one has ever put Indrik down.

"There's always a first time," Arval said smiling. "Now do you know Plistral or not?" Revan took a step towards the incredulous street general, his balled fists held up menacingly.

"Of course, I know him. He's the leader of my Khet," he replied, holding his hands up as if to ward off a blow from Revan.

"Then he's the leader of my Khet too," Arval said.

"Your Khet?! Who are you?"

"I'm Arval," he replied simply.

"Arval?! You're Arval?!. He said you were dead."

"Do I look dead?"

The boy gulped, realizing in that moment that he'd committed a serious crime by accosting one of his own Khet.

"You won't tell him about this will you?" he asked, fear evident in his eyes and voice.

"The rules are the rules."

"But we didn't know who you were," the boy said in a tone bordering on pleading. "We'd never have fronted up on you like that if we'd known who you were."

"You didn't bother to ask. And when I asked you about Plistral, you pretended you didn't know him.

That should have been your first clue that I wasn't just some lost merchant or Heavy Chest Crescent worm looking for fun with a street girl."

"I beg forgiveness and the mercy of my Khet-brother Arval," he said meekly.

"Well, you have some clout around here, eh?" Revan asked, glancing at Arval.

"People know me. I have a bit of a... reputation on these streets."

"I imagine you do."

Arval turned from Revan to the terrified former street general in front of them. "Where's Plistral?" he asked. "I won't ask again."

"He's, he's... in the, the Hive," he stammered.

"Take us there. Now." Arval's tone left no doubt in the boy's mind that should he decide not to take them, it would not go well for him in the end.

"Right away. Come with me," he said.

Plistral was ecstatic to see Arval again. The reunion was loud and joyous, with tears on both sides. Revan smiled at his friend's happiness at being back with his Khet. Arval had given Plistral a brief account of what had happened since he'd been taken and promised a more detailed explanation later. The boy he'd knocked out had come around not long after the general (his name was Asplan, Revan found out) had agreed to take them to Plistral. The big boy, Indrik, walked around holding his head and moaning about how much it hurt until someone told him to sit down and be quiet because he was giving them a headache with his complaining.

Plistral had welcomed Revan as if he'd known him as long as Arval. He even laughed when he heard the story of Revan facing down eighteen of his Khet. "We could use someone with your stones in this Khet. And I hear you're faster than anyone this lot has ever seen. That's a desirable trait in our line of work."

Revan smiled and made non-committal comments. Food was brought and everyone ate heartily. It was a banquet in honor of Arval's return. There were fresh fruits and vegetables, most of which Revan had never seen before, dried meats and bread. Even though he wasn't hungry after Yelun's biscuits and gravy, he sampled some of everything, marveling at the new flavors. A cask of ale appeared after the food was gone and all enjoyed a mug before they began to drift off to bed. The Hive was located in the basement of a burned down building not far from where the earlier confrontation had taken place. Plistral explained to Revan that The Hive was the name they gave to whatever place they slept in. It changed frequently. His Khet was always on the lookout for places where a new Hive could be established.

"Tomorrow you'll have to tell me what else happened since I last saw you," Plistral said to Arval.

"I will. Some of it I can't tell you but know this – I wouldn't be here right now if not for Revan. He's saved my life more than once."

"Then you are a member of our Khet whether you want to be or not," Plistral solemnly told Revan.

"Thank you," he replied simply and a bit sheepishly.

"I'm tired," Arval said. "Where do we sleep?"

"There's a bunk in the far corner," Plistral said gesturing to a corner of the basement. "See you in the morning."

As Arval wandered off to find his bed, Revan turned to Plistral. "That boy who led the gang, Asplan? Where can I find him?"

"Why do you want to know?"

"I'd like to talk to him if it's alright with you."

"He's been put out of the Khet for a season. It's his punishment for accosting one of his Khet brothers. Well, two now."

"Where would he go?"

"I don't know. Wherever he could find a place to sleep I suppose. Why are you so interested in him?"

"I think something's wrong with him."

"Of course, something's wrong with him – he's an idiot. Good for bossing around the muscle, but not much else."

"No, not that. I mean I think he's very sick."

"What makes you think that?"

Revan pondered for a moment, then made up a story. "My mother taught me a bit about healing. I could see in his eyes that something is wrong with him. I'd like to ask him a few questions. Maybe I can help him."

"Why would you help him after what he did to you?"

"He didn't know who we were. He was only doing his job, as he sees it. I wish you hadn't made him leave. Anyone could have made the same mistake."

"If I hadn't run him off then what good would our laws be? It is forbidden to accost a fellow member of a Khet. He did."

"I understand that. I just think it was a mistake and I hope you take him back. None of the others recognized Arval either."

"I'll think about it. In the meantime if you really want to find him, I'd look upstairs in what's left of this building. I'll bet he didn't go too far. He's probably under what's left of the stairs to what was the upper level of this place."

Revan thanked Plistral and made his way up to the main floor. As he moved over and around the burnt wooden remains of the building, he heard a quiet cough from a dark corner of the room. The silhouette of a set of stairs stood out against what was left of a wall. Beneath it he could make out a shape.

"Asplan? Is that you?" he asked quietly.

"Who wants to know?"

"It's me, Revan."

"What do you want?" Asplan asked, anger and sadness in equal measure were apparent in his voice.

"Can I come talk to you?"

"What do you want to talk about? I really don't feel like talking. Especially to you." Another cough punctuated his words. It sounded wet and deep.

"How are you feeling?"

"What kind of question is that?"

"I think you're sick. And I think I can help."

"No one can help me," Asplan said. "My father had the cough and it killed him. It'll kill me too. Go away. I won't live long enough to rejoin the Khet. If they even let me."

Revan ignored him and knelt down next to where Asplan lay.

"I told you to go away," he said, sitting up.

Revan seized Asplan's head between his hands and instantly saw white.

The tunnel flew past, turning and twisting as it had on the other occasions when Revan had been here. He let himself be pulled towards the room he knew was at the end. When he arrived in it, he was surprised to find it empty. He'd thought that maybe a part of Asplan would be here to talk to him like Drannal and Jinirlyn had, but there was only the white. He looked around, hoping something would materialize, that a form would take shape, but nothing happened. There had to be something here though. He knew Asplan was sick, and he was sure that he could heal him, but how? Revan paused to get his thoughts under control. When he was composed he looked around slowly. This room was much larger than the others he'd been in. He moved across it until he detected a wall, then began to follow it. After what seemed several minutes of searching, he found himself in front of the entrance to another passage. It was the same as what he'd seen in the room when he spoke to Jinirlyn, except that there was only one this time. It had no door but was simply an opening; the white tunnel stretched on inside it.

Revan moved into the doorway and was in another tube of light, but this time he didn't go flying down it. He moved through it as if he were walking. And if he stopped, he stopped. There was choice in this place, not like in the other tunnels where it was as if he was a passenger on a bird as it flew. He moved deeper and in a very short time sensed a change in the color of the tunnel. It appeared to be turning pink. The further he moved, the darker the pink became until eventually it was a dull, dark red the same color as the threads he'd seen in Asplan. Ahead of him he could make out the end of the tunnel and what appeared to be a void. As he emerged into it, he was amazed at the size of it. The entire city of Kessar could have easily fit inside. The ceiling rose up to an immense height. Revan thought that mountains could have nestled comfortably underneath it's roof. Across the floor, around the walls, and above on the ceiling writhed innumerable red threads, interspersed with a few gold ones, slithering here and there. Most were the same dark shade of red as the tunnel, but a few looked normal. Revan understood somehow that these normal looking threads were healthy and that the dark ones were somehow the source of Asplan's illness. As he watched, a few of them actually changed color to something much closer to black than red, and a few bright red ones turned dark. When they were all black, Asplan would be dead. How he knew that he wasn't sure, but Revan was certain it was true.

Something drew his attention to the healthy threads, called to him in a way he'd never experienced and didn't understand. He knew that in order to heal Asplan, he had to do something, make something happen with the healthy threads that still existed. Even as he pondered this new development, several more normal ones turned that dark, sickly red.

Without thinking and with no understanding of what he was doing, Revan stretched his mind towards the healthy threads. It was if he was using his voice to call out to another person across a distance, but it was in his mind. The threads slowed their movements, then stopped. The healthy ones raised straight up in the air, then began to glide towards him, like snakes swimming on the surface of a pond. As they reached him, they began to circle him. Faster and faster, they spun around, until they were nothing but a nearly solid red blur. Revan felt something in him join with them, some deep part of his essence. It was as if Asplan's threads were communicating with his own. There was a hint of sound, like a rumble deep in the earth that penetrated to the core of the part of Revan that was in this place. If he'd been in his body, he would have stopped still, the feeling was so intense. He had no idea how long it went on; his sense of time had been interrupted, like he was asleep, yet aware of his surroundings.

The whirling threads suddenly stopped, and Revan apprehended that time had started moving again. Asplan's healthy threads had changed. They were still the brilliant, vibrant red he was used to, yet they now possessed another quality – they had threads of their own. Much smaller versions of the red threads were twisting and turning around Asplan's healthy ones. Slowly, they moved away from Revan in the same manner they had come to him. As they got further away, they began to split up, some rose toward the ceiling, others made for the floor and walls. When they reached their destinations, they resumed flowing in their old patterns among all the other threads. Revan watched spellbound as the small threads that had been circling Asplan's healthy ones darted off and wrapped themselves around the dark red and black threads. In moments those threads had returned to the healthy red color. When one thread had been changed, the small thread moved on to another, and another, until most of them in the vast room had returned to their normal shade. As the small threads began to work their magic on the remaining ill threads, Revan felt himself pulled backwards into the tunnel. Soon he was flying back through the white, and in moments found himself back in his body, looking into the amazed and unbelieving eyes of Asplan.

"What did you do to me?" he asked, his voice low, yet unmistakably full of excitement.

"I healed you. I think," Revan replied.

"How?"

"I don't know. I just did it."

"I could feel the cough leaving me. There was a noise, no a rumble… no it was both. Inside me. Then I started to feel better. Now I feel completely normal." Asplan's eyes were wide with wonder and appreciation.

"I'm happy I was able to help," Revan said, dropping his eyes. He felt a little embarrassed at the look of gratitude on Asplan's face.

"Why would you help me after what I did to you and Arval? I broke the laws."

"It was a mistake. You didn't know who we were. You were just doing what you thought was your job."

"I wish Plistral had seen it that way."

"Well, your Khet has rules. And you broke one. He had to do what he thought was right too… I asked him to take you back."

"You did?!"

"I told him the same thing I told you. Whether he will or not, I don't know. But you shouldn't be put out of the Khet for a mistake."

"I don't know what I can do to thank you," Asplan said. "But if you ever need my help, or need anything, I'm there." He was silent for a moment, his eyes distant. "I wish I could have met you before my father died. Maybe you could have healed him too."

"What was your father like?"

"He was the best man I've ever known. My mother left us when I was a baby; I don't remember her at all. My father took care of us. He drove teams of horses for the merchants here, hauling loads of goods around Jarradan. I went with him since there was no one to care for me. He taught me many things before he died."

"Was he an honest man?"

"The most honest I've ever known."

"Then this is how you can repay me: live your life like he did. Be an honest man. If you ever have a son of your own, care for him the way your father cared for you. Make your father and your son proud of you."

"You have my word," Asplan said, grasping Revan's hand to seal their agreement. They looked into each other's eyes a moment, then Revan rose and went back into the hive to find a bed.

Revan woke early. Most of the rest of the Khet were still asleep, but a few were up preparing the morning meal. He stretched and yawned as he threw back the light cover he'd slept under. Arval was still sound asleep on the pallet beside his. Moving quietly so as not to wake him, Revan stood and pulled on his boots. He stepped gingerly around the sleeping boys and made his way to the cookfire where a couple of the Khet were stirring something in a large pot and another had just put a smaller pot with a lid on it next to the coals after pouring something into a mug from it.

"Sleep well?" the one who had handled the small pot asked.

"Very well, thanks."

"The food isn't ready yet. Would you like some coffee?"

"Coffee?" Revan asked.

"Yes coffee."

"I suppose. I've never had it. What is it?"

The young man gave him a puzzled look. "It's a drink most people have in the morning. Helps wake you up. You've never heard of it? Really?"

"No, I haven't. But sure, I'll try some.

The boy took the pot out of the fire, lifted the lid, and slowly poured a portion of the dark liquid inside into a mug. Steam rose from it, as did a thick, heavy, but not unpleasant aroma Revan had never smelled before.

"It smells wonderful."

"Try it. But just take a sip – it's very hot."

Revan poured a little into his mouth. The boy was right – it was hot. But delicious. He felt it burn all the way down his throat. The heavy, slightly smoky flavor was unlike any food or drink he'd tried yet. After a couple more sips, he realized the boy was doubly right, it had definitely helped chase sleep away; Revan felt invigorated in a way he never had before from food or drink.

"I'm not hungry, but thanks for the coffee. When Arval wakes up tell him I'll be back later. I want to go explore a bit."

The boy nodded and told him not to get lost.

Revan finished his coffee and climbed the ladder up out of the basement and into what remained of the burned-out building. Where to go, he thought as he looked both ways down the street in front of him. Maybe he should go to The Needle and Thread, tell Endanna that Fendalon said hello. But shouldn't Arval be with him? He was better at talking to strangers than

Revan was. No, he needed to learn how to do that for himself. They could always stop in some other time and Arval could introduce himself. His decision made he set off in the direction of the shop.

The city was mostly still asleep. A few people were moving about. Some street vendors were setting out their wares on tables, preparing for the day's customers. As he passed a very run-down building with a sign that said The Full Mug, he saw two men in grubby, threadbare clothes struggling to hoist a dead man into a cart. Curious, Revan walked up to them.

"Excuse me?" he said. "What happened here?"

"So, who might you be that you want to ask questions this early in the morning?" one of them said gruffly.

"Just someone new to the city."

The man sighed, as if he was used to people asking him his business, but also annoyed that he had to explain it again. "Well, this fellow's dead and we're cleaning up the mess."

"So, are you cleaners then?"

"For someone new to the city, you seem to know a bit about it. Enough to know about cleaners anyway."

"My friend told me about you. About your job that is. That you clean up the city."

"Well, yeah, that we do. What's it to you?" he asked defensively and with more than a hint of aggression.

Revan could tell he didn't really want to talk. The other man ignored him completely.

"I'm just trying to learn about this place. Sorry I bothered you."

"Off with you then," the man said brusquely, returning to the body.

Revan could see a cut in the middle of shirt the man wore, and a dark stain all around it. A drying pool of blood lay on the ground where his body had been. This place was probably a tavern, and it looked like someone had stabbed the man sometime last night, probably in a drunken rage. Sensing he wasn't going to get anything else from the two cleaners, Revan walked away.

He found The Needle and Thread not long after passing by the dead man. Its door was locked. Since it wasn't open yet, he turned onto one of the main roads and headed north towards the Azure Palace. Some time later he found himself on the edge of White Square. Its gleaming white stone stretched out in front of him for a good distance. He guessed that it could hold several thousand people with room to spare. To his left the hill on which the palace lay rose high into the sky. At its summit stood the far eastern end of the palace itself. The blue stone glowed in the morning light, its battlements, ramparts and towers soared above him. Revan stared at it in awe. How someone could have conceived such a magnificent structure, let alone built it, was beyond his comprehension. Seeing it from a distance was one thing. Standing right underneath it was quite another. Its size and intricacy left him speechless.

"Never seen the palace before?" a voice behind him said.

Revan turned to look at the person the voice had come from. He found himself looking into a face hidden in the shadows created by a dark blue cowl. Below it he saw light grey leather armor embossed with a familiar symbol – a scroll crossed with a sword.

"You're Jix!" he said excitedly.

"Never seen one of us before either, I take it?" the man asked, a tinge of amusement in his voice.

"No Sir! Never! But I've heard of you."

The man sighed. "Yes, I'm afraid our reputation precedes me. Don't worry. I'm not going to kill you, if that's what you're thinking. We only kill if we have to."

"No Sir, I don't think you're going to kill me. It's just that I met someone once. Someone who used to be one of you. But you're the first... active Jix I've ever met."

"Who would that be? Maybe I know him."

'I probably shouldn't have said anything,' Revan thought, suddenly remembering Fendalon's admonishment not to mention meeting him to anyone else. "I didn't actually catch his name. But he said he'd been one of you."

"And you just believed him?"

"He didn't seem to be a liar."

"So, you know how to judge the truth and lies people speak?"

"I can usually tell when someone is good or bad," he said.

"That didn't really answer the question though, did it?"

Revan gulped. His mind suddenly went blank. The man laughed then and clapped him on the shoulder. "Don't worry about it. I just like to watch people squirm. You seem like a good lad. Whether you know one of us or not doesn't matter." His playful tone changed suddenly to a more serious one. "Be careful around here. The City Wardens don't like trouble. And they're quick to deal harshly with anyone they even think might cause some."

The man turned and started walking away. Revan's mind was spinning. He'd just met a Jix. One of the men who lived in the place he was trying to get into, and he'd just let him walk away without even trying to find a way in.

"Wait, Sir!" he called out after him.

The Jix turned back to him, his face still hidden in the shadows of his dark blue cowl. "Yes?" he said, much less friendly than he had been a moment before.

Revan walked up to him. "If someone wanted to, uh, learn your history, how would he go about it?"

The Jix considered him for a moment; it seemed forever to Revan. It was unsettling not seeing the man's eyes, shrouded as they were in his cowl. At last, he spoke. "That person would have to be one of us," he said simply.

"How would someone go about joining you? Become a Jix that is?"

The man stared silently at him again for another long moment. "Do you seek to join?"

Revan's mind whirled with conflicting thoughts. He might not get another chance, if this actually was a chance. But what about Arval? What would Arval think if he ran off to join the Jix? Would he ever see him again, or be able to tell him what had happened? Would Arval think he'd been murdered somewhere, his lifeless body thrown into a cart by a crew of cleaners like the dead man earlier? He was torn between loyalty to his friend and his desire to learn where the other Kryxaal were.

"The man I met, his name is Fendalon," he said, his decision made.

The Jix stepped closer. "Did you say Fendalon?" he asked quietly.

"Yes."

"And how would you know him?" the Jix asked skeptically.

"I met him several days ago. He allowed my friend and I to stay a night with him in his home. He made us promise not to tell anyone we'd met him or where he was."

"Then you've broken a promise."

"Yes, but I have my reasons."

"And what might those reasons be?"

"I can't tell you that."

"So, what should I think? You play coy with me, then break a promise you made to a man I greatly respect, whom I regard as a brother, now you won't tell me the reason why you broke it. Why should I believe anything you've said?" the Jix said menacingly. His hand rested on the hilt of his sword. Revan realized he had moments at best to convince this man or his chance was gone for good. And who knew, maybe his life too. Desperate, Revan raised his right hand and showed the

Jix the small silver ring he wore on his short finger. The man leaned in closer and grabbed Revan's wrist, pulling it towards his cowl.

"Where did you get that?!" he asked, anger evident in his voice.

"I found it. On a skeleton in the desert. After I escaped from the pit."

The Jix' hand relaxed on his wrist. "So, you were at the pit. You were a digger then?"

"Yes. I escaped when it… disappeared."

"Come with me," he said, turning and striding away.

Chapter 25

arittin strode through the halls of the Azure Palace lost in thought. The sound of his boots on the blue stone floor echoed back to him across the enormous hall as he entered. The throne room was one of his favorite places to think, and to conduct meetings with his eyes and ears. Its vast openness provided no vantage for spies. He was certain that his chambers had ears, as did most of the rest of the palace. The throne room was the only place where he could be sure he wouldn't be overheard. The guards posted at evenly spaced intervals around the enormous room were too far away to hear anything clearly. Meeting someone here was risky, but only in the sense that a spy could report that he'd seen two people talking, not what they'd actually said. Barittin didn't care who saw him talking; he talked to people all the time – it was part of his duty to the king. And that staff was well aware of his penchant for thinking while strolling through this room. He'd made a point early on in Vraniss' reign of making sure they got used to seeing him here. The man he was going to meet in a moment wouldn't arouse suspicion from anyone watching. A moment later he saw him emerge from a corridor on his left. Barittin kept pacing, pretending not to see him.

"My Lord Barittin," the man said.

Barittin looked up, pretending to be startled out of his reverie.

"Virta, what can I do for you?" Barittin asked. Voices carried in this room the way his footsteps had, but the vastness of the space caused words to become garbled and indistinct the farther away from the speaker a listener was. And there was no one close to the two of them.

"I've learned that the mission the king plans to send Clammalod on is not to research the history of King Travorik, but to look into a completely different matter."

"And what might that matter be? Do you know?"

"It has something to do with that giant stone box that was dug out of the ground up in the northern desert. The one that disappeared under such… unusual circumstances."

"Specifics man! What is the king looking for?"

"It would appear," Virta said, "that the structure was not the only one of its kind."

"What do you mean not the only one?"

"There are apparently three more of them secreted in various places around the world. The king is going to send Clammalod to discover their locations."

"Well, this is an interesting bit of news. But why would the king care where the others are. More importantly, what are they? What purpose do, or did, they serve?"

"They seem to contain a power of some kind. Its exact nature remains beyond my knowledge, but it is a power that the king desires. And he isn't the only one."

"What do you mean not the only one? Who else is looking for these things?"

"Otarab."

"And how would you know that he is looking for them too?"

"The palace isn't the only place I have ears. And eyes. A man who works for me in Otarab's villa was able to partially read the contents of a letter he wrote to someone in the Udron Library named Clatri. The letter stated that Otarab would be coming to Enrat personally to look into a matter they'd discussed on one of Otarab's previous visits. The last thing my man was able to read before he had to run to escape discovery was something about the structure in the desert, the three others, and how it's power could lead them to their ultimate goal."

Barittin frowned at Virta. He'd had no idea that this palace functionary was as well connected as he'd just revealed. Even the king hadn't been able to get someone into Otarab's palace. As far as he knew. Barittin himself had tried on numerous occasions to place ears next to Otarab, and had had zero success. Perhaps Virta was more resourceful than Barittin gave him credit for. He'd have to watch this one more closely from now on. But what was more important at the moment was the interest the king and Otarab both seemed to have in these structures and the power they were said to contain. He wondered idly what it could be. Whatever it was, it must be something quite powerful to have prompted such unusual actions from them both. Maybe it was time for Barittin to visit Enrat himself.

"Thank you Virta. Your services are, as always, invaluable. You'll find your payment in the usual place."

Virta nodded, and with a deferential, "Thank you My Lord Barittin," turned and walked away.

Otarab's head cracked into the ceiling of the carriage. "Watch the ruts you worm," he yelled at the driver. A muffled reply of contrition came back to him through the open window. The ride so far had been mildly unpleasant. It was too warm, the road too rough, the food too plain. Otarab wondered briefly if perhaps there wasn't a better way to travel than by carriage over these cursed roads. He'd been away from his villa in Kessar for over a week, and looked forward longingly to arriving in Enrat. The letter he'd sent ahead to Clatri would probably arrive in another week. Correspondence between kingdoms was usually carried by horse and rider – a significantly faster method of travel than by carriage. But Otarab would never ride a horse. The smell alone revolted him. Not to mention the road and the filthy animals would ruin his immaculate and expensive robes. That was what galled him the most

– the destruction of his apparel such a journey would surely cause. Otarab was not a man to change his ways, or his dress, simply to ride a horse. What he didn't like to admit to himself was that he was afraid of horses. They threw people all the time. His sedentary lifestyle had made him soft; being thrown from a horse would surely be his end. His physical weakness was not something he acknowledged to himself either, except in the deepest recesses of his mind, where the darkest parts of him dwelled. Otarab preferred not to ponder his weaknesses unless they were forced into his view somehow. And he was quick to bury them again as soon as he could.

The guard that rode next to the driver leaned back and called in the open window, "It's getting late My Lord. We'll be having to stop for the night soon."

"Is there a traveler's rest nearby?" He'd hired this carriage to take him to Enrat, and these men were well-traveled; they should know where all the best places to sleep indoors were along the route. Otarab had chosen them for their skills and knowledge and had been required to sleep outside only once so far on this journey. The men had told him that he would inevitably have to; traveler's rests were just too far apart in some areas. For these occasions Otarab had brought a tent and a number of pillows, which he'd paid the men to erect and lay out for him. That night hadn't been terrible. The sounds of the forest at night were the worst, but the men had taken turns on watch while he slept as best he could. They were both skilled with weapons, another requirement Otarab demanded when he'd decided to make this journey. He didn't really fear for his life from bandits; most of them worked their schemes closer to cities where the prey was more plentiful. The wilderness where they were now was inhabited mainly by animals and the occasional hermit or homesteading family, scratching a life out of the dirt. Those people were no threat.

"No, My Lord, the next traveler's rest is far too distant to reach before sunset."

"Fine," Otarab sighed. "Find a decent flat place to put up my tent if I can't have a proper room and meal tonight then," Otarab replied to the man. With a tip of the cap in acknowledgement, the face disappeared from the window.

Another night outside listening to the creatures of the forest was not his idea of time well spent. But there was nothing for it. He'd have an extra mug of ale from one of the casks he'd brought. That would help him sleep. He would have brought cloud wine, but he'd been told the glass bottles wouldn't survive the trip. So, he'd have to make do with ale stored in sturdy wooden casks like some city cleaner in a tavern.

It wasn't long before he felt the carriage slowing, then turning to the right. The driver and his companion seemed to have found their spot to stop. When the carriage came to a halt, he heard the men jump down from the driver's seat. The one who'd spoken earlier, Otarab thought his name was Lofser, told him it would be a few minutes before his tent was ready. He briefly pondered staying in the carriage but decided to get out and walk a bit. A stretch would do him good after hours of sitting and bouncing.

He saw that the driver (he didn't care what that man's name was, one name for men of his status was enough for him to know) had indeed found a fairly flat place to stop. They were on top of a low hill that strangely wasn't covered by trees. Most places in this part of the world were. Later, once they entered Drisava, the trees would give way to rolling grassland and plains dotted with ponds and lakes. Otarab glanced to the south and saw the enormous black sphere spinning slowly, its arms disappearing below the horizon, the gold and red threads shooting through them like lightning. He wondered idly what lay beyond it. There were stories to be heard if one had ears for them. But Otarab suspected they were all just conjecture or boasting. No one he'd ever heard of had been beyond that gigantic spinning black mass in the sky. It was said that the swirling arms touched the earth far to the south, and that anyone who attempted to pass through them disappeared forever. Otarab had never been far enough south to see if the arms actually did reach the earth, but he suspected the stories were true about that part. He watched the violent undulations for a moment, the shiny ebony peaks lifting up from the arms and collapsing down into shadow-dark valleys, before turning to his escorts. They had erected his tent and were just finishing filling it with pillows. A cask of ale sat next to the tent's opening. Otarab walked over and filled a mug which had been set on the ground beside it. As he was finishing his first sip, the sound of a wagon reached his ears. It seemed to be coming from the same direction his carriage had. A moment later he realized there was more than one. When the first wagon drew abreast of their camp, it slowed to a halt and an older man jumped down, raising his hand in greeting.

"Hello! Mind if we share your camp for the night? It's just myself, my wife and son."

Otarab's escorts looked at him for approval. "Of course. There's safety in numbers and all that, right?" he said.

"Thank you Sir," the man said. He led his horses off the road and to a spot a little ways from Otarab's tent. A second and third wagon followed him. A young man and an older woman alighted from their seats and began unharnessing their horses. When they'd finished setting up their camp and caring for their teams, the three newcomers walked over to Otarab's camp where his escorts were just finishing cooking an evening meal of stew.

"Would you like to join us?" Otarab asked.

"We've already eaten, but we'd enjoy some company if that's alright with you," the older man said. He spread a blanket on the ground and sat down, his wife and son following suit.

"Well, if we're going to share a camp, we should have each other's names," Otarab said as he extended his hand to the man. He shook it and introduced himself, "I'm Anden," he said, "and this is my wife Poli and my son Denen."

"Pleased to meet you, I'm Otarab. My companions can introduce themselves – they're big boys," he said, not wanting to let on that he only remembered one of their names.

"I'm Lofser and this is Denival," the wagon driver said.

After handshakes all around, Otarab offered the newcomers a draught from his cask of ale. He'd brought four and this one wasn't even half empty. There was plenty for all. Even though Otarab generally didn't associate with people of lower social status, as these obviously were, he'd found that on occasion they could be useful. In this instance he put his prejudices aside and welcomed them.

"Where are you coming from?" Otarab asked. His escorts wouldn't speak unless spoken to; they knew their place. And his, as the client with the links.

"We're on our way home from Kessar. Just finished selling our early summer wheat to the bakeries there."

"Ah, merchants then are you?"

"Not really, just farmers. We play the part of merchant when we sell our crops, but we're people of the land at heart, happiest digging in the soil and watching things grow."

"Truly a noble profession," Otarab said, and not sarcastically. While he had disdain for most people he believed were below his station, there was a soft spot in his heart for farmers. After all, they were the ones who produced much of the food he so loved to indulge in. Their vocation was one worthy of respect. He was secretly glad that he'd offered them his ale.

"Thank you My Lord Otarab," Anden replied.

"No need to use titles with me," he said. "I'm not a lord, just a man traveling as you are. Please, just call me Otarab."

"As you wish, Otarab," Anden replied with a nod of his head. "Your rich garb made me think you must certainly be a representative of the king or some high palace official."

"No, I'm just a man on my way to visit a relative I've not seen in a long time."

"I wish your journey to be a safe one," Anden said. "These roads can harbor bandits. Why my family and I were accosted by ten of them on our way into the city. We were quite fortunate to have encountered two young men who were able to deal with them. I swear, I never saw anyone move so fast."

Otarab's curiosity perked up at the story. "Two young men you say? They dealt with them? What did they do?"

"They killed them. All ten of them. Well, one killed nine, the other killed one. The first one, for my eyes I never saw anyone move like that. I'm an old man and I've seen any number of strange and odd things in my life. That boy was the fastest I've ever seen. He could move like a gale. The bandits didn't have a chance against him. He cut them down like we cut our wheat."

Otarab was intrigued. He recalled the report of two of his diggers escaping from the pit. And how fast they'd run across the ramp of light. Could this be them? His instincts told him it was. "Did they offer their names," he asked.

"They did. They were very nice young men. Had they wanted, they could have cut the three of us down and stolen our wheat, sold it for themselves. But they were as polite as a petitioner at the king's court. The first one's name was... I don't recall. Poli! Denen! What were those boys' names?"

"The fast one was Revan," Poli said.

"The other was Arval," replied Denen.

Make sure this gets to Kessar as quickly as possible," Otarab told the man behind the bar at the traveler's rest. After parting from Anden and his family that morning, they'd come upon the rest in the early afternoon. Otarab had insisted they stop even though Lofser had told him there was another rest further up the road which they could still reach before sunset. He'd relented when Otarab offered more coin. Money could make just about anything happen. The owner of the rest had been happy to have customers with links and had provided Otarab with paper, pen and ink, which he'd used to write a letter to Hento. In it he described the incident Anden had told him about, including physical descriptions of the two boys and their names. He'd made clear that Hento was to find those two boys at any cost. When he had them, he was to hold them until Otarab returned. There was a place, a tiny room, in the bowels of his villa in Kessar where they were to be housed under heavy guard. He'd also made sure to tell

Hento how dangerous they were and to use every caution and plenty of men when apprehending them. His letter finished, Otarab had folded it into an envelope and affixed his wax seal to the flap.

This traveler's rest was a waypoint for the messengers who carried letters and correspondence throughout the kingdom. That was something else Otarab thought he should look into – getting a piece of the messenger service for himself. It was privately owned and operated; the king and his functionaries had nothing to do with it, other than using it (and taxing it of course), and he'd heard it was quite profitable. He sighed. That was something for another day.

After he'd made certain that the man knew how quickly this letter was to get to Kessar and receiving assurances that it would be there within three days, he'd ordered a plate of roasted meat and vegetables, with the best wine the man had, and retired to his room. He had more plans to make

Chapter 26

evan was gone when Arval woke. A quick look around and a couple well-placed questions confirmed his suspicion that he'd left to explore the city. Arval doubted that he'd find Revan simply by wandering the streets; that boy's sense of adventure and inquisitiveness was going to get him in trouble. Instead of rushing after him, Arval sat down at one of the tables set up by the cookfire and enjoyed the first cup of coffee he'd had since he'd been abducted and sent to the pit. He was in ecstasy at the first sip. Coffee had always been one of his favorite drinks, and there was nothing like a hot mug of it first thing in the morning when sleep's armies still occupied territory in his mind. The breakfast that had been prepared was hearty, full of eggs and potatoes, and left Arval feeling like he wanted to go back to bed, despite the coffee. With a sigh he stood up and made his way up the ladder to the street. He'd meant to tell Plistral more about his adventures since being abducted, but his friend was nowhere to be seen. Story time would come later then.

It was late morning now and the streets were busy with people about their day's business. Arval decided to go to The Needle and Thread first to see if Endanna had perhaps seen Revan. It didn't take him long to find it; he knew these streets and all the good shortcuts. The door to the shop stood wedged open when he arrived; it was turning into a very warm day.

Arval walked in and immediately noticed the beautiful girl working on some fabric at a long table. She looked up and smiled as he stepped closer.

"Good day," she said in a cheerful voice. "Can I help you find something?"

Arval just stared at her a moment. She seemed to be about his age. Her blond hair cascaded down the sides of her round face and fell across her shoulders in waves. She had dark brown eyes that sparkled as she smiled and perfect white teeth behind full lips. "Are you looking for something?" she prompted, her eyebrows slightly raised.

"Uhh, yes, um, that is, I'm looking for my friend," Arval stammered. Ordinarily he was perfectly comfortable speaking to strangers, but this girl's beauty had utterly disarmed him.

"Well, do you see him in here?"

"No," Arval gulped. "But he might have come in earlier today."

"What does he look like? What's his name?"

"His name is, um, Revan and he's, uh, tall."

"That's it? He's tall?"

"Well, he has these blue eyes. They're the same color as the, the... stone of the palace. And he has this, er, black hair that comes to his, ah, shoulders."

"That's a little better description. But no, I haven't seen anyone who looks like that come in here today. Why do you think he'd be here?"

"We, uh, a friend of ours, um, wanted us to deliver a message to the woman who, ah, owns this shop. Endanna?"

"She's my grandmother. She's not here right now, but she'll be back soon. Would you like me to give her the message?"

"No, that's all right... I'll come back later," Arval said.

"Fine. Good day to you then," she said.

Arval wandered out the door in a daze. He couldn't get her face out of his head. A sudden thought caused him to go back into the store.

"What's your name?" he asked.

The girl smiled knowingly. "My name is Valbirnia," she said. "What's yours?"

"Arval," he said with a smile that wasn't forced or awkward.

He wandered the streets for a few hours, reacquainting himself with his old haunts. Not much had changed in the months he'd been away. Vendors still cried out for customers, each trying to be louder and more vociferous than their competitors. It seemed they believed vocal volume alone would attract customers. The cacophony didn't even register on Arval. His thoughts were occupied with Valbirnia. Her beauty dwarfed that of any girl he'd ever seen. He kept trying to think of a reason to go back and talk to her. Since he'd left the shop, he'd been berating himself for being so tongue-tied in talking to her. Talking to people had always been easy for him. Up until he'd met her. She'd utterly destroyed his capacity for wit and banter just by looking at him. Maybe he could bring her a bunch of flowers. Girls liked flowers. But he didn't have any money. Well, he thought, his old pickpocket skills could be put to use. He just needed a rich merchant with deep pockets. White Square was the place for that. The market there would be going full bore by now, and there'd be lots of rich folk looking to spend their links. He didn't much like White Square because of the memory of his mother, but he'd been able to put most of that pain behind him and walk through it like anyone else visiting the market. Flowers for Valbirnia helped dissipate his melancholy and focus his resolve.

He soon reached White Square and was not disappointed in the number of available pockets. Normally Arval would have worked the crowd with a partner, but since he didn't have one, he'd have to resort to other tactics. It didn't take him long to spot a potentially lucrative mark, and he quickly formulated a plan. The pocket was a middle-aged man who was carrying something in a sack made of rough brown fabric. The man was dressed in obviously expensive clothes, but what caught Arval's attention was his beautifully embroidered green jacket on which was a pocket that fairly bulged with what he suspected was a purse full of links.

The man was perusing jewelry on some vendor's table, the sack cradled in his right arm, when Arval approached and stood next to him, pretending to look at the jewelry. He leaned to his left, closer to the man, and reached out with his left hand, intentionally bumping into the bundle, and knocking it to the ground. The man turned quickly towards him, irritation on his face. Arval affected a surprised and chagrined face and bent down to retrieve the bundle, apologizing profusely to the man for his clumsiness. As he rose with the sack in his right hand, his left went to the man's pocket where he'd seen the bulge and deftly lifted it out. A quick movement placed it into the pocket of his trousers where he felt its weight settle next to his thigh. "I'm so terribly sorry Sir," he said, handing the bundle to the man. "Forgive me. I was just trying to get a better look at a necklace I believe my girl might enjoy."

"You should be sorry. Don't be so self-absorbed. Try thinking of others instead of just yourself," the man admonished him.

Arval was about to reply when he heard a commotion behind the man and someone shouted, "Thief!" He looked up and saw three black clad Wardens coming straight for him led by a man in common clothes. He knew instantly they'd seen his play on the man with the bundle and that he had to get away, and quickly. Spinning around, he ran off into the crowd, the shouts of the Wardens and their leader close behind him. If he could get into the warren of streets away from the square, he could lose them easily. In this open space they could call other Wardens to head him off and box him in. He was closest to the southern edge of the square, but that's where the Wardens were coming from. He'd have to head north and hope to evade any others that might join the chase. His decision made; he increased his speed as he made for the far side of the square.

He skirted and wove through people and vendors as he ran, occasionally leaping over a table or display of some item or other. Once a woman walked right in front of him and he knocked her to the ground without slowing. She should have been looking up and around instead of down at whatever trinket she had in her hands, he thought. People were always so distracted by the things they held. The north side of the square was rapidly approaching; Arval could see several streets ahead of him across the immense open area. He chose one to the left and made for it in as straight a line as he was able. There weren't many vendors on this side of the square, which consequently meant there were fewer people browsing. The way being fairly uncongested, Arval increased his speed again. The opening of the street loomed large in front of him. He was now running as fast as he had on the ramp of light when the Kryxaal was disappearing behind him. The voices of the shouting Wardens were growing fainter as he distanced himself from them. Wind blew his hair out behind him, and people turned to gape at how fast he was moving. Their amazed expressions barely registered in his thoughts; he was consumed with escape, not in how he was impressing people with how fast he could run. The mouth of the street suddenly was to either side of him, the walls of buildings rose to either side and shadows fell across his path. Arval didn't know this part of the city as well as he did the southern part of it, but he knew enough to find his way out. A couple quick turns took him completely out of sight of his pursuers, and he slowed to a pace that wouldn't attract as much attention. He remembered that there was another bridge on the north side of the city. If he could get to it and cross to the other side of the river, he could make his way back south to the Hive.

He no longer heard the Wardens behind him, so he slowed to a jog and began angling back towards the river. In a short time, he came out onto a broad avenue that ran parallel to it, the river's waters sparkled in the sun. Ahead a short distance he saw the bridge. It was only a few moments before he turned and began to cross it, walking now to avoid any extra attention. He was sweating and panting, which was enough to make people look askance at him. Running would just cause them to look harder.

Midway across the bridge he paused to catch his breath. Arval stood looking down into the water flowing below when a hand on his shoulder caused him to jump and turn around. He found himself looking into the shadows of a dark blue cowl. He knew without looking down that underneath the hidden face he'd see light grey leather armor embossed with the image of a scroll overlaid by a sword.

"That was some performance, getting away from the Wardens like that," the Jix said.

"I suppose," Arval stammered.

"You do know that the man you robbed was just a decoy, right?"

"A decoy? What do you mean?"

"The Wardens have been investigating thieves in the city. One of their favorite places to work is White Square. So, the Wardens put a man out there dressed as a rich merchant, and put a purse full of rocks in his pocket to attract thieves. Once the purse gets stolen, they are able to arrest the offender."

Arval reached in his pocket and pulled out the purse. No sense hiding it from the Jix; the man knew all about it anyway. If he was going to be arrested or die, then he wanted to at least know what was in the purse. He untied the drawstring and peered in. Rocks, as he'd been told. Arval held his hand out over the river and upended the bag, watching as the stones splashed into the water below.

"I can't believe I fell for that," he said, more to himself than the man in grey leather in front of him. The Jix laughed heartily.

"Been doing this a while have you?" he asked good-naturedly.

"Yes," Arval muttered. "It's how I've survived since my mother was executed in White Square when I was a child."

"I'm sorry to hear that. Lots of people have lost loved ones in that square," he said, his mirth fading. "Its sometimes hard to think that people sell and buy things there considering how many people have died on that spot. Its morbid."

Arval remained silent for a time. Thoughts of his mother's death had suddenly invaded his mind. He pushed them away with effort and regarded the Jix in front of him. He realized that this was the first time he'd ever actually spoken to one. He sighed, resigned to whatever his fate was to be.

"So, what are you going to do with me now that I'm caught?" he asked.

"Do you think I'm going to arrest you? If you do, forget about that right now. The Wardens arrest people; the Jix don't. Actually, I was going ask if you'd like to join us."

Arval was speechless. His mouth had suddenly gone dry, and words had fled in fright from his mind.

"Caught you by surprise did I?" the Jix asked, his voice hinted that he was smiling.

"Uhh, yes," Arval stammered. He couldn't remember ever being struck nearly speechless twice in one day before. But it had happened on this day. Things surely had changed since he met Revan.

"So, would you like to try to join us? Or shall I leave you for the Wardens. The lot of them will have your description by now. It's unlikely you'll make it back to wherever your home is without being caught. With me, you'll be safe. For now."

"Not much of a choice is it?" Arval asked.

The Jix laughed again. "Not one I'd want to have to make. But it's not my choice. It's yours. Now make it quickly before I rescind the offer."

"Of course, I'll try."

"Good. Let's go then," the Jix said as he turned and walked back the way Arval had come. Yes, Revan had created all sorts of chaos in Arval's life.

Chapter 27

anar couldn't believe his eyes. Arval had just run past him faster than he'd ever seen anyone move. He'd been certain that his two former companions would die in the mountains. They hadn't known much of anything about how to survive in the wild. Apparently they were more resourceful than he'd given them credit for.

Kanar had been in the city for several days, trying to find a way to join the Jix. He'd been completely unsuccessful. Every time he'd approached one of them, on the infrequent times he actually found one walking the streets, he'd been gruffly told to disappear before something bad happened to him. The methods they used for recruiting members to their order were a mystery to him, and he was beginning to lose heart in his self-appointed mission.

On the other hand, he'd seen plenty of Nojii. The city was fairly crawling with them. After the events at the pit, it seemed that all of them who'd been there, and many more besides, had migrated to Kessar. The city's taverns attracted them like rats to a midden heap. Not many days went by when he didn't see cleaners loading up another body whose life had departed thanks to a Nojii blade. The cleaners had been busy since they'd arrived. Kanar hadn't tried to hide from them; there were only one or two who he thought might recognize him. Diggers had been faceless objects to the Nojii at the pit. One looked much like another to them.

What Kanar had done since he'd arrived was listen to them. He'd been able to scrounge a few links performing odd jobs for vendors, which in turn had allowed him to buy the occasional meal in a tavern, where he'd been sure to sit close enough to the Nojii to overhear their conversations. He kept hearing Hento's name mentioned in regard to some order issued by a high ranking Nojii official. They were looking for someone, but he'd been unable to learn who or why.

Hento. He was in the city. Somewhere. If Kanar could find out where, he could set a trap for that hated man and rid the world of his vile presence. Since joining the Jix was not working as he'd hoped, Kanar decided that he'd just have to have his revenge some other way.

He turned back to the merchant who'd hired him for the day to help guard his wares against thieves. This particular merchant sold pottery plates and bowls. They were roughly made but sturdy, and the man charged a fair price for them. Most thieves weren't interested in stealing kitchenware, unless they needed a bowl to eat from, so Kanar, while employed for the day, was bored. Business was slow here in the northern part of White Square. The best places for merchants were in the southern section. Yet even here the man sold a few things.

Kanar knew there was no way he'd have been able to catch up to Arval, as fast as he'd been running. The boy must have a bit of that magic that Revan had told him about. That was the only explanation for his speed. He'd suspected there was much that Revan hadn't told him about that particular subject. What he'd just seen seemed to confirm it. The merchant and some other people were still marveling at the sight they'd witnessed. One of them claimed that the boy had been moving faster than even the swiftest horse. They were all wondering how it was possible to move like that. Kanar kept quiet and looked around, maintaining his vigil for the non-existent thieves even as his mind raced.

Arval had told them of his Khet and how he'd lived with them after his mother's death. They were coming to the city to join with them, but what they planned to do after that was a mystery to Kanar. He sighed in resignation. The plan to join the Jix seemed to have died like a nascent fire in the rain. He needed a new plan. Working as a watchman for a merchant was not how he wanted to spend his days. His thoughts turned to the Nojii. He wanted them dead. All of them. Especially Hento. But how to get close to him? He'd have to find him first. But how to do that? They kept mostly to themselves. He rarely saw people with the Nojii who weren't of the Nojii. But he had seen a few. Young men like himself. He wondered idly if someone could join the Nojii like they could the Jix or the Wardens. Only one way to find out - try. But he needed an angle, a story, something that he could tell one of them or do in order to be accepted. Kanar knew a tavern where several of them liked to congregate in the evenings over drink. When he was done working on preventing thievery, he'd pay that tavern a visit. He had the rest of the day to come up with a story.

Kanar sat on a stool at the bar slowly eating a plate of steaming meat covered with gravy. A mug of cheap ale sat next to the plate, half of it gone. There were five Nojii at a table behind him, their voices getting louder with each mug of ale that disappeared down their throats. He'd decided that the best way to get their attention was to show them that he could be as violent as they were. The Nojii loved nothing more than a good brawl, and Kanar intended to give one to them. He was just waiting for his opportunity. It didn't take long for it to arrive.

One of the Nojii had come to the bar to harangue the barkeep, a frail looking woman with ratty hair and a greasy, stained dress. He'd demanded better ale than the swill they'd been served earlier. The barkeep was obviously terrified of the big man and was trying her best to placate him while trying to make him understand that what she'd served them was the best the tavern had. But the Nojii was having none of it. He was yelling and cursing at the poor woman while his arms gesticulated wildly. Kanar leaned slightly to his right as the Nojii entered a particularly vociferous portion of the diatribe and made sure to get his head in the way of the big man's elbow. It only glanced off his temple, but Kanar still saw a flash of light from the unintentional blow he'd made sure to receive. The force of it caused him to swoon a little, but he recovered quickly and hopped off his stool to face the Nojii.

"Hey! Watch your elbows you rancid cow!" he said. Kanar knew the insult would turn the man's anger away from the frightened barkeep and to him. He was right. The Nojii balled his fists and swung one at Kanar without a word. He was fast. The fist was at his head before Kanar could really react. All he was able to do was turn his head a bit as the blow connected with his cheek. Pain exploded in his head and he staggered a few steps to the side. Shaking his head to clear it, he ran straight at the Nojii and wrapped his arms around the big man's waist, driving him back into the bar. With a whoosh the man's breath left him and he slumped a little, just enough that Kanar was able to drive his knee up into the man's stomach, further separating his breath from his lungs. As the man sank to the floor, Kanar swung a fist at his head which connected with his temple. The Nojii's eyes rolled back in his head, and his journey to the floor was punctuated with a groan.

The four Nojii at the table, none of whom had risen to help their fallen comrade, all roared with laughter. "Nolik finally met his match! And it's just a boy!" one of them cackled.

"Come on, get him up," another said. "He's supposed to buy the next round!"

"Just take his coin and pay the barkeep," shouted another. "He's not looking to be too interested in spending it!"

Kanar stood looking down at the fallen Nojii. The man's eyes had rolled back in his head, the whites stared up at him sightlessly. First part of the plan was complete, now came the second. He turned to the mirthful Nojii at the table and glared at them.

The first one to have spoken glanced at him as his laughter subsided. "So, you're good enough to take down one of us. Think you can take us all?" he asked.

Kanar shook his head. "Not four of you at once, but I'll take you one at a time if that's what you want."

"No need," the man said smiling. "It's not often one of us gets bested by a sprout. Come, sit and have an ale!" His tone wasn't menacing, and since this was what Kanar had been aiming for, he sat in the seat that had been vacated by the man on the floor. His eyes had closed, and he looked like nothing more than a passed out drunk. As Kanar watched, he groaned and began to stir.

"He'll be fine," the other Nojii said. "Let's have your name then."

"I'm Kanar," he said simply.

"I'm Adir. You already know Nolik. These others aren't worth the breath to introduce," he said as he grinned at his companions. "Drink up," he encouraged Kanar as he pushed a mug of ale towards him. "This is swill, but it'll put a man in the mood."

"Mood for what?" Kanar asked.

"For whatever we decide to do when that lump of grease finally wakes up."

"What do you usually do?"

"Whatever we want," Adir replied simply.

Nolik had come around and was trying to stand, his hand rubbing his temple where Kanar's fist had connected. Kanar watched him warily, ready to move quickly if the man decided he wanted retribution. He seemed more intent on regaining his senses than anything else, so Kanar relaxed a bit, but kept an eye on him. Adir had turned to his companions and was extolling the virtues of a well-aimed punch. He seemed to have a wealth of experience in such matters and was telling stories of punches he himself had thrown. The others roared in delight at these tales of pugilistic prowess and the effects they'd had on the unfortunate victims.

"Well, you're awake finally," Adir said to Nolik. The big man was standing now, still rubbing his head, but most definitely returning to the world of the conscious. "Our young friend here has taken your spot. Get a chair from another table."

Nolik glared at Kanar but did as he'd been told and sat down with the rest of them. "Give me a mug," he said testily.

"Yours is being used. Get another one from the barkeep."

The terrified woman had been watching them since the fight and had heard Adir. She quickly placed another mug on the bar, along with a full pitcher of ale. Nolik stood and retrieved them, and with a glare at poor woman, rejoined the revelers.

"I should take you outside and show you how to fight with a knife," he said to Kanar. Adir clapped him on the shoulder and admonished him for challenging their new friend in such a manner. Kanar just stared back at Nolik. After a moment he dropped his eyes to the table, and a sudden grin broke out on his face. "You certainly can throw a punch for one as skinny as you," he said looking back up at Kanar. He couldn't help it, and a smile broke out on Kanar's face in return.

"I've been known to throw one now and again," he said.

Nolik laughed. "Well, you fit in just fine with us."

Adir motioned to the mugs scattered around the table. "Drink them up," he said. "I've a sudden desire to see what we might find at The Full Mug. Let's go have a look, shall we?"

The others voiced their agreement. "Come on lad, let's see if we can find you some more trouble to get into!"

Chapter 28

evan followed the Jix up the winding, switchback road towards the Grey Keep. He could see its massive black gate looming above where the road ended. He really was about to enter that imposing building, he thought, slightly amazed. Fendalon's story had created an image of the place in his mind, and he'd seen it from a distance, but just like the palace had been, it was very different when you were close to it. The grey stone walls climbed straight up from the steep hillside; they looked almost as smooth as the walls of the Kryxaal had been. The towers and merlons looked like they could hide any number of soldiers. Revan idly thought that an army attempting to besiege this place could send every soldier it had against it and still not come remotely close to breaching the walls.

The Jix had been silent since he'd shown him the ring. Revan, not knowing the man's mood, had not tried to engage in conversation, but had simply followed. Now that they were approaching the keep, he felt anxiety welling up in his stomach. Would he face the same kinds of tests that Fendalon had described? He looked up from the road in front of him and was jolted in surprise - they'd arrived in front of the massive black gates. Soundlessly and without a call or signal from the Jix, they swung open just far enough to admit the two of them. Revan recalled Fendalon's tale of the tests he'd faced upon entering the keep, and he remained vigilant even as he tried not to look awed. The size of the keep made that somewhat difficult.

He heard a muffled thump and turned to see the gate had closed behind them. It was just as Fendalon had described – animal pens to the left, archery targets and various training tools to the right. Windows dotted the walls that soared above the courtyard, and Revan suspected that any number of eyes were watching as they made their way towards a simple door directly across the courtyard from the gates. Revan kept expecting the Jix to pull his sword or an arrow to fly at him, but neither thing happened. Instead, they reached the small door, which also swung open without any signal from the Jix. Revan hesitated a moment, looking at the darkness inside the door.

"Aren't you going to give me the tests?" he asked.

The Jix had stopped just inside the open door and turned to look back at him. "And why should we test you? Do you think you could pass?"

Revan nodded.

"Some other time perhaps. Right now, we have more important things to deal with. Follow me or you'll never leave this place, unless it's in the cart of a cleaner."

Revan didn't doubt the man's words. He could feel the eyes watching him, their arrows aimed at his chest, swords ready to cut him down. With no real choice, he walked through the door and into the darkness beyond.

Arval followed the Jix up the twisting road to the enormous black gates. When they were within a few paces, one of them swung silently open just enough for them to walk through. The courtyard beyond was just as Fendalon had described it. He tensed with the expectation of the sword to come swinging at his torso, the arrow to fly towards his head. The tests would happen any moment now… Except they didn't. The Jix just walked across the courtyard. No swords or arrows came his way as they had at Fendalon. Bewildered, Arval simply followed as the Jix led him to a small door on the far side of the courtyard. It too opened silently, and they passed into the shadows beyond. The door closed behind them immediately and Arval found himself in darkness.

"Where are we going?" he asked.

"Follow," the Jix responded.

"But I can't see anything."

The Jix remained silent. Arval could hear his boots on the stone floor of the passageway or room they were in and followed the sound. After several paces his right shoulder bumped into the corner of a stone wall.

"Ouch," he said, moving to his left into what appeared to be another passage; it seemed they had been in a room. The sound of the Jix' footsteps changed and Arval could tell he was climbing a set of stairs. Not wanting to fall, he moved forward gingerly until he found the first step, then began ascending behind him.

Several minutes later he heard the Jix stop. Ahead he could see the outline of a door; light filtered through cracks to either side of it. With a creak it opened, and sunlight poured in, temporarily blinding Arval, whose eyes had gotten used to the dark.

"Come," he heard the Jix say.

Blinking, Arval emerged out onto a rampart high above the courtyard. It stretched off to the left and right in straight lines, only ending at the enormous round towers at the corners of the keep. The Jix turned left and strode away. When he reached the tower, he opened a door and passed through. Arval followed him into big circular room with a number of windows that let in plenty of light. A set of stairs on the far side curved up around the wall and disappeared into the upper sections of the tower. A second set descended in the same manner. The Jix turned right upon entering the room and immediately proceeded through another door. This one led out onto a very long, straight rampart that went directly to the tower at the farthest corner on the long side of the rectangular keep. Arval paused a moment and looked to his left between two merlons. The outer wall dropped away below him and ended on the slope of the hill, which descended steeply even further down to the city below.

A noise behind Arval made him turn. Inside the tower room he saw a second Jix just coming to the top of the stairs that descended into the lower reaches. He was preceded by three enormous, slavering, growling dogs.

The Jix who'd found him on the bridge with a pouch full of rocks was ahead of him on the rampart, watching. Without turning his cowled face from Arval, he pointed his arm towards the far tower and said one word – "Run."

Revan followed the Jix down a hallway dimly lit by lanterns hanging from iron rings embedded into the stone walls. At a plain wooden door, they stopped and the Jix knocked softly. A voice inside told him to come in and he opened the door. They walked into a plain stone room containing a simple wooden desk with one chair behind it and two chairs in front for visitors. Bookcases filled with volumes lined the walls from the edge of the door, all the way around to the two windows that were set side by side in the opposite wall. Outside them Revan could just see the tops of the enormous black gates. This room must look down onto the courtyard, he thought idly. Standing with his back to them, looking out one of the windows, was a man in the same grey leather armor, but without the cowled cloak. He ignored them for a moment before turning and facing Revan. "Sit," he said in a courteous tone. Revan sat in one of the chairs facing the desk. His Jix escort remained standing behind him.

"You wear a ring on the short finger of your right hand," the man said as he took his seat at the desk. "Show it to me."

Revan raised his hand and held it out to the man. He gently took Revan's wrist and pulled it closer to him. "Extraordinary," he muttered softly. "Where did you get this? The truth now," he said, not unkindly.

Revan knew that he was in mortal danger in this place. Either of these men could probably kill him without even breathing hard. But he also felt that he could trust them, that they didn't mean him harm, like a Nojii would. He took a deep breath as he pondered how much to reveal. A moment of reflection later, he decided to just tell them everything. He turned to the Jix behind him and said, "This is sort of a long story. You might want to sit down."

Arval was panting hard by the time he reached the far tower. The dogs had charged him as soon as the Jix had said 'run' and Arval had. He'd easily outdistanced the barking and snarling animals, reaching the far tower while they were still only about halfway down the rampart. Another Jix had emerged from the far tower and walked towards the dogs. A sharp chopping motion of his hand caused them to stop instantly. A backward flip of the same hand and they all turned and trotted back the way they'd come. In the distance the Jix who'd first brought Arval here was walking towards them. When he reached the far tower, he stopped and looked at him. He still had his hood up, his eyes invisible in it's deep shadows. "Come," he said and led the way into the tower. The other Jix followed Arval, who now found himself bracketed by these deadly warriors.

The inside of this tower was the same as the other, and the Jix in the lead took the stairway down. After passing a number of different levels, they emerged into a long hallway lined with torches. They passed a number of closed doors on either side along its length. Arval wondered where they were going and why. A few turns of the passage later they entered a large room full of long tables lined up end to end and flanked by benches. The lead Jix motioned to one of the benches at the end of a table and said, "Sit."

Arval sat and looked around. The Jix walked through a door on the far side of the room and left him alone with the other. That one wasn't talking. A moment later the first one emerged from the door carrying a plate of steaming food and a mug of something. He placed the meal in front of Arval and said, "Eat."

Arval ate. It had been several hours since he'd woken up in the Hive and had breakfast, and he was hungry. The food was a jumble of pieces meat and vegetables with a dark brown gravy spread over what looked like pieces of bread sliced into small chunks. It was magnificent. Arval devoured the entire plate and drained the mug, which had been filled with water. He leaned back when he was finished and looked at his Jix guardians. "That was marvelous," he said. "I've had good food before, but that was some of the best I've ever had." He thought he saw the chin of one of the Jix move as if with a smile, but it was hard to tell since they were still wearing those cowls.

"Come," the one who'd brought the food said. Arval was starting to wonder if they only spoke one word at a time inside the keep. When he'd met the man on the bridge, he'd seemed almost chatty, now he seemed more like an ambulatory statue than a man. With a sigh Arval rose and followed him through yet another door in the room. A short time later they walked out into the courtyard. There was a half circle of about twenty Jix, all in their grey armor and cloaks, facing them.

"Am I to be given a meal and executed then?" Arval asked. "Didn't I pass your test with the dogs?"

The Jix all remained silent. From his right Arval detected movement and turned. Yet another Jix was approaching him from across the courtyard. This man, while wearing the armor and cloak, did not have the cowl pulled up over his head. He was totally bald and clean shaven, with deep lines of age on his face which exhibited an unreadable expression. His sword swung at his hip. Walking right up to Arval, he stopped and stared silently and intently into his eyes.

"Did I fail?" Arval asked softly.

The man remained silent, simply regarding Arval with that unreadable look. Suddenly he raised his right hand into the air. One of the Jix on the far end of the half circle came forward and stopped next to them. The man held out his hand and the Jix threw back his cowl and took off the cloak he was wearing, handing it to the bare-headed older man. He took it and immediately draped it around Arval's shoulders. Arval didn't know what to do, so he just stood there gaping at him. The Jix whose cloak he was now wearing walked back and resumed his place in the half circle. Seemingly without a signal from anyone, the whole line of them all slowly raised their arms, hands fisted, until they crossed on their chests. The bare-headed man looked at Arval and the slightest of smiles touched the corners of his mouth. "You did not fail," he said.

Arval was dumbstruck; he could barely form a thought in his mind, let alone respond to the man. A real smile now bloomed on his face. "The warriors of the Jix offer you home and sanctuary as the newest wearer of the grey."

"I passed?" Arval managed to croak out of his now dry throat.

"Of course. You'd be outside the gate by now, and probably in the custody of the Wardens had you failed. Instead, you have been offered a place with us, but before anything else, you must accept it."

Arval, now knowing anything about such matters, knelt before the man, bowed his head and said simply, "I accept."

Revan felt drained as he finished his story; he had told them everything, omitted nothing. The two Jix sat, one in front of him, one to the side, regarding him with inscrutable expressions. At last, the one behind the desk rose and walked to one of the windows that looked out on the courtyard. He sighed deeply and dropped his head, as if in sorrow. "So, it has happened at last," he said. Revan remained silent. The man remained at the window for a few moments before taking a deep breath and sitting back down at his desk. His intense gaze found Revan's face. He was older that he'd appeared when Revan had first seen him. Deep lines of age gouged his clean shaven face and formed furrows in the cheeks under his bald pate.

"My name is Ulvar," he said after regarding Revan for a moment.

The man next to you is named Tandan."

"Pleased to meet you both," Revan said.

"We are honored to have met you," Ulvar said quietly but emphatically. Tandan nodded to Revan, silently echoing his comrade's words.

"Fendalon mentioned you," he said to Ulvar. "You're one of the ones who tested him when he first joined the Jix."

"That's correct," Ulvar said with a wistful smile. "Fendalon was my friend. And a great leader. He is missed terribly by most of us here. I'm relieved to know that he is well and happy in the life he's chosen. But Fendalon is a matter for another time. We've graver concerns at the moment."

"What concerns?" Revan asked.

Ulvar sighed and threw his head back in thought. "Many things are now in motion. Things we have no influence on or control over. Did you know that the Nojii are hunting you?"

Revan was caught completely by surprise. "No! I didn't! How do you know they are? We got away from them..."

"One of them has learned your names, yours and Arval's. Instructions have been given to the Nojii here in the city, and others throughout Jarradan, that they are to find you. Since the Kryxaal disappeared, they've had little to do other than drink, fight and accost innocent people. Particularly women. Now that they have a mission, they're intent on accomplishing it. They are patrolling the streets in groups, searching for any word or sign of you."

Revan was at a complete loss as to what to say. Ulvar noticed his distress and sought to allay his fears. "You're safe with us," he said. "Nojii would never attempt to enter this keep. But they aren't the only problem. King Vraniss has learned of your existence and is also looking for you. He knows about your escape from the pit."

"How do you know all this?" Revan asked.

"We have eyes and ears in various places who report things to us. And we listen, we watch, we learn."

"How am I supposed to find the other Kryxaal before the king?! If he gets to them first... And what do the Nojii want with Arval and me?!"

"Patience lad," Ulvar said. "He has no idea where they are, although we have reason to believe that he has taken steps to learn the locations of the other three. It will be some time before he has any reliable information. We must use that time wisely."

"What are we going to do?"

"First we are going to eat. Then I will convene the Council of the Grey, and we will discuss this further. You will remain here with us for now. At least until we decide what actions to take. You must be hungry. Come, you'll like the food here," Ulvar said as he rose from his desk and led them out into the hallway beyond.

Chapter 29

ing Vraniss walked slowly down the dank stairway. Water seeped through cracks between the enormous stone blocks that made up this part of the palace. The walls fairly dripped greenish black fungus, and the smell of wet and rot permeated the air. He was deep underneath the main floors, making his way to the lowest level. It was in these dark, slimy passageways that the worst and most dangerous criminals were brought for confinement. There were dungeons with cells a few levels above, in a drier and less oppressive part of the palace. But this place, this was reserved for the worst of the worst.

Vraniss liked to come down here from time to time. It reminded him of where he could end up if he wasn't vigilant against his enemies. He was under no illusion that the people of the city loved him. In fact, he was quite sure that most of them would like nothing better than to see him lose his head in White Square. Or to know that he'd been imprisoned down here, never to see daylight again. This awareness kept him sharp, made him look hard at everything, examine every angle of every decision he made and person he dealt with. He hadn't ascended to the Throne of the Firmament through luck.

The stairs ended and he found himself in front of a rusty iron door. He took a ring of keys from the pocket of his jacket and fed one into the lock. The mechanism yielded reluctantly, and he pushed the door open. It swung silently on well-oiled hinges. He'd made sure that his jailers kept this door maintained, but apparently they'd forgotten to service the lock. He'd speak to them about it on his way out. Beyond the door the passageway stretched on for a short distance. Five iron doors on each side of the passage were the only variations in the stone walls. Vraniss walked up to one of them and flipped a small latch. A flap of iron dropped down opening a square viewing port into the cell beyond.

"Still alive in there?" Vraniss asked.

A muffled cough was the only reply.

"It would appear you are."

"Yes. I am still breathing. If it can be called breathing in this filthy air," a man's exasperated voice replied.

"Good. I may have need of you soon. Perhaps you'll yet have some fresh air in your lungs before I remove your head."

"And I thought you wanted my head to stay attached so I could rot alive down here," the voice said.

"In all honesty I'm still not sure what I want to do with you."

"I wish you'd decide. If you'd like my blood to water the stones in your square, then have at it. If you want to just keep me locked in here until I die from the smell, or just from boredom, then tell me and I'll get on with it."

Vraniss laughed at that. "You know, it's generally accepted practice to address the king as Sire or your majesty. Have you forgotten your courtly manners?"

"Am I at the king's court? I think not. Here we are just jailer and jailed. You can take your courtly courtesies and shove them up where your meals make their exit. Your majesty," the man said, his voice full of defiance and sarcasm.

Vraniss laughed again. "You've not lost your sense of humor at least! Stay alive a little longer. Maybe I'll send for you soon, allow you to breathe some of that fresh air."

"I'll hold my breath until then."

Vraniss chuckled all the way back up the stairs.

Back in his study, in the much cleaner air of the palace proper, Vraniss pored over a stack of reports. There were the usual notes about the condition of the army and the sea forces, requests from any number of private citizens for one boon or another, updates on farm production, all very boring but necessary to the efficient management of the kingdom. Vraniss usually designated a subordinate to read through these and bring him anything needing his personal attention. But today he wanted to immerse himself in minutiae in order to divert his mind from the emissary he'd sent to Drisava. There had been no word from Queen Andissa as of yet, and Vraniss was becoming concerned. He'd dispatched a messenger to Drisava with his official request that his scholar be allowed into the archive vaults. The plan was to send Clammalod and one of his royal attendants, along with an escort of ten of the king's personal guard for protection. They'd take the fastest and strongest horses in the royal stables in order to make the journey as quickly as possible; a carriage, while more official, would slow the party down. All he needed now was Andissa's permission.

What to do if they were refused access to the library in Enrat was the worry that truly occupied his mind. The information contained in the restricted vaults had to be retrieved. As he saw it there were two options if diplomacy failed. He could mass his armies on the border and threaten invasion, or he could use the man in the deep dungeons he'd just visited. Neither option was attractive. A war would cause chaos, destruction and disorder. Vraniss hated disorder. But releasing the man in the dungeons would create an entirely different variety of disorder. He was imprisoned below because he'd attempted to assassinate Vraniss in his bed some months ago. The only thing that saved the king's life was his inability to sleep more than a few hours at a time. He'd been awake and staring out the window of his bedroom when the man had silently entered the room behind him, armed with a knife. Vraniss' own instincts and prowess at feats of arms had barely saved him. The man had rushed him when he realized his target was awake. Vraniss had heard him coming and spun to meet the attack. In the ensuing struggle, he'd disarmed the assassin and been able to call for his guards while restraining the man. All while wearing only his smallclothes. He'd immediately had the man imprisoned and questioned. But even his best inquisitor had been unable to get the man to provide even his name. And oh, how he'd tried. The questioning room had been awash in blood when he'd finished, but the man had never even groaned, let alone screamed. That in itself was cause for immense concern. Anyone would have answered questions under that kind of duress, even lied just to make the pain stop. But not this man, no. He was unique in Vraniss' experience. If he could be turned into an ally, he would be invaluable. What still bothered, and intrigued, Vraniss, was how the man had gotten into his chambers in the first place. There was no way he could have scaled the outside wall without being seen, and there were guards posted right outside his door and all down the hallway. How had he done it?!

The king was so lost in thought over the enigmatic man in his dungeon that he was totally unaware that he had a visitor. A polite cough roused him from his reverie, and he looked up at the man in blue and gold palace livery in front of him.

"Your highness," he began. "We've received a message from Drisava," he said, holding out an envelope. Vraniss broke the wax seal and removed the letter. It only took a moment to read it. Its words did not tell him what he'd been hoping to hear. With a growl he slammed it down on his desk, scattering the stack of reports.

"Find Barittin. Now," he said.

"At once Sire," the official replied. He turned and ran out of the study. The palace staff knew when the king was not to be trifled with, which was almost never. Instances like this were ones when the staff were doubly quick to depart his presence, lest they end up in the dungeon. Or White Square.

Vraniss sat at his desk fuming. Perhaps he would make a deal with the man in the dungeon after all.

"The queen has refused my request to allow Clammalod into their library vaults. She gave no reason. But she did also mention that should we be involved in any way with Drisava's dispute with Bentravirri, she would declare war on us." King Vraniss, his message delivered, turned to the window behind his desk. Barittin, standing in front of it, pondered this news for a moment.

"I'd actually expected her to decline the request to visit the library. But Queen Andissa has expressly stated that if we get involved in their border dispute then she will declare war on Jarradan?" Barittin asked.

"Yes," was all Vraniss replied.

"We may not have any choice. The land in dispute runs right up to our southern border. If it comes to blows, which I'm betting it will, the fighting will surely spill into Jarradan. That area is home to our prime farmland. Agriculture could be devastated for years."

"I've thought of that," Vraniss said acidly. "That's why you are going to lead one of our armies down there to make sure nothing happens. Or to put a quick stop to it if it does. You know how I despise chaos and disorder. There will be no disorder in Jarradan while I sit on the throne."

"But Sire, I'm needed here. Surely one of your generals would be able to maintain order. And wouldn't Andissa consider us placing one of our armies there to be a hostile act?"

"I don't care what she thinks about our army being there. They will remain on our side of the border unless they're forced into something. We will protect our farmlands! And no, you are going. You'll have General Remerska with you. He'll keep the soldiers in check and see to it that they respond appropriately to any aggression. You will be there to gather intelligence for me. Make sure that you take captives from both sides. The higher their rank, the better. I want to know what their orders are. And alert your eyes and ears that the king will pay for information regarding the intentions of Queen Andissa and King Zeryph."

"Very well Sire," Barittin said. "But what are you going to do about the library? You seemed very intent on gaining access to it the last time we spoke of it."

"I don't know yet. But I do have some options I'm considering."

"Might you be able to infiltrate it somehow? Bypass Andissa's permission?"

"Not likely. Clammalod knows a bit about the Udron library, and he informed me that only a very select few are allowed access to their most sensitive documents. The vaults where those records are stored are deep under the library and are heavily guarded by hand-picked sentries."

Barittin was even more intrigued now than he had been. What could be so sensitive that it had to be buried that deep and held under such heavy guard? He knew it was something to do with the structure in the desert that had disappeared and the power it was thought to contain, but what? If something was that secret, that dangerous, better to destroy the records and kill anyone who knew anything about it. He had to find out what Vraniss was searching for.

Chapter 30

evan sat down at one of the tables in the dining hall and watched as more and more Jix filed in, taking their places at tables and chatting amongst themselves. The room was filling up quickly, and he watched as men brought platters of food out from the kitchens and placed them on tables. He'd never seen such a variety. The smells were making his mouth water. There were a number of different roasted meats, fruits and vegetables both raw and cooked, and bowls full of green leaves that he heard someone call salad. Everyone was helping themselves, so Revan followed their example and filled his plate with a variety of foods he'd never tried. It was all as delicious as it smelled. Except for the soft orange things. They weren't good at all. He turned to one of the Jix sitting next to him and asked what they were. Yams was the answer.

"Yams?" he asked.

"Yes, yams. Have you never had them before?"

"No. I've not had any of this before."

"How can that be? Everyone's had potatoes and meat with gravy, salad and fruits."

"I was at the pit until recently."

The man straightened. "So, you're the one I've heard mention of."

"You've heard of me?"

"Of course. There are important, and not very nice, people looking for you. You seem like a good lad. I'm glad we found you first."

Revan was about to thank him and say that he was glad too, when a voice yelling his name rang out across the room.

"Revan!!! What in the dark depths are you doing here?!" It was unmistakably Arval. As he stood to look for his friend, he spied him walking quickly across the room.

"I should ask you the same thing," Revan said.

"I've been accepted into the Jix!"

Revan stared speechless at him a moment. "You... have?"

"Yes. Sit down, I'll tell you all about it."

As they ate Arval filled Revan in on the events of his day, the race across White Square, how he'd been found on the bridge by the Jix, and how he'd ended up running for his life from huge dogs who seemed determined to rip his limbs from his body. Revan laughed out loud at the part about the rocks in the pouch. "Couldn't you have found some honest work for an hour or two?" he asked.

"Sure. But that would have taken too long. I wanted to get some flowers right that moment." He'd only mentioned Valbirnia in passing, and the mention of flowers sparked Revan's interest.

"Flowers then? For the girl?"

Arval blushed a dark shade of crimson. "Well... you would want to give her flowers too if you saw how pretty she is," he said defensively.

Their companions at the table had been listening intently to the story, while trying to appear uninterested. Revan knew they'd been paying attention and couldn't resist the opportunity to needle Arval. "My friend here is in love," he announced, rather loudly to those in earshot. "He almost got arrested trying to get flowers for a girl." Grins and snickers broke out among the Jix. Arval glared at him, obviously embarrassed. But after a moment he just laughed, which caused Revan to laugh too. Soon the whole table was laughing with them. "You'll make a fine addition to the Jix with an attitude like that!" one of them said to Arval. "Don't lose it."

Revan told Arval his story, which was much less exciting, and they both ate silently for a time when he was done.

"How are we going to get word to Plistral?" Arval asked. "I hadn't seen him in months, he thought I was dead, now I'm gone again."

"We'll ask if we can visit him to let him know we're ok and not going to be back for a while."

"You think they'll let us go?" Arval asked.

"Probably. If we ask nicely. Or maybe they'll send someone to tell him. We can figure that out tomorrow."

One of the Jix looked up at the sound of a bell from the kitchen.

"Dessert tonight! Don't get dessert here too often, except on special days. Nothing special about today, except that you two have joined us. If you're the reason – thank you!"

"What's for dessert?" Revan asked.

"Won't know until they put it in front of us." Just as he said that several men carrying large platters emerged from the kitchens. They placed large round pottery dishes on the tables and left.

"Well look at that," Arval said, looking at the steaming dish in front of them. "You're about to have your first taste of ironberry pie!"

"Are you telling me that this lad has never had ironberry pie before?" one of their tablemates exclaimed.

"He really hasn't had much of anything," Arval replied. "I've been waiting to see him get his first taste of this."

Revan helped himself to a large slice of the pie. Its aroma was divine. He carved off a piece with his fork and lifted it to his mouth, Arval, and the rest of the Jix at their table, watched intently. As he chewed the flavor released in his mouth. He moaned in ecstasy and leaned away from the table; head thrown back. "This might be the best thing ever!" he said.

"Gentlemen, fellow wearers of the grey, my brothers," Ulvar said as he stood at one end of the room. His raised hands caused the room to fall silent. "We've some new arrivals with us tonight. I see some of you have already met them. I'd like to welcome our newest initiate Arval," he said as he gestured to Arval. "Stand that we might see and welcome you."

Arval stood hesitantly and the crowd erupted with cheers of "Welcome" and "Hail initiate." He smiled sheepishly and sat back down.

"We welcome another tonight, who while not an initiate, is no less worthy of our consideration. Revan, stand that we may welcome you."

Revan stood and looked around the room; there were several hundred faces looking back at him. The room rang with calls of "Welcome," but not as vociferously as had been those for Arval.

"Both of these young men were, until recently, slaves at the pit in the northern desert. Through a series of fortunate occurrences, they were able to make good their escape, and have found themselves among us. Tomorrow Arval will begin his training as a Jix. Revan, on the other hand, brings news of a most dire and important nature. You all have been instructed in the history of the Jix, in the formation of our order, and what our first task was upon our creation. As you will recall from your lessons, it was to find four places throughout the world where Kryxaal could be concealed when it was determined that magic must be sent away from this world. The first of the four has been found. It was the structure that was excavated at the pit. That Kryxaal has now disappeared, which means that the cycle of events which will bring about the return of magic has begun. Revan will be assisting us with this matter. Tomorrow I will convene the Council of the Grey and we will decide what actions are in the best interests of the Jix. That is all I am able to tell you at this time. Cloud wine will be served shortly, and there is ale aplenty. Enjoy yourselves tonight. Tomorrow the world will begin to change."

Chapter 31

anar watched impassively as Nolik and Adir finished with the woman in the alley. Her cries had stopped when Nolik's fist connected with her temple. Their companions had remained in The Full Mug, preferring ale and a fistfight, or a knife fight, to this variety of sport. Given the clientele of the tavern and their level of inebriation, it wouldn't be long before one or the other, probably both, happened.

"What do we do if Wardens come by," Kanar had asked when they'd first dragged the woman off the street and into the alley.

"Ask if they'd like to join in," had been Adir's reply.

Kanar found these actions disturbing and grotesque, but he kept his mouth shut and didn't protest. His ultimate goal was to get close enough to Hento to kill him. If he had to endure the abuse of a few innocent people, well, sacrifices had to be made. Still, he'd found the whole affair difficult to watch. He'd turned his head away several times, reminding himself that he'd survived the pit and the camp. This was nothing compared to that. Except maybe for the unfortunate woman. As long as they didn't kill her, she'd be alright, he told himself. As long as he got to Hento, everything would be worth it. Avenging his parents was worth enduring anything for.

Their sport concluded, Adir and Nolik rose from the prostrate form of their victim and ushered Kanar back into the tavern. "That was thirsty work! I'm ready for another ale," Nolik exclaimed.

"Why haven't you found some sport, Sprout?" Adir asked Kanar. He'd taken to calling him that since they'd met.

"I'll find some. Just waiting for the right game," he replied.

"Don't wait too long. If you're going to carouse with us, you need to partake. I'm just starting to like you. I'd hate to see you laying in the street with your entrails on the outside instead of inside where they belong."

"Try it," was all Kanar said.

Adir laughed and clapped him on the shoulder. "Good lad! That's the spirit! Find yourself someone to gut," he said, handing Kanar a wicked looking knife. "There's got to be someone in that place deserves a gutting. Find him and give it to him. Or her, I don't care."

Kanar realized that Adir, while acting jocosely, was entirely serious. If he didn't kill someone this night, he'd be the one dead before morning. He'd better find someone and soon.

As they walked back into the tavern, Kanar noticed the eyes of the patrons on them. These were mainly poor people, working folk who lived on the fringes of the city. The Nojii were interlopers here and were not well liked. He could almost feel the hate radiating off them. And the fear. They never directly confronted the Nojii, but their sidelong glances and scowls were evidence enough. There was an undercurrent of anger flowing through this city that was palpable. Many of the conversations he'd overheard had to do with the Nojii and their antics, and how the king and the Wardens weren't stopping them. There was so much animosity towards the king, the Wardens, and the Nojii, that Kanar was mildly surprised there weren't riots in the streets. Wardens were good at cracking skulls and keeping an uneasy sort of order. Nojii were just good at killing and abusing people. Between them, they had the whole populace cowed. But all it would take, Kanar thought, was one person to find some courage and there would be mayhem and bloodshed. He hoped he'd be able to find and kill Hento before that happened. He wanted to finish his business and be away before this place exploded.

They rejoined their companions at the table, and Kanar began looking for someone to kill. There didn't seem to be anyone in the tavern who was worth accosting. He wanted to find someone bad, a criminal. Everyone here was just a worker, like his parents had been. Like he'd been. These people hadn't done anything to him; they were only in that tavern to have an ale after toiling the day away in some thankless, low-paying and unrewarding job. Most probably had families at home that they were trying to support. Could he really deprive some woman and her children of the man who put food on their dinner table and a roof over their heads? Sacrifices must be made, he told himself again. He picked out a solitary man nursing an ale at the end of the bar and decided that he'd be the one to die tonight. Now he just needed a ruse to goad him into a fight. The knife Adir had given him was tucked inside the waistband of his trousers, it's handle concealed under his shirt, but easy to get to. Its weight felt comforting and terrifying at the same time.

He rose from his chair to approach the man when he saw someone come in through the back door. The figure was swathed in a black cloak, hood up, face concealed in its shadows. He couldn't tell if it was a man or a woman, but the way it moved made him think it was a man. He was about average height and build, but moved smoothly and confidently, while also remaining silent and unobtrusive, which was not easy to achieve. This looked like the perfect mark. But who would come into a tavern with the hood of their cloak up? If this person was trying to remain anonymous, then wearing a cowl indoors was sure to attract attention. Better to leave it down and let people see your face, make them think you are not worth paying attention to. The person was speaking softly with the barkeep, who drew an ale and placed it in front of the newcomer. Kanar changed direction from the lone man and moved towards his new target.

He sat down next to the person and ordered an ale. After taking a few sips, his mark silent next to him, he turned and spoke. "Hello friend. What brings you in here tonight?"

"I'm not your friend," the person replied. It was definitely a man. "I'm just here for an ale. Leave me be." His tone was calm but stern; the man didn't want to be bothered. It should be easy to get him to fight, Kanar thought.

"Now that's not very nice. I've not been rude to you, but you've been most rude to me."

"If you're looking for a fight, and from the look of that knife you carry you are, I'd suggest you find someone else."

Kanar was caught off guard at the mention of the knife, but he'd committed to his strategy and was determined to see it through. The Nojii were watching from behind him, grinning in anticipation of violence.

"Maybe I would like a fight. Maybe I'd like a fight with you."

"Your Nojii friends there aren't going to be of any help to you if you continue to push me. Now I suggest, strongly, that you rejoin them at their table and leave me be."

Kanar didn't hesitate - he pulled the knife from his waistband and swung it at the newcomer. With more speed than he'd ever seen, the man caught his wrist with one hand and wrenched the knife from it with the other. The Nojii, sensing their friend was in trouble, rose and began to move towards them. The stranger, still holding Kanar's wrist, flung the knife at them where it buried itself in the forehead of Nolik. He dropped without a sound. The other four roared in anger and rushed at the man who'd just killed one of them. With his free hand the man drew a short, slender, wicked looking sword with a curved black blade. Strange red markings adorned its length; they looked as though they'd been rendered in blood. As the first Nojii closed in, he swung it smoothly, but incredibly quickly, and caught him across the cheek. The blade carved through his face like it was air and he fell dead instantly. Two of the others hesitated slightly but not Adir, he raced forward screaming, a knife in his right hand. The man, still holding Kanar's wrist in a grip he couldn't break, calmly waited for Adir to get close enough, then with that amazing speed, swung the short black sword in a X pattern and promptly lopped off both Adir's arms. He fell screaming to the floor, his blood rapidly draining from his body. The other two, seeing their leader and two others dead, decided not to die and quickly ran from the tavern. The patrons were all stunned. No one ever stood up to the Nojii. Many left their ales unfinished and quickly left the tavern. Only the barkeep and the lone man Kanar had initially targeted were left, and he was getting off his stool to leave.

"Tradan's Pocket, you killed three of them with one hand!" Kanar said.

The cloaked man didn't respond. He calmly sheathed his black blade, after wiping it clean on Adir's shirt, then reached into his pocket and removed two gold coins. He placed them on the bar in front of the stunned and terrified barkeep. "These are for you, and for the mess I've made. You have my deepest apologies. I only wanted an ale, then I would have been on my way." Kanar realized the man was still holding his wrist; his hand had begun to go numb; the grip was so tight.

"Are you ever going to let me go?" he asked.

"Depends. Do you deserve to be let go of? After all, you're the reason I had to do this. If you'd just left me alone like I asked you to, none of this would have happened."

"I'm s-s-sorry," Kanar stammered. "I was just trying to impress those Nojii so I could get close to one of them and kill him."

"Really?" the man said, more patronizing than intrigued. "So, you were going to kill a man. Ever killed one before?"

"No. But I've seen plenty killed."

"It's not as easy as some of us make it look."

"You sure made it look easy."

"I've been trained. You, quite obviously, haven't. If you'd had even the least bit of training, you'd not have tried to swing that knife at me like it was a sword. You'd have thrust it straight at my chest. Swinging takes too long, and unless you've been instructed to do it right, its fairly simple to evade. A thrust on the other hand, that's more difficult to avoid. Your chance of scoring a hit on me would have been much greater."

"Alright, so I don't really know how to use blades. I'm pretty good with a bow though. Will you let my hand go now?"

"I still haven't decided if you're worth releasing. In other words, I haven't decided whether or not to kill you too."

Kanar's heart was beating out of his chest. He hadn't been this scared since he'd been taken to the camp. Was that only just a few short weeks ago? It seemed an age. He had no idea what the man wanted, what he could do or say to save his own life. In desperation he blurted out the only idea that occurred to him.

"I'll be your servant if you teach me to use weapons the way you do."

The stranger threw his head back and laughed, a mirthless, mocking sound. "Do you think I need a slave? That I can't take care of myself?"

"Then just teach me what you know. I'll do whatever you ask and not complain. I need to learn to use weapons if I'm to kill... who I need to kill," Kanar said.

The stranger looked directly at him; his eyes still hidden within the black cowl of his cloak. "You're serious aren't you. You really do want to kill someone."

"Yes."

"If I accept your offer, you won't like what happens to you. And we will be leaving this city at once. The place we will be going is not pleasant. Do you understand?"

"I was at the pit. I know what torture is like. I think I can handle whatever it is you're talking about."

"You've no idea what I'm talking about. But if you're still willing, then I accept your offer." He released Kanar's wrist and blood began to flow back into his hand. He rubbed it as he studied the man. He wished he could see his face, his eyes. There was something amiss about this man. Even when he'd thrown his head back and laughed, the cowl had stayed on his head, his face concealed in its shadow. He had a moment of regret for his hasty words. But maybe they had saved his life. If he had to endure more suffering in order to learn to kill as easily as this man had, then he would. Sacrifices and all that, he thought.

"You said we have to leave here. Where are we going?"

"Beyond the Blackfire," the stranger replied.

"Hento, how lovely to see you again," Bhinja said, his voice fairly dripped with sarcasm.

"Bhinja, how've you been? I've been so worried about your welfare. Things must have been difficult for you since your big stone box disappeared," Hento said, smiling unkindly. He knew that Bhinja had resented being posted at the excavation, and that he'd taken out his frustrations on the diggers. It was impossible for Hento to resist needling him about his former profession. They were sitting at a table in an inn that the Nojii had appropriated from the owner. That unfortunate man had been forced to sleep in the small stable behind the main building. When he'd tried to protest the theft of his business, two of the Nojii had held him down while Hento took a hammer to his left arm and hand. He hadn't needed any more persuasion.

"Don't patronize me Hento, I'm not at all in the mood."

"Oh alright," he sighed, a little disappointed to have the banter be cut short so quickly. "To business then. You've heard the reports of three of ours murdered last night?

"I have. What of it?"

"Do you have any information on the identity of the perpetrator? There must be justice for our departed brothers."

"All I know is what the barkeep told me. It was a person wearing a black robe who carried a black blade unlike any he'd ever seen. When he was finished with his work, he left with a young man who'd been drinking with Adir and his crew."

"And who is that young man? Does anyone know?"

"There are two Nojii who were with Adir who survived. They said his name was Kanar. He'd joined them earlier that night in some other tavern."

Hento sat back in his chair, his expression thoughtful. He glanced around the room, then up at the ceiling. "That name is familiar," he said softly. "Where have I heard it before?"

Bhinja stood patiently. It rankled him to no end that he had to report to Hento. How could this wretch, this braggart, this swine possibly outrank him? He knew yet hated to admit it. It was because Hento payed obeisance to Otarab. He could never lick the boots of that pile of rat dung the way Hento did. But wasn't that politics? Bhinja was not a political man.

While his superior was lost in reverie, Bhinja took the opportunity to fetch another ale from the bar in the inn. With the innkeeper relegated to his stable, there was no one to serve the clientele, not that there was much clientele in an inn full of Nojii, so they simply helped themselves.

"Isn't it a bit early for ale Bhinja?" Hento said, apparently back in the present moment.

"I'm a Nojii. It's never too early for anything. If it's too early for you, maybe you should have stayed in bed."

"Too much to do for sleeping in," Hento replied. "Otarab will want a full report on how three of us were murdered yet have not been avenged."

"They will be. I have teams scouring the city as we speak. Your assassin in black will be found and dealt with."

"He'd better be. And I want him alive. We have something special in store for him once he's ours."

"Whatever you wish," Bhinja said dismissively. Once the murderer was found, he didn't care what happened to him. All he wanted right now was someone to pummel. "I will take some men and find him myself."

"There's a sport!" Hento exclaimed. "Bring him here directly when you've found him."

"Yes, yes. Am I free to go now?"

"Go find him," Hento said with a dismissive wave of his hand.

Bhinja stalked out the door into the warming day, his sightless left eye rolled madly in it's socket, the glare on his face as fierce as it ever was.

Chapter 32

rval couldn't believe how tired he was. The Jix were working him harder than he'd ever worked at the pit, or anywhere for that matter. From the time he woke in the morning until he dropped into bed at night, his days were a blur of activity. He was awakened at dawn in the large room where he and a number of other Jix slept. They hurriedly donned their grey leather armor, then dashed downstairs to breakfast. After a hurried meal they split into groups, and each went to a different part of the keep for training and instruction in various subjects. Since Arval was new his first lessons of the day were with Ulviq, The First of Armaments, a title that was well-deserved; the man knew his weapons. The lessons consisted mostly of running and jumping, climbing, and lifting heavy things. On the first day, utterly winded and dripping sweat, he asked Ulviq why he had to run up and down stairs.

"Have you ever been chased by someone who wants to end your life?"

"Yes… I've… run… plenty of… times," Arval replied, gasping.

"And since you're here you obviously got away. What would have happened if you'd been caught? Would you be alive and gasping for breath in front of me right now?"

"Probably... not."

"Exactly. We Jix don't run from a fight. But we are also wise enough to know when we are in a fight we can't win. When that happens, we have to be able to get away. If you can't outrun your pursuers, you'll be dead. I know you're some kind of fast, but how long can you run? We need to be able to run for an entire day without stopping. You've not even made it halfway to lunch before being short of breath. Stamina boy! You must have stamina! Now run!"

And Arval had run. He'd run up and down flights of stairs, up through the towers and onto the long ramparts, then back down to the courtyard, only to do it all over again. He climbed up and over walls, both by hand and with ropes, and was made to carry crates that weighed as much as he did around the courtyard. By lunch he was so tired he could barely walk. After a brief meal it was training with weapons. His arms grew so fatigued from swinging swords that he could barely lift them to feed himself at dinner. His fellow Jix smiled at him knowingly, yet not unsympathetically. They knew what he was going through.

The last part of his day before dinner was spent in a classroom where he received instruction in writing. Arval had never learned to read or write, and he found it difficult at first to decipher the bizarre symbols his instructor called letters. Over the days and weeks though, they began to make sense, and soon Arval was reading on his own without difficulty. He found that he enjoyed the written word very much. There was an enormous library deep within the keep that was overflowing with literature. Scrolls filled racks on the walls and were stacked on tables, books in their thousands lined shelves that formed aisles that stretched from one end of the enormous room to the other. Arval often wondered what secrets lay hidden in those books and scrolls. What amazing stories were in there, just waiting to be found? If he ever completed his training and had some free time, he'd find out, he told himself. But before he could lose himself in the library, he had to master the other things he was learning.

Weapons training was his favorite part of the day, in spite of how tired he was by the time he got to it. He'd never had any idea how much there was to learn about using a sword. He'd always thought it was just a matter of swinging it at your opponent and hoping you hit them. Ulviq had taught him differently from the first day. He'd learned that there were numerous different stances, forms, methods and techniques that could be used for any number of purposes. Most were used to kill or wound, but others were used to disarm an opponent you didn't wish to kill, or to buy time so that a wounded comrade could escape. Knowing what to do in a given situation was just as important as knowing how to wield a weapon and made up a good portion of what he was learning.

While Arval developed a proficiency with blades, he'd found that the bow was a weapon he had a true talent for. The first time he'd been allowed to fire an arrow towards a target, he'd been able to hit very close to the center. Ulviq and the other instructors had been surprised. "Looks like we've found your weapon, haven't we?" Ulviq had said. Arval had been as surprised as they were. "Hinbladd, this one needs special instruction in bows. You'll see to it," Ulviq said to the older man next to him. Hinbladd, the ancient bow master of the Jix, nodded at the order. "I'll make sure he can pin an ant's leg to an ironberry from three hundred paces." Ulviq clapped Hinbladd on the shoulder and smiled.

"We'll make a Jix of you yet," he said to Arval. Coming from Ulviq this was high praise. Arval couldn't help but smile. Hinbladd had been true to his word. He'd worked Arval hard, and the results had amazed even the grizzled old bow master.

"I swear, in all my years teaching Jix the bow, I've never seen anyone able to hit as accurately and consistently as you." Arval was proud of his growing skill with a bow. Some of the other Jix, hearing about the prodigy in their midst, had come to watch. Wagers were made and links changed hands. Arval's skill became so reliable that the wagers ceased after only a few days.

But what concerned Arval more than fatigue and bows and books was Revan. They'd seen each other at meals, where they'd exchange stories about their days, but that was the only time he'd seen him. Until one day Revan wasn't there at all. When he asked his instructors about him, the answer was invariably some form of 'mind your training – there's nothing else for you to think about.' That was the most frustrating part, not knowing. Revan had been there one night at dinner, the next day he hadn't. He'd simply vanished. Arval didn't even know where in the keep Revan's room was, so it wasn't like he could sneak out at night to talk to him. If there was one consolation it was that they'd allowed him to send a message to Plistral about where he was. He'd not received a response, but Ulviq had assured him that the message had been delivered. Yet his thoughts returned always to Revan. Where was he?! It was infuriating and worrisome not to know. One day, many weeks after beginning his training, Arval saw Ulvar walking through the courtyard. He stopped his sword practice and stalked over to him.

"Where is Revan?" he asked forcefully.

Ulvar halted in mid-stride and stared at Arval. Arval just stared back.

"Are you sure you want to speak to me in that tone?" Ulvar asked, his authority clear in his voice.

Arval was chagrined but determined. "My apologies Captain, but I'm worried for my friend. I haven't seen him in weeks, and no one will tell me anything."

"Your friend is fine. He is working on something for us. That is all you need to know."

Arval hesitated a moment, debating whether or not to push the issue. This man was his superior and could have him thrown out into the street, or worse.

"I understand Captain, I am only concerned for his safety. He doesn't know this world very well yet."

Ulvar smiled slightly at Arval. "Your concern and loyalty are laudable. We praise those traits here. I assure you – your friend is safe. I don't know when, but you will see him again. Now if you'll excuse me," Ulvar said as he brushed past Arval and into the keep.

"That was not a wise thing to do," said one of the blade teachers, a man named Ganaf. He twirled a knife, his specialty, around his fingers so quickly it was hard to tell which end was blade and which was hilt. "That is our Captain, Commander, and the First of Tomes you just accosted. Lucky for you he seems to like you. You do know that the keep has dungeons much like the Azure Palace don't you?"

"I know. I just had to have some news of my friend."

Ganaf smiled. "I would have done the same."

Despite Ulvar's assurances and Ganaf's good nature, Arval was still uneasy about Revan.

Asplan begged for the pain to stop. The Nojii had been working on him for two days. He'd been slipping in and out of consciousness almost from the moment they'd gotten him into the basement of this inn. The one called Bhinja had beaten him into unconsciousness with his fists. He didn't even ask any questions. When Asplan awoke Bhinja was gone and there was a different Nojii in the room. This one had introduced himself as Hento and had offered him water. He was lying on his back on a table, tightly bound to it, and Hento had allowed him to sit up to receive a sip of water. Asplan had drunk greedily until the waterskin was taken away. Hento had asked questions. The first one had been whether or not he knew Revan and Arval. Asplan wasn't sure what to say, so he told them the truth, that he did know both of them. But that wasn't enough, Hento wanted more, like where they were, who they were with, what their plans were. He tried to tell them he didn't know, but they didn't seem to believe him. That was when the pain had really started. Hento brought in a Nojii named Nillit and introduced him to Asplan. The man's black tattoos, in the murky and dim lamplight of the basement, made Asplan shiver with fear. All of the Nojii had tattoos, but this man's were somehow worse than most. They were more spiky than swirly; they reminded Asplan of the blood vine that grew in some of the deepest parts of the forest. He'd heard tales of it ensnaring humans with its barbed thorns and feeding on their flesh and blood. Asplan had never seen a blood vine, but the stories he'd heard as a young child had filled him with terror. The tattoos of this Nillit brought those fears roaring back into his consciousness, and he felt very much like how he imagined those poor victims of the blood vine must have felt. If the stories were true. His present story was certainly true.

Nillit didn't bother to use his fists like Bhinja had. He simply removed a wicked looking knife from his belt and proceeded to slowly carve skin from various parts of Asplan's body. He was very careful in his work. Nillit had a practiced hand and knew not to cut too deeply. The small patches of skin he removed from Asplan were cast into a bucket and salt was placed on the open wound. Once in a while he poured some sort of liquid on the skinless area. That pain was exquisite and always caused Asplan to scream. Hento sat in a chair on the far side of the dim room, watching, but not speaking while Nillit did his work. Asplan cried and begged as his skin was cut away, but neither Nojii spoke. He had no idea how long this went on, and he lost track of how many spots on his body had lost flesh. When he passed out from the pain, there was always a bucket of cold water to revive him. After some interminable length of time, Hento finally stood and approached the table where he was still bound.

"What do you know of Revan and Arval that you haven't told me?" Asplan, gasping for breath against the agony, couldn't think clearly. The pain consumed his thoughts and prevented him from forming a coherent answer. His mouth worked soundlessly as he tried to form words. Nillit raised his blade to begin again, but Hento stayed his hand.

"It looks like he's trying to speak. Give him a moment."

Asplan realized this might be his last chance to make the pain stop.

"How did you find me?" he finally gasped. "How did you know I knew Revan and Arval?"

"Well, now that's not the way to answer a question – with another question. But I'll tell you. One of our friends overheard you telling someone on the street that a boy named Revan had healed you. We'd like to talk to Revan, and you were the only person we could find who knew anything of him. Satisfied?"

Asplan cursed himself for his inability to keep quiet about things. It had gotten him in trouble with his Khet numerous times. Nothing for it now but to tell them what they wanted to know. Asplan had no illusions that the Nojii would let him live. He'd seen far too much of their handiwork around the city to believe that they had any intention of letting him go. The best he could hope for now was to get them to kill him quickly; the pain was unbearable, and he'd held out as long as he could. If they hadn't found Revan yet, then it was likely they wouldn't, so he didn't see any reason not to tell them. Asplan silently asked Revan for forgiveness for betraying him. He told them everything he knew from first meeting Revan and Arval in the alley, how Revan had knocked out Indrik (and how amazingly fast he was), and how he'd been healed by him. When he was finished with his story, Hento just stood looking at him. The pain rose and fell in waves, and at this moment it was rising again, every injury screamed. His entire body felt as if it had been submerged in acid. The pain would soon get so intense that he'd beg for them to end it. He already had. Many times. Hento continued to just look at him, then with a resigned sigh, he gestured to Nillit. Asplan had passed out again. He never felt the knife as it was plunged into his heart.

Chapter 33

evan had gotten used to being on a horse after three weeks in the saddle. The first week had been torture. His legs and back were so sore he could barely sleep at night. But as the journey went on, he was getting more and more adapted to being in the saddle. His companions sometimes laughed at the way he walked at night when they made camp. "It looks like he's riding a barrel," Edro said to the whole camp once. "Probably would look the same if I was riding your sister," Revan had replied to uproarious laughter. Edro smiled wickedly. Revan was getting as used to being around these Jix as he was to riding horses. In the keep they were all business and formality. Out here in the wilderness, away from Kessar, they were more like a bunch of ruffians drinking in an inn. He enjoyed the banter and camaraderie he'd developed with them. He'd not been formally accepted into their ranks like Arval had, but they'd taken to him like he was a little brother. Sometimes when they camped at night or during breaks in their riding, they'd teach him things about using weapons. He hadn't been instructed in weaponry during his stay in the Grey Keep; Ulvar had told him it was forbidden to teach anyone but Jix and their initiates any of their fighting secrets. But these Jix he was traveling with had felt that another sword could be useful and had disobeyed the rule. "I won't teach you everything, mind," Lenys said during the first lesson. "But you should know enough to protect yourself and help us if need be." So, the instruction had begun. Revan seemed to have a natural ability for swords, and combined with his speed, he was a difficult match for even the best of them. "You keep on practicing with that blade, you'll be challenging Ulviq before long," Lenys told him one afternoon after battling to a draw.

When Revan had found out that they were going to Enrat, he was as excited as he'd ever been. The tales he'd been told of the city on the promontory high above the sea filled him with wonder. He couldn't wait to wander its streets, see Stormtide Castle, and, of course, try the food. His companions had told him that the people of Drisava ate a lot of things from the sea. That was another food he hadn't tried yet. In addition to his excitement, he also felt fear and anxiety. When he thought of his purpose for visiting Enrat, his palms started sweating. He tried to keep his anxiousness from his companions, but Lenys was too perceptive.

"She's just a woman. Yes she's a queen, but she can be talked to just like any other woman," he'd said one day. They were riding along a deserted stretch of road in the far south of Jarradan. Farms and fields stretched away to the horizon. The land in this region was relatively flat, with low hills and very few trees. It was a beautiful day with sparse puffy white clouds dotting the sky. Birds circled high above, and the air was redolent of tilled earth and green, growing things. Off to his right, the Blackfire spanned the southern sky, spinning its mysterious purpose to an unknown end. He watched it for a moment, saw the red and gold threads shooting through its inky fringes, and wondered again if they were akin to the ones he sometimes saw.

"I've never talked to a queen before!" Revan said, suddenly refocused from pondering the Blackfire to the purpose of his journey. "I don't know what to say!"

"You're just going to ask her to let you into the vaults on behalf of the Jix. Ulvar already told you about the protocol when speaking to a monarch of Drisava. And he told you how to approach the request. They trained you for days just for that one moment. Have some faith in yourself. You'll do fine."

"Easy for you to say. You don't have to talk."

Lenys laughed and clapped him on the shoulder, leaning over in his saddle to do it. "Quit your worrying. You're as bad as an aged innkeeper's wife whose cat just left a dead mouse on the bar. 'Oh, what will the customers think!?' Come on boy, get your back straight!"

Revan smiled at the jibe; he liked Lenys. They rode on in silence for a time. He was enjoying seeing the world. It was hard to believe how big it was. And there was ever so much more to see. They were riding roughly southeast, following a road that Edro said would lead them to a much larger road that would ultimately take them directly to Enrat. Including Revan there were nine of them. Eight Jix for protection was like a small army, and Revan had no fear of meeting bandits on the road like he had when he and Arval had been with Anden and Poli. Besides, all the Jix were wearing their grey armor and blue cloaks. They were instantly recognizable anywhere in the three kingdoms, and people were not interested in picking fights with them. Most travelers they saw either diverted their eyes and hurried away or raised their hands in greeting to show no hostile intent.

Revan let his thoughts wander as he rode, and they eventually turned to the Council of the Grey that had convened the day after he'd arrived at the keep. Ulvar, acting in his capacity as Captain and First of Tomes, had opened the meeting by introducing Revan to the council. It was made up of Ulvar, his twin brother and First of Armaments Ulviq, and eleven other Jix. Ulvar had asked Revan to tell his story to the council, and he had – all of it. When he'd finished, there was silence around the long, ornately carved wooden table. They were in a room one floor above Ulvar's office that contained the large table and chairs, and nothing else. Several windows looked out onto the courtyard and the black gate. Sunlight streamed in rays through the mullions in the glass and illuminated small dust particles that floated in the air. Revan didn't know what else to say when he'd finished his story, so he remained silent. Tandan was the first to speak.

"When Revan arrived here yesterday, he told this tale to Ulvar and I. It is the same as it was yesterday. I believe it to be true. If he was lying, some parts of the story would be different or missing altogether, but they aren't. And he bears Jinirlyn's ring. Show them."

Revan held up his hand and displayed the small silver ring on his short finger. Murmurs swirled around the table, looks of incredulity broke out on several faces.

Tandan continued, "As you all know, only four of these rings were produced during Jinirlyn's time. One was given to the commander of each of the detachments who were assigned the task of finding locations for the Kryxaal. The only depictions of these rings are contained in our records, so no one other than us knows what they looked like, or that they were even created. This is not a fake. Revan did truly find Jinirlyn's remains. And I believe he spoke with the part of him that was still tied to this world by the magic that was infused in this ring upon its creation."

"The question before this council is what to do now that the first Kryxaal has been found and it's powers activated. We are fortunate that Revan ended up with us first. King Vraniss and the Nojii are also hunting him, and his friend Arval. Our source in the Azure Palace has informed us of this development. It would seem that the Nojii were the first to discover their identities, which were subsequently passed on to Vraniss through other channels."

"Nest of spies and snakes," one of the Jix exclaimed.

"Indeed," replied Ulvar. "But they have their uses. With this knowledge we can keep Revan safe from their questioners and formulate our own plans with regard to the remaining three Kryxaal."

"Where are they?" asked the man who'd just spoken.

"We don't know," Ulvar said simply.

Exclamations of surprise and anger rose around the table, growing louder until Ulvar raised his hand for quiet.

"Those records disappeared from our archives many years ago. No one who is currently a member of the Jix knows the locations of the Kryxaal. We believe the records are now in the restricted vaults in the Udron Library in Enrat."

More exclamations and oaths were uttered, and again Ulvar had to raise his hand.

"Brothers, please. This council has been convened so that we can find a solution to this problem. Not so we can bicker, curse and lay blame. We've known for some time that these records are gone and have been working diligently to discover their location and recover them. We are still unsure as to who is responsible for their theft and how they carried it out, but if that person is still alive, we will find him, and he will be dealt with most severely. Now, if our information is correct and the records are in Enrat, does anyone have any suggestions on how we might gain access to them?"

Silence had fallen around the table. An older man with white hair to his shoulders and a short white beard finally spoke. Revan thought he remembered the man's name being Hinbladd. "Queen Andissa must be petitioned. The Garnassis line has always been a friend to the Jix. If we humbly request that we be allowed access to the vaults, perhaps she will grant it."

"The restricted vaults at the Udron Library are as closely guarded as ours. It is unlikely that she will allow anyone, other than her highest-ranking resident scholars, to enter them, let alone read anything they contain," Tandan said.

"She has no love for King Vraniss," said Ulvar. "Perhaps if she is informed of his desire to access the vaults, and is made aware of what's at stake, she'll assent."

"Then we have to tell her Revan's story," said Hinbladd. "If she believes it, as I think everyone here does, she'll have no choice but to allow him in. If for no other reason than to keep Vraniss from learning the locations of the other Kryxaal and getting to them first."

"I agree with all but one thing you said. We will not tell her Revan's story. Revan himself will," Ulvar replied.

Shouts of dissent rose around the table. One grizzled old veteran exclaimed, "We're going to send a boy to do our work?! He's not even a true Jix! Why would she even grant him audience, let alone allow him into her vaults?!"

"Silence," Ulvar said. His air of authority and command was so intense that he didn't need to shout. The room instantly quieted. "This 'boy,' Malor, has accomplished much in his short time. Doubt his mettle if you will, but I have faith that if anyone here can persuade her, its him."

Mumbles and mutters circulated around, finally growing quiet. No one spoke for a time as they all pondered Ulvar's words. Revan himself sat petrified in his chair. They wanted him to talk to a queen! He could barely get a few sentences out in front of most ordinary people, now they wanted him to appear in front of a monarch on her throne and ask that he be allowed to view her most closely guarded secrets. Were they mad?!

"Revan, I can see the doubt on your face," Ulvar said. "Don't fear lad, we'll teach you all you need to know about how to behave in the court of a queen. There are protocols, but they're fairly simple once you know them. And we'll help you with a strategy for approaching her, in other words, we'll help you figure out what to say."

"Thanks…" Revan replied uncertainly.

"I still say it's a bad idea," Malor said.

"We will know in time. Right now, we have no other options, as far as I can tell," Ulvar said. Tandan nodded his agreement. "If anyone else has a better idea, please speak it." Silence fell around the table. A couple Jix shook their heads, others glared at nothing. Hinbladd smiled at Revan in a reassuring way.

"If no one has anything else to add, this council is adjourned. You are all dismissed," said Ulvar. Everyone slowly rose from their chairs and made their way out of the room. Hinbladd clapped Revan on the shoulder on his way out. Tandan and Ulvar remained behind.

"Well lad, tomorrow we start your instruction in courtly protocol," Tandan said.

And Revan had learned. Ulvar and Tandan had combined to teach him all about etiquette and manners - how to address a sovereign, how to bow, how to walk. It was all a bit too much for him to process, but over the days, he began to improve. They also sent him to Aat I'n in the library for lessons on reading and writing. "Just call me Aat, everyone does," the kindly old man said to him on his first day. "Most can't pronounce my kinname, so just leave it off."

"Ok, Aat," Revan replied.

"Do you know anything about reading and writing?" Aat asked.

"I read some Denoran in a place we found in the desert," he said.

"You can... read Denoran?" Aat asked, incredulous. "But that language has been dead for thousands of turnings. No one even speaks it anymore!"

"Well, I can read it," Revan said simply.

"You're just a fountain of surprising things aren't you?!"

Revan smiled. "I surprise myself sometimes."

"Well, you're not going to learn any Denoran here, but maybe you could teach me sometime."

"I'd be happy to teach you what I know, although it's not much."

"It's more than anyone currently alive knows, and that's enough for me. But for now, let's just focus on our language. You may have to sign your name in Enrat or read official court documents; it wouldn't do to have you be an illiterate in front of the queen. Besides, if she lets you into her vaults, you'll have to be able to read what's in there. And who knows, maybe someday you'll write a book about your adventures."

So, Revan began to learn how to read and write. He found, after a few days, that he loved reading. And he picked it up quickly. Aat was mildly amazed at what a fast learner he was. Within a week he could read almost without assistance. Writing was a little more difficult since he wasn't used to holding the quill pens, but eventually he was proficient enough that Aat thought e would be fine in Enrat.

"Keep studying and you'll be a scholar to rival me someday," he said kindly.

Revan smiled at the compliment. Ulvar and Tandan checked on him regularly and were pleased with his progress. He didn't see Arval at all, which worried him. His meals were served to him in his room deep in the keep; he wasn't allowed to eat with the rest of the Jix in the large dining hall. When he asked Tandan about it one day, he was told that only members of the Jix were allowed to eat there for safety. Can't ever be too vigilant against someone putting poison in the food. He'd been permitted to eat there the night he'd arrived only as a special circumstance. But he'd been assured that Arval was fine and doing well in his training.

Ulvar had forbidden Revan from telling anyone that he was going to Enrat to meet with Queen Andissa, so while he yearned to tell Arval that he was going on another adventure, he was sad that his friend wouldn't be coming and that he couldn't even tell him about it. "Utmost secrecy is required for this journey," Ulvar had said. "If word reaches the Nojii or King Vraniss, they'll set an ambush somewhere and you'll be captured. Only the council knows of our plans. When the time for you to leave arrives, those who will be travelling with you will know as well. But until then do not speak of our plans to anyone."

And Revan hadn't. Several weeks after arriving at the keep, Ulvar came to him in the library one evening and asked him to come with him. Revan had followed, mystified. They'd walked through hallways and passages that Revan had been down before, but at the end of one corridor deep in the keep, Ulvar reached behind a tapestry and manipulated some kind of device. A large section of the stone wall swung out silently, revealing a dark tunnel roughly hewn from the bedrock of the hill. Two Jix in grey leather and cloaks stood waiting with torches. "This is where we part ways," Ulvar said. "Tonight, you will begin your journey to Enrat. These men will guide you directly to Stormtide Castle. Do as they say, and you'll be fine. And remember – we trust and believe in you." One of the waiting Jix held out a sword out to him and Revan buckled it around his waist. "I hope you'll not need this on the journey," Ulvar said.

"Thank you for all you've done for me. I'll do my best not to disappoint you."

"I know you will lad. Safe journey. Take care of him boys," Ulvar said to the waiting Jix. Then he turned away and was gone. The stone door closed behind him.

Chapter 34

t begins tonight," Yelun said. The group of men gathered around him in The Short Wall nodded in agreement. "The Nojii have murdered and abused us long enough. And if the king and the Wardens won't do anything about it, we will. Are the weapons caches in place?" A young man in front nodded. "Good. Everyone knows what to do. Get back to your homes and alert your teams. The signal will be a fire at the first bridge south of Heavy Chest Crescent. When you see it, move quickly to your assigned areas. Not a single Nojii is to be spared. And if the Wardens interfere, do for them too. Good luck to everyone."

The men filed out of the tavern quickly and Yelun was left alone. He walked slowly to the bar and poured himself a mug of his finest ale. If he was going to die tonight, then he'd enjoy the best before the end. He sat on a stool and gazed into nothing until he heard the door open. Turning around he saw an older woman closing the door behind her. He recognized her as she turned to face him.

"Endanna! What are you doing here?!"

"Nice to see you too Yelun."

"I didn't mean it wasn't good to see you, it's just that its late."

"I'm aware of the hour. What I don't fully understand is what's about to happen."

"Happen?"

"Don't play dumb with me Yelun. I've known you too long. Something bad is going to happen. Probably tonight. And I want to know what it is."

Yelun sighed, knowing he was caught out. "Bad things are going to happen tonight Endanna. You really should be home with Valbirnia."

"I will go straight home as soon as you tell me what's going on."

"There is going to be a revolt."

Endanna raised an eyebrow but didn't speak.

"What I mean is that we are going to kill the Nojii."

"Who is we?"

"Most of the men in this city. Except the Heavy Chest Crescent worms. They'll stay behind their wall, with their guards, while we do the work they won't do."

Endanna let out a long breath. "I was afraid this was going to happen."

"These outrages can't go on anymore. And if the Wardens try to stop us, we'll deal with them as well. You really should get home now. It won't be very long before it begins. I fear once it does, it will get out of control quickly."

"You're right I'm sure. Things like this never seem to turn out the way they're intended to. I should get home now."

"If you have a weapon of any kind, get it and go down into your cellar with Valbirnia. Bring water and food. It may be a few days before it's over. And barricade the door once you're down there."

"Thank you Yelun. I could always count on you to tell me the truth." Endanna hurried out of the tavern leaving Yelun alone again.

The fire was started in a large wagon filled with hay which had been soaked in oil. When the torch was tossed onto it, the flames rocketed up into the night. The signal was seen by observers throughout the city who spread the word to groups of men who fanned out to find Nojii. They weren't hard to locate. Most were in taverns, drunk on as much ale as they could swallow. The men of the city attacked them where they sat at tables, on barstools or standing in corners. Most were dragged outside after a scuffle and executed in the street. The teams then moved on to the next inn or tavern.

But word spread quickly among the Nojii that something was happening, and it didn't take long for them to start to organize themselves. Nillit, Bhinja, and Pinsi were in the inn they'd appropriated, drinking and deciding what to do with the rest of their night, when a

Nojii none of them knew burst in. He was bleeding profusely from a ragged slash on his left arm.

"They're killing us," he gasped.

"Who?" Bhinja asked, rising from his chair.

"Everyone! The whole city is attacking us!"

Bhinja knew instantly what was happening. "Get that gash tended to," he said as he checked his sword and the knives in his belt. "Let's go," he said to Nillit and Pinsi.

They rushed out the door, collecting four other Nojii who had been drinking in the small yard in front of the inn. "Get your weapons," Bhinja roared as he stalked by. The men were quick to arm themselves and fell in with Bhinja's group. They could hear cries and the clash of steel from a street just ahead. As they rounded a corner, they saw a large group of men attacking a much smaller group of Nojii. They'd been backed against the wall of a building and were battling for their lives. A guttural scream emanated from Bhinja's throat as he drew his sword and crashed into the rear of the group. He slashed left and right, his rage fueling his strikes, and many men fell to the ground stricken or ran before him. His companions were equally as fierce. This was what Nojii were made for, and they'd finally gotten to do it.

Endanna had been true to her word. After waking Valbirnia she'd taken her granddaughter into the cellar. They'd brought food and water, just as Yelun had suggested, and Endanna had also brought a stout club she kept in The Needle and Thread for unruly customers. There was no lock or bar on the door to the cellar, so they'd tied a rope from the handle to the railing leading downstairs. They hoped it would hold. Moreover, they hoped no one would find them. Outside they could hear the screams and cries of men fighting and dying, the clash of arms and the sound of horns sounding alarms. The Wardens would be responding to those horns soon. It wouldn't be long before the entire city was a battleground.

There were number of shelves and cabinets in the cellar that they moved to block the bottom of the stairs to slow anyone coming down them. But the reality was that if anyone did get the door open and came down, they were trapped.

Arval was awakened by a strange sound. As he rose from his bed, he noticed several other Jix staring out the window towards the center of the city and talking animatedly. He walked up behind them and could clearly hear the sounds of steel on steel and cries of men. Smoke rose from several places throughout the city.

"What's going on?" he asked sleepily. Horns began to sound just as he finished his question.

"There's fighting in the city," one man said.

"Fighting? Why-" he stopped himself in mid-sentence. Of course, he knew the answer: the people had finally had enough of the Nojii and were exacting their revenge. As he watched out the window, more fires sprang up. It looked like entire sections of the city would soon be in flames. His thoughts turned immediately to Plistral and his Khet, and Valbirnia.

"I have to go," he said as he raced back to his bed and started pulling his clothes out of the chest next to it.

"What do you mean go?" someone asked. He didn't bother to look at who it was. He donned his grey leather armor, strapped his sword to his hip and threw a black cloak on over it all. He didn't want anyone to know he was a Jix unless he wanted them to know; the blue cloak would identify him too quickly.

"You can't go. We haven't been summoned yet."

"I have friends there who will need my help. I'm going."

"But, but.." Arval didn't hear the rest. Once dressed he dashed down the stairs and out into the courtyard, stopping only long enough to pick up a bow and quiver of arrows that had been left by the archery targets. The enormous black gate was closed for the night, but since he'd been accepted into the Jix, he'd been shown other ways into and out of the keep. He turned left instead of heading for the gate and ran to the tower at the corner of the wall. Passing into it he hurried down a flight of stairs which ended in a tunnel deep below the keep. There was no light, but he'd taken a torch from the inner wall next to the gate, and with its flame flickering from the speed of his movement, he found his way to the end. In front of him was a wall of stone. He reached for a rough knob of rock on the right, gave it a twist, and the whole wall swung out. As he exited the tunnel, he found himself behind a cleverly constructed screen of boulders that hid the doorway. He had to drop to his hands and knees to crawl out of the small passageway, but in moments he was out and onto the lower reaches of the hill. The keep towered high above him. He gazed at it for a moment, wondering if he'd ever be inside it again, then turned and ran towards The Needle and Thread, using all the speed he had.

Yelun and his team were tiring rapidly. The Nojii had been utterly surprised at first and they'd been able to kill several. But a few had escaped and alerted others. They were now forming into groups of their own and counterattacking. And the Wardens were in the mix too. Yelun wasn't sure which side they were taking, or if they were just cracking any skull they ran across, but he needed to find out. There had been over twenty in his team at the beginning, they were now down to twelve, and only three had not been wounded in some fashion.

"Those Nojii are fierce," one man said. "Do we have a chance at getting them all?"

"We will get as many as we can," Yelun replied. "I'm in this to the end. Are you?" he asked the group. A few nods and halfhearted murmurs of assent were the only response. These men were not warriors, trained to fight and with the stamina for prolonged combat. They needed to find another team to join up with and soon, or the next group of Nojii they ran into might be the last one they saw.

They'd crossed the river a short time back and were now on the same side as the Azure Palace. Horns of alarm were sounding from its ramparts and towers. Surely everyone in the place must be awake with all that noise. Yelun smiled at the thought of that worm, King Vraniss, running around beside himself with fury over the fires and fighting in the city. Everyone knew how he hated disorder. Yelun was leading his team in the general direction of The Needle and Thread, but they were still a bit to the north of it. They'd been staying off the main road; the side roads provided more cover and better hiding places should they need them.

As they came to an intersection, Yelun saw a group of about ten Nojii standing in the street to the left. A group of eight Wardens were with them. They appeared to be talking. Motioning his men to stop, Yelun peered around the corner of a building and watched. They were definitely talking. That was not a good sign. If the Wardens and Nojii had joined forces, the men of the city were going to be massacred. Those not killed this night would surely greet death in White Square in the days to come. Both groups suddenly turned and began walking towards Yelun and his men.

"Go back, quickly," he urgently whispered. The men, looking perplexed, began to turn back the way they'd come. "Move!" he admonished. Suddenly cries rang out behind them. Yelun turned to look back just as a group of about thirty men poured out of the street opposite his adversaries and rushed the Wardens and Nojii. There was a fierce clash of steel as the groups joined in combat.

"Let's go!" he cried to his group. Yelun led them in a charge to join their comrades. The Nojii were vicious and deadly in a fight. Two or three would attack one man, finish him off, then turn to another.

"We have to break them away from each other," Yelun cried. Three of his men, instantly seeing what he meant, rushed one of the Nojii and separated him from his comrades. With quick slashes and thrusts of their old and rusty swords, they finished him. But just as quickly four Nojii attacked Yelun's men. Three were slain almost immediately, and Yelun himself barely evaded a thrust from one of his enemies. He danced back out of their reach while his remaining companion went down. A quick glance told him that although the Nojii and Wardens were outnumbered, they were going to win. A fire was burning in a building across from the battle, and the flames painted the gory scene in hues of orange and red.

"Regroup!" Yelun shouted. His men turned and ran several paces back and formed into a tight knot. There had been over forty of them. In mere moments they were less than twenty. Four Nojii and three Wardens lay dead, but that wasn't enough. Groans and cries of dying men rang out in the smoky air. Blood ran down the street like rainwater.

The Wardens and Nojii had taken advantage of the respite to regroup as well. Now they split into two groups, with the Nojii coming up the street on the left, the Wardens on the right. Yelun could see they intended to catch his group between them.

"Take the Wardens first. There's only five of them. Eight of you guard our backs from those Nojii. We'll deal with them when the Wardens are dead." Yelun said. The men formed themselves into their groups, ready to resume the fight. Just as the Wardens and city men resumed their clash, loud screams were heard from behind them. Yelun glanced over his shoulder and saw at least ten more Nojii rushing his men's backs. They were led by a huge man with a ropy white scar running across his chest from his waist to his left shoulder. His swirling and spiky tattoos stood out starkly against his skin in the hideous light of the fire. Strangely, his left eye, white as a cloud, whirled crazily. Yelun stared at it in amazement for a moment. How odd that in this moment, with life itself at stake, his attention should be riveted by a blind eye in one of his enemies. He recovered his senses quickly.

"Run!" he yelled. "We can't win this fight!" But there was nowhere to go. Nojii and Wardens to either side, had fanned out just enough to prevent them from running forward, and more Nojii were coming up from behind. Yelun decided that if this was where his life ended, then he was taking as many Nojii with him as he could. He raised his sword and began stalking towards the closest one when the man suddenly sprouted and arrow between his eyes. The Nojii on his left just as quickly had one through his throat. Both men fell and Yelun rushed into the gap, swinging his sword at the

Nojii on his left. A huge gash opened down the man's left side, exposing his ribs and opening a door which his viscera used to spill out onto the ground.

"This way!" he screamed as he charged out of the opening and toward the empty street beyond. His men followed quickly. A few of them fell as they tried to cover the escape, but so did two more Nojii and three Wardens, all with arrows in various lethal places. Who was shooting those things?! Yelun didn't know but swore that if he ever found out, that man would have free ale in The Short Wall for life. If it was still standing after tonight. He glanced over his shoulder one last time as he ran and, although it was hard to be sure in the smoke and the firelight, he thought he saw a figure in a black cloak and holding a bow disappear into the shadows of a side street.

"Where did those arrows come from?! Did anyone see?!" Bhinja roared. He was furious. Bhinja always was, but this was a special kind of anger. The kind displayed by a man who has seen his quarry, had it right in front of him, only to have it escape at the ultimate moment. The Nojii around him shook their heads, a few muttered 'no's' were audible. The Wardens had run off to some other part of the city. Probably to find more of their kind. Bhinja didn't care. Let them run, he thought. Most of them were cowards who weren't any good in a fight anyway. The only way they were effective was in numbers. He'd take one of his Nojii against ten of them any day.

"Fan out and find that archer," he ordered. His men didn't need to be told twice. In groups of two and three they ran off down various streets, hunting their leader's prey. Bhinja himself, along with four more Nojii jogged off down the street in pursuit of the men who had escaped. He would not leave them alive for long.

Arval drifted through the smoke and shadows away from the battle he'd just turned. He'd seen Yelun in the middle of the fight, saw that he was about to be cut down, and had fired his arrow without thinking. He was still slightly amazed at how easy it had been. And at how accurate a shot it was. Practicing on archery targets was one thing, even when they were at a great distance. Actually, hitting a man, a living being, who was moving, was beyond anything he'd imagined. He wasn't sure if he was happy about it or not. His first shots had killed Nojii, the last had gotten three Wardens, and while he had great enmity for both groups, he still felt a twinge of regret. What if they'd had families? Children? Hinbladd had told him that the first time he killed someone with an arrow, he would probably feel this way. But still, actually having these feelings was very different than just thinking or hearing about them. Strangely, he hadn't felt this way when he'd killed the bandit on the road with Revan. Maybe it was because that man was trying to kill him, and he'd just defended himself. These kills were from a distance, and he hadn't been directly threatened. It didn't matter.

They were dead and he'd saved Yelun and his men. That was what counted.

As he moved silently through the shadows of the city, he could see even more smoke rising. Sounds of battle rose up from streets close and far. The city was destroying itself. And for what? Why would King Vraniss ever have let those Nojii into the city? He must have known what they were doing. Why didn't he put a stop to it? Too late now, he thought. All he could do was try to get to Valbirnia and make sure she was safe until this was over. And Plistral! He had to find his Khet. He stopped for a moment, pondering. He couldn't do both; there were too many Nojii and too many Wardens out and about. Plistral could take care of himself. The Hive had been in a good spot if they hadn't moved it. The whole Khet should be in the cellar of that burned out house. The fighting hadn't started until well after dark, and the Khet was almost always inside before nightfall. So, he'd go to Valbirnia. It was only her and her grandmother in their store; they had no one to protect them. The Khet had ways of protecting itself. His decision made, he moved out of the shadows where he'd been and back into the street, breaking into a run as he made his way toward The Needle and Thread.

Nillit saw a shadow dart out of a darkened building two streets ahead of him. It was very dark in this part of the city, but he thought he saw a bow slung across the figure's back.

"This way! Hurry!" he said. Pinsi and the other Nojii with them ran after him.

Nillit's eyes were fixed on the spot where he'd seen the shadowy figure disappear into the murk. As they ran he thought he saw glimpses of the person up ahead of them. But the figure was a lot more than two streets ahead now. How could that be?! It's just a man. How could anyone move that fast? Maybe it was a different person and the figure with the bow had gone another direction. Just as the thought occurred to him, he saw the figure stop and look at a building. There was a structure on fire a street away, and in the glow of the firelight he clearly saw the outline of the bow across the figure's back. He was right – this was their quarry! The figure suddenly disappeared inside the building.

"Keep quiet," Nillit said as he slowed. The building where the figure had disappeared was only half a street ahead now. "This is the swine who killed our boys with those arrows. We're going to get him. Keep your heads on and your eyes open."

They were now in front of the building. Nillit could read the sign above the door in the orange light from the fire, The Needle and Thread, it said. He wondered briefly why the figure would be going into a clothing store. No matter. Whoever it was would be dead soon and whatever was inside would belong to the Nojii, or he'd just burn the place down. He stepped through the open door and into the shop.

Yelun was very winded. They'd run he knew not how far. In their already fatigued state, it probably wasn't a great distance. He hadn't had a destination in mind but had simply run to get away from the Wardens and Nojii. Now that they were, he thought, a safe distance away, he'd stopped to catch his breath and figure out where in the city they were. He had a small barn behind The Short Wall where he kept a few chickens and some stores. In the floor was a concealed trapdoor that led to a small cellar where he planned to hide until the fighting was over. If he could get to it. There was room for maybe four others if they squeezed, but he wasn't planning on entertaining guests. The men with him, most bent over with their hands on their knees, gasping, would have similar hiding places they would go to. He did a quick count. The band of over forty when they'd joined the battle not long ago had been whittled down to sixteen. Over twenty men dead, he thought. Actually, almost thirty. How many more would die before this was over? He collected his thoughts and looked around. They were still on the opposite side of the river from The Short Wall. He'd have to get back across. Another look at his men told him that their fighting was about done for the night; they were exhausted, and many were bleeding from a variety of wounds.

"I don't know how much more you men have in you, but I'm about spent," he said. A few murmured agreement. "I'm going to try to make my way back across the river to my hiding spot. I trust most, if not all of you, have places to hide?" There were nods all around. "Good. You should get there. Does anyone live on this side of the river?"

No one nodded.

"Alright. Then we travel together until we get across. We go our separate ways as we all get close to wherever we're going. Agreed?"

They all nodded.

"First, we need someone to scout ahead, make sure there aren't any Nojii or Wardens waiting for us. It should be someone who still has some energy."

One younger man raised his hand.

"Good. Go on ahead of us, but make sure you keep us in sight. Don't call out – use hand gestures to let us know if we should keep moving or stay put."

The man nodded his agreement and moved out. The rest of the group followed with a last admonishment from Yelun to keep quiet. As they moved down the street, they broke into two groups, one on each side of the road and up tight against the buildings. It would be easier to duck inside somewhere to hide if they were already close to a place of concealment. Being in the middle of the road could be deadly. The sounds of combat were distant now, and Yelun felt good about their chances for getting across the river unseen. He'd swim it if he had to.

A few streets on he realized that he was getting close to Endanna's shop. When the scout turned to gesture that it was safe to move forward, Yelun gestured to him to come back.

"There's a clothing store called The Needle and Thread a couple streets up," he said to the man when he'd rejoined the group. "It belongs to a friend of mine and I'd like to look in on her before we get to the river. If anyone objects, you're free to go on alone if you'd like. It'll only take a moment."

No one said objected, so they kept on, the scout resuming his place in the lead. A few moments later the man stopped and pointed to a sign above his head. Yelun could see from the light of a nearby burning building that it was the place. The rest of the group quickly caught up with the scout and stopped outside the shop. Yelun made his way to the door and was surprised to hear the sounds of combat inside.

Arval walked cautiously through the dim interior of the shop. It appeared that no one had been in here; everything was intact. But strangely the door was unlocked. Maybe Valbirnia and her grandmother had gone somewhere to hide when the fighting started. He'd only ever been in the main room of the shop, but he knew they lived here, so he moved quietly to a doorway in the rear of the store that he assumed led to the living quarters. It was very dark in this part of the building. The fire across the street had let some light in through the door and windows, but this part of the shop was completely cloaked in shadow.

He was in a hallway with doors on either side, all closed. One by one he opened them slowly and whispered Valbirnia's name inside. All was quiet. At the end of the hallway was a door with a window that looked to the outside, a set of stairs led up on the right, and another closed door on the left. He decided to try upstairs first. Slowly and as quietly as he could, he started ascending. Some of the steps creaked as he put his weight on them, but that was the only sound, other than the faint din of battle from outside somewhere. At the top of the stairs, he found himself in a wide room with a bed at each end. A large curtain on a cord that stretched across the room hung on one side of the wall. It looked to serve as a divider. Valbirnia and her grandmother must sleep up here and the curtain was for a bit of privacy. Other than some miscellaneous furniture and clothes, the room was empty. Only one place left to look.

Arval started back down the stairs, going a little faster now that he was sure he was alone in the building. The stairs creaked a little louder and his boots made faint echoes in the stairwell. When he reached the bottom, he saw the only door he hadn't tried directly across from him. He stepped out into the hallway and a sword flashed in front of his face, missing his nose by a hair's breadth.

Valbirnia looked at her grandmother, her eyes wide with fear. They'd lit one small candle because neither one of them liked sitting in the inky blackness of the cellar. They'd been there for several hours, listening to the sounds of men fighting and dying, but with no real idea of what was going on outside.

Now there was someone in the shop above them. The boards creaked as whoever it was walked down the hall toward the door to the cellar. The steps paused right outside. Valbirnia's heart was beating as fast as she'd ever felt it. Her grandmother was holding her hand, both their palms sweating so much that their grip kept slipping. She finally dropped Valbirnia's hand and hugged her close, the club in her right hand.

But the person upstairs decided to go up to their bedroom first. They heard the stairs creak with the person's footsteps. When it was silent again, they knew that the intruder was in the bedroom they shared. It would be very soon before the steps creaked with the person's descent. Just then another sound reached their ears – more footsteps up above. These had come in through the shop the same as the first person. Only there was more than one this time. There was no way the two of them could fight off more than one person. And maybe not even one if he was armed and knew his business. They were alone and there was no one to help them.

Arval was so surprised at the sword flashing in front of his face that he staggered back a step. It saved his life. As he did, another sword was thrust through the air he'd just occupied. His instincts took over at that moment. He realized instantly that his bow was of no use here and drew his sword. The days of practicing with it had served him well; it was out in a flash. The window in the door to the outside let in just enough light for him to see that he was facing at least two Nojii, one on either side of the opening to the stairs. He attacked the one to the right first. His sword flashed up in a short arc and caught the Nojii's sword hand across the back. His fingers and half his hand, along with his sword, fell to the ground. A scream of pain and anger escaped his lips even as his good hand grabbed what was left of the ruined one.

The other Nojii hadn't wasted any time, and he slashed at Arval's back. The sword made contact with his left shoulder; the grey leather armor he wore kept him from being grievously injured. But the force of the blow caused him to stagger, and his right shoulder crashed into the Nojii with half a hand. Arval took the opportunity to shove his sword through the Nojii's neck. He quickly pulled it from the dying man and spun to face his attacker. Except there were two of them. Arval's sword flew up to meet a thrust from the Nojii in front, barely knocking it aside. The one behind didn't have room to attack in the narrow hallway, but his eyes were fierce with the delight of battle and desire to kill. Arval swept into a form he'd learned in the keep called Hummingbird. It consisted of short, swift swings of the sword, specifically created for fighting in confined places like this. The Nojii was quick and strong, but he didn't have Arval's training, even though he'd only had a few weeks of it. Most Nojii were brutes who attacked through sheer force. They didn't have much finesse, nor had they been instructed in the ways of weapons like Arval had. A few quick and short swings had disarmed the man and a fast thrust had done for him, leaving Arval's blade buried in his stomach. The second Nojii, sensing his chance, had tried to shoulder past the dying man to get at Arval, and when he had, the movement of the soon to be dead man's body had wrenched the sword out of Arval's grip.

Weaponless, he backed toward the door to the outside. If he could run up the stairs, he might be able to find something in the bedroom to use as a weapon. But this Nojii was fast and was on him before he could get turned to the stairs. Just as the man raised his sword to bring it down on Arval's head, a blade erupted from his chest, spraying Arval's face and cloak in the dead man's blood. As he fell Arval looked behind him and found himself looking into a familiar face.

"Yelun!" he exclaimed. "Where in the dark depths did you come from?"

"I just saved your life and you're going to question me?" Yelun replied, smiling.

"Tradan's Pocket am I glad to see you!"

"And I you, lad."

"Have you seen Valbirnia? I came here looking for her, but she's not in any of the rooms I've searched. The only place I haven't looked is behind this door."

"That's the cellar. I told Endanna to take her and hide down there earlier tonight. I'll bet that's where we'll find them." He knocked on the door and called out to them. After a moment they heard muffled scraping noises, like furniture being moved, then the sound of footsteps on the stairs.

"Yelun!" a woman exclaimed as the door opened. "It's you! Thanks be to all that there is!"

Arval could see Endanna and Valbirnia in the dim light.

"Do I know you?" Endanna asked him.

"No, but I'm a friend of Fendalon's. And I've met your granddaughter."

Valbirnia looked closely at him in the gloom. "I've met you?" she asked.

"We can talk about everything later," Yelun said. "Right now, we have to get out of here. The Wardens have joined with the Nojii and they're slaughtering any of us that they find. I have a place behind The Short Wall where we can all hide until this is over. Let's go. There's a group of men outside waiting for us."

The four of them stepped gingerly over the bodies of the Nojii, Arval paused long enough to retrieve his sword, then made their way down the hall and out into the street. Yelun's men were still waiting for them.

"Let's get moving men. And we have some company."

Most of the group eyed Arval and his bow for a moment, then began walking off down the street. They hadn't gotten far when a scream of rage rang out behind them. The group turned almost as one and saw five Nojii sprinting toward them from three streets away. Arval didn't hesitate. He pulled his bow from his back, drew an arrow from the quiver, and loosed, all with a speed and fluidity that made the eyes of everyone who saw it bulge with amazement. A Nojii on the left fell dead with an arrow in his chest. He drew and fired again and one on the right fell. The other three slowed, now only a street away from them, their battle cries dying in their throats. Arval had nocked another arrow and was about to loose it when they turned and ran off down a side street. Just before they passed behind a building, Arval was shocked to see a distinctive white scar running diagonally from the left shoulder to the waist of the one in the lead. Bhinja! He made to go after him, but Yelun caught the shoulder of his cloak.

"Not now lad. We need you if we're all going to live."

Arval couldn't believe Bhinja had been right in front of him. He burned with rage at that hated Nojii and wanted nothing more than to chase him down and end him. But Yelun's words broke through his anger, and he calmed himself.

"You're right," he said with a deep sigh. "But one day I will kill that man."

"I've no doubt," Yelun said. The others were staring at Arval as if he was made of solid gold. A couple smiled and clapped him on the back. His cloak had fallen open, revealing his distinctive grey leather armor, and one man, staring at it said, "I can't believe the Jix are out here! And on our side!"

"I'm not a Jix. Not yet anyway. Let's go," Arval said. He led the way as they moved toward the river.

They were able to get across without incident. The bridge was unguarded and unoccupied. The streets, while filled with debris and the bodies of the dead, were deserted. The sounds of fighting were still audible, but they were distant and diminishing. As they reached different streets, men began to peel off by ones and twos, bidding farewell and good fortune to their comrades. Almost all had a special word of thanks to Arval. He smiled abashedly and muttered some banality about it being nothing.

"You'll be famous by this time tomorrow," Yelun said. "Those men will tell their friends and families the story of what you did, and they will tell others. The whole city will soon know of your exploits tonight."

Valbirnia glanced at him out of the corner of her eye. It was clear she still didn't know who he was but realized that now wasn't the time to discuss it.

"I'm not sure I want that kind of notoriety Yelun," Arval said. The last two men turned off on a side street, also praising Arval and thanking him for saving their lives before they left.

"The Short Wall is just ahead. We'll go around the back to my secret little spot," Yelun told them.

They followed him through the gate and to the rear of the building where he showed them into the barn and opened his hidden trapdoor. Once they were safely inside and the door was closed, they all breathed a sigh of relief.

Yelun lit a lamp and regarded his tired and dirty guests. "I've a cask of ale in the corner. Only two mugs, but we can share. Don't know about you, but after tonight I could use a drink." Everyone nodded and Yelun filled the two mugs. He shared his with Arval, Valbirnia and Endanna took the other. In a moment he was filling them a second time.

"Where do I know you from?" Valbirnia asked.

"I came into your shop several weeks ago to give your grandmother a message. She wasn't there and I never got a chance to come back."

"I remember you now!" she said. "I wondered what happened to you. When you didn't return, I figured it wasn't a very important message."

"What message?" Endanna asked. "From who?"

"From Fendalon," Arval replied.

"Its true Endanna," Yelun said. "He and his friend came to me too with a message from Fendalon."

Endanna's face had gone white. "He's still alive..." she whispered hoarsely. "I can't believe it. What did he say?"

Arval told them the story of meeting Fendalon with Revan and gave her his message.

"I'm so glad he's alright," she said. "This night has been full of surprising things."

"How did you come to be in that armor?" Yelun asked.

Arval sighed and told them that story too. "I'm not sure I'll be allowed to rejoin the Jix. I left without permission or orders. And I'm not truly a Jix yet, just an initiate in training."

"Worry about that tomorrow," Yelun said. "Right now, we should get some rest. Tomorrow we'll decide what to do."

The four of them made themselves as comfortable as they could in the small, cramped space, and soon sleep found them all.

Chapter 35

"Who is responsible for this?" Vraniss asked acidly. The group of advisors and officials standing before him remained silent. "Surely with all of your resources one of you has some idea of how this happened and who started it." He glared at them one by one, focusing on each face in turn. Many were openly sweating; most couldn't meet his gaze. Visions of White Square and scaffolds, of crowds and headsmen whirled through their minds, the fear of which was writ large on their faces.

"So, whom shall I execute first?" Vraniss asked. They were gathered in his office, two rows of them stood across the desk from him as he paced back and forth. The carpet he trod was getting very threadbare, but Vraniss didn't give it a thought. "For the last time, who has some information for me?" Virta, who had remained silent, now chose his moment to speak.

"Sire, I believe I may have information that could be of some assistance."

"At last! Someone has something and has found the fortitude to share it! Speak!"

"It has come to my attention that two young men have been seen in the city who were at the, uh, excavation where so recently… unusual circumstances, er, caused such… distress. It is my opinion that they were involved in the events last night. Their names have become known to me." Virta had already shared this information with the king, but he sensed that it was the right time to share it with everyone else. They'd had no luck finding the two boys on their own. Perhaps with the help of the rest of the palace staff they'd have more success. Besides, Vraniss had told him to tell everyone. This meeting had been planned in advance with that express purpose. The events in the city had simply added another topic for it.

"And what would they be?" Vraniss asked, his voice low and dripping with deadly menace.

"Revan and Arval, Sire."

Vraniss stalked down the stairs to the deepest part of his dungeon. The wet and moldy walls, the stale and dank air made no impression. His destination was clear, his thoughts fixed on his singular purpose. It didn't take long for him to arrive in the corridor he sought. The door that was his destination loomed before him; he opened the small latch and let the metal plate fall, revealing the small window into the cell beyond.

"So have you finally decided to kill me then?" a hoarse voice asked from inside.

"No. I have a proposition for you." He heard muffled movements inside, then a pair of eyes became visible at the small opening. Their whites were bloodshot, the brown around the pupil lusterless, but there was still something in them Vraniss didn't like. A spirit of defiance, he thought. This man would die before he broke.

"I have two people I'd like you to capture for me. None of my men seem to be capable of accomplishing the task. Perhaps you are."

"You'd have to let me out of here if you want me to capture someone for you. Then I'd have to bring them to you. Assuming I decided to come back. And what do I get if I succeed? My old room in your dungeon back?"

"Your life with a full pardon from me."

The man was silent for a time. "What if I just disappear once you let me loose?"

"If you do, I will send the entire Jarradan army after you. They will have orders to take you alive and keep you that way. Until you can be returned to me. And when you arrive, you'll wish I'd kept you here in the first place."

"I'll tell you something. Because I like you so much," the man said. Vraniss thought from the tone of his voice that he was smiling. "Where I'm from they have a name for me."

Vraniss remained silent, although his interest was piqued. This man hadn't offered any information about himself since Vraniss had overpowered him in his bedchamber. Even when he'd been under the most extreme duress.

"Would you like to know what it is?"

"I'm breathless with anticipation."

The man chuckled softly. His eyes suddenly lit up with a fierceness Vraniss hadn't seen since they'd grappled the night he captured him.

"I have a reputation in my homeland. And in other lands. It's well deserved. Until I met you, I'd never failed in an assignment and never been captured."

"Yes, I'm sure you're peerless in your choice of vocation. So, what do they call you?"

The eyes just stared at Vraniss for a long moment. Finally, he spoke. "They call me The Vanishing Man."

Barittin stood next to General Jaradlik Remerska on the edge of the low plateau looking down into Bentravirri. The army they'd brought here to the southern border of Jarradan was camped behind them. The smell of cookfires wafted towards them, the sounds of the camp clear even though they were a good distance away. Armies in camp were always noisy when they weren't about to go into battle.

"See that there," Remerska asked, stretching his arm off towards the left. "That's Andissa's force." In the far distance, on the grassy plain below the plateau was a dark blotch on the landscape. Smoke drifted from their fires, but they were far too distant to smell them. To the right was another, larger blotch on the plain. Remerska gestured toward it, "And there is Zeryph's force. They'll meet in the middle tomorrow. It'll be a banquet for the worms by nightfall." The Blackfire, as mysterious as ever loomed high above the scene. Barittin watched its violent revolution. The rising and falling of the inky peaks and valleys as they grew and collapsed fascinated him for a moment. He'd never been this close to it, and from their vantage on the plateau, even though it wasn't very tall, the enormous spinning mass blotted out nearly all of the southern sky. Red and gold lines shot through its ragged fringes, light lightning in a spring storm. He wondered idly what they were. Remerska had spent his life campaigning throughout the three kingdoms; this sight was nothing new to him. But Barittin was transfixed by it. He'd heard the stories and rumors of those who had supposedly passed through it and returned. Being this close he didn't believe them. Anyone trying to penetrate that would surely be destroyed instantly. Its violence made him shiver. Somewhere to the south, he was sure, the very earth was being torn apart by that savage spinning wheel of black.

"There are no natural features for either army to use to its advantage," Remerska said, drawing Barittin out of his reverie. "They'll meet each other head on. The slaughter will be enormous. Whichever side has the best cavalry will probably win the day."

"Drisavan cavalry is well-regarded," Barittin said.

"Yes, they are professionals. But the Bentravirri are no slouches in horsecraft either. If I was a betting man, I'd not lay a wager on this battle. Should it happen."

"You seemed sure it would a moment ago. Have you changed your mind?"

"Someone down there has got a trick or two. I would, in their place. If it works, it could stop the battle before it really begins, or turn it at a critical point. Or perhaps the commanders will see what I just described to you and decide the risk is too great."

"What kind of trick?"

"Any number of things. One of them could have sent a force far to the south to circle in behind the other and attack from the rear or during the night. Or maybe one of them coated the field in oil and is just waiting for the enemy to walk into the area before shooting a flaming arrow into it."

Barittin nodded thoughtfully. "Our scouts say that each side is preparing for battle. Seems that they want to fight."

"Perhaps," Remerska said. "A good general always has his soldiers ready for battle."

"Whatever their intentions, I'm hungry and tired. Time for me to find a meal and my bed."

"Until tomorrow then," Remerska said.

Barittin found his meal, and his bed soon after.

Shouts woke him seemingly as soon as he'd fallen asleep. Springing from his bed, Barittin hurriedly pulled on his clothes and rushed out of his tent. He wasn't terribly surprised to find it was still dark, although a glow lit the eastern horizon; day would be on them soon.

"What's all this about?" he asked the guard outside.

"I don't know My Lord."

Growling Barittin hurried toward the command tent where he could see lamps burning through the open doorway. Remerska and several of his lieutenants were inside, gathered around a sweating man who was also bleeding from a slash on his shoulder.

"...and that's how I got away General," the man said just as Barittin walked in.

"What's going on," he demanded. Remerska turned to him.

"This man is one of our scouts. He was just attacked by what he claims was a group of Bentravirri cavalry. Another of our scouts reported seeing a large mass of horse galloping north of our position. Toward the Drisavan side of the field."

"On the plateau? On our side of the border?" Barittin asked, incredulous.

"Yes," Remerska replied simply.

"That constitutes an invasion! It's an act of war!"

"We know. Our men are being roused as we speak and told to prepare for battle."

"We're going to war?"

"The King gave me very specific instructions. Any incursion into our land is to be considered a hostile act and met with swift retribution. If soldiers from one of those armies are on this plateau, that qualifies."

Barittin was mortified. He was not a military man, his skills were in diplomacy and management, not soldiering. While he'd received some rudimentary weapons training, he was far from a warrior. Now here he was about to be cast into battle. Perhaps he'd stay in the command tent, offer assistance to the commanders.

"You are in charge of the army General, I just hope you know what you're getting us into."

"I'm following my orders. Nothing more. You may want to find some armor and a weapon. Sometimes battles end up making their way towards the rear."

He could hear the crash of steel and the screams of men from where he stood on the edge of the plateau. The scouts had been right – the Bentravirri had sent a detachment of cavalry to the north, through Jarradan, in order to attack the Drisavans from the rear. They'd hit them at daybreak just as their foot soldiers had begun their charge across the open ground. The Drisavans had been ready for the frontal assault. Waves of arrows from a large cadre of archers had mown down scores of the Bentravirri soldiers as they raced across the plain. But the cavalry had wreaked havoc on the rear of the Drisavan camp until enough men had been mustered to stop them. What had at first appeared to be a rout in favor of Bentravirri had turned into a free for all. Then the Jarradan army had joined the fracas. Their orders had been to attack only the Bentravirri, but the Drisavans, seeing another force entering the field, had attacked them. In short order the Jarradans were fighting both armies. The carnage was immense. Dead men and horses lay scattered all over the plain below.

The grass had turned red. Only on the fringes where the battle was the lightest was there any green left.

Remerska had retained a force of about two hundred men to guard the camp from any sneak attacks. He'd also had the horses saddled in case they needed to make a quick escape. The rest of his force was fully engaged. Three men stood to Barittin's right, each holding a flag on a long pole in each hand. They were of various colors and were used to signal the commanders below. From time to time a runner from the command tent would arrive with orders that were then relayed via combinations of flags. Messengers on horseback running to and from the battle below reported regularly to Remerska and his close aides in the tent. Late in the afternoon, the general finally emerged from the tent and came to stand next to Barittin.

"We've lost a lot of men, but it seems we're winning."

"Against two armies?" Barittin said, disbelievingly.

"They slaughtered each other for a time before we joined in. And kept at it once we joined. Each force has been dramatically reduced."

"When will it stop?"

"When it gets too dark to see, everyone will retreat, or perhaps one commander will order his force off the field if he decides his losses are too great."

They stood in silence for a time, watching the battle below. From this far away Barittin couldn't tell who was who. It was such a jumble of men and horses, lances and arrows, blood and dead, that he marveled that any commander had a clue what was happening. Shouts from behind caused them both to turn quickly around. Some of the soldiers left to guard the camp were pointing to the left, others to the right. Barittin looked both ways and was aghast at what he saw - large groups of soldiers on horseback approaching the camp at a gallop from either side. Riders in front of each group held long poles atop which pennants flew.

"Those are the standards of Bentravirri and Drisava!" Remerska shouted. "They're attacking our command post! We've got to ride. There are too many for us to fight." At that he broke into a dead run for the line of horses behind the command tent, shouting for everyone to evacuate as he ran. Barittin didn't need to watch any longer to see that the general was right. He too ran towards the horses as fast as he could. In a moment he could tell that he wasn't going to reach the horses in time. The soldiers bearing down on them would reach the camp before he could get mounted. He slowed, confused, and looked around for somewhere else to go. But the plateau was too open, too exposed. There were no trees or rocks to hide behind, no river to dive into. There was only a wide path leading from the plateau down to the killing field below, and that was out of the question. He was certain in that moment that he'd seen his last day.

The soldiers guarding the camp had formed into two lines, one facing each group of cavalry. These were brave men. Their enemies outnumbered them at least two to one, if not more, yet here they stood facing death fearlessly. Barittin wondered if he'd do the same in their place. The soldiers held long pikes pointed at the onrushing horses, the ends buried in the ground. But the attackers were seasoned, experienced warriors, and they didn't ride their mounts onto the deadly spears. Instead, they reined in their horses and several produced short bows with which they fired arrows at the pikemen. Many fell, but the others, also knowing their business, dropped their spears, drew swords, and rushed stationary the cavalry. Slashing and hacking to either side, they began to cut down riders and horses alike. Some twenty of them had picked up bows and were returning fire at the attacking enemy. But their numbers were too small; they were being cut down too quickly by the superior numbers of mounted men. Barittin realized that only moments remained until the entire contingent of guards was wiped out. He would follow soon after. General Remerska suddenly appeared in the midst of the battle, a short sword in each hand. He screamed as he whirled and slashed at the attackers, cutting them down from their horses. His presence bolstered the morale of his men, and they fought fiercely beside him. But he was just one man and would soon be overwhelmed.

The horsemen, seeing the general engaged in battle, began to form a ring around him, knocking Jarradanian soldiers out of the way with their horses. Barittin realized that the general would be cut down in moments, then the battle would really be over and his life with it. Just then screams rang out from the far northern side of the camp. He looked up and saw a small group of mounted men riding at full speed toward the ring of horsemen around the general. Everyone stopped for a moment and looked at these newcomers. Blue cloaks streamed out behind them, while their grey leather armor gleamed orange in the rays of the now setting sun. Barittin could hardly believe his eyes. The Jix were here!

The blue cloaked warriors crashed into the Bentravirri and Drisavan cavalry like a storm wave on the beach. Their sudden appearance rallied the remaining Jarradan soldiers who redoubled their attacks on their enemies. The Jix carved their way through the cavalry like fire through dry grass. Laying about them with their swords, they cut down scores of men. Somehow they could ride at full speed and still swing their swords so accurately that they killed men before they could even be challenged. But one thing confused Barittin. He'd counted nine mounted men when he'd first seen them, but only eight wore the armor and cloaks of the Jix. The other was wearing a black cloak and simple riding clothes. Yet he fought as fiercely as his deadly companions. Maybe more so. His sword arm flashed so quickly that Barittin could hardly see it. But he certainly saw the damage it caused. Men fell before him in numbers equal to those of the storied Jix. It seemed the Bentravirri and Drisavans couldn't even scratch a Jix, let alone slay one. It was soon apparent that the Jix were going to kill them all; in conjunction with what was left of Remerska's rear guard, they were simply decimating the attackers. Barittin was so stunned at the violence and effectiveness of the Jix' actions that he felt rooted to the spot where he stood. No one seemed interested in him. One man, unmounted and alone, was no real threat. As he watched, he began to understand just how deadly the Jix were. They had a reputation, and he'd seen many walking the streets of Kessar, even spoken to a few. But he'd never seen them fight. Until now. And it was an awesome sight to behold.

A horn sounded from the right side of the battle, where the Drisavans had come from. At its call, their soldiers spun their horses around and fled the battle. A moment later the Bentravirri did the same, albeit without a horn. Barittin considered it a wise move. The Jix didn't pursue either group as they galloped off but dismounted and began tending to their horses. Several had minor wounds that they wiped with cloths wetted with water from their skins. He watched them go about this mundane task as if they'd just stopped to camp for the night in an empty field in some uninhabited land. The fact that they'd just been in a battle didn't seem to faze them. They weren't even breathing hard after their exertions.

Barittin finally rediscovered the ability to move and began walking toward where Remerska was talking to one of the Jix.

"… heard the battle from the road and came to investigate," the Jix was saying as Barittin reached them.

"Again, thank you – we owe you our lives," Remerska said.

"You're our countrymen and brothers in arms. It's our duty to fight with you," the Jix replied.

"My Lord Barittin," Remerska said turning to face him. "This is Lenys. We are more than fortunate to have had his assistance, along with that of his comrades."

Barittin grasped Lenys' hand in both of his. "Thank you, thank you!" he said. "We'd surely have been slaughtered without your intervention."

"It was our pleasure My Lord. None of us has had a good fight like that in some time. It's good to stretch the arms and draw some blood now and again, don't you think?"

Barittin was confounded by the question and stumbled over his words, unsure of how to respond for a moment, before Lenys laughed and clapped him on the shoulder.

"We're not all warriors, and you look more like an administrator than a soldier, even though you're wearing that pretty armor you obviously got from the king," he said laughing. "The world needs men like you too. But if you ever want to learn how to really fight, let me know. I'll teach you!" He clapped Barittin so hard on the back that he stumbled forward a half step. Remerska smiled at them both.

"I believe I'll find something to drink. There's a cask of Cloud Wine around here somewhere. Lenys, would you and your men care to join me for a libation?"

"Would we ever! We'll be along after we've tended to our mounts."

A rumble behind them, toward the edge of the plateau caused them to turn and look. Just coming over the ridge was the first of the Jarradanian soldiers returning from the battlefield below. Night was very near, and it looked like the fighting was done for the day. A shout from Remerska caused the soldiers in the camp to start boiling water and preparing mats on which to lay wounded men. There would be many to tend to this night. Others began to light cookfires to feed the surely hungry soldiers, and another group began to harness horses to carts and load dead enemy soldiers into them. The bodies were driven to the edge of the plateau and dumped over the side. The dead Jarradanian soldiers were laid out in lines for identification, and graves were dug in the loose soil. Dead horses were dragged into a pile and set ablaze, injured ones beyond treatment were mercifully killed and also burned.

Barittin watched the grim doings with a detachment he'd never felt before. He'd heard enough stories of warriors and battles to know that one was changed by combat. But having actually seen it, and now it's aftermath, he felt himself changed. Life was so easy to end, he thought. So many years went by for a man to reach fighting age, so much effort went into arming and training a soldier, and his life could be over in seconds. It seemed such a waste. Perhaps one of those dead soldiers out there would have created something that made the lives of all easier or more pleasant. It would never happen now. Where was that Cloud Wine?

The Jix, General Remerska and Barittin sat around a campfire next to the command tent. Mugs of Cloud Wine were drained and refilled liberally. The conversation was subdued, the excited emotions immediately following the battle having subsided. Fatigue was beginning to set in, and many were beginning to yawn.

"What brought you to this part of the country?" Remerska asked Lenys. He seemed to be the leader of this small band of Jix.

"We are on an assignment from Ulvar. More than that I can't tell you. You understand?"

"Ah, secret missions. Been on a few myself," Remerska replied, nodding his comprehension. "Still, it was to our great good fortune that you were here."

"Yes, for you. Our actions today may end up hindering our goal though. Time will tell."

"Well, this battle is over. But I fear we may now be at war with our neighbors."

"The three kingdoms have been fighting each other since the Era of Disruption. It's nothing new."

Barittin looked at the young man with the Jix who was not dressed as one of them. He was listening intently to the conversation. His black hair hung a little past his shoulders, his blue eyes, nearly the color of the stone of the Azure Palace, were intent and betrayed a keen intellect. This one was an enigma. Barittin determined to find out more about him. But now wasn't the time. He was surprised when the young man spoke up.

"Era of Disruption? What's that?" he asked. Everyone turned to look at him.

"You don't know about the Era of Disruption?" Remerska asked.

The young man shook his head.

"What's your name lad?" he asked. "I saw you fight with these Jix as though you were one of them. You cut down just as many men as any, yet you don't wear the grey."

"My name is Revan. They've taught me a few things since we've been traveling together."

Remerska looked at him keenly. "Indeed," was all he said. The boy blushed a little but didn't drop his gaze. Barittin thought that a bit unusual. Generally, one of this boy's age would be cowed by a man of the general's authority and air of command. But not this lad. He was more intrigued by him than ever.

"Our history is divided into six eras," Lenys said patiently. "This is turning 3793 of the Era of Apprehension. The first is the Era of Cataclysm, after that came the Era of Disruption which was just mentioned. If you want to learn more about the others, read a history book," Lenys said grinning. Revan smiled back. Barittin could see that they liked each other and were comfortable bantering. It was that way with soldiers, he'd learned. He'd discovered that he enjoyed these men. Most of his adult life had been spent in the service of the king. Protocol and palace intrigues had been his vocation for most of his adulthood. The simple life and close friendships these men had were new to him; he found their candor refreshing. Idly, he imagined himself as one of them. Would he enjoy it? He thought he would.

"We've much to do on the morrow," Remerska said. "And the wine has made me sleepier than I'd care for. Drink as much of it as you'd like; I'm off to my bed."

The Jix bid him a good rest and a few of them, Revan included, meandered off to find a place for their bedrolls. Barittin remained in front of the fire, his mug of wine forgotten in his hand as he pondered who that young man was and what he was about with the Jix.

Revan woke with the dawn. The dew that had settled on the ground overnight had wet his blanket and made him shiver with cold. Summer was ending and fall was approaching. He'd seen yellow leaves on some of the trees they'd passed on their journey. Not knowing what they meant, he'd asked his companions who'd told him about the seasons and what signs indicated they were changing. There was so much to learn. Sometimes he felt as ignorant as an insect. But the Jix knew who he was, where he'd come from, and they answered his questions with a patience that made him feel, while not smart, at least not stupid. He loved them for it.

The camp was waking up; soldiers were cooking a morning meal, tending to wounded and repairing equipment. The army would be moving on when they were ready.

"He's awake then," Lenys said when he saw Revan gathering up his bedroll.

"He's got his beauty sleep," Edro said. "Look how pretty he is!"

"Your mother would love me Edro," Revan said. "More than even you."Edro and Lenys roared with laughter and went about preparing to leave.

Remerska walked up to them as their mirth was dying and laid a hand on each of their shoulders. "I know you have to be on your way, but I wanted to thank you again for what you did yesterday. Know that if you are ever in need of anything, Jaradlik Remerska is your friend, as are all these men with me."

Lenys and Edro grasped his hand in acknowledgment and bade him farewell. Revan watched from a distance as he fastened his bedroll to the saddle of his horse. Hearing footsteps behind him, he turned and found himself facing Barittin.

"We weren't really introduced last night," he said. "I'm Barittin D' Otrand, Chief Advisor and Facilitator to his highness King Vraniss Antra."

"I'm Revan. It's good to meet you."

"Likewise. I don't wish to impose, but would you be amenable to me riding with you?"

Revan was taken aback for a moment, confusion in his eyes. "But shouldn't you stay with the army?" he asked.

"The army can take care of themselves. I was mainly here as an observer at the request of the king. That duty is ended. Returning to Kessar is not attractive to me at the moment. I'd like to learn more about the Jix and what it is that makes your bond with them so strong. I'd ride with you for a time if you'll allow it."

"I'm not really in charge," Revan said hesitantly. "You'd have to ask Lenys. He's our leader."

"Yes, I observed that. But a word from you would go far with him, no?"

"Well... I... We are going a long way... It's..."

"Good! I'll speak with Lenys. Riding with you shall be educational. In my position as the king's advisor, it's one of my duties to learn as much as I can about his subjects. And I'll make sure to tell him how welcoming and cooperative you were. Perhaps one day you too will be employed by the king."

Revan could only stare at Barittin. How had this man just wormed his way into traveling with them? He'd not given his blessing, yet somehow he'd been made to feel like he had. Barittin turned and strode over to Lenys, who was just finishing his preparations. They spoke briefly for a moment; Barittin gestured toward Revan once or twice. Lenys looked his way, obviously confused, then finally nodded a grudging assent. Barittin, grinning with his victory, quickly gathered his belongings and tied them to his horse.

Revan, not seeing any graceful way out of this new predicament, sighed and mounted his horse. The rest of the Jix were already mounted and had moved away from the main camp toward the north, where they waited for the others. In a short time, Revan and Lenys were joined by Barittin, still grinning, and together they urged their horses into a trot towards the road a few ranges to the north.

Barittin rode next to Revan, and looking over at him, said "I've been in the Azure Palace most of my life. Adventure was never something I pursued, or even gave much thought to. Now that I've been on one, I find I'm enjoying it immensely."

Revan glanced at him but didn't reply. Barittin smiled and turned his face forward, into the wind, grinning all the while.

Kanar glanced at the Blackfire, its ominous shape loomed overhead. He still had trouble believing that he was going to pass through it. As it grew in the sky, so did his fear. Whatever end he was going to meet, he was sure it would be painful and prolonged.

His companion exhibited no emotion. No fear, no happiness, no trepidation, no excitement. He was as a stone and nearly as silent. Kanar had tried to talk to him many times over the weeks that they'd been traveling together, but he was not conversational. Questions were met with grunts or very short, vague answers that left him with even more questions. He'd resigned himself to just walking and waiting. He'd soon enough have answers.

They'd passed a battlefield a week or so back, and Kanar had recognized sigils on the armor of some of the dead. Jarradan, Bentravirri and Drisava had all fought there. Most of the dead had been buried or piled up and burned, but they'd run across a few bodies that had been missed. He'd availed himself of a sword from one of the dead Drisavans. But his companion, whose name he still didn't know, had urged him to move on.

He'd barely had time to buckle the sword belt around his waist before the man was moving again. And that black cowl. It never left his head. Even in full sunlight Kanar couldn't see his eyes, just the bottom part of his chin. The man's skin was a ghastly white, like marble. He wore black gloves on his hands, so Kanar couldn't see if his skin color extended to his whole body or just his chin. Whatever the case, it was unsettling. So was the fact that he didn't eat or drink. How was that possible? Everyone needed food and water. But apparently not this man. Kanar told himself that he ate at night when he himself was asleep. That had to be it. Maybe his teeth were bad, and he didn't want Kanar to see them. Some people were vain or ashamed of their appearance. It had to be something like that. For himself, Kanar had brought three waterskins and some dried meat, which had long since run out. But somehow when he woke in the mornings, his skins were full and there was food of some variety in his ration bag. Never fresh fruit or vegetables, it would generally be more dried meat, or perhaps some hard biscuits. He wondered, each time it happened, where the man found water and food out here, in this nothingness.

Still the ranges passed, and the enigmatic man remained so. The Blackfire grew larger in the sky and the days passed uneventfully. The pace the man set was brutal and Kanar had a hard time keeping up at first. They would set off early in the morning, before dawn, and travel until long after sunset. Kanar was so tired the first week that he considered abandoning the journey and returning to Kessar. But somehow he knew that if he did, the man would kill him. So, he kept his own council and bore the strain. Over time he grew stronger and more accustomed to the strenuous exercise until it was fairly easy to keep up with him.

The grasslands they were passing through in the northern part of Bentravirri quickly gave way to a flat, arid plain dotted with rocks and dun colored dirt. Very little grew in the unforgiving soil. The only plant life consisted of some small, stunted shrubs and little clumps of yellow grass that looked more dead than alive. The grasslands had been quite fertile, and they'd passed a number of farms. If all of Bentravirri was like this, he wondered how they fed themselves. Jarradan certainly had no problem with food, unless there was a drought or an invasion of insects, but out here very little grew and even less resided. Once in a while they'd see scaly reddish-brown creatures about half the length of a man's arm scurry into holes in the ground. Their bodies were long with even longer tails and eight short legs, four on either side, and round heads with pointed snouts from which protruded long stalks tipped with things that looked like small feathers. Kanar thought they might be good to catch and roast over a fire, but when he'd tried to pick one up, his companion had caught his wrist in that iron grip. "That little thing will bite you if you touch it. If it gets its teeth into you, you'll be dead before sunset," was all he'd said. Kanar hadn't tried to pick one up since.

They passed no towns or cities in this desolate region of Bentravirri. Nor did they see any other travelers. For ranges around they were the only humans. Sometimes birds flew high above, but they didn't circle like some did when they were seeking prey. These flew in straight lines, like they wanted to leave this area behind as quickly as they could. Kanar sympathized. Some weeks after passing out of the grasslands and into the plain, Kanar looked up from the ground before him and saw what looked like the tips of mountains in the distance ahead. As the day wore on, the mountains grew until they loomed tall in their path, the Blackfire hanging over them like a violent black carpet about the be laid over the earth. Kanar looked at its round, black center and noticed for the first time that there were different shades of black swirling and colliding within it. The intensity of its movement was even greater than that of the enormous arms that spanned out towards the earth and sky. Kanar's fear of it grew as he watched.

The next day they entered the lower hills of the mountains. These weren't as tall as the Blue Crag mountains he'd crossed after escaping from the camp, but they were still imposing. There was no snow on them, which he found encouraging for ease of travel, but the rocky and loose soil made trekking difficult. Still his companion didn't slow but led him on steadily higher until they reached a pass between two peaks. Two days later they emerged on the other side and Kanar found himself looking down into a dense forest of tall brown trees, their leaves as brown as the trunks. Was everything in this land dead? Sure seemed that way.

They descended the far side of the pass, and in a few hours walked into the trees. Kanar saw that his initial impression that the trees were dead wasn't exactly correct. They looked sick, like the ground had been poisoned. Sap oozed from cracks in the trunks of many, but it wasn't clear like that from the trees around his home. This was a hideous yellow color and smelled like rotting things. There were no sounds of animals, no birds flitting from branch to branch; all was silent. It didn't seem to bother Kanar's companion any; he simply kept on towards the south. The trek through the forest went on for days, and Kanar wondered if they'd ever emerge from it. The Blackfire was hidden from view most of the time, the canopy of the trees being too dense to see through except in small glimpses. The light was muted and tinged brown as it filtered through the sickly leaves high above. There was very little wind and not much air moved; the smell of rot was always present, a stinking miasma invading Kanar's lungs. He began to feel ill just from breathing it but remained silent and followed the strange man. This journey had a purpose, and its name was Hento. When Kanar felt like abandoning the man and turning for home, he thought of that hated murderer, and sometimes of Revan. He wished on occasion that he'd had another chance at him. He'd be ready for Revan's speed the next time, and he'd finish him. But Hento was his true motivation. He would learn what his strange companion would teach him, then he'd kill that vile Nojii. And any others he could. Even if it cost him his own life, the murders of his parents and the life that had been torn from him would be avenged.

Many days after entering the forest, they finally reached its far southern edge. As they emerged, Kanar saw a small city off to the right and several ranges away. The ground was still flat here, and the city shimmered in the heat of the day. None of the buildings was more than two or three stories tall, and it looked to be about one third the size of Kessar. It had no wall, but a dirt road led to it. For the first time since setting out, his companion deviated from his due south course; he angled toward the city.

"We're going there?" Kanar asked.

"Yes. I've something to do before we pass the Blackfire."

Kanar hadn't thought of that giant black mass much since losing sight of it in the trees. Now he looked up. It loomed almost directly overhead. The only way he could see the sky was to turn and look back behind them. The contrast between the blue of the north and the black of the south was startling. It even seemed darker here, like the Blackfire had tainted some of the light from the sun. Probably it had.

"Does that city have a name?"

"It is called Jursafar."

Kanar and his companion rented rooms in an inn in the town. From somewhere inside his black robes the man had produced two gold coins that he'd used to pay for the rooms, and food for Kanar. The city was grimy and decrepit. Buildings were in various states of decay; nothing looked new or well maintained. Even the people looked ill-used. Most of their clothes were merely rags that hadn't been washed in who knew how long. Their faces were smeared with dirt, their eyes dull and usually downcast. He saw scabs and bruises on their faces and arms. This was not a place that contained much, if any, happiness or comfort. The food he ate in the inn, while better than the meager fare he'd had on the journey so far, was not good. The vegetables, such as there were, had a wilted, nearly rotten flavor. The meat was tough and flavorless, and even the water tasted like it had been strained through muddy cloth. The only thing that was relatively decent was ale, and it had obviously been imported from somewhere else.

The man left Kanar in the inn and disappeared for most of the day after they'd arrived. Kanar didn't really care where he went; he was happy to have a real bed to sleep in and a washbasin with which to bathe. Even after washing he still felt dirty. He slept for a time then rose and went downstairs to the dining room of the inn. The innkeeper, a skinny and skittish man with hair only growing around the sides of his head, received him obsequiously, fawning over him as he pulled out a chair and sat him down at a table.

"Does the Master require anything?" he asked, fidgeting with the dirty apron he wore.

"A mug of ale would be wonderful."

"Yes, yes, I'll fetch it right away," he almost screeched. The odd man practically ran behind the bar and poured an ale so quickly he slopped half of it on the floor. He gestured to a serving girl who was wiping a table and she scurried over to clean up his mess. Kanar found the whole scene a bit surreal. He pondered a moment and realized that the man wasn't afraid of him so much as his companion. They'd come in together and the innkeeper must know something about him, or he wouldn't be acting so deferential towards Kanar. He was obviously terrified of what might happen if Kanar wasn't treated well. Maybe this would be a good place to learn more about the man in the black cowl. An idea occurred to him. He beckoned the innkeeper over to his table. The terrified man was jolted by the gesture but ran to Kanar.

"What can I do for you Master?" he asked.

"Is the serving girl… available?"

"For you, of course, anything you wish, anything at all."

"Send her to my room when she's finished with her chores. I'll be waiting."

"Yes, yes, but immediately. There will be no waiting for you Master."

Kanar frowned but finished his ale and went upstairs. He hadn't been in his room long and was sitting on the edge of the bed when there was a knock on the door. "Come in," he called. The door opened and the girl entered. She'd taken some time to clean herself up and tried to apply some rudimentary makeup, but her terror was evident.

"You wanted me to visit you Sir?" she asked, trembling.

"Yes. Come here, sit down," Kanar said, gesturing to a chair in front of a small table. "I'm not going to hurt you; I just want some information."

The girl sat tremulously in the chair, her hands folded in her lap. She wouldn't look up. Kanar put his hand under her chin and raised her face until her eyes met his. He realized that she was quite pretty, despite her fear, the poorly applied makeup, and the ragged condition of her clothes. Tears threatened to fall from her terrified eyes.

"I promise you I won't hurt you. I just want to talk."

Her lower lip trembled, but she nodded.

"Do you know anything about the man I came in here with?"

She nodded but didn't speak.

"What do you know?"

"He's deadly," she said, her voice quiet.

"I know that. Is he from beyond the Blackfire?"

She nodded. Kanar had to get her to talk. He didn't know when his companion would return, but he didn't want him knowing he was asking questions about him. Maybe he should try something else.

"My name is Kanar and I'm from Jarradan. What's your name?"

She looked at him disbelievingly. "You're from Jarradan?" she asked.

"Yes."

"Truly?"

"Yes."

She hesitated a moment, as if deciding whether he was telling the truth, or maybe if she should talk at all, but finally said, "I've heard of it, but never met anyone from there. It's so far away."

"It has been a long journey. We've been traveling for weeks. Your name?" He reminded her.

"My name... is Irulia."

Kanar took one of her hands in both of his and smiled calmly. "It's very nice to meet you Irulia." She smiled back at that.

"You too, Kanar."

"I don't know when my companion will be back, but I need to learn as much about him as I can. What can you tell me?"

"He is from beyond it. Sometimes those who live beyond come here. Not many of them, but they do come."

"What do they want? Are they all like him?"

"Usually just a room. Sometimes... more. And yes... they're all like him. You can never see their faces."

"Do you know his name?"

"No. But people here call his kind The Bloodless."

"Do you know why?"

"No. I always guessed it was because their skin is so white. What you can see of it anyway. But I don't really know."

"What else do you know about them?"

"Only that when they come here, everyone is afraid. If we don't give them what they want, they kill people until they get it."

"What do they ask for?"

"Most times people."

"People?"

"Yes. Children usually. But sometimes adults too."

"They take children? What do they do with them?"

"No one knows. They take them off to the south. Through the Blackfire is what everyone says. To the Bone Grinders."

"Bone Grinders?" Kanar asked.

"I don't know what it means. It's just what people say."

"Alright. Go on."

"People who have children are terrified that they'll be taken. Everyone wants to leave, but no one has enough money to travel. We're all stuck here."

She paused for a moment, then looked out a window at the Blackfire and gestured toward it. "Are you going through it?" she asked.

"I don't know. I think so. He told me that I was and that he would help me if I came with him."

"Help you with what?"

"It doesn't matter. Irulia, thank you for what you've told me. You've helped me greatly. You're free to leave now."

"I can't go back right now!" she exclaimed. "Cerquintas will beat me! I haven't been up here long enough to have... pleased you. He'll know nothing happened." The terror was rising in her voice. This city was full of fear, Kanar thought.

"Slow down," he said. "You can stay here for a while. Then when you think it's safe, you can go back downstairs."

"I can't. He will… check me," she said.

Kanar frowned but didn't say anything. Irulia stood from her chair and began unbuttoning her ragged dress. Kanar's eyes widened at that. They practically bulged when her dress fell to the floor, and she pushed him back on the bed.

His companion, The Bloodless as Kanar now thought of him, returned late that night. He walked into Kanar's room unannounced and said, "We leave at first light. Be ready." And Kanar was. They'd left the inn when everyone was still asleep and made their way through the darkened city to its southern fringes. The Bloodless was carrying a long bag that clinked once in a while as he walked. It looked heavy, but Kanar didn't ask about it. For three days they walked straight towards the Blackfire. It didn't seem that it could grow any larger, but Kanar was slightly amazed to find that it did. It covered almost all of the sky this far south. There was just a small crescent of blue to the north.

The land south of the city was like a dry riverbed. The dirt was cracked and dusty. Nothing at all grew here. As the city faded behind them, Kanar felt a pang of regret for Irulia. She was a sweet girl who had been born into a life of servitude and terror. Like so many others he'd met throughout the three kingdoms. Did suffering never end? He supposed not. As long as one person wanted to dominate another, there would be anguish and pain. Maybe one day people would just leave each other alone and live in peace. But that day was far in the future. He idly thought that if he ever passed back through this city, he'd find Irulia and take her with him back to Jarradan. Maybe he could help one person live a better life.

The fourth day out from the city, Kanar looked up from the ground in front of him and stopped suddenly – he could see where the Blackfire met the earth. He'd wondered what it would look like when he finally saw it and was surprised now that he did. What he'd expected to see was a massive cloud of dust and debris rising up from where those black edges and their gold and red threads spun against the earth. But there was nothing. They just met. The junction point was only a few ranges away and there wasn't even any noise. How could that be? Something that big, spinning as it did and full of all that violence should have carved a furrow deep into the earth, with a roar to accompany it. But it looked like it wasn't even making contact, even though he could see where they met. He'd heard people say that they thought someone might be able to walk around one of the edges, but he realized now that was impossible. The Blackfire met the earth all the way to the horizon on either side of where he stood. The only way past it was directly through it. The Bloodless stopped ahead of him and looked back.

"Scared?" he asked.

Kanar just stared.

"It's where we're going. Unless you want to turn back. I wouldn't advise that though."

It was difficult to get moving again, but Kanar forced his legs to move and caught up with his companion.

Sometime later, Kanar thought it was far too quickly, they drew near to the spot where the Blackfire met the earth. He peered intently at it, trying desperately to see what lay beyond, but it was just one enormous swirling black wall far up into the sky. The red and gold threads flashed and swam through the fringes where they touched the earth. An occasional small fissure opened in the wall of black right at the ground, and Kanar could see a pace or two into it. The earth didn't look any different inside it than it did where he was standing. His fear welled up in him, overpowering for a moment his hatred and desire for revenge. He almost bolted, but his companion, perhaps sensing his feelings, took him by the upper arm and forced him to walk towards the black spinning wall.

"We're here now and we're going through. This is what you wanted, remember?"

Kanar stared at him dumbly for a moment, took a deep breath and nodded.

"Alright," he said. "What do we do now?"

The Bloodless drew his curved black sword, the strange runes carved along both sides of its blade glowed a hellish blood red. Kanar thought he could see the red changing in spots from dark to light red and back again.

"Take hold of the sword. Put your hand under mine." Kanar gripped the hilt as instructed. "Do not let go for anything. If you do, you're lost forever. Understand?" Kanar nodded. "Walk next to me at the same pace at which I move. And do not let go."

The Bloodless turned to face the swirling dark wall, Kanar with him. "Walk," he said, and together they passed into the Blackfire.

Word of Thanks

Thank you, dear reader, for reading

The Blackfire Chronicles, Volume I

Please take a minute to leave a review for this book on Amazon and Goodreads. All feedback and reviews are helpful for authors. Thank you in for your purchase, your reviews, and sharing this book with others.

Mark hopes you have enjoyed this book as much as he did writing it. He is working diligently at creating, he can often be found writing at his desk. Follow him as an author on Amazon to make sure you are notified of his latest publications. Mark works hard to reply to all reader emails. His blog page has an email form you can use to write to him. You can also follow Mark:

at Parler, @MarkSowersBooks

on Minds, @MarkSowersAuthor

his blog at: http://www.marksowersbooks.com

About the Author

Mark grew up in Tacoma, Washington, and currently lives in Wasilla, Alaska. When he was very young he lived for two years in a suburb of Athens, Greece. This experience to this day shapes and informs his perspective on other cultures. After spending much of his twenties working various labor and construction related jobs, he decided it was time to get an education.

He began attending Tacoma Community College, where he received an Associates in Arts and Sciences in 2005. Mark, with an ever-persistent desire to improve himself and challenge himself to reach his goals, decided to continue his education and enrolled at the University of Alaska, Southeast (UAS). Obtaining a Bachelor's degree had been a personal goal for many years, and in 2013, he achieved it graduating magna cum laude from UAS with a Bachelor of Arts, Social Science. He majored in History and minored in Economics and Political Science.

In between college endeavors Mark met his amazing wife Marcy and they moved to Juneau, AK and married in 2009. They have raised three incredible children, Jade, Iris and Harold. The couple eventually moved to Wasilla. They have a dog who entertains them on a regular basis in addition to moose watching, gardening and enjoying Marcy's culinary delights, always created with much love.

He enjoys music and has been an avid musician since he started playing guitar at age 12. Mark is a talented musician who is mostly self-taught. After guitar he took on the challenge of teaching himself drums and bass guitar. Mark has been in several bands throughout his life. He and his wife dream of creating an incredible jam space for Mark to pursue his love of music.

A short time after graduation he landed a job working in the Arctic oilfields of Kuparuk which is west of Prudhoe Bay. With the catastrophic effects of COVID19 and the oil price depression Mark was let go from his position on the north slope. However, during that time Mark was able to see some things most people never get to see such as arctic foxes, herds of caribou, brown bear roaming the tundra (he did not get to see a polar bear), but unfortunately did see the thick, black swarms of mosquitos in summer. Mosquitos are affectionately known as the Alaska state bird. Mark worked long hours, twelve-hour days for fourteen days straight. He commuted to and from work to and from Kuparuk on a flight that took an hour and forty minutes by jet (in state)! This schedule while rigorous allowed him to pursue another goal - writing.

During Covid-19 quarantine Mark completed the second in the series The Blackfire Chronicles, Volume 2 which is close to publication! He is currently working on Volume 3 along with several other exciting works. A new job allows Mark to work closer to home and his schedule provides him more time to pursue his writing career. In summer, when he is not helping his wife in the garden he is writing or mowing the lawn, (which is so big it takes 8+ hours on a riding mower!) he is finishing other books, short story collections, editing and writing. Ultimately he would love to retire to spend his days at his true passion, writing! Your support reading his books, writing reviews are what can help him get there!

Next in Series

Turn to the next page to read a free excerpt from the next book in the Blackfire Chronicles Series, Volume 2.

The Blackfire Chronicles

Volume 2

Mark Sowers

From whence did it come? The accepted theory of our age contends that it has always been, as if it sprang, fully formed, from the ground, in that long ago age when the land was created. Yet questions persist. If the Blackfire has always been, then what is it? What purpose does it serve? Or does it even have a purpose? Most simply gaze at its ominous and striking presence in the southern sky, watch its slow spinning, the mountains within it thrusting up with their unfathomable force, then crashing down as if their very foundations suddenly vanished. Perhaps they did, like so many who have attempted to cross its boundary. I have devoted my life to the study of the Blackfire, and it often seems I know less now than when I began, so many years ago.

Transcribed from a lecture by
Wurfavend Mentrana, Udron
Library, Enrat, Turning 3480,
Era of Calm

Blackfire Chronicles Volume 2, Chapter 1

The further east he traveled, the more uneasy Otarab became. It wasn't for lack of familiarity or an uncertainness about his destination; he'd been to Enrat before and was comfortable within its walls high on the promontory above the sea. This feeling was deeper, more disturbing, as if events had outpaced him. Otarab did not enjoy feeling as if he wasn't in control, or at least aware of what was happening. All his life his instincts had served him well, and he'd learned to trust them. They screamed at him now to be cautious. Perhaps I should have brought more men, he thought.

No. After the events at the pit, anonymity was his ally. The two men he'd hired to convey and protect him on this journey were capable, if unimaginative. What were their names again? It didn't matter. They'd be released from his service as soon as he reached The Drowned Gate that opened into the city. Its name was appropriate if a bit misleading, given the city's location on the sea, and the fact that no enemy had ever breached it. They'd all drowned under a rain of arrows and steel, if not in the actual roiling waters that pounded the cliffs on three sides of the enormous promontory, on top of which the city was built. He knew they were close to the city and the safety it's walls provided, but the feeling of unease grew stronger as the ranges fell away behind them.

"How much longer?" he called out to the carriage's driver.

"We should be there by nightfall," came the reply. Otarab frowned a little at the lack of an honorific. His hired help had been calling him 'My Lord' and 'Master' since they'd departed Kessar half a season ago. Had it been so long? There were only four seasons to a turning, and he'd spent half of one on the road. Otarab sighed. There was so much he could have done in that time. So spins the Blackfire, as the saying went. Some things were simply more important than others. He gazed out the window at waves of grass. This part of Drisava was mostly flat, covered in a sea of yellowish-brown grass, and was quite probably, Otarab thought, the most boring landscape in all of the Three Kingdoms. At least the road was well maintained here. Queen Andissa was nothing if not savvy. She understood that roads were essential to her kingdom's prosperity and did a fine job of maintaining them.

Drisava did not have rich farmland like Jarradan, and most of the produce its people consumed was imported. What Drisava did have were animals. Herds of boslin, those enormous six-legged beasts, were raised on huge farms in these vast grasslands. Most were butchered for meat and leather, both of which were traded with Jarradan and Bentravirri. On the coast fleets of boats braved the stormy seas to catch fish and other varieties of sea-meat, which were also food trade items. Otarab despised sea-meat.

Just thinking of the smell as some slimy creature roasted on a spit or in a pan made him feel like vomiting. How could people eat that offal? The city was rife with the stink, permanently permeated by its stench. He shuddered a little in anticipation of the putrid miasma he was soon to encounter.

"We're approaching the coastal mountains," a voice called out from the front of the carriage. Good. It won't be too much longer then. Otarab remembered the pass through the mountains. It rose and fell in mostly gentle slopes, skirting a mountain here, going straight over a low hill there, until it finally became a narrow ramp that rose higher and higher, ending at The Drowned Gate well above the sea and shoreline below. They hadn't encountered any bandits or robbers on this journey, but Otarab knew that this road, especially through the coastal mountains, was quite popular with criminals, despite Andissa's best efforts. It was the only route, other than the sea, to reach the city, and as such was the only thoroughfare for all of the goods coming into and leaving Enrat. It was a bandit's paradise.

The pass through the mountains was dotted with outposts manned by the Queen's soldiers, who also patrolled it on horseback, but even they couldn't stop all thievery. Out here in the grasslands there were few places to hide, no favorable spots to wait in ambush. But in the mountains there were many. Most merchants who traded with Enrat employed groups of mercenaries to guard their persons and their wares. But the problem with mercenaries was that they worked for whomever paid the most. Many a merchant had found himself at the point of a sword held by a mercenary he'd hired, who had in turn led him into a trap on this very road. Otarab knew – he'd paid a few of those mercenaries to steal the shipments they'd been hired to protect. That was another reason Otarab hadn't brought more men. Although there was only one carriage, the presence of more than the two he'd hired would have attracted attention. In this guise he was simply a man who'd hired a carriage to convey him to Enrat. Perhaps he was a man of means with a little gold to be had, but not really worth the effort to accost. Or worth the penalty should the thieves be caught by the Queen's soldiers.

Enrat had a unique deterrent to crime - and punishment for those convicted. The preferred method of dealing with criminals was to bind their arms and legs, then throw them off the city walls to their deaths on the rocks below. There was one place in particular – a wide, flat specimen below the southern side of the promontory, known locally as The Anvil - where the impact of the body could be heard even on the walls high above. Bets were made on gruesome potential outcomes, such as whether the condemned's head would remain intact, or how far the blood would splatter upon impact. Otarab had lost and won a few coins betting on this most macabre of pastimes.

He felt the road rise under the carriage as they began to climb the pass through the mountains, and sat back to ponder his options once he arrived in the city. Even here the salt scent of the sea reached his nostrils. It was not as unpleasant as cooking sea-meat, but still carried more than a hint of the death and decay that was so prevalent near the ocean. Lost in his thoughts, Otarab cried out as the carriage suddenly lurched to the right and began rolling and crashing downhill. His head hit something hard and the last thought he had before everything went black was – *I should have brought more men.*

Books by the Author

The Blackfire Chronicles Series Overview

The Blackfire - that mysterious and gigantic wheel of black flame spinning in the southern sky has been an enigma for thousands of turnings. What is it? Who created it and why? Magic – it once existed, but no longer. Where did it go? Will it return someday? Revan and Arval – two young men, slaves, who seek to escape their tormentors, the brutal and vile Nojii. How will they win their freedom? What will they discover when they finally escape, and where will fate lead them? Will secrets and knowledge, long hidden and lost, be revealed and understood?

The Blackfire Chronicles, Volume 1

From the depths of a pit in a barren desert rises an enormous stone box. Slaves toil in the broiling heat, digging out the mysterious object which has no door, no windows, no features of any kind. Revan has spent nearly his entire life here. He has only vague and indistinct memories of a time before he dug for his life. Unseen and unknown to him, above the rim of the pit and far to the south, looms the Blackfire – a gigantic rotating wheel of black flames that obscures and dominates the entirety of the southern sky. Red and gold lightning flash threateningly and ominously in its fringes. Can Revan escape the pit, find his freedom, and discover the secrets of the Blackfire?

The Blackfire Chronicles, Volume 2

In the aftermath of the violence in Kessar, Arval learns what it means to disobey the Jix. Revan reaches Enrat and resumes his search for the documents that may help answer some of his many questions. Kanar passes through the Blackfire with the mysterious cowled man. What does he find on the other side, and will it help him in his mission for revenge on the Nojii? New characters, new places, and new adventures are waiting inside The Blackfire Chronicles, Volume 2.

Mark is currently writing the next in series, The Blackfire Chronicles, Volume 3.

Enders & Associates

Adrian Blake just knows things, which for a time made him one of the FBI's most successful investigators. Some might call him psychic, but whatever his power is, it couldn't prevent the tragedy that changed his life forever. When his mother passes away unexpectedly several years later, Adrian's life is upended when he learns that he has inherited a silver mine. Researching the mine and how it came to belong to his mother reveals an ancestor he hadn't known existed - the enigmatic Bertram Fields. Who exactly was he? When Adrian travels to the small town of Boot Mesa, Arizona to find out, he discovers that strange and terrible things have been happening there for many years. Was his family somehow involved in the mysterious deaths and disappearances? Adrian, with the help of park ranger Mandy Moretti and his old FBI colleague Pete Sparks, will soon find the answers to his questions – and they are far from what he expected.

Society's House of Intractable Tension

Bryce Ingman doesn't know anything different. His entire life has been spent under the steel-shod boot of oppression. In this, the Federated Territories of North America, freedom and self-determination are forgotten notions from a dusty past. But there are those who still remember. Follow along as Bryce discovers what it means to be free, how absurd and self-aggrandizing tyrannical governments actually are, and how much politicians and the institutions they create deserve to be ridiculed. At turns poignant, tragic, sarcastic, parodical, and philosophical, Society's House of Intractable Tension is cautionary tale of what has been and what could yet be if certain elements in society aren't opposed by those who believe in true freedom.

33339691R00277